RIDE INTO HISTORY WITH THE BRAND-NEW SAGA STARRING THE HOLTS, THE BRAVE YOUNG MEN AND WOMEN WHOSE MOST PRECIOUS HERITAGE IS THEIR PIONEER FOREFATHERS' SENSE OF JUSTICE . . . AND THEIR UNQUENCHABLE DESIRE TO EXPLORE NEW HORIZONS, TO LOVE WITHOUT LIMITS, AND TO FIGHT FOR AMERICA'S VALUES FROM SEA TO SHINING SEA. . . .

THE HOLTS ARE THE LEADERS, THE PATHFINDERS, THE RISK TAKERS AS A BRAWNY, COLORFUL, FAST-GROWING COUNTRY SPEEDS TOWARD A NEW CENTURY ON IRON RAILS AND IN NEW HORSELESS CARRIAGES . . . ON RAW COURAGE AND UNSTOPPABLE IDEALS.

TIM HOLT—

A young, hotheaded newspaperman, he dreams of building a publishing empire on the dusty prairies of Oklahoma, but the boomtown of Guthrie may be a hope crusher as one fire consumes all he owns . . . and another begins to burn recklessly in his heart.

ROSEBAY BASHAM—

A hillbilly beauty, she looks fragile and corn-silk pretty, but her backbone is pure iron as she fights to make a life on the prairie. Good men and bad will soon be fighting for her . . . and the battle may get Tim Holt killed.

TOBY HOLT—

As an influential senator he is willing to risk his career to stand up for human rights, but the sight of an old love revives dangerous passions as his tumultuous past now comes back to jeopardize his future, his family . . . and finally his life.

MARTHA LECLERC—

Once a mob boss's daughter, she is still a sinfully beautiful woman now married to a Southern senator. But the price of her social position has been to pledge herself to a madman . . . instead of the one man she has never stopped loving.

CLAUDIA BRENTWOOD—

A proud matriarch, at eighty she is shockingly unable to settle for less than living life—and loving—to the fullest. But her heart is breaking as she sees her family heading toward tragedy, and only her daring can save a precious grandchild.

ROWELL BASHAM—

A "man of God" with a jug of moonshine under the pulpit, this cowardly villain will use arson, rape, and even murder for his own evil ends . . . unless someone in the town of Guthrie stops him.

MAYOR ABEL DORMER—

The new mayor of Guthrie, he hides his greed and ruthlessness behind a cloak of respectability, but Tim Holt will endure a horsewhipping to expose him—and make an enemy who will plot to see Holt hang.

PETER BLAKE—

The precocious son of Henry Blake and a German baroness, he is, at fifteen, ready to strike out for adventure, and no place better suits his desire to make fast money, to jump without looking into life, and to learn to be a man than Oklahoma.

CATHY MARTIN—

The gorgeous, irrepressible daughter of Rob and Kale Martin, she's run away to the bright lights of New York City, where her dreams of becoming an actress may expose her to a nightmare . . . or make her a star.

HUGO WARE—

A blond, handsome Englishman, he's an aristocrat on the outs with his noble family. Drifting into Oklahoma looking for love and trouble is either going to make him into a hero . . . or a corpse.

The city of Guthrie, Oklahoma stands today very much as it did when it was the territorial capitol in 1889. With 400 blocks of turn-of-the-century architecture, it is one of the largest districts on the National Register of Historic Places.

THE HOLTS: AN AMERICAN DYNASTY
VOLUME TWO

OKLAHOMA PRIDE

DANA FULLER ROSS

Created by the producers of
**Wagons West, The First Americans,
White Indian,** and **The Australians.**

Book Creations Inc., Canaan, NY • *Lyle Kenyon Engel, Founder*

OKLAHOMA PRIDE

A Bantam Book / published by arrangement with
Book Creations, Inc.

Bantam edition / May 1990

Produced by Book Creations, Inc.
Lyle Kenyon Engel, Founder

ISBN 0-553-28446-0

Published simultaneously in the United States and Canada

Bantam Books are published by Bantam Books, a division of Bantam Doubleday
Dell Publishing Group, Inc. Its trademark, consisting of the words "Bantam
Books" and the portrayal of a rooster, is Registered in U.S. Patent and
Trademark Office and in other countries. Marca Registrada. Bantam Books,
666 Fifth Avenue, New York, New York 10103.

PRINTED IN THE UNITED STATES OF AMERICA

KRI   0 9 8 7 6 5 4 3 2 1

Toby flailed with his fist and caught Leclerc in the jaw. The jolt knocked the knife from Leclerc's hand and sent it spinning down into the air.

But Leclerc, intent on killing himself, kicked out, and his foot caught Henry in the chest, knocking him backward. Henry pulled himself up and watched with impotent horror as Toby and Leclerc teetered in the gaping emptiness of the arch.

© BOOK CREATIONS INC. 1989

RON TOELKE '89

She tried to go on singing, but she couldn't remember the next verse. Some of the audience were pounding with their beer bottles on the table tops, and half of the rest were standing up, shouting at her.

© BOOK CREATIONS INC. 1989

R. TOELKE '89

I

The *Virginia City Beacon* office looked much too small a space to contain anyone as angry as John Ormond, owner of the Ninevah Mine. His bowler hat was jammed straight on his head, and the cigar in his teeth practically quivered with fury. He was accompanied, as he always was since the Ninevah silver miners had gone on strike, by two burly company guards, whose main function was to break heads that John Ormond thought needed breaking. They stood just outside the open door, like truculent cigar-store Indians, and passersby gave them a wide berth.

The editor of the *Beacon*, Timothy Holt, sat behind his desk, sleeves rolled up for work and a green eyeshade pulled down over his blue eyes. He gave Ormond a serious look, from which he couldn't quite keep a trace of amusement. He had riled Ormond up but good, as he was well aware, and he took an unholy delight in that fact.

"You think about it, Holt!" Ormond snapped. "I've offered you far more than your paper is worth!"

"Then you ought to be glad I won't accept," Tim replied. "I'm just looking out for your pocketbook, Ormond." When Tim had been a junior engineer in John Ormond's mine, and courting Ormond's daughter, he had addressed the boss as "Mr. Ormond." Since they had fallen out over the miners' strike, in which Tim had frequently taken the miners' side, formalities had been abandoned.

1

"You'd better think about it," Ormond informed him. "There might be other ways to make you take an offer." He indicated the company thugs, whose attention had been momentarily diverted by a giggling parade of women coming out of the white frame house across the street: Roseanna Dawn's "girls" taking their noontime constitutional. Possibly feeling Ormond's eyes boring into their back, the company men turned and glared at Tim through the open door.

A cold wind whipped in and rustled the papers on the editor's desk. Tim took a pistol out of the drawer and put it down for a paperweight. John Ormond would be aware that it was loaded, for no one in Virginia City bothered with an unloaded one.

"I'm warning you, Holt—"

"I wouldn't suggest trying anything," Tim commented. "You and your boys better get out of here—while you still have their interest." The guards had let their eyes stray again as Roseanna Dawn and her flock passed by, winking and waving.

"Damn it!" Ormond erupted, and the guards jumped to attention. Ormond pointed his cigar at Tim. "You're going to sell out, Holt."

"Not to you. I worked for you, Ormond. I spent four days in the bottom of your damned mine, and I thought I was going to die down there. I can't say it's any thanks to you I didn't. That cave-in was as close to hell as I ever want to get. And as far as I can see it, any man whose conscience would let him sell a newspaper to someone like you is bound straight for hell."

"I don't take any responsibility for that cave-in!"

"Sure . . ." Tim drawled. "That drift fell in all by itself. Faulty timbering and cheeseparing management didn't have a thing to do with it. That's why all the miners are on strike, just for the heck of it. I'll put it in an editorial, so folks'll understand that."

"You print one more editorial about my mine, Holt, and you'll pay for it!"

"I *am* paying for it," Tim said. "I get to look at you and your ugly boys out there, don't I?" He grinned. It was just amazing how much reaction a little ink and type could stir up. Then the grin faded, and Tim sighed. Fighting with John Ormond wasn't as much fun as it would have been if he wasn't reminded of Isabella Ormond every time he saw her father's face. He put his hand on the pistol. "Get out of here," he said, suddenly irritable. "You're letting all the cold air in, and I have work to do."

"You're going to be sorry," Ormond growled. He threw his chewed cigar on the floor, stomped on it, then stalked out into the frozen mud of D Street. As he turned up the fur collar of his coat, his breath made angry clouds of steam in the air. The company guards followed him.

Tim replaced his pistol, closed the door, and watched Ormond's departing back through the glass. Gradually the temperature in the office rose again, due to the potbellied stove in the corner. The *Beacon* building was small—just the office in front and the composing room in the back, with the editor's bed in a curtained-off corner—and definitely in the low-rent district, next door to a Chinese laundry and across the street from a whorehouse. The building's appearance had improved considerably in the last three months, though. Tim had hired the laundress next door to scrub it from top to bottom, and the gilt lettering on the front window was no longer gap toothed, having been lovingly refurbished by Timothy Holt in his capacity as editor, publisher, and amateur sign painter.

Circulation was up, too, which hadn't been hard; when Tim had won the paper from Waldo Howard in a drunken poker game, there hadn't been any. Now almost everyone in Virginia City read the *Beacon*, mostly to see what Tim Holt was going to have the nerve to print next. The war between the striking silver miners and the big mine owners was in full swing, and Tim was an editor who didn't hesitate to put his opinions into print. Not that the miners' union always cared for his editorials, either, due to certain past differences and the fact that Tim had an annoying capacity for being objective. But with circulation up, advertising was beginning to come in, even if some clients insisted upon a line in their copy indicating that the editor's opinions were not their own. Even the staid *Territorial Enterprise*, which was published by a coalition of mine owners and Virginia City bankers, had been forced to take notice of the *Beacon* with an editorial castigating Tim Holt as a loudmouthed upstart who had no notion of what was good for the town.

Tim went back to the composing room, where he was in the process of setting a reply to that editorial: He intended to point out that before it had sold out to the big business interests, the *Enterprise* had held much the same opinions as his own. Whistling through his teeth, he started spiking letters into the type stick, but Ormond's offer stayed in the back of his mind. Tim wanted to get out of Virginia City, not because of John Ormond but because of his daughter. Isabella Ormond had not loved Tim enough to risk her comfortable life for him.

Virginia City was too small to give Tim a respite in which to grow numb to that jilting. Every time he saw her in the street, he felt as if a cold hand had closed around his guts. Matters were not helped by the fact that Isabella owned a spaniel as brainless as she was friendly. Whenever Tim's and Isabella's paths crossed, Columbine would hurl herself to the end of her leash, tail wagging, lunging and yipping as if saying, "Ooooh, there he is! Let's go talk to him!" And Tim, ears burning, would duck around the first handy corner.

His diversionary strategy was to spend a lot of his time in the *Beacon* office or to chase stories in the kind of neighborhood that Isabella didn't frequent. The result was material a lot livelier than what the *Enterprise* offered. Tim slapped another line of type into the form and ran his hand lovingly over the old Washington flatbed press. Since he had overhauled it, the press pulled a perfect impression.

"Got me a new girl," Tim murmured to the press. "Name's Newspaper." Even though the newspaper had, in effect, snared him on the rebound, the love affair was genuine.

The brass bell over the door jangled, and Tim put the type stick down. Moose Pearum, the driver of the dray that had pulled up in front of the office, was warming his hands at the stove.

"Got your Readyprint," Moose said. "Want to help me unload it?"

Tim went out with him, and they hauled the baled sheets of newsprint into the office. Readyprint held national news and advertising on one side, with a blank sheet on the reverse for local copy. It was a boon to the small-town editor who had to hand spike all his own type. After cutting the string on one of the bales with his pocketknife, Tim picked up the top sheet and read what had been going on in the world since Monday. Moose peered over his shoulder.

"Hurricane in Samoa," Moose read. "Where's Samoa?"

"It's in the Pacific," Tim answered. "If you ever read this stuff instead of just lugging it around, you'd know. We've been mixed up in a civil war there, and I thought sure we were going to get into a fight with Germany over it, but this hurricane's smashed up everybody's warships in the harbor."

"Hand of God," Moose observed.

"Could be," Tim murmured. "Thou shalt not fight, at least not over a coaling station in Pago Pago." He scanned another article.

2 MILLION ACRES
IN INDIAN TERRITORY
TO OPEN FOR SETTLEMENT

The government will purchase for settlement some two million acres of unassigned land in the Oklahoma section of Indian Territory, to be opened for claim on 22 April.

Still reading, Tim walked around his desk, bumped into a corner of it, and sat down in his chair.

"It's going to be like Virginia City was in the old days," Tim predicted. "Instant city. Bang, like magic, right out of the ground."

"They got silver in Oklahoma?" Moose asked.

"No, they have land. A hundred and sixty acres of good prairie for each man or woman who can grab it."

Moose grinned. "You got a yen to be a farmer?"

"I have a yen to own a newspaper about ten times the size of this one," Tim said. "And this looks to me like a mighty fine place to work up to it. All the land's going to go at once, which means a whole new city. That many people will need banks and stores and lumber. And a newspaper." Tim grinned. "Can't get by without a newspaper."

"Before you buy your ticket, you want to pay me for hauling the Readyprint?" Moose inquired.

Tim dug in his pocket. "Do me a favor, will you? Go over to the miners' union hall and tell Billy Pitts and Joe Yellan I want to see them."

"What makes you think they'll come here? You ain't exactly their favorite person," Moose said.

"Tell them I'm considering selling the Beacon to John Ormond," Tim said. "I'm more favorite than he is."

"That ain't hard." Moose gave Tim a long look. "You ain't really gonna do that?"

"Between you and me, I'd set fire to it first," Tim confided. "But you just kindly don't mention that to Billy Pitts."

He put his feet on the desk and sat back, thinking, while he waited to see if Pitts and Yellan would show up. Billy Pitts was the union organizer, sent to orchestrate the strike, and Joe Yellan was head of the miners' union. Despite having taken the union's side even while he was working as an engineer for John Ormond, Tim was persona non grata with the union management, due to his courtesy cousin Sam Brentwood (a connection that Tim could now well do without) having proved to be a company spy. Tim had prevented the miners from lynching Sam, but it had been his last act as a union member. Pitts and Yellan had tossed him out on his ear.

Maybe they had toned down some by now, Tim thought. Sam had married Annie Malone and left town for a European honeymoon on which Sam was no doubt spending Annie's money like water and having a fine time. Tim doubted that they would come back to Virginia City. And ever since Tim had won the *Beacon*, the paper had mostly supported the union cause. Of course Tim hadn't approved of the union's beating up of scabs or collecting donations by strong-arm methods, and when Tim didn't approve of something, the *Beacon* generally said so in print. It was hard to say how Pitts and Yellan would react, but the intimation that he might sell out to Ormond ought to get them over here—maybe with a shotgun. Tim put the pistol back on the desktop.

He listened to the rumble and clatter in the Virginia & Truckee rail yards behind the *Beacon* office and dreamed of Oklahoma. It was very bright in his mind, a sudden dream sprung full-blown out of the Readyprint. The sound of the rail cars seemed to sing to him: *Ok-la-ho-ma, Ok-la-ho-ma . . .*

A new start, a new town, a new paper. Aside from its unpleasant associations, Virginia City was fading, its boom days long over. When the mines had dug the last of the low-grade ore from the earth, Virginia City would cease to be. It had been built on silver, and silver was finite. But land endured, and the creation of a new city, built from the ground up, was something a newspaperman could get his teeth into. Tim pulled from his desk an advertising flyer he had been saving and read again the specs of a new portable press. *Ok-la-ho-ma, Ok-la-ho-ma*, sang the steam cars in the rail yard.

The door banged open, and Billy Pitts and Joe Yellan stalked in on a cloud of cold air and fury.

"Moose Pearum says 'ee're selling the paper to that bastard Ormond," Yellan said. He was a tall, black-haired Cornishman with the muscular build of a man who could swing an eight-pound sledge all day. He looked as if he would like to swing one now at Tim Holt.

"You better hope there's no accident first, like a fire," Pitts cautioned. He wore wire-rimmed glasses and looked more like an accountant than a union tough, but he was an accomplished brawler and ruthless enough to make good on the threat.

"Simmer down, Joe," Tim said. "And, Pitts, you shut up. You're the second idiot to come in here and threaten me today. You do it again, and I'll throw you out of here and put it in print. This paper's been on your side most of the time, and I can't say you've been grateful."

"I'm rarely grateful when someone calls me a thug," Pitts snapped. "I didn't like that last editorial."

"And I didn't like your tactics," Tim said. "You *are* a thug. I've supported you because by and large I support the miners." He glanced at Yellan. "You know that, Joe."

Yellan looked uncomfortable. He and Tim had survived a cave-in together and come out of it through sheer stubbornness and muscle. Both were aware that neither would be alive without the other.

"Listen to what Holt has to say, Billy," Yellan said. "If he was selling to Ormond, he wouldn't be telling us about it, I'm thinking."

"Ormond will just shut it down," Pitts said. "The mine owners don't need but one paper."

"Then why are you threatening to burn me out?" Tim asked. "On principle?"

"Yeah," Pitts answered.

"You've got interesting principles." Tim picked up the revolver from his desk and put it across his lap. "I didn't say I was selling to Ormond. I said I'd had an offer from him. I thought you boys might want to make me another offer."

"We can't match Ormond's price," Yellan said.

"Are you trying to blackmail the union?" Pitts demanded.

Tim looked at the organizer with disgust. "Pitts,

you are the most suspicious bastard I have ever met. I thought the union might want to *buy* the damn paper and *run* it, to have its own voice, instead of letting Ormond fold it. Because I am going to sell to someone, and I don't want it to be Ormond if I can help it, since I like him even less than I like you."

"Joe just said that we can't meet Ormond's price."

"I didn't ask you to," Tim said quietly.

Some other sound was coming over the shriek of the steam engine's whistle. Tim leaned out the window of the slowly moving passenger car.

"Holt, you cowardly son of a bitch, you come out of there!" John Ormond screamed.

"Come and get me," Tim suggested as Ormond came abreast of Tim's window. A number of curious faces popped out of other windows along the car.

Ormond was puffing with anger. "I'll have the sale stopped! They'll have no credit, and you'll never see a dime!"

"They paid me in cash," Tim said. "You're up the creek, Pops."

"You're insane, Holt!" Ormond began to chase the train. "What did they pay you?"

"Half what you offered." Tim cackled and watched Ormond's face turn beet red. Now that he was leaving, the urge to prod John Ormond until he had apoplexy was overpowering. "I gave them a little discount." The train picked up speed. "Give my love to Mrs. Ormond," Tim shouted, "and all the little Ormonds. You'd better keep looking for a husband for Isabella. People as dumb as I was don't come along every day."

As the train lurched out of the rail yard and into the E Street tunnel, Tim pulled his head back in and slammed the window closed. A grimly satisfied look on his face, he relaxed in his seat.

Across the aisle, Graham Tucker, an acquaintance heading to Reno on business, shook his head in wonder.

"I call that a lot of money for a 'discount,' " Graham remarked.

"It came out of my entertainment fund," Tim said.

As the Southern Pacific train screeched its way out of the Reno depot two days later, Tim slit open a letter from his sister Janessa, which he had found awaiting him there. With the suspicion that he might be departing Virginia City in a hurry—as soon as the miners' union scraped together five hundred dollars—he had suggested that Janessa write to him in care of the Reno post office. Also awaiting him had been his copy of the waybill for the new press that was to meet him in Oklahoma. Tim had arranged to have that delivered to the M Bar B Ranch, near the soon-to-be-opened lands. The *M* in M Bar B stood for Rob Martin, an old family friend who wouldn't mind having a printing press dumped on him without prior permission.

Dear Tim,

Charley and I labor on, halfway to being doctors and up to our elbows in the torso of a cadaver so old that I think it predates the medical school.

Meanwhile, you are going where I long to be, at a family reunion at the Martins'. Charley doesn't know what he is getting into, marrying into our family, but he has another eighteen months to change his mind—not that he will, bless him. Now that we are officially engaged, all the other boarders at Mrs. Burnside's have been giving me advice and watching us like hawks whenever poor Charley comes over. Most of the time we're both too tired to misbehave even if we had the opportunity. Actually being a doctor cannot possibly be harder than learning to be one, and assisting at an amputation with one's true love is not exactly conducive to romance.

I think you are doing the wise thing to leave Virginia City. Our family does tend to have wandering feet. I think it is because we are driven to search for something. May you find it in Oklahoma.

Your loving sister,
Janessa

Tim folded the letter back into its envelope. It was written on scented stationery, although he thought he detected a faint hint of formaldehyde, too. Janessa's happiness with Charley left him feeling rather at loose ends. He didn't *want* to get married, he reminded himself; Isabella Ormond had been a narrow escape. He wanted to follow his wandering feet, pack up his press, and move on to wherever the action and the opportunity might be.

The train was beginning to pass through a darkening desert landscape, the low sun casting rippling shadows beside the track. Tim leaned back and pulled his hat over his eyes to sleep until dinner.

His wistful reflections on marriage might have been only a passing aberration, because he didn't dream of Isabella Ormond; he dreamed of a printing press, shiny and solid and new, waiting for him in a packing crate in Oklahoma.

II

The Cumberland Hills Select Academy for Young Ladies prided itself on its strict adherence to decorum, its healthful regimen, and its fine teachers. Miss Maria Cumberland had devised emergency procedures in case of fire, flood, and measles in the dormitory . . . but none to deal with Miss Cathy Martin, nineteen years old, who had run away to New York to become an actress.

Cathy's cousin, Eden Brentwood, who was twelve, sat on her trunk in the downstairs foyer of the dormitory. It was the beginning of spring vacation, and a half-dozen girls were awaiting carriages to the station. Next to Eden, on a settee, was Miss Cumberland, who held a handkerchief to her temples. Cathy's letter of explanation lay across Miss Cumberland's lap.

The headmistress reminded Eden of a picture that her mother had in the parlor at home. Entitled *Dead for His Nation's Honor*, it depicted a swooning maiden who had apparently just read the tragic news of her lover's death in the missive abandoned among the folds of her hoopskirt. Eden thought that Miss Cumberland looked even more agitated than the lady in the picture, who couldn't be blamed for the fatality. On the other hand, Grandmother, who was due any minute, could most certainly blame Miss Cumberland for Cathy's lack of supervision.

"I must telegraph Mr. Martin," Miss Cumberland said dolefully.

12

"You could let Gran tell him," Eden suggested.

Miss Cumberland appeared to find a faint flicker of hope in that, but duty reasserted itself. "No. We stand in loco parentis to you young ladies. The responsibility must be mine."

Cathy's friends Lulie and Nell stood at the end of the foyer, wide-eyed.

"Who'd have thought she'd really do it?" Nell whispered.

"Miss Bailey!" Miss Cumberland rose and advanced on them. "If there is any idle gossip about Miss Martin's departure, I will be extremely disappointed. Do I make myself clear?" Miss Cumberland's buxom figure, encased in whalebone and black bombazine, loomed over them.

"Yes, ma'am." They tried to appear pious, but Eden could tell they were enthralled. Cathy had done the most scandalous thing that anybody at Cumberland Hills had ever heard of.

A carriage rattled to a stop outside the door, and Eden bounced off her trunk. "Here's Gran!"

Miss Cumberland turned to face her fate, in the form of a white-haired old lady with a walking stick. Claudia Brentwood at eighty was still a Tartar, albeit an attractive one. Shrewd green eyes gleamed from a pale, softly wrinkled face, and the walking stick was her only concession to age. Although she staggered slightly as Eden hurled herself into her arms like an exuberant puppy, she seemed in no danger of being knocked over.

"Gently, child."

Eden beamed. "I'm so glad to see you." She buried her face in her grandmother's shoulder. As an afterthought, she looked up at Claudia and asked, "Are Mama and Papa with you?"

"They're at the hotel in Versailles, dear, waiting for you. Your mother wanted to rest." Claudia's voice was noncommittal. "You look very well." She straightened Eden's shoulders and inspected her navy-blue sailor dress and straw boater. "Where is Cathy?"

Miss Cumberland came forward and, with a mournful sigh, presented Cathy's letter to Claudia. "I was preparing to telegraph her father when you arrived. I'll go and do so now."

"Not until I've read this," Claudia said, having taken in the first sentence.

"But, Mrs. Brentwood—"

Claudia pointed at the settee. "Sit down, Miss Cumberland, and say your prayers." She took a gold pince-nez out of her purse and put it on her nose. "She has vile handwriting," Claudia announced when she had finished reading. "If that is the best you can teach these girls, it's no wonder the world is in the state it is in today."

Miss Cumberland struggled to regain her place in the pecking order. "Really, Mrs. Brentwood, I do not see that that is germane to the issue. Miss Martin has behaved in a fashion to disgrace this institution—"

"Well, Miss Martin wanted a better eye kept on her, didn't she?" Claudia remarked acidly.

"I did not expect such extremes to be necessary," Miss Cumberland said. "That is not the behavior we expect of—"

"For heaven's sake, woman, what do you think you're raising here? Buttercups? With two hundred and fifty girls in your charge, you should have expected anything!" Claudia folded the letter into her purse along with the pince-nez.

Miss Cumberland sagged. "It doesn't matter how it came about, Mrs. Brentwood. I'll take full responsibility."

"The time to take responsibility was before my niece took a train to New York," Claudia retorted. "However, since you appear to have been incapable of that, you may leave any further steps to me."

"But her parents—"

"You leave them to me, too. That's not a piece of news one wants to receive in a telegram."

Miss Cumberland didn't much want to send it, either, but she looked determined. "She may be in danger."

"Not until I catch up with her," Claudia said grimly. Her expression softened a little at Miss Cumberland's obvious agitation. "I know where she's going; she's going to see Lucy Woods, who *is* an actress and, unless I miss my guess, the unwitting inspiration for this adventure. I am sufficiently well acquainted with Miss Woods to wire her to meet the little devil's train. Then her parents can receive a telegram from Miss Woods that Cathy is safe with her, rather than one from you that she is heaven knows where."

"Very well," Miss Cumberland said stiffly. "Since you know this woman." Her expression indicated that knowing an actress was unfortunate.

"You may send any of Miss Martin's things remaining in her room by rail to her home," Claudia said. "I rather doubt that she will be returning."

"I doubt it myself," Miss Cumberland said with meaning.

Claudia sniffed. "Come, Eden."

"Gran, what are you going to do when we get to the Martins'?" Eden asked as the carriage rattled down the drive with her trunk strapped to the back.

"I don't quite know yet, dear," Claudia said. "I'm thinking about that."

"What about me? Do you think Mama and Papa will send me back to Cumberland Hills after this?" Eden sighed. "I don't like it much, but I don't want to go someplace else. At least I know people there."

Claudia patted her hand with a certain irritation in her eyes that was not for Eden. "I'm thinking about that, too, but don't ask your papa about it yet. I have an idea, but timing is very important."

Claudia leaned her head back against the slightly musty upholstery of the carriage and prayed, not for the first time, for charity toward her daughter-in-law. Her widowed son, Andrew, had fallen so in love with Lydia von Hofstetten while he was in Switzerland on army business as to forget that she was married. Claudia, who had led a long life, buried two husbands, and was no prude, found that less distressing than the fact that Andy had also allowed himself to be inveigled, through the scheming of Lydia's in-laws, into getting Lydia pregnant—a task beyond the capabilities of her invalid husband. An heir, it seemed, was all-important to this royal family. And when Lydia's husband died, the in-laws kept the heir and threw Lydia out. Andy and Lydia had tried to run away with baby Franz but failed, and a heartbroken Lydia had come with Andy to the United States.

Claudia had had nothing but sympathy for her as they had unsuccessfully pulled every conceivable diplomatic string to retrieve the child. But her sympathy had waned when Andy and Lydia devoted themselves to this crusade at the cost of ignoring little Sam, Andy's son by his first wife, and then their own child, Eden.

Sympathy had vanished entirely when Franz, aged six, had died of scarlet fever and Lydia had turned the house into a kind of perpetual tomb in his memory. His crepe-draped portrait still hung in the parlor, an eternal reminder to Sam and Eden that they didn't matter very much.

As a result, Eden had been farmed out to boarding schools, and a rebellious Sam had first been thrown out of three separate universities and then capped his career by marrying a silver nabob's widow eleven years older than he and bringing her home to Independence for Christmas—probably for the spiteful amusement of seeing his stepmother have hysterics.

Claudia sighed, frustrated. Lydia was obsessed with Franz, but Andy was obsessed with Lydia. The more emotionally fragile Lydia grew, the guiltier Andy felt. When Lydia took to her bed for six months to mourn Franz, Andy understood. When Lydia began not to get up until noon, Andy understood. When she became terrified of being without him, he resigned his commission in the army. They had not been out of Independence in years when Claudia ruthlessly uprooted them for this visit with the Martins. Andy had been a gregarious soul before Lydia's emotional problems had rearranged his life. Claudia thought that Andy must feel rather like Mary Shelley's Dr. Frankenstein, having created a monster that had gone beyond his control.

After their arrival at the hotel in Versailles, Claudia and Eden found Andy pacing dolefully in their sitting room and Lydia in bed in the chamber beyond, with a damp cloth on her head.

Eden hugged her father dutifully, perfunctorily. Certainly it was all that Andy could expect, but it made Claudia feel sad. She watched Andy and Eden looking at each other, as if each wanted something more but didn't know how to go about it.

"What's wrong with Lydia?" Claudia inquired briskly.

"She has a headache." Andy gave his mother a look that dared her to make something of that. Andy at fifty was still a handsome man, dark haired and energetic looking, but the energy was overlaid with wistfulness.

"Well, our train leaves in twenty minutes," Claudia said, "so she'll have to finish her headache on the train."

Andy looked at the empty doorway behind Eden. "Where's Cathy?"

"On a train to New York, preparing to turn her parents' hair gray overnight," Claudia replied. "She intends to star immediately on Broadway. She left us a letter."

"Good God." Andrew looked at his daughter. "Did you know about this?"

"No, Papa," Eden said.

"Has anyone wired her parents?"

"No," Claudia answered. "I wired Lucy Woods to meet the little wretch's train and keep her out of trouble. I sent it from the desk downstairs. We should have a reply by the time we get to the Martins'."

Andrew cast a glance into the bedroom, as if he felt incapable of dealing with anything beyond his own domestic difficulties. Lydia was still lying on the bedcover with her eyes closed, but a faint movement of her hand indicated that she was listening. "I hope you know what you're doing, Mother," Andy said.

"Interfering," Claudia said, and gave him a long look. "I'm good at that."

Cathy Martin edged herself a little closer to the train window, and her skirts a little farther away from the drummer who had a plug of tobacco in his cheek and a gleam in his watery eyes.

"What a coincidence, ain't it, girlie, me going to New York, too? Maybe I can show you around some." He propped his feet on his sample case and spat a stream of tobacco juice into the aisle.

Cathy closed her eyes and shuddered faintly. "I don't think so. I have friends who will be meeting me."

With luck, Cathy thought, she would be able to dodge him at the station in New York before he found out that wasn't true. She was certain Lucy Woods would take her in, but she hadn't dared to wire Lucy ahead of time, for fear Lucy would try to dissuade her from leaving school. It wasn't fair, Cathy thought irritably. Lucy Woods's parents were friends of the Holts, of Cathy's father's, and her father's partner, Edward Blackstone. Cathy had heard numerous times how Alexandra Holt had cured Lucy of her childhood stutter, by teaching her to recite poetry with her mouth full of pebbles. Everyone thought it was just splendid how Lucy had overcome her speech impediment and become an actress. Unfortunately, nobody thought Cathy should follow in her footsteps. No, they all wanted her to marry some nice man and have babies. Well, they would just have to change their minds.

"Maybe we could all go out, do the town," the drummer said. "I ain't introduced myself. Name's Smates—traveler in ladies' better corsets. I got some right pretty samples here—you wanta see 'em?"

"No, thank you." Cathy gave him a freezing look meant to indicate that no gentleman would discuss undergarments with a lady, much less offer to show her samples.

Smates was undaunted. "Best whalebone and canvas. Guaranteed to give any lady a winsome, youthful figure." He eyed Cathy with appreciation. "Not that you need much help, girlie." He nudged her in the ribs with his elbow, and Cathy's eyes widened in indignant surprise. "Some of 'em got lace and ribbons on 'em, too—all the fancy doodads a gal likes. I sell to all the best stores in New York. I could give you a special price, seein' as we're friends."

"No, thank you." Cathy looked at the watch around her neck and realized that she was going to have to spend the night on this train, with Mr. Smates and his corsets lurking in the berth above her. It was going to be a long trip.

The next morning, peering through the window at the outskirts of New York City, not even Mr. Smates could daunt her. Everywhere she looked, there seemed to be buildings, and more people than she could count. Cathy, raised on the plains of Indian Territory, had been to St. Louis and Kansas City and New Orleans. But nothing had prepared her for this.

"It's something, ain't it?" Mr. Smates said. "I'm going to have me a time."

Cathy sat back primly and adjusted her hat, trying not to look like a rube—like Mr. Smates. Sold to all the best stores in New York, indeed. Cathy was aware that the best stores in New York did not buy their goods from the likes of Mr. Smates.

The train pulled into the Grand Central depot in a cloud of steam, and Mr. Smates felt under the seat for his sample case. He stood up, plainly waiting for Cathy to precede him, and as she did, his fingers touched her rib cage in a kind of proprietary guidance. He appeared to have attached himself to her like a barnacle. *The ladies' lounge*, she thought desperately. She could hide in there until he went away.

She stepped from the train, clutching her pocketbook and trying to look like someone who was being met by a respectable aunt and five burly and protective male cousins. The platform was crowded with travelers. They all seemed to know where they were going.

"I don't see your friends, girlie," he said cheerfully. "Maybe you'd better let me give you a hand. This is a big town."

"I'm to meet them inside," Cathy said, preparing to bolt, when miraculously over the hubbub of the crowd she heard someone call her name.

Startled, Cathy peered through the jostling crowd and saw Lucy Woods coming toward her. Lucy deftly dodged around a fat woman sitting on her steamer trunk and a thin child younger than Eden who was selling apples from a wooden tray, which was attached on both sides to a thick ribbon that went around her neck. Lucy took Cathy by the hands and instantly appeared to take in the significance of the unwanted Mr. Smates. "My dear, there you are! I'm so very glad to see you. I have a cab waiting, so we'll just collect your trunk."

Mr. Smates held out his hand. "Name's Smates," he told Lucy. "I been looking out for her."

"How kind of you." Lucy gave Mr. Smates two gloved fingers, retracted them almost immediately, and bent icy blue eyes on him until he melted into the crowd.

"Oh, thank you," Cathy breathed.

"That's one of the hazards of traveling alone." Lucy gave her a stern look. "You have been *extremely* naughty."

"I know, but I had to come. How did you know I was coming?"

"Your great-aunt Claudia sent me a wire," Lucy answered. "She was quite explicit about what she wanted me to do with you."

Cathy smiled. "Starting with putting me over your knee?"

"It may come to that if you don't behave yourself," Lucy informed her.

"Then I can *stay*?"

"For the time being," Lucy said. A faintly wicked

gleam lit her eyes. "Unless you'd rather put yourself under Mr. Smates's protection?"

"Heavens, no." Cathy tucked her arm through Lucy's. "I'll be angelic, truly I will."

"You will indeed. We'll begin with a contrite wire to your parents."

Indian Territory, April 1889

Cathy's telegram arrived in a packet by messenger from the Indian Territory rail depot in Folsom, Oklahoma. Also enclosed were Lucy's wire to Claudia and a telegram to the Martins from Miss Cumberland, whose conscience had refused to allow her to hide behind Claudia Brentwood's skirts. The Brentwoods arrived at the same time, in the buggy that Rob Martin had sent for them, resulting in considerable chaos.

The telegraph boy had to cough loudly several times before anyone remembered to pay him, and Lydia Brentwood made her contribution by fainting on the Indian rug in the front hall.

"I'm going to New York this minute," Rob Martin decided.

"You might want to change your garments," Claudia suggested mildly. Rob's work clothes were covered with a fine layer of prairie dust. "Now don't go tearing off anywhere until you've heard me out. Cathy is just fine for the moment." Claudia indicated the small fortune in telegrams clutched in Kale Martin's hand.

Kale put a hand on her husband's arm, in case he was planning to turn the buggy around and drive to New York in it. He looked as if he might be.

"Mama's fainted," Eden announced.

"Good heavens!" Kale knelt over Lydia and found a bottle of smelling salts in her reticule.

Lydia opened China blue eyes and whispered plaintively, "It's all been just more than I could bear. You have no idea how dreadful this journey has been."

Kale looked baffled and a little annoyed. She had never cared much for women who fainted, and it was *her* stepdaughter who had run off to New York, not Lydia's child.

"Mama always faints," Eden assured her.

"To lose a child . . ." Lydia's eyes spilled over with tears, and Andy picked her up in his arms.

"We'll put you to bed," he said helplessly. "Let you rest."

Eden, stone faced, backed off a little from her mother.

"Andrew!" Claudia thumped her walking stick on the oak floor.

Everyone turned to look at the elderly woman.

"I am aware," Claudia announced, "that I have no authority in this situation, other than by virtue of advanced age." She didn't look all that advanced, and her green eyes sparked in a fashion that made Lydia struggle to sit up in Andy's arms and glare back at her.

"I do, however, have a plan," Claudia said.

"I've got a plan, too," Rob muttered grimly. His red hair was standing on end from having run his fingers through it in frustration.

"Well, I have a sensible plan," Claudia said. "So you just listen to it before you go off to New York half-cocked and prod that child into doing something worse. She's your daughter, Rob Martin, and she comes from very pigheaded stock, as you ought to know."

"Perhaps we should go into the parlor," Kale suggested, "and close the door before the house fills up with geese." Two of them, Kale's pets, had been eating bugs in the carefully tended square of lawn in front of the ranch house. One had come up the steps and was peering with interest into the hall, its neck snaking out from behind a pot of geraniums.

Rob threw his hands in the air and shut the door, then followed the others into the parlor.

Andy lowered Lydia gently to a settee and sat holding her hand. Claudia settled into a wing chair and beckoned to Eden. "Come here, child."

Eden sat on the ottoman by Claudia's feet, and Kale pulled Rob down onto a second settee. The adults looked at Claudia expectantly. Eden studied her parents and the Martins with interest, wondering what was going to happen.

Eden knew that her mother and grandmother didn't like each other, and she had tried dutifully not to take sides. But it was hard, Eden thought guiltily, not to love Gran better.

"Andrew, I am taking Eden out of school," Claudia announced. That snapped Andy's head around in a hurry. "And this time you are not going to argue with me."

Eden looked at her wide-eyed. She had not known that they *had* argued about it.

"Well, in view of— Well, I guess that that school isn't the best place for her," Andy said.

"I am taking her out of school entirely. I will see that she has a suitable governess, but she is going to live with me."

"Nooo!" Lydia moaned. "You aren't going to take my baby. Oh, it's too cruel." She burst into tears.

"Stop it!" Claudia ordered. "You put your baby in a boarding school when she was seven, and she saw precious little of you before that. Spare me the histrionics."

The Martins looked embarrassed.

"Andrew, my smelling salts . . ." Lydia's eyes were wild. "That's how they took my Franz. . . . That's how my first husband's family took my baby!" Her voice rose to a wail, and Andrew put his arms around her.

"I think, Andrew," Claudia said quietly, "that you had better think about this seriously." She flicked a glance at the Martins' stunned expressions and went on, speaking now to them. "Rob and Kale, I propose to take Eden with me to New York City. I will buy her some clothes, take her to the theater and the ballet, the opera—give the child some fun with her education. While I am there, I can take your Cathy under my wing for a while."

Eden, overcome with emotion, buried her face in her grandmother's skirt.

"Give consideration to this, Rob," Claudia urged. "Lucy won't let the child come to any harm, and she may give her a little food for thought. How long has she had this bee in her bonnet about acting?"

"Several years," Rob muttered. "Of all the foolish—"

"We just don't know *why*," Kale cut in. "She doesn't need to earn her own living. She doesn't know what it's like." Kale's eyes were unhappy. "Before I married Rob, my life had more hardship and sacrifice than Cathy could possibly know. I want to spare her from all that."

"That's my point, dear," Claudia told her gently. "Lucy hasn't come as far as she has in her profession without seeing the—shall we say—seedy side of things. Let Lucy talk to her, and Cathy may find some of the glamour wearing off."

Rob looked uncomfortable. "Maybe we've protected Cathy too much."

Kale appeared to weaken. "And you would watch over her?"

"Like a hawk," Claudia assured her. "I have friends in New York who are so respectable, one almost goes to sleep in their presence. But they have sons and daughters Cathy's age who are lively but do not move in theatrical circles. Cathy can see the sights with Eden and me, go to parties, have some fun—and feel that she has rebelled just enough to satisfy her sense of independence but not enough to give you heart failure."

"Well . . ." Rob ran his hands through his hair again.

"Yes," Kale decided abruptly. "If we bring her home like a bad child, Rob, she might run away again, and then she wouldn't have Lucy and Claudia for a safety net. I couldn't bear that."

"I've usually left decisions on her upbringing to you," Rob said. "You've always done a good job of it, so I'm not going to stop now." He looked at Claudia. "If you're willing to let her try her wings a little, we'll be grateful. Heck, maybe I should have seen this coming. Maybe *we* should have taken her."

Claudia smiled. "You can't run away from home and take your daddy with you. Now quit worrying."

"I have not agreed to this," Lydia said.

"I think maybe it's a good idea," Andy muttered.

Lydia sat up, clutching her handkerchief. "I never thought that you would bring me to a foreign country only to turn on me. Abandon me!"

"Now, that's not it—"

"You're upsetting Eden," Claudia warned sharply.

Lydia looked at them all furiously. "You are all against me! Your whole family is conspiring against me! First I am humiliated by Sam's marriage to a common, vulgar peasant! And then you drag me here, in the middle of desolation, where there are Indians. You know I can't sleep away from my own bed. I am not strong, Andrew. You are killing me. And now you let your mother take our child—" Lydia got up from the settee, swaying on her feet. "I am going to bed. You have made me ill again. No, Andrew, don't come with me. I can manage." Tears rolled down her cheeks, and she pressed one hand to her breast. "One day I shall die, and then you all shall be free of me." She turned and moved toward the door.

Kale, stunned by the outburst, got up and followed her. "I'll show you to your room."

"I've got a cow I've got to see about," Rob said.

"Take Eden," Claudia suggested. "She's a city child. She'd like to see the ranch."

"Right. You come with me, honey." Rob held out his hand. They both knew they were being told to stay out of the parlor for a while and were only too happy to oblige. Rob looked as if he would have gone through the window if it had provided a faster exit.

"How long has this been going on?" Claudia demanded when she and her son were alone.

He sat down on the settee again and put his head in his hands. "It does seem to me like maybe she's feeling worse lately."

"Feeling worse!" Claudia fumed. "That woman is probably as strong as a horse; otherwise, she couldn't have survived all the hysterical fits she's thrown over the years."

"She's had so much tragedy in her life," Andrew defended. "It's not her fault. She was brought up to lead a gentle life, and she's been through hell."

Claudia snorted. "Most of the people we know haven't had a bowl of roses for breakfast every morning. Look at Rob and Kale. Look at Toby Holt. Look at me, if you will. I lost two babies after I had you, and I doubt that I found it any less distressing than Lydia did."

"No one stole them away from you," Andy said. "That's different."

"God stole them away from me," Claudia said. "And don't you ever dare tell me it was different." She raised her hand, and for a moment Andy thought she was going to hit him.

"I'm sorry, Mother. I didn't mean—"

"No, and you didn't think, either, because you're so wrapped up in Lydia. You think it's your fault, the state she's in. Well, allow me to present you with a couple of basic truths." Claudia thumped her walking stick on the floor.

"Yes, Mother."

"Lydia is a weak person. She probably would have been fine if her life had been a constant tea party. But she simply cannot handle adversity, and you haven't tried to teach her to. And now you have a selfish, insecure woman who's bitter at the world and afraid of it. So what are you going to do?"

"That's a heck of a question. If I knew what to do about it, things wouldn't be in this mess." Andy looked harassed. "I love her. I can't bully her."

"Do you think Lydia is happy right now?"

"No." He sighed. "I don't think she's ever been happy. That's why I feel so rotten."

"Happy is as happy does. Do you think she'd be less happy if you quit cosseting her?"

"I don't know." Andy looked nearly as miserable as Lydia had.

Claudia thought he was pretty close to the end of his rope. It was a thirteen-year-old rope—and certainly a mark of Andy's devotion to his wife that it hadn't frayed sooner.

"Well, I suggest you make the experiment." Claudia marched to the door, her stick punctuating her every step.

"Where are you going?" Andy looked abandoned.

"Out for a walk." Claudia looked at him over her shoulder, a faint sly affection in her eye. "Believe it or not, I find it quite exhausting to be such an imperious old woman."

That wasn't far from the truth, she thought as she set off down the walkway, with Kale's geese honking around her skirts. She was eighty, and Andy was fifty, and she had chided him as if he were five. Certainly a wearing experience for them both.

Claudia wondered if anything would come of it. She had voiced her opinion before—it wasn't in her nature not to—but never with such candor. On the other hand, she had never seen Lydia quite so bad before. Lydia perceived Sam's marriage as a personal affront to her own good breeding and had complained numerous times that dear Franz would never have done that to her.

I should have stepped in sooner, Claudia thought. *I should have taken Sam.* Well, she would make amends with Eden. She sat down to rest on the carriage block. In the distance she could see Rob and Eden, walking companionably through the paddock, admiring the Brahma-longhorn crossbreeds that were Rob's pride. India and Winslow Blackstone, the children of Rob's partner, Edward, skipped out of the barn, towing a pet calf. Edward and his wife, Ramedha, who was from India, half-English and half-Hindu, lived in the white frame house that Claudia could just see under a grove of trees half a mile away. The Blackstone children displayed the calf proudly, and Eden ran over to admire it.

Now that Claudia had everyone's consent to her scheme, she wondered briefly if she had lost her mind.

Children rarely sat still, and she was proposing to take charge of Eden and a headstrong nineteen-year-old. She couldn't admit that to Andrew; he was only half-convinced as it was.

Down the dirt track that led to Folsom, Claudia could see another carriage coming. She brightened. Maybe it was Toby, bringing Lee and Eulalia with him. The children raced down the road to meet the carriage, the little calf cavorting along beside them.

Eden broke from the group and swerved toward her grandmother. Her face was alight. She threw her arms around Claudia.

"Oh, Gran, I do love you!" Eden hugged her hard, then raced away again, following India and Winslow.

Well! Claudia thought. There really wasn't much question that she was doing the right thing, was there? Smiling, she rose from the carriage block. When it came down to it, she thought, you could probably always do anything, as long as you didn't tell yourself you couldn't.

III

The surrey rattled to a stop by the carriage block, and Toby Holt got down and stretched. He was a tall, sandy-haired man with a strong-boned face and a determined chin. He looked up at the Martins' house appreciatively. It was more elegant than a farmhouse but big and sprawling. Its wide porch had a swing and was surrounded by tall cottonwoods for shade. Toby thought that the house had grown since he had last seen it. Every time Rob thought about it, he decided the house was too small and added a room or two. To Toby, after a jolting three days on the train, confined with his restless offspring, it looked like heaven.

He held out his arms to Claudia Brentwood, and she hugged him and then hugged his family in turn as Toby handed them down from the surrey: Toby's wife, Alexandra, auburn haired and remarkably elegant, considering the journey; his mother, Eulalia, and his stepfather, General Leland Blake, whose first wife had been Claudia's sister; thirteen-year-old Mike, a thin, red-haired boy with a resemblance to Alexandra; six-year-old Sally; and finally Juanita, Alexandra's maid and Sally's nurse, huffing a little with the exertion of getting her girth out of the surrey.

Rob came up from the barn, while his wife and Andy Brentwood came down the steps from the house.

Andy shook Toby's hand. "Good to see you, Senator."

Andy sounded jovially congratulatory, and Toby

29

grinned. This was their first face-to-face meeting since a vituperative exchange of telegrams, occasioned by their respective sons having run off to Nevada together to dig for silver. Toby was gratified that both he and Andy had given up trying to argue out whose fault it all was.

"Good to see you, you old reprobate." Toby looked around cautiously. "Where's Lydia?"

"Resting," Andy answered.

Toby thought he wouldn't ask anything more. His eyes lit on a monstrous packing crate in the yard outside the horse barn. Even from here he could read the word *Holt* scrawled across it.

"What in tarnation is that?"

Rob chuckled. "Printing press. Its owner is due any day now."

"Good," Toby remarked. "He owes me a hundred dollars. I lent Tim enough to get the *Beacon* on its feet again, and he's assured me that he's ready to pay up." Toby intended to collect, too, in reparation for a great deal of fairly recent gray hair.

They went into the house in companionable conversation, and Kale took the women upstairs to wash off the dust and train soot. The children stayed in the yard in a swirling mass of what looked to Toby like about fifty youngsters, introducing themselves to each other and showing off the calf.

"Henry and Cindy should be here in time for dinner," Rob said. "They're bringing Peter and the young ones with them. And Edward and Ramedha are coming over. We're going to have a houseful."

"Where's Cathy?"

Rob rolled his eyes heavenward. "I'll tell you as soon as I pour us a drink. I feel as if I could use one."

By evening the house could have been mistaken for a good hotel, with casual service and excellent food. It overflowed with laughing, hugging kin and good friends. Toby's sister, Cindy, and her husband—Lee and Eulalia's adopted son—Henry, had arrived with their two boys and a girl. The two young ones, Frank and Midge, were out on the lawn in the dusk with the other children, chasing lightning bugs with a jar. Fifteen-year-old Peter, too old for bugs and not quite an adult, hovered on the edge of the group while his father and stepmother cast anxious glances in his direction. In the way that large families have of soaking up information by osmosis, everyone knew within an hour or two of their arrival that Henry and Cindy were having trouble with Peter.

Tim Holt arrived in time for dinner and made an elaborate ceremony of presenting his father with five twenty-dollar gold pieces tied up in a handkerchief. "With all the radicals getting sent to Washington these days, I figured we shouldn't trust paper money any-more," Tim said with a grin.

Toby chuckled and stuck the money in his pocket. "Probably a good plan," he said solemnly.

The older generation nodded approvingly. Tim Holt had grown up. It gave the other assembled parents a good deal of hope.

Kale, who loved nothing better than a houseful of people and didn't have one very often, had master-minded a dinner of quail, peas, biscuits, quince pre-serves, and a standing roast of M Bar B beef. For dessert there was ice cream, which the children had been set to churning on the back porch. There was now a spirited argument going on at the children's table as to who had done the most cranking and thus deserved the biggest helping.

" 'From each according to his abilities, to each ac-cording to his needs,' " Peter Blake quoted. "That's what Karl Marx says."

"Who's Karl Marx?" Mike Holt asked him.

"A man with a theory," Peter said. "I think it's got holes in it, but it sounds good on the surface."

"Well, I need lots," Winslow Blackstone assured them. "Two helpings."

Tim Holt, overhearing this exchange, looked at Henry Blake. "Good Lord, has he actually read Karl Marx?"

"In the original German," Henry answered, then sighed. Peter was Henry's son by his first wife, Gisela, a German baroness from whom Peter had inherited a considerable fortune. With the fortune came a trio of trustees who wrote him long, stern letters in German on the subject of money management, with which Peter, whose grasp of finance was precocious, invariably disagreed.

Tim's aunt, Cindy, Peter's stepmother, lowered her voice and leaned across the table. "Peter's with us because the commandant asked Henry to take him out of school. It's not that he's done anything wrong—but Peter's so logical. That doesn't seem to act in one's favor in a military school." Cindy cast a glance at her husband, then at his father, Lee Blake—career military men both. "I mean, if Peter can see a more efficient, more sensible way to do something, he can't see any reason to do it the old way, just because it's traditional." She caught Tim's sympathetic eye and smiled. "The commandant wrote Henry a letter that said, 'Cadet Blake constitutes a sort of ticking bomb, ready to blow an otherwise orderly regiment to Hades. Please find something else for him to do.'"

"That's not exactly humorous," Henry protested.

Cindy eyed her husband affectionately. "You'd think it was, darling, if he wasn't ours."

Lydia Brentwood gave a mournful sigh. "No one knows what a mother goes through," she said, apparently to the company in general.

Some of the other mothers at the table opened their mouths to dispute that and then, in a collective burst of tact, closed them again.

"We brought along a marvelous letter from Janessa," Alexandra said brightly, changing the subject.

"Oh, read it to us," Ramedha Blackstone urged.

Toby pulled the letter out of his pocket, along with a pair of spectacles. The spectacles were new, a concession to middle age that he did not much care for. He began to read:

"We're in the middle of the rainy season now, and so everything is green. For the moment we have spring, and the season is investing all my fellow boarders at Mrs. Burnside's house with a certain giddiness.

"Only Mr. Anderson's health was declining in some mysterious way, which he would not explain to Charley or me. He pestered us with questions so oblique that neither of us could decipher precisely what was ailing him.

"Then Charley and I both noticed that Mr. Anderson hadn't sat down all evening. Charley hauled him into the next room and ordered him either to strip and present us with the problem, or to be quiet about it.

"The poor man turned out to have a very large boil on his backside. Charley sent me for my bag and put the protesting patient over his knee and ruthlessly held him down while I lanced the boil. When Charley finally turned him loose, Mr. Anderson yanked on his trousers and fled.

"This morning at breakfast, Mr. Anderson looked right through me, as if I were a dressmaker's dummy propped in the chair. Mrs. Burnside, who I suspect was listening at the door last night, very solicitously presented him with a pillow."

By the time Toby finished reading, Rob Martin was laughing heartily. "This Charley sounds like a man after my own heart. I hear Janessa's going to marry him."

"A man whose sensibilities are so calloused?" Lydia shuddered delicately. "It is unfortunate that his lack of delicacy appears to be rubbing off on his intended wife." She laid her fork down and rose weakly from the table. "I shall go and rest. I have no appetite after such an unpleasant description."

Alexandra and Kale watched her go, then exchanged

a speaking glance across the table. Toby put the letter back in his pocket and began to talk to Rob and Edward about cows. Andy applied himself to his roasted beef in silence for a minute or two, then got up and followed Lydia.

"Really," Alexandra said, "that woman is a wet blanket." Then she saw Eden at the children's table, sitting with her shoulders slumped, and wished she had kept quiet.

Mike Holt tapped Eden on the arm. "Come on," he said. "Let's get the ice cream."

When they got to the back porch, where the can was chilling in its rock-salt bath, Mike sat down in a wicker chair by the steps and motioned Eden to another. "We can wait out here till you feel better."

"Does it show?"

"Some." Mike looked embarrassed. "I was . . . I was kind of watching you."

"Why?"

"I think you're nice," Mike said. "And I think you're pretty, too."

Brooding, Eden put her chin in her hands. "I probably look like Mama. Nobody thinks Mama's nice."

"Hey, now don't you pay any attention to what my mother said. She didn't mean it."

"Your mama always looks so happy," Eden said with longing. "As if everything is fun."

"I don't know about that," Mike said. "She spends a lot of time worrying about me." He looked self-conscious again. "I have a funny heart. I had rheumatic fever when I was a kid." He shrugged. "I'm not supposed to do too much. Sometimes I think it's going to make me crazy."

"What would you like to do?" Eden asked.

Mike tucked his feet under him in the chair. He wore knickers, with long black stockings and button boots, which made him look even thinner than he was. "I'd like to be a photographer, like Aunt Cindy's friend Marjorie White." He sighed. "The only trouble is, you have to go places to do that."

"You're going to Washington," Eden pointed out.

"I know." Mike brightened. "I guess that's better than nothing. But everybody is always checking on me to see if I'm all right. Mama does it all the time, and Dad does, too, and Grandmama Eulalia and Grandpa Lee. We were going to stop here on the way to Washington even if there hadn't been a get-together planned. Mama was afraid the trip would be too much for me and wanted me to rest."

Eden smiled at him. "Well, I'm glad you did."

Mike smiled back. "Me, too."

The M Bar B was a working ranch, so the day began early. At dawn Rob was in the barn with Edward Blackstone, and Kale stood in the kitchen mixing and baking biscuits.

Tim was among the first to awake. Now that he was here, with nothing to do but cool his heels until 22 April, he felt restless. None of the others were his age. The Martins had been delighted to hear that he was coming, and Tim suspected that they had been hoping that Cathy would be delighted, too, but she had had her own plans. Tim wasn't interested in courting, but at least Cathy would have been company. He walked into the kitchen, said good morning to Kale, filched a biscuit when her back was turned, and then roamed, looking for something to do.

Peter Blake found him in the parlor, taking the mantel clock apart, fifteen minutes later.

"That's a lot of pieces," Peter observed. "You know where they all go?"

"Mostly," Tim replied. "It wasn't running, so I thought I'd fix it." He fiddled with its insides and slipped a spring back into place. "It's all a question of logic," he added, poking another piece gently into its slot. "Mechanics is a logical progression of working parts. A moves B, and B moves C, and so on."

"I never thought of it that way," Peter said, interested. "I thought you were a newspaperman."

"Oh, I am. That's my baby out there in that crate. Brand-new Washington press. But I like machinery. You can see what makes it go. If a lever moves up and down one day, it won't turn around on you and go sideways the next."

"Logic in its physical form," Peter murmured. "Interesting. You could work up a whole philosophical theory about that, I expect."

"Well, it has its surprises," Tim said when a spring shot out and rocketed across the room. He retrieved it and squinted at the back of the clock. "Got any tweezers?"

Peter produced a pocketknife with tweezers among its attachments.

"You strike me as mighty serious for fifteen," Tim commented.

"Probably," Peter said. "The trouble is, I can't get serious about what Dad gets serious about."

"Like military school?" Tim asked. "I can't say I blame you there. Ha! I got it."

"I don't mind the discipline," Peter continued. "It's just the way they go about it."

"I believe the general idea is to teach you to jump when they say jump. People who stand around saying 'Captain! Oh, Captain! Yoo-hoo! *Why* are we supposed to jump?' very often end up with their hair on some Apache's belt."

"I didn't mean in a battle," Peter said indignantly.

"Well, I expect one is training for the other. Still, you don't sound like much of a candidate." Tim was quiet for a moment as he concentrated on working on the clock mechanism. "Just let me finish this up. Then we'll go outside."

"The trouble with you is," Tim observed later as they ambled through the barnyard, going nowhere in particular, "you've got a passel of family traditions to uphold, and they're grating on you."

"Tradition is important in my family," Peter said stiffly.

"Yes, tradition's a fine thing. Lots of change in the air now, though. When it butts heads with tradition, we're going to see something."

"What do you mean?"

"There's a whole new world out there—electric lights, telephones. Everyone's going to have them in the house in a few more years. The internal-combustion engine. When I was a kid in Portland, there was an old man who'd been tinkering with one of those. He used to let me into his workshop. Everyone thought he was as mad as a hatter. Maybe he was. But a German named Karl Benz has built a horseless carriage with one. Have you got any idea what that's going to do the entire economic structure of the country? Lord. If you ask me, when you get your hands on your mother's money, you ought to go look up old Karl."

"My trustees," Peter informed him, "generally view any recent inventions as bound to explode—literally as well as financially."

"Prototypes always explode," Tim said cheerfully. "That's why everyone always thinks any inventor has a screw loose."

"A lot of people in the family seem to think *you* have a screw loose."

Tim laughed and was relieved to see the flicker of an answering smile on Peter's face. Peter's blue eyes crinkled up, and the prairie wind lifted his chestnut hair. His thin face seemed both adolescent and oddly adult, as if he were adrift and somewhat baffled between the two states.

"Maybe I do," Tim admitted. "Maybe that's why I'm out here waiting to land a piece of a city that's not even built yet. Oklahoma's going to be an invention. It's going to be the damnedest thing anybody ever saw." He started off again toward where Mike and Eden, with Sally in tow, were drawing a bucket of water at the pump. He felt restless just talking about Oklahoma and wanted to poke at something else to work it off.

Peter followed him and stood looking northward toward where Tim's "invented" city was going to rise from the prairie just beyond the horizon.

"We're going to bathe the calf," Mike told his half brother.

"Let me look at that pump," Tim said. "It's not pulling near enough water, with all three of you hanging off the handle." They relinquished the pump handle, and Tim lay down on his back and squinted up into its works.

India Blackstone came up with the calf on a lead. It didn't look much as if it wanted a bath, but India had an apron full of apples. "Uncle Rob's going to be sore if you break his pump," she declared.

"Trust me, India."

"My brother can fix anything," Mike assured her.

India turned up her nose. "I heard you set fire to your house with a steam engine."

"Nobody's going to let me forget that, are they?" Tim grunted as he poked at the pump. "I was about your size, little girl, and it was a road locomotive. I didn't set fire to the house; I bulldozed it. *Then* it caught fire. You've got a busted lever in here. Peter, you want to see if you can find a wrench?"

Peter, who hadn't been listening, was still staring across the rolling prairie, watching the wind stir the distant grass into waves. "People are going to make a lot of money out there, aren't they?" he asked suddenly.

"I fervently hope so," Tim said. "Where's my wrench?"

"I'll get it!" Peter raced for the toolshed.

By the end of the day, Tim found that he had a shadow. Peter Blake had attached himself to Tim with the fervor that only an adolescent who has made his first adult friend can summon up. Tim was not so far from Peter's age, and he also had spent time as the family misfit. He listened sympathetically to Peter's unhappy speculations as to whether or not he would ever fit in anywhere. Discovering that Peter had an uncanny grasp of any facts concerning money, Tim answered seriously the boy's questions on the financial end of the newspaper game and the economics of boomtowns.

Peter followed happily while Tim jiggered with the works of the windmill and rigged a new set of pulleys for the hay lift in the barn, and they discussed with great seriousness a further theory of logic and mechanics that Tim predicted would make them famous if they had the time to work the kinks out of it.

"What makes you think it has kinks?" Peter asked. "It sounds right to me."

"There are always kinks," Tim said. "There's always a wild card. It's called life. That's what makes things explode. And exploding logic is a force that goes way beyond dynamite."

Peter laughed; he had started to laugh more often. "You know a lot about life, don't you?"

Tim sighed. "Well, I've been blown sky-high a time or two."

When he couldn't find anything else to take apart, Tim took Peter with him into town, to the stockyard next to the rail depot, where he bought a saddle horse, a wagon, and a team. He set the seal on Peter's devotion by letting Peter dicker with the stockman for them.

As they drove back to the M Bar B with the new horse and the two mounts they had borrowed from Rob Martin tied behind, Tim was beginning to get a notion—a wild-card notion.

"Well, here's my idea," Tim said to Henry Blake at the end of dinner, "about young Peter."

"What idea?" Alexandra and Cindy inquired together.

Cindy cast a cautious glance around the dining room. The children had all been sent to bed, except for Peter, who was too old to go to bed at nine and was, she suspected, lurking somewhere not quite out of earshot.

"Give him to me," Tim said.

"Give him—? He isn't a parcel!"

"I, uh, sort of figured he was at loose ends," Tim said. "It might do him good to have a job for a couple of years, take a little time, and figure out what he wants."

"That is the most irresponsible—"

"He has to go to school!"

"What would you do with him?"

"I need a printer's devil," Tim answered when the family had expressed its collective opinion that he was insane. Only Toby hadn't said anything. He was looking at Tim with fascination and barely suppressed amusement.

"I need someone who can handle money, too," Tim continued.

"Someone to keep you out of poker games," Toby murmured.

Tim ignored that. He looked at Henry Blake. "Peter doesn't need to go to school. I think he just needs time to find his niche."

"He has a niche!" Henry said indignantly.

"He does not, however, seem to be staying in it very well," Lee Blake commented.

"Dad, are you proposing we let him do this?" Henry demanded.

"Not at all." Lee sipped his whiskey. "It's your decision, yours and Cindy's. I was just offering an observation."

"As long as we're observing," Toby said, "I think this is a fine idea."

Andrew Brentwood snorted. "You were mighty upset about Tim's leaving school."

"So were you about Sam's," Toby said mildly. "Now that's water under the bridge, Andy. And I'm just going to say this once, so everybody make it last." He looked around the table, particularly at Tim and Andy. "I was wrong. I think leaving Harvard was the best thing Tim ever did. If any of my other kids try it, I'll probably scream like a stuck pig, but right now, I'm admitting he was right. Some people just seem to need to jump into life and see what it brings them."

"I'm afraid we do not agree with you, Toby," Lydia

said with a sniff. She fixed baleful eyes on Tim. "We hold Tim responsible for Sam's tragic marriage."

"Tragic, hell," Toby said, irritated. "You sound like Sam fell down a hole."

"He might as well have," Lydia pronounced.

"Well, it was full of money," Toby consoled dryly. He caught Alexandra giving him a will-you-be-quiet look and turned to Henry again. "I don't think you need to worry about Peter. He'll have someone with sense in charge of him, which those two idiots didn't."

Cindy burst out laughing. "The 'idiot' and the 'person with sense' happen to be the same person, my dear brother."

Peter appeared in the doorway. "Does anybody want to know what *I* think?"

"I told you to let me handle it," Tim grumbled.

"You weren't getting anywhere." Peter sat down among the adults on a chair dragged over from the children's table. He looked at his parents, who looked back at him with troubled, questioning eyes. "I want to stay with Tim."

"What if you don't like it, dear?" Cindy asked him.

"I'll stick it out anyway," Peter answered.

"Do you mean that?" Henry asked seriously.

Peter nodded.

Henry leaned back in his chair, considering. He caught his wife's eye, and she gave him the ghost of a nod. "We'll think about it," he said.

"Good-bye!"
"Good-bye!"

The whole gathering of kin and clan was setting off almost at once, in ways as separate as those by which they had converged: The Holts and Blakes to Washington, the Brentwoods back to Independence, and Claudia and Eden to New York.

"I'll take care of Cathy!" Claudia called from the train window to Kale, who was standing on the narrow platform. Eden leaned out the window beside her and waved at Mike, who was waiting for his own train.

Something landed at his feet, and Mike picked it up. A little gold locket lay in his hand, with the initials EB on the back. "I'll write!" he called as the train chuffed away from them.

Settled into the compartment of their own train, Alexandra looked at Mike turning the locket over in his hands, but she didn't say anything. She smiled out the window, so he couldn't see.

Sally was bouncing on the seat, waving out her window at Tim and Peter, who were getting into the loaded wagon by the tracks. Juanita had her hand on Sally's sash to keep her from falling out.

"Good-bye, good-bye!" Sally called, and Tim blew her a kiss.

Lee and Eulalia Blake settled in the seat across the aisle, with Henry and Cindy and the two younger children behind them. Midge Blake squeezed in beside Sally to hang out the window, too. Juanita grabbed Midge's sash and hung on, like a woman with a brace of puppies on a leash.

Henry looked dubiously past his daughter's backside at the face of his elder son. Peter was sitting beside Tim on the wagon seat, his face shaded by a broad-brimmed hat, and he was wearing clothes borrowed from Rob Martin—blue-denim work pants and a collarless shirt more suitable for the coming adventure than the brown worsted city suit he had brought from Washington. The work pants were a little too big for him; the hat sat a little too low on his ears.

"I've lost my mind," Henry groaned.

Cindy and Toby looked at each other conspiratorially. Henry had been saying that ever since Cindy had convinced him to let Peter stay with Tim.

Eleven-year-old Frank kicked his heels against the seat. "I wish I could stay."

"Not on your life," Henry muttered.

Alexandra smiled at the pair in the wagon. Tim seemed to have matured enormously since he had gone to Nevada. Really, he looked just like Toby. "Relax," she told Henry. "That's what big families are for: to let the young ones try their wings without having to do it among strangers."

The train began to move, and Peter stood up on the wagon seat to wave again. They could just see his grin under the hat.

IV

New York City, April 1889

Cathy Martin sat in the drawing room of Lucy Woods's New York apartment and sighed with pure pleasure. Her father's telegram was clutched in her hand. He was going to let her stay.

Lucy lived in the Dakota apartment building across from Central Park, in an elegant six-room suite. Scattered about were copies of playscripts, directors' notes, and letters—mash notes, really—from stage-door Johnnies. Lucy laughed about them. They weren't serious, she said. Just boys with money, out "slumming."

Cathy longed to remake herself in Lucy's image. Lucy was at the theater now, but she would be home soon, bringing with her friends who swam in the same glittering theatrical current that Lucy did. Sophie, Lucy's Polish maid, was in the kitchen fixing food for them: little sandwiches of potted meat and a platter of oysters. There would be champagne. Maurice and Georgiana Barrymore might come with Lucy. Cathy loved the Barrymores. Once they had brought their children with them, and Ethel, Lionel, and Jack had danced a soft shoe on the hearth while Lucy had played "Tavern in the Town" on the grand piano.

Lucy had already taken her backstage at the theater, a wonderful, mysterious world that smelled of greasepaint and hot pressing irons. Mr. Smates and his corsets and the sooty peddler children at the railway station had faded from her mind already. New York was fairyland, just as she had known it would be.

Oklahoma, Indian Territory, April 21

To Tim Holt, Oklahoma was El Dorado—streets paved with gold . . . or would be, as soon as there were streets. Just now there was only a swelling sea of gold seekers who held the same view he did. Along the northern border their campfires stretched endlessly under the prairie sky, and their restlessness seemed to crackle in the air. Everyone was moving, twenty thousand people stirring in the night, dragging a wagon forward to jockey for a better position, settling back, getting up again, pacing . . . sleepless, eager, nerves strung tight. Too much hung on the next day's noon gun to sleep.

Beyond the campfires, mounted federal marshals patrolled, searching for any wily soul who might use the darkness for a head start. Three men had been found hiding in trees and gullies already and hauled back across the line. Rumors were circulating that the marshals themselves had let their friends in early . . . that a hiding place across the line could be bought for a hundred dollars . . . that an eastern land company had mounted three hundred men on racehorses to claim the best sections . . . that—well, that anything. The moonlit night was wild with speculation.

Tim and Peter couldn't sleep, either. They had been there for a day and had a good spot. Tim's saddle horse had been loafing and eating grain and was ready to challenge any hypothetical racehorse.

Now they sat by their fire, listening to the stirrings in the night, watching their hopeful fellow settlers with interest.

To one side a pair of cowboys, a little drunk, was playing poker and betting shares of the land they hoped to claim. Beyond them, an immigrant family from Sweden, with a cluster of fair-haired children, had all their household goods piled in a wagon, chair legs sticking out from under the tarp lashed over it all. On the other side, a portly man in a derby hat was reading the *Police Gazette* by lantern light. A sleek-looking horse was tethered nearby, and except for the magazine and the lantern, its owner seemed unencumbered by any worldly goods.

Just beyond the man in the derby was a young couple, also with everything they owned piled in a wagon, although that didn't seem to amount to much. The man, in a flannel shirt and a slouch hat, prowled along the perimeter of their campfire's light, glaring into the darkness. He looked drunk. The woman sat by the fire, a shawl around her thin shoulders, stirring a pot of beans. Tim didn't blame the fellow for the smoldering glare he was giving any man who looked their way. The woman was beautiful—young and slim, but with blue eyes about twice as big as anybody's had a right to be and a small, delicate mouth. The cloud of hair that framed her heart-shaped face was so pale in the moonlight that it looked almost white, and between the moonlight and the firelight, it made a glowing aureole around her face.

The man in the slouch hat, catching Tim looking at her, shot him such a venomous glare that Tim turned away. *Just admiring the sight, friend,* he thought. *Don't get worked up.*

Rosebay Basham saw the look that Tim had given her, and he seemed so nice and friendly that she almost smiled back. But then she noticed Wedge scowling at him, so she looked into the bean pot instead. Rosebay scooped a steaming ladleful onto a plate.

"Sit down and eat, Wedge. You got to eat."

As he took the beans, the scowl faded into that crazy look again—excited and triumphant. Rosebay smiled. Wedge wanted this land more than he had ever wanted anything, except maybe her. They'd come all the way from the Appalachian mountains for it.

Rosebay looked out across the prairie. It didn't look so bad now at night when you couldn't see how it just went on and on; but in the daytime—Lord, it was ugly. Not green or wet, like Mossy Creek Hollow back home, where the pines and the sycamores and oaks were so thick they nearly blocked the sun.

Rosebay had only been married six months when Wedge's father died, and Wedge had taken the notion to sell everything and light out for Oklahoma. Wedge was a restless soul, a brawler and a hell-raiser afflicted with a wandering foot and a quick temper. He wasn't as bad as his brother Rowell, but he was bad enough.

Rowell called himself a preacher, but he had more than a handshake acquaintance with the devil. He only preached when there was somebody's pretty wife to pray with. After he'd tried to "pray" with Rosebay, she had known she couldn't stay on at Mossy Creek with Rowell there. And maybe it was just as well they'd lit out, Rosebay thought, because without his father around to stop him, Wedge might have shot Rowell, and then he'd have a blood sin on him that wouldn't ever wash out.

Wedge wolfed down his beans, and Rosebay poured him a cup of coffee, but Wedge took a drink out of his bottle instead.

"You won't be able to drive the team if you're liquored up," Rosebay warned. The team was a horse and a mule, and they didn't travel together so well, but the mule was needed for plowing.

"Ain't liquored up," Wedge said. He reached for her. "Got a mind to prove it, too."

His hands reached for the buttons of her dress, and Rosebay pushed him away. "You quit that. There's people all over." But she let him sit beside her and put one hand under her shawl where it didn't show. Rosebay put her head on his shoulder. There was no denying that Wedge was a loving man, and his love was a comfort to her out here in the middle of this flat, empty country. He was prideful and jealous and footloose, but he loved her true, and she knew it.

Wedge clutched his bottle, got up, and began to pace, looking out through the night toward where his land would be.

*   *   *

Nobody seemed to be able to sit still. One of the cowboys who had been playing poker for land tossed his cards into the other one's lap and got up.

"Where you goin'?"

The first man grinned. "Gonna find me someone better lookin' than you."

"Such as?"

The cowboy shrugged. He took a last drink out of his own bottle and dropped it, empty, on the ground. "Hell, Newsome, you don't get a crowd of folks like this without some girls workin' for it. Half the whores in Wichita are probably down here tonight."

"You're drunk as a skunk. They'll probably roll you. Why don't you wait?"

"I ain't in a mood to wait." He stumbled a little, picking his way among the camps.

"Get on back here, Yates!" Newsome yelled.

Yates didn't pay any attention to him. He wavered on in dogged concentration on his goal. But as he passed the man in the derby, still reading, he caught sight of a beautiful woman with white-blond hair, bent over her campfire.

Rosebay looked up at the cowboy who had suddenly lurched into the circle of firelight. "You get out of here," she hissed.

"Gawd. If I had you, lady, I wouldn't ever need no whore ever again."

Wedge lunged into the firelight with his pistol in his hand. "You get away from her before I kill you!"

"Who the hell are you?" Yates saw the gun. "I don't take orders from no son-of-a-bitch farmer."

Rosebay looked from one to the other in desperation. "Wedge, don't!"

"I'm gonna *kill* you!" Wedge's gun came up, and Yates slapped his hand down on the pistol in his own belt.

Beyond them, Rosebay saw that the man in the derby was scrambling for cover. The friendly sandy-haired man in the next camp started to rise as if to help, but there was a quick double crack of gunfire.

She screamed as Wedge toppled slowly into the fire. *"No!"*

Rosebay dragged him from the flames and beat the embers off his shirt. All around them people were shouting, but she didn't look up. Wedge's hat had fallen off, and his pale face and dark hair were as motionless as rock. His eyes were open and empty. When she put her ear to the spreading red stain on his chest, there was silence.

"This 'un's dead," someone said.

Another voice said, "Aw, geez, Yates."

Rosebay lifted her head to see the sandy-haired man and another cowboy bending over the man who had shot Wedge. He lay still, too, the pistol just beyond his empty, outflung hand.

The sandy-haired man got up and came over. He knelt and put a hand on her shoulder. "Someone's gone to get a marshal."

Rosebay looked down unbelievingly at Wedge and then up at the vast night sky. They heard a horse coming at a gallop, moving down the clear land along the starting line. A man with a federal marshal's badge on his coat pushed his way through the campsites. Nearly all the interested faces that had crowded around them faded back into the night.

The marshal glared around him. "Anybody that saw anything, I want him up here pronto."

Tim stood. "I reckon I saw as much as anybody."

"And who the hell are you?"

"Timothy Holt. Editor of the *Prairie Recorder*." Tim held out his hand.

"Hodge Landrum, U.S. marshal. What happened?"

"They shot each other," Tim said.

When the marshal looked around at the crowd of settlers camped on either side, his face got hard. "They started shooting in a crowd like this? I'd say they both got what they had coming."

"Ease up," Tim said. "That's the man's wife over there."

Landrum looked at Rosebay. She had pulled Wedge's head into her lap and sat cradling it. The front of her worn calico dress was dark with his blood, and one side of her face was smeared with it. Landrum stalked over.

"This fellow says they shot each other. That what happened?"

Rosebay nodded.

"What was it about?" Landrum demanded.

"He looked at me." Rosebay's voice had a soft southern mountain twang. "He said something to me, and Wedge got mad."

"That's all? He just *looked* at you?"

"He'd been drinking," Tim said. He toed Wedge's empty bottle.

"I drink myself," Landrum said. "And I don't generally shoot somebody 'cause he looks at my wife. What did you say *back* to him, gal?"

"Nothing." Rosebay started to cry. "I tried to make him git."

The dead cowboy's companion got up from beside his body and came over. His sunburned face was shocked and grieving. "Yates was drinkin', too, Marshal. He was out lookin' for a whore. I don't reckon she did nothin'."

"I reckon she did enough," the marshal said. "What's your name, gal?"

"Rosebay Basham," she whispered.

"And his?" He pointed at the still head in her lap.

"This is Wedge." Tears slid down her cheeks.

The marshal nodded grimly. "I got enough on my hands tonight that I got no more time for you. But I'll tell you this: You stay out of my way. I got no sympathy for any damned hillbilly who shoots a man in a crowd." He stalked off, and a minute later they heard a furious tattoo of hoofbeats.

The cowboy stood miserably between Rosebay and his dead friend. "I—my name's Walter Newsome, ma'am.

I don't reckon you want the sight of me around right now, but—well, I don't reckon it was your fault. If I can help, you let me know." He picked up Yates's body, put it over his shoulder, and trudged off through the darkness.

Rosebay hadn't moved. Suddenly, just before he was out of sight, she called after him, "It warn't your fault, neither, Mr. Newsome!" She looked up at Tim, shaking off the shroud she had pulled around herself and Wedge. "Mr. Holt, I got to get him in the wagon. Will you help me?"

"You show me where you want him." Tim saw Peter standing hesitant and wide-eyed on the edge of the firelight and beckoned him over. "This is Peter Blake, Mrs. Basham. We'll lift him for you."

Rosebay got up slowly and climbed into the wagon. She pushed the iron bedstead, the cane-bottom chairs, and the old trunk, which held nearly all they had, to the front and took her wedding quilt out of the trunk. She ran her hand over its starry pattern, then spread it on the wagon floor.

"Put him on this, Mr. Holt."

Tim and Peter picked up Wedge and laid him in the wagon. Rosebay folded the quilt over him gently. She found a piece of rope and tied it around the middle. Then she ran her hand along the quilt one more time.

"It don't seem right, but I guess he'll have to rest in the wagon awhile."

Kneeling beside him, with her hair falling over her shoulders, she looked pitifully young.

Tim watched her with worried eyes. "Mrs. Basham, what are you going to do now?"

Rosebay stood up. "I'm gonna pray, Mr. Holt. I'm gonna pray to Jesus to take Wedge and give him some peace. After that, I don't know."

"How old are you?"

"I'm nineteen."

"You have to be twenty-one to claim land," Tim

said gently. "You might want to be a little older tomorrow—if you're staying."

Rosebay gave him a level look. "I'm a sight older now than I was an hour ago. But I thank you for your counsel."

Tim's horse jigged under him, feeling the tug of movement that seemed to sway the whole crowd stretched along the starting line. The horse was a big dun with heavy, muscular shoulders and hindquarters. He had a mouth like a piece of old railroad track, but he could run.

Tim leaned down and to get Peter's attention swatted the brim of his hat. The boy looked a bit too ready, with the wagon team's reins clenched in white-knuckled hands. "Don't you try to keep up, you hear? You aren't a stagecoach driver, and I don't want that press knocked to hell before I get it out of the crate. We don't need but one of us on the lot to claim it."

"I promise," Peter said. "Honest."

They had planned it all out: Tim was heading for the rail depot at Guthrie, which wasn't much more than a water tower and the place where the Santa Fe Line crossed the Cimarron River. But Tim knew that Guthrie would be a city by the time he got to it. There were town-site company runners with plats in their pockets already.

It was nearly noon. A marshal cantered along the line, kicking up dust, and the site where twenty thousand people had camped the night before was churned to powder. There were probably nearly as many people waiting on the starting line on the southern border. In the distance, Tim could see a faint puff of black smoke from the first of the Santa Fe trains scheduled to make the run. To keep the land grab fair, the trains were restricted to a fifteen-mile-an-hour speed, and the passengers could disembark at any depot stop or drop off along the way if something took their eye. It was all very disorganized, but nobody seemed to be bothered.

Tim checked his watch. Two minutes to time. He

looked around for Mrs. Basham, but he didn't see her in the mob. Maybe she had decided to turn back.

A bugle sounded, echoing up and down the line like a cavalry call, and six gunshots split the air. The whole seething mass rolled forward over the prairie in a cloud of dust so thick that Tim couldn't see where he was going and just let the horse have his head. He passed buggies and racing sulkies, which appeared and disappeared in the cloud, and thundered by a driverless wagon, with two men at the tail heaving sacks and barrels overboard to lighten it. Beyond them, a woman with a corncob pipe clenched in her teeth grimly whipped her lathered team. Tim's dun shied at a man on a bicycle, who popped suddenly from the dust, pedaling furiously.

Then they were out of the cloud, and Tim risked a quick look back over his shoulder. Behind him still came the surging wave of horses and wagons. The man in the derby hat shot past him on his sleek mount, and Tim quit looking back and put his spurs to the dun's flanks. The horsemen were well ahead of the wagons now, and as the air cleared, Tim could see the rolling, pale-green land stretched out ahead of him.

The other riders fanned out around him, yipping and shouting like cowboys on a Saturday-night spree. Already a few were pounding stakes with their names on them into the ground, but most pushed on, certain that better land was farther ahead.

Another racehorse flew past him, with the rider leaning low in the saddle. Tim grinned. That fellow was serious, but he was going to wind his horse before he got anywhere. Tim reined the dun in just a little. The horse had a gait like a sack of rocks, but he would eat up the ground with it all afternoon if Tim paced him.

Suddenly he felt happy, wildly happy with the exhilaration of a kid let loose from school . . . happier than he had been since Isabella Ormond had leveled his life into a pile of rubble. He was over Isabella, he thought. With each thud of the dun's big hooves he was outrunning her memory across Oklahoma.

* * *

Peter Blake, caught in the press of the second wave, saw the dun receding until it dwindled and winked out across the blue and gold horizon. Peter grinned, too, and shook out the reins. He knew he couldn't keep up—Tim would chew him out good and proper if he even tried—but he couldn't resist racing just a little, to feel what it was like to be a part of this surge of human energy, this hell-for-leather gallop toward hope and opportunity and growth.

The whole land is growing, Peter thought. When his grandfather had gone to Oregon, there hadn't been anything between Missouri and the Pacific Coast. Now there was no stopping the growth of the United States. Peter didn't know whether that was good or bad, but it was exciting to be part of it.

Tim's big dun came plowing past the Santa Fe rail line and into Guthrie, blowing like a bellows and lathered in sweat. Tim cast an eye over the staked-out lots that were no more than little surveyor's flags in the grass. An awful lot of people seemed to be ahead of him, considering the fast time he'd made, and he snorted at the pious speeches he'd heard about the marshals hauling back people who tried to claim land early. Tim suspected that most of the people who had beaten him into Guthrie were marshals and Santa Fe workers.

He wasn't about to waste his time yelling about injustice, though. There were still empty lots. Speed, not equity, was the measure of the day. Everything around the depot and the land office was taken, so he wheeled the dun and galloped north until he came to ground with no one sitting on it. He reined the dun in, threw himself out of the saddle, and wrote "Timothy Holt" on the corner flag's wooden stake. As an afterthought he looked at his pocket watch and added "1:34 PM."

The dun stood with heaving flanks, head down and eating spring grass.

"I've got to get you some water," Tim muttered. He slapped the horse on the rump to indicate to it that it was not forgotten. He pulled a tether stake out of his saddlebag, tied the dun to it, and then took out a piece of paper and a thumbtack. He wrote "This Land is Claimed" in large letters on the paper and tacked it to the dun's saddle. He didn't have any tent to put up until Peter got there, but, he thought, that note ought to do the trick. He took his canteen and set out for the land office and the depot water tower.

People seemed to be coming from everywhere, with more pulling in every minute. Outside the land office, some joker had put up a sign that said:

Guthrie Station
Pop. ~~35~~
10,000

A line was already forming for water, and inside the land office was the kind of chaos achievable only by a government that hasn't thought things out. The townsite companies were still trying to register their own plats, with individual claimants wrestling their way into the process. No one had thought to take streets into account. There weren't any drawn on some of the plans.

A harassed clerk instructed, "Write your name here. You'll get a certificate when the town plat's been registered."

"When do you think that might be?" Tim inquired.

"When hell freezes over, the way things are going," the clerk snarled.

Tim chuckled and headed back toward his claim, swinging the canteen by its strap. As he got closer, his eyes narrowed, and he started to run. His horse was ambling toward him, reins lashed around its saddle horn. And the notice on the saddle had disappeared.

Tim grabbed the dun and swung up on the horse. On Tim's lot, a man in a grimy buckskin vest was writing his name on a stake. Tim's marked flag was stuck in the intruder's back pocket.

Tim pulled back on the reins. "You're on my land," he said quietly.

The man in the vest just grinned. "I didn't see no claim."

Tim slid down off his mount. "You saw my horse here. And I just registered this lot."

The man lifted a hand and pointed a finger at him. "Your claim ain't worth horse manure if you ain't on the land. I reckon you lost out, friend."

Tim sighed. "I can't shoot you, with marshals crawling all over. But I *can* get rid of you."

The man's expression turned ugly. There was something vaguely familiar about him, but Tim didn't bother to wonder what. "You better run off, sonny," the intruder said menacingly. "While you can."

That ended the preliminaries. The horse threw up its head and snorted as Tim and his opponent began to swing at each other. Tim's fist connected with the other man's jaw, and then the man came back at Tim with a bellow of rage. Tim staggered as a fist landed in his eye, but he kept his footing. The man swung again, and Tim ducked and then hit him in the stomach, hard enough to knock him down. Tim, feeling his eye beginning to swell, jumped the man before he could get up. The intruder writhed under his grasp and tried to knee Tim in the groin. Tim hit him again, knocking his hat off and revealing dark hair and glittering eyes.

He hit his opponent just one more time. The man's head snapped back. He wasn't quite unconscious, but he was past fighting. Tim got up, hauled the man to his feet, and took the flag back. Then Tim threw the man bodily off the claim, with a foot in his backside for good measure.

The man landed with an explosion of air on the churned-up ground, where hooves and wagon wheels had cut the prairie into dust. When he pulled himself to his feet, his face was caked with the red dirt. He staggered slightly and made no move to come back, but the look in his eyes was bright and as malicious as a snake's.

"You better watch your back," the man threatened.

Tim drew his pistol just in case the intruder might get the same thought. "Right now I'm going to watch yours."

Tim made good on that until the man was out of sight in the jumble of tents that was already rising in Guthrie.

Rosebay Basham's team was slowing, but she could smell water now and hear the shouting of other wagon drivers. The piebald horse and the plow mule pricked up their ears and lurched down the slope toward a wide loop of river fringed with sycamore and cottonwood. The ford was churned to mud, and the team slithered down the last few feet of bank. Out toward the middle, where it was clearer, Rosebay drew rein and let them drink. Her own mouth was caked with dust, and she got down from the wagon and drank, too, bunching her skirts around her hips, feeling the heavy, cold pull of water against her legs.

"How far to Guthrie?" she shouted to a man in a Conestoga wagon.

"Right across the river, God willing," he shouted back. He whipped up his lathered team.

Rosebay checked on Wedge before pulling herself back up on the wagon seat. His body had rolled from side to side in the wagon so much that the quilt was torn and caked with dust. She shook out the reins, and the team splashed wearily across the ford.

It was late afternoon when she came to the out-skirts of Guthrie, already a tent town. She plodded past a banner staked in the grass. It said Bank of Guthrie, and a man was sitting on a folding chair beside it. She pushed on another mile and, with no clear notion of how to choose, came to a stop at the first empty land she saw.

It was just a square of grass like all the other squares of grass, but there was a trickle of a creek on it to water the stock. She stood still a moment, the wind blowing her hair and skirts around her. Then she got a piece of pencil and the stake that Wedge had sharpened, and wrote her name laboriously down the side. There was a sledge in the wagon, and she pounded the stake into the ground with it, then picked up the shovel.

Rosebay buried her husband on the land he had come west for.

V

The Prairie Recorder

"Let the people know the facts and the country will be safe."
— A. Lincoln

Guthrie, Oklahoma Territory   Tuesday, April 23, 1889

Timothy Holt, Editor and Publisher

Tim, holding the coal-oil lantern up in the tent for better effect, admired his new masthead. "Mighty pretty," he said. "Mighty pretty."

Peter Blake, laboriously hand spiking type and trying to remember that he had to arrange the type backward, looked less enthralled. "Why are you so determined to print this thing tomorrow?" He peered at Tim's handwritten copy. "Is this thing an *m* or an *n* or a *w*?"

"It's a *u* and an *m*," Tim said. "*Triumph.*"

"Oh. It looked like *harrumph* to me. You're going to have to practice your handwriting if I'm going to set your type."

"Spike it," Tim said. "You spike type. Might as well learn the lingo."

"Oh, for—" Peter peered into the font, holding another lantern over it. "I can't see a damned thing."

"You aren't old enough to swear," Tim said. "Go on. You go cook us some dinner, and I'll finish up."

"I can't cook."

"You probably cook better than you spike type," Tim guessed, inspecting Peter's efforts. "Don't worry. You'll catch on."

"To which?"

"Both, I hope. I can't cook, either."

Peter got the potbellied stove going, grinning in spite of himself. His grumbling was mostly for show, because Tim had had all the excitement of the run and a fistfight and a black eye, while Peter had had to plod along playing nursemaid to the press that was now looming in the corner of their tent.

He had arrived to find Tim, a pistol across his lap and a notebook in his hand, holding his ground on a good lot near the center of Guthrie and writing his first copy. Tim intended to beat any other newspapers to the punch by circulating an edition of the *Prairie Recorder* the next day and sending Peter around with free copies to solicit advertising. Peter wasn't complaining about that; he wanted to get a look at Guthrie.

Guthrie was already a tent city of some ten thousand people by Tim's estimate. Peter could see their fires, like a camped army, from the doorway.

Nor were they the only souls working into the night. Peter could hear hammers and saws and the occasional crack of gunfire. The marshals had their hands full. Tim still had his gun belt on, as did Peter. Tim had given the boy one after making sure that he knew how to shoot.

"Just for rattlesnakes," Tim had commented.

Peter suspected Tim wasn't the only one who had fought for his claim and that there might be considerably more rearranging before it all settled down. Most of the arguments had erupted between the settlers who had raced from the border with the noon gun and the sooners who had been in residence when they got there.

It was wonderful and exciting to be here, Peter thought. It was history in the making, in the way that Grandpa Lee had described the Oregon wagon train that he and Tim's grandfather Whip Holt had led. Peter leaned dreamily against the front tent pole and watched other tents still going up across the street.

"Cooking your overshoes?" Tim inquired.

Peter turned around and groaned. The beans he

had put in a pot on the stove had boiled dry. They looked like adobe and were beginning to smoke.

"One of us has got to learn to cook," Peter grumbled the next morning, "or I quit."

"Summer soldier." Tim had the brayer in hand and was rolling ink on the form for his first edition. At the bottom of the single page was a big box with a curlicued border. Inside the box it read: "Let Guthrie Know You Are Here. Consult Our Representative for Rates."

Tim put a sheet of paper in the tympan and closed it over the inked form in the bed. He slid the bed under the platen and pulled down on the bar.

"Oh, you beautiful gal," he said when he had lifted the tympan to see a perfect impression, crisp and black, the masthead solid and prosperous looking in Old English display type. Tim pinned the sheet up on a line stretched across the tent and got ready to pull another. When he had twenty-five, he gave the stack to Peter.

"Start with the businesses. Give them a free copy and line up subscriptions if you can, but the advertising's more important."

"How about a free ad if they buy a month's worth of advertising today?"

Tim chuckled. "You'll go far, friend. You've got the touch. That's a fine idea."

Peter put the sheets under his arm and stuck a pencil and notepad in his jacket pocket. He stopped outside the *Prairie Recorder*'s tent and took stock of the street. It was labeled Oklahoma Avenue on the plat, but it was really only a dirt right-of-way. Already it had achieved something of the look of a main street, however. On the west end it led toward the land office and the depot; to the east it stretched nearly two miles, as far as there had been settlers to lay it out. In the lot next to Tim's, a burly man in overalls was painting a sign: Hallam's Livery and Cartage. Toward the land office, the Bank of Guthrie was conducting business from a tent in front of its construction site. The building was going up in sections. Guthrie was a town in a hurry.

The man behind the big oak desk in the bank's tent shook Peter by the hand. "Abel Dormer, bank president and member of the Guthrie town council," he said.

"I didn't know there was one."

"Elected last night. Got to have guidance, you know. Got to have guidance."

Dormer was a portly man in striped pants and spats, with his shirt-sleeves held up with red garters. His coat hung on a coat tree at the back of the tent, where a clerk on a high stool sat at a table with a ledger. Dormer's gray hair was slicked down on either side of a center part, and he had the florid complexion of a man given to good living.

Peter wondered just who had elected Abel Dormer to guide them. Tim had sat up late, covering Guthrie's first town meeting, and had come back to report that nobody knew what they were doing. Maybe Dormer had elected himself. Peter gave him a copy of the *Recorder*.

"First edition, eh?" Dormer admired the Old English masthead and the paragraphs in praise of Guthrie. "This Mr. Holt seems to be a sound man. Well, the Bank of Guthrie will subscribe, son."

"If the bank would like to advertise for depositors," Peter suggested, "we have a special rate for our charter subscribers. The First Oklahoma Bank over on Cleveland Avenue has taken this offer greatly to their advantage, sir. . . ."

Peter gave the president of the First Oklahoma Bank his most earnest expression. "Yes, sir, Mr. Dormer at the Bank of Guthrie felt it was an excellent way to reach prospective depositors. . . ."

"Fifteen accounts," Peter told Tim triumphantly. "And did you know we had a town council?"

Tim snorted. "They're mighty unofficial. They've been arguing all morning about which one of them's going to be mayor. I got another fifty sheets pulled. And I made soup. How's Guthrie looking, for a day-old town?"

"I never saw anything like it. I counted two dry-goods stores, a livery, a couple of boardinghouses, and two hotels. A bakery and a bathhouse. Three churches. And about a dozen saloons."

Tim grinned. "The devil always outnumbers the righteous. I call that enterprising in a town that can't sell whiskey." Oklahoma was still officially Indian Territory, where whiskey sales were forbidden. The saloons were getting by on beer, but Tim would bet on that being a short-lived situation.

"There were a bunch of tents full of ladies, too," Peter added. "Well, not ladies, exactly. . . ." He blushed.

"You stay away from that side of town," Tim warned. "Your father would shoot me. You can try the saloons for advertising, but don't you order a drink." Playing surrogate father in a fast-moving boomtown had complications that Tim had not anticipated.

"I already did," Peter said. "In case you told me not to, afterward. I sold two ads. The Yellow Rose and the Jack of Diamonds."

"You're going to be a trial to me. Who else did you get?"

"The bathhouse. Boy, were they doing a business. But one guy who had been telling people the bathwater hadn't been changed all morning was having a fistfight with the owner. I got the ad after the marshal hauled the customer off for disturbing the peace. The jail's full already."

"How do you know all that?"

"I went over there after I got the bathhouse ad. The marshal is the same man we met after Mrs. Basham's husband got shot. He said if you'd come over, he'd tell you what everyone was arrested for. I think Marshal Landrum wants his name in the paper."

"I don't suppose you saw Mrs. Basham?"

"I did look for her," Peter said, "but she could be anywhere. She may not even be near Guthrie."

"Well, I hope she's all right," Tim said. "Let me see the ads and subscription orders you brought back." He gave Peter the stack of newspapers. "Go round up more advertising. Get some water, while you're at it."

Peter took the bucket and the new copies of the *Recorder* and set out again. A work crew was digging a trench along the street, and the wagon following them was emblazoned with red and gold paint along its side: Guthrie Waterworks. Water was the most essential civic improvement, Peter thought as the bucket bounced against his leg.

The brassy Oklahoma sun was burning through his shirt, drying up the trodden "avenue" until it was soft with thick red dust. The whole town was made of wood and canvas. If Abel Dormer and his free-lance city council were in a hurry to get water mains in, it was the specter of fire that motivated them. Anything out there would burn like tinder, Peter thought, if it was beyond the reach of the depot water tower. Well-drilling companies would do a good business, too, until every farmer had a well sunk.

And then there would be electric lines, gas mains, and sewers, miles of wire and conduits, making up the web of the city. Abel Dormer had shown Peter on a map of the town where the trolley lines would run. Everything was going to be up-to-date in Guthrie; progress at ninety miles an hour.

As Peter passed the land office, two men spilled out the door, swinging at each other. They tripped and rolled in the dust, still fighting. No one looked inclined to interfere, but after a few moments, the marshal's office door banged open down the street, and Hodge Landrum stalked out. He took the combatants by their collars and knocked their heads together.

One of the men spat bloody dust out of his mouth and glowered at Landrum. "The arbitration board's been paid off! Dormer and these damn sooners are stealing the town blind."

"You calling me a liar?" The other man lunged at him again.

"I'm calling you a thieving polecat! I got a certificate for the lot!"

"Yeah? Well, so do I."

"Save it for the arbitration board!" Landrum bellowed.

Progress had a few kinks in it, Peter decided. Or maybe the nature of progress was order out of chaos, eventually. Guthrie was just trying to do it overnight.

Committed to the *Prairie Recorder*'s advancement, Peter ducked into the land office. Land claim notices had to be published to be legal.

"Who are you?" the land agent demanded. "You're too young to claim a lot."

"I represent the *Prairie Recorder*," Peter said grandly. "Timothy Holt, editor and publisher. I am Mr. Holt's assistant. We publish all land claims and legal notices and have extremely reasonable rates."

"Then you're the only bargain in town, boy," the land agent grumbled. "I just paid twenty-five cents for a cup of coffee."

Peter mulled that information over as he strolled back to the *Recorder*'s tent with a bucket of water and the sheaf of legal notices the land agent had given him. Everything was expensive because everything had to be shipped in by rail. It would stay expensive until Guthrie was self-sufficient. The first businesses to get on their feet stood a good chance of getting rich—unless they had to borrow from the Bank of Guthrie to do it. Peter had already heard howls about Abel Dormer's interest rates. There wouldn't be a crop out of any farm around Guthrie until fall. Money would be tight until then.

A man with a little money to invest, Peter reflected, might buy a piece of some of the more promising concerns. Peter had fifty dollars that his stepmother had given him, and Tim was paying him ten dollars a week and a commission on all the advertising he could sell. Even with coffee at twenty-five cents a cup, it wouldn't cost him that much just to eat, and there wasn't anything else he wanted to spend money on.

Peter began to pay attention to the smaller establishments, the shoestring operations that lined the side streets. He had always had a knack for spotting a venture that was going to succeed; even his father admitted that. But no one had ever let him test his theories with real money before.

Rosebay Basham stood in the doorway of her tent and looked at the wind blowing down the endless prairie grass. *I got to get it plowed,* she thought. *And I got to get me a house built and a well sunk by summer.*

Even in spring, the sun burned her face through the shadow of her slat bonnet. It was like an oven in the tent. She slumped, head bowed, overwhelmed by it all. Wedge was supposed to have done the plowing and hired himself out to work betweentimes, to bring them some money until the first crop.

She surveyed her stores. Everything was low. She had some money—not much, but enough so she wouldn't starve for a while. At least she had a stove. They had lugged it all the way, knowing it would be too expensive to buy one here. But there wasn't any wood in this empty place, and she would have to buy a load of coal. She hitched up the team, alternately missing Wedge and cursing him, while the sun got higher and hotter.

She stared curiously at the town as she drove through it again. So much had changed, just since yesterday. Sawing and hammering were constant background sounds. Rosebay climbed down off the wagon seat outside a tent with Dry Goods painted on its side. The tent was full of people, mostly men, and it was stiflingly hot. She swayed a little, and a hand caught her arm.

"You all right, ma'am?"

She blinked at him. It was Walter Newsome, the cowboy whose pal had shot Wedge. "Just tired," she said flatly. "I dug a grave last night."

"Me, too," Newsome replied. "Sorry I bothered you, ma'am." He turned away to the man behind the counter. "Gimme a sack of coffee," he said brusquely. "And tell me where I can get a square meal, if you know."

"There's the hotel."

"I ain't no land baron," Newsome said. "I'm just looking for a little home cooking."

There were hoots of laughter from the rest of the men in the tent.

"Try the boardinghouse?"

"I *did*. Near to killed me."

"I hear she uses them biscuits for paperweights."

Rosebay sidled through the crowd and touched Newsome's arm. "Mr. Newsome, if you want a good meal, I can give you one. And I didn't mean to speak to you so sharp."

Newsome looked at her curiously. "You don't look old enough to know how to cook."

"I got eight brothers and sisters back home," Rosebay said. "And my ma died when I was twelve. If there's one thing I do know how to do, it's cook. And I got a living to earn. You come out to my place tonight. If the meal ain't good, I won't ask you to pay for it." She looked around at the other men. "Anyone else is welcome, too." She counted her money carefully. "Biscuits and stew and dried apple pie. I'm Rosebay Basham, and I got a place about two miles east down the road."

"Given the sorry state of the cuisine in this town, you'll probably have more customers than you can handle," a voice said. It was an odd voice, with a strange accent, and she looked at the speaker cautiously. He was a tall man, very fair-haired, with a sleepy expression. His mouth was just curving up in a faint, lazy smile, so she thought he was teasing her.

"Mister, you got no idea what I can handle," Rosebay said.

"Well, I don't suppose I do," he said mildly. "What kind of stew?"

Rosebay narrowed her eyes. "Whatever I can shoot

between now and then," she informed him. Might as well let him know that she *could* shoot, in case anyone took the notion that she was offering more than cooking for sale.

They all stood looking after her as she shook the reins over her team and turned the wagon in the road.

"You reckon she can really cook?"

"I don't reckon I care. I wouldn't mind just looking at her."

"Venus of the prairie," the fair-haired man murmured.

Walter Newsome looked him up and down. The fellow was dressed too elegantly and was too clean to be a farmer. But he didn't look like a banker, either. "What the hell kind of an accent is that?"

"English," the fair-haired man answered. "And I was under the impression that it was you gentlemen who had an accent. But I suppose it's all in one's point of view."

"Well, Mrs. Basham's just been widowed, and she ain't looking to be courted," Newsome told him.

"Farthest thing from my mind." He held out his hand. "I'm Hugo Ware. It appears we're to be dinner partners."

Newsome shook it grudgingly. "Wally Newsome. I got a little spread outside town. Gonna raise cattle on it. And just what the hell do you do, Ware?"

"Not much." Hugo's mouth twisted a little. Newsome couldn't tell whether it was a smile or not. "But that pays better than you might think." He strolled out, leaving Newsome looking after him suspiciously.

Rosebay lifted the rifle to her shoulder and sighted in on the jackrabbit. She squeezed the trigger, and the rabbit dropped. Lord, she was weary, and she still had the rabbits to clean before she could start cooking. But if all those men came and bought dinner, maybe she'd have found a way out of her troubles. Her spirits lifted a little as she slung the rabbit behind the piebald's saddle with the others. Maybe she could learn to like it out here, when she had a garden and a house—things to anchor her to the ground. Right now she felt as if the prairie wind could just lift her and blow her along over that bare horizon.

She rode back toward her tent and unsaddled the piebald to lead him over to the creek. She was just about to pick up the rabbits when she felt the hair going up on the back of her neck. Another horse was staked out by the creek, cropping grass beside Rosebay's mule. She spun, staring back at her tent, and saw a pack on the ground beside it. Rosebay grabbed her rifle and ran.

He was in the tent. Rosebay cocked the rifle.

At the click, he stood and turned. His face was coated with the red prairie dust, and he looked as if he'd been fighting, but Rowell Basham wore that cat like smile he always put on when he wanted to be ingratiating.

"What're you doin' here?"

"That ain't no way to greet your brother."

"You ain't my brother." Rosebay didn't put the rifle down.

The smile faded, as easily as it had come. "Where's Wedge?"

"Wedge is dead."

"The hell you say." Rowell looked more interested than grief stricken. A little light flickered in his eyes. He was tall and thin, like Wedge, with the same dark hair and pale eyes. "How'd it happen?"

"He got in a fight," Rosebay said. "He's buried yonder. If you want to pray for him."

"Maybe," Rowell said. "When I get settled in."

"You ain't settling in here. What're you doin', Rowell?"

"Looking after my kinfolk in time of need."

"You didn't even know Wedge was dead. What have you done?"

"Had to kill me a man," Rowell said.

"And you came lookin' for Wedge to take you in."

Rosebay lowered the rifle, but she kept a grip on it. "Who'd you kill?"

"Jonas McCormack. He come hunting me. I didn't have no choice."

"And you left Dory McCormack a widow with all those children," Rosebay said. "He find out one of those children was yours?"

"Must have." Rowell sat down. "Get me a drink."

"There ain't none!" Rosebay snapped.

"Then get some."

"I ain't your wife, and I ain't your sister, and I ain't here to do for you."

Rowell leaned forward in the chair, giving her the look that had always made her skin crawl. "There ain't no land left. I had me a claim, but some son of a bitch stole it. Maybe it ain't such a bad thing old Wedge is passed on. Maybe I'll just take unto me my brother's widow, like the Good Book says to do."

Rosebay glared back at him. "I'm through with reckless men. I'm going to make something out of what Wedge left me stuck with, and I'm going to do it myself. I'll feed you if you'll plow the garden for me, but I won't let you stay here."

Rowell stood up. "A viperous woman is a sin before the Lord. I'll be back when you got dinner cooked."

"You going to plow for me?"

"I got no calling to the plow." Rowell slapped the pocket of his jacket, where she could see the tattered edge of a bible. "I got the word of the Lord to preach."

She watched him untether his horse and climb in the saddle. His hat covered his eyes with a masklike black shadow. Rowell had no calling to the Lord, either, Rosebay thought, but he had a gift for terrifying sinners with his vision of hell. There weren't but three things Rowell knew how to do: preach, make whiskey, and slip between some other man's sheets.

After picking up the rabbits, Rosebay got out her skinning knife and started cleaning them, wishing viciously that one of them was Rowell. He'd do someone a hurt if he stayed here long enough, she thought; it was his nature. Dory McCormack should have known better.

I'll feed him, she thought, *whether he plows or not. I got to do that much because he's Wedge's brother. But he ain't going to sleep here.* He would try, she knew.

Rosebay put the rabbits in the pot with some onions, relieved now that she had told those men she would cook for them. Having them out there wasn't near as chancy as having Rowell alone.

Wally Newsome showed up at dusk, and Rosebay blinked when she saw six other men ride in behind him. One of them was the tall, fair-haired man who had spoken to her in the dry-goods tent. He introduced himself as Hugo Ware. Some of the others she hadn't seen before.

"I kind of spread the word," Newsome explained as Rosebay accepted their coins.

"Lord," she said. "I hope I got enough. Well, sit down. You can eat till it runs out." She pointed at a cloth laid in the grass. "I ain't got but three chairs."

Hugo smiled down at her. "Our interest is purely culinary." He sat in the grass by the spread cloth and watched Rosebay take a pan of biscuits out of the oven. "And what did you manage to shoot?" he inquired.

"Rabbits." Rosebay put a bowl in front of him.

Hugo sniffed at it. Everyone else around the cloth was wolfing it down like starving hyenas. He took a bite. "Madam, you amaze me."

Rosebay looked at him, her head cocked to one side. "Do you mean it's good?"

"It's first-rate," Hugo said. "Will you stop hovering and sit down?"

"I'll eat when everyone's through."

"You'll eat right now," Hugo commanded. When she hesitated he said, "Will you sit down and eat if I pay for two dinners?"

She looked shocked, but she didn't answer because at that moment Rowell rode up, dismounted in a hurry, and stalked up to Rosebay. He grabbed her by the wrist and pulled her toward him.

"What you doin' here with these men?" he raged.

Rosebay jerked her wrist away. "They're paying customers here for supper," Rosebay hissed. "If you want to eat, Rowell, I'll get you a plate, but you keep your mouth shut."

The cowboys inspected the newcomer, who gave them a malevolent look and stalked over to the kettle behind Rosebay. She filled a plate for him and then took a small portion for herself. When she came back, she sat beside Hugo, as far away from Rowell as she could get.

"You aren't paying for my dinner," Rosebay said to Hugo.

"Who's that?" Hugo asked.

"He's my brother-in-law," Rosebay said uncomfortably. "Don't pay him no mind."

"I come to look after her," Rowell declared loudly.

"Looks to me like she's doing all right," Wally Newsome observed.

"And what do you do in Guthrie, Mr. Basham?" Hugo inquired.

"I preach the word of the Lord," Rowell answered.

There didn't seem to be much to say to that, so no one spoke.

"I preach the righteous wrath of the Lord," Rowell added. "Against the sinner." He pointed a finger at Rosebay and glared at Hugo from the other side of the tablecloth. "This woman's newly widowed. And under my protection."

Rosebay flushed. "I ain't."

Rowell didn't say anything further. He finished his bowl of stew and went and got another one. When he had finished it, too, he stood up, wiped his mouth on his sleeve, and spoke to Hugo. "What do you do, mister?"

"I write," Hugo said mildly. "I paint a bit."

Rowell gave a bark of laughter. "That ain't no job for a man."

"I hunt a little, too," Hugo added, his hand brushing the pistol at his side—not threateningly, only calling attention to its existence.

"That was a fine meal, ma'am," Wally Newsome said. He stretched and got up, easing his way between Hugo and Rowell. "Best I've had. I reckon you've got you some steady customers if you want 'em."

"Yes, sir, I do," Rosebay said. She realized that the men Wally had brought were edging Rowell along with them, toward the horses. As Rowell mounted his, she called after them, into the dark. "Thank you, Mr. Newsome!"

Wally lifted his hat and said with a faint chuckle, "Glad to oblige, Miz Basham."

Relieved, she turned back to clear the dishes and saw that Hugo Ware was still there.

"I'll help you with the dishes," he offered. "Since you won't let me pay for your dinner."

Rosebay looked him over carefully. He didn't appear dangerous or even very solid, not like Wally Newsome with his grizzled beard and his cracked, tanned hands. This one looked almost like a drifter, except that she had never seen a drifter who wasn't poor. His gun was expensive, with a fancy chased grip, and his clothes were good, and clean, as if they had never been really dirty.

"You're a puzzlement," Rosebay said.

"Can I stay and help with the dishes?"

She nodded. "Are you really a writer?"

Hugo stacked the bowls and brought them to the pan of dishwater Rosebay was heating on the stove. "Shall I confess?"

Rosebay smiled. "Depends on what you got to confess to."

Hugo sighed. "Not very much, I fear. I'm what they call a remittance man."

"What's that?"

"Nothing to be proud of." Hugo's voice took on an angry edge for a moment. "A remittance man is an English gentleman of good birth who has so troubled his beloved family that they have packed him off to America—or some place equally inaccessible—and support him with regular remittances from home . . . on the condition that he stays where he is."

"Your own kin sent you out of the country?" Rosebay was incredulous.

"My own father," Hugo said. "Aided by my elder brother. Gerald is the self-appointed conservator of the family name, and it was beginning to be felt that I wasn't an asset to it."

"What did you do?" He didn't look wicked enough to have made anybody that angry.

"I declined to enter my proper place in the world," Hugo said. "My father is a baron, you see, and all his property is entailed—that means it all goes to the eldest. Younger sons are supposed to take up the army or the Church, both of which seemed to me entirely too much alike to suit me. I read for the law for a while, sporadically I'm afraid." He took a washed bowl out of Rosebay's hands and dried it. "I also drank too much, and I had unseemly friends. I did some things I won't tell you about. So one day Gerald decided I had gone too far, and he worked on our father until he thought so, too."

Rosebay looked at him as she might if he had just said that he came from the moon. "I guess you must be telling the truth," she said finally. "Nobody could make that up."

Hugo began to laugh. "I can see you don't read novels. No, of course you don't. That's the stock plot of countless dreadful epics. I happen to be the genuine article, and it's not nearly so romantic in the doing as the telling. They sent me to India first, to work for an uncle who has a company. I didn't take to that, either, so here I am. I do write a little when I feel that I must do something. My entire literary effort rests in one unpublished volume."

"Why isn't it published?"

Hugo shrugged. "I never tried. It isn't much, just

my impressions of America. Collections of stories. It's only for my amusement."

"Amusement . . ." Rosebay said faintly.

Hugo flinched. "Don't tell me you never amuse yourself," he said defensively.

"We had quiltings," she responded. "And storytellings. And I always liked to go out a-pickin' greens in the spring. I reckon that was amusement." Her eyes spilled over suddenly, and she pushed another bowl at him. "This one's ready to dry."

"Here," Hugo said. "I'm sorry. I didn't mean—"

"I know you didn't. I was just missin' home. I reckon we just come from two different kinds of worlds, is all. I can't imagine you throwing yours away just for not wanting to work. But I won't be faulting you," she said hastily. "I don't know enough. Maybe you'll tell me about your home sometime. I miss hearing a storytelling."

A storytelling, Hugo thought. *Well, that's put you in your place, old man. She doesn't even think you're real.*

VI

Over the next few days, civic order came to Guthrie, in a way. Tim followed it closely and reported it with a proper awe for the process. It began on the morning of 23 April, when the city council, which had been elected by no one but itself, tried to get the proceedings ratified. Because everyone fancied himself a statesman, a sharp struggle developed for the position of mayor. It took the better part of the day to reduce the candidates to three, Abel Dormer being one of them. And there, as Tim reported in the *Prairie Recorder*, matters stuck.

When a voice vote degenerated into a shouting match, the candidates hit upon the happy idea of lining up three wagons, with a candidate in each. Voters were to pass by the wagon of their choice to have their noses counted. When the total reached a number larger than the male population of Guthrie, it became obvious that some noses had been counted more than once. The election committee gave up and went home.

They tried again the next day, this time with paper ballots, with similar results. Matters only came to a head two days later when a delegation of homesteaders armed with pitchforks threatened to run the three candidates out of the territory if they didn't quit fighting and pick somebody who could deal with the crises of conflicting claims, block-long lines at the water tower, and hair-trigger tempers.

One candidate, eyeing the pitchforks, withdrew. The other two appointed a nominating committee, which, after some consultation with the candidates, nominated Abel Dormer, who hired the loser as a vice president of the Bank of Guthrie.

Tim sat happily through the entire meeting, taking notes. He didn't think much of Abel Dormer but was consoled by the fact that the mayor would probably provide good copy.

Dormer, duly elected, came up to pump his hand. "Glad to see you here, Holt. We need a sound man for the press in Guthrie."

Tim, with his piece on Guthrie's first election already composed in his head, knew that this was probably the last time that Dormer would be glad to see him. But he shook his hand anyway. "I call 'em as I see 'em, Mayor," he said with a faint grin, and let Dormer draw his own, probably erroneous, conclusions from that.

At the end of the week, Tim Holt and Peter Blake exited the third boardinghouse dinner tent they had tried so far, and Tim clutched his stomach dramatically. "Cross that one off your list."

"That's the last one," Peter said. "We'll have to go back to cooking for ourselves."

"You set fire to the stove last time," Tim said. "And I didn't become an exalted editor to go on eating beans and tomatoes. I had my fill of that when I was a starving silver miner."

"There's still the hotel."

"I'm not that important yet. The *Recorder's* circulation is coming along, but I've got to put the money back in the paper." It was just dusk, and he stood looking down the street disconsolately. Across the way, a fiery-eyed preacher was conducting a revival meeting by lantern light inside a tent.

"The Lord knows the man who is in sin!" he shouted.

"What about the man who is in indigestion?" Tim muttered.

"There's Marshal Landrum," Peter said. "He looks like he's got a touch of it himself."

Tim snorted. "He's got a wife. I bet *she* can cook. I wonder what he's so fired up about."

They ambled across the street to where the glowering marshal was leaning against a hitching post.

"How's the crime rate, Hodge?" Tim asked him. "Keeping up with progress?"

"Outstripping it," Hodge grunted. "I need about three more deputies, but my head office says it's up to the city council to provide them, and the city council says it's the government's job. It's my personal belief they're all too busy making money hand over fist to care."

"Marshals being above all that," Tim murmured. Half the sooners had been U.S. marshals.

"Don't start with me, Holt," Landrum said. "I got as good a right as the private citizen. Better maybe, seeing as I go out and get shot at regular, keeping the private citizen's hide in one piece."

"You defending us citizens from bad preaching tonight?"

Hodge Landrum didn't look as if he cared much for the man, either.

The preacher was tall, and his black hair hung over his eyes. Tim looked at him more closely and was startled to recognize his combatant for the *Prairie Recorder*'s land claim. It struck him as a novel way to acquire a church site. "The Lord knows who supports His works and who don't! The man who don't give to the Lord's work will look down on the fiery pit!"

"That man is vermin," Landrum muttered. "He's got a jug under the pulpit, and I ought to run him out of town. I heard somebody is making bootleg whiskey, and I wouldn't put it past these damn hillbillies to be at it. That Basham woman got two men killed flaunting herself around."

"I thought the accent sounded familiar," Tim said. "Hodge, you can't lump every soul to come out of the Appalachians in one pot."

"The hell I can't," Landrum said. "He's her brother-in-law. I tell you, these people are no good. She better watch out I don't run her in for soliciting."

"She's a baby," Tim protested. "Hodge, you've got rocks in your head. Where is she? I've been meaning to see if she's all right." Especially now that he had met her brother-in-law.

"She's got a spread about two miles down the road," Landrum growled. "Been cooking for drifters and lazy cowpokes."

"Cooking?" Tim's ears pricked up. "Can she cook?"

"Yeah," Hodge said grudgingly. "I ate there when I went out to see if she was running a still. Couldn't find it, but that ain't to say it ain't there. She was sashaying around feeding about ten men. She had some layabout Englishman hanging around, too. You watch out for her, Holt. She ain't your kind."

"Hodge," Tim said, "I don't care if she's a houri out of Arabia as long as she can cook."

The last time Tim had seen Mrs. Basham, she had been half-frozen with shock, but he thought she was tougher than she looked.

"Everybody out here is tougher than they look," Peter said the next afternoon. "Or they get out."

Tim nodded. Some of the land had proved to be arid and some of it malarial, so settlers were pulling out already. But there were always more to take their places. Construction companies in Guthrie, Oklahoma City, and other smaller towns along the Santa Fe lines were making fortunes. Guthrie's streets were being graded, and about half the tents had been replaced with wood-frame buildings. The cellar of the *Prairie Recorder*'s permanent quarters had been dug, and the flooring laid over most of it. Abel Dormer's bank had a fancy false front with scrollwork and curlicues.

A flock of lawyers had descended on the town to register land claims and represent quarreling claimants before the arbitration board, which was quickly acquiring a reputation for resolutions in its own best interests.

Tim had printed a couple of irate editorials about that, so Abel Dormer no longer considered the editor of the *Prairie Recorder* as sound a man as he had.

The population, which had begun as almost completely male, was beginning to acquire a respectable female element. Farmers' and storekeepers' wives joined them, and a dressmaking establishment and a milliner's shop had appeared down the street from the *Recorder*. The city council had decreed the construction of a town hall, which Abel Dormer referred to as the Opera House, on the theory that it sounded more cultured. So far no operas had been booked, but the Savoy Shakespeare Company had announced its intention of presenting *Romeo and Juliet*, preceded by a performance of snake charming and Arabian magic.

The company had posters plastered all over town: "Direct from their triumphant Continental tour!"

"The only continent that company ever toured was this one," Tim said, laughing. "They played Virginia City while I was there. We'll review it for the *Recorder*. I've always wanted to be a theater critic."

Peter looked at him thoughtfully as they strolled into Hallam's Livery, where they saddled their horses. "How serious are you about this newspaper business? Sometimes you make it sound like a toy."

"I believe that a man's livelihood ought to be fun," Tim said. "But I'm dead serious. A newspaper's got an obligation to stir things up and shed light on what some people don't want lit up. Injustice is real easy to get comfortable about if nobody mentions it out loud."

After they trotted through the outskirts of Guthrie, they detected an appetizing aroma. Peter sniffed the air. "Food," he announced. "Real food."

Tim sniffed, too, and shelved the rest of his discourse on journalistic responsibility. He was only twenty-two and had yet to outgrow the ravenous appetite of youth—an appetite he shared with Peter Blake. They followed the scent of chicken pie along the breeze.

Rosebay Basham had installed a hitching rail where

a now well-worn road ran past her land. Tim drew rein beside it and looked around him, impressed. Whatever Hodge Landrum thought about Mrs. Basham, she was a worker. A dozen speckled hens clucked and scratched under a sycamore tree, oblivious to their companions' fate. Beyond her tent, a garden had been plowed already, the red furrows as neat as if they had been laid out with a ruler. Under a second tent were two long trestle tables, with benches on either side and gingham tablecloths. There were a dozen men at them already.

Rosebay was carrying bowls of biscuits to the tables, each of which was laid with tin plates and cups and a handful of prairie wildflowers in a jar.

"You got room for two more?" Tim asked her.

Rosebay blinked at him, and then she smiled. "Mr. Holt! I surely do."

She bustled back into the kitchen tent and returned with chicken pie. Tim and Peter took a seat on one of the benches next to a blond man who, Tim judged by his speech, must be the "layabout Englishman." Rosebay's preaching brother-in-law was seated across the table, glaring at the rest of the company. His eyes flickered as he recognized Tim.

"Evening, Reverend," Tim said genially. He gave the title "Reverend" just a faint emphasis of sarcasm. "You find yourself a plot in Guthrie yet?"

Rowell's hand tightened on the knife beside his plate. "I got no need for land. I preach the gospel of the Lord; the Lord sees to my keep."

"I'm glad to hear that," Tim informed him, with meaning. He thought that Rowell looked as if he had been drinking. Not enough to incapacitate him, just enough to make him mean—unless that was his natural disposition.

"Calling himself a man of the cloth," Peter whispered indignantly. "If there's anything I can't abide, it's a hypocrite."

Tim took careful stock of Rowell. "Watch your back" had been the man's parting words, and he looked as if he would make good on that, given half a chance.

When Rosebay had everything on the tables, she took a seat on the end of the bench next to Tim, while the men watched her expectantly. The lantern light in the tent made her face look soft and ethereal.

She folded her hands and bowed her head. "Lord make us mindful of our blessings."

There was a muttered "amen," and then the diners tore into the chicken pie.

Tim chuckled. "You've got a firm hand."

"They won't stand for a very long blessing," Rosebay said. "But I figure it ain't right not to say one." She smiled at him again. "I never did thank you, Mr. Holt, for helping me that night."

"I didn't help much," Tim said. He had been feeling a little guilty about that, although he didn't know what else he could have done. "And why don't you just call me Tim?"

"All right. I'm real glad to see you. It's kind of like meeting a friend. I saw you and your boy had your newspaper set up."

"He's not my boy," Tim said, horrified. "He's my cousin. Don't tell me I look that old."

"Can I call you Pops?" Peter asked.

"You don't look that old," Rosebay said quickly. "You just kind of seemed like a person who takes charge."

"You've taken pretty good charge yourself. This is the best meal I've had since I got here. Hodge was right. You sure can cook."

"The marshal?" Rosebay frowned. "I'm surprised he sent you. He don't like me."

"It's not really you," Tim said. He flicked a glance at Rowell.

"Yes, it is," Rosebay said. "You don't need to soften it none. He holds me to blame for Wedge. But I guess Rowell ain't helped none, either," she muttered.

"I didn't know he was with you," Tim said.

"He wasn't." Tim thought she looked as if she could do without Rowell now. "But he's kin. I got to feed him."

"You're feeding about half of Guthrie," he teased.

"I'm cooking three meals a day now," Rosebay said proudly. "I plowed my garden, and I'm gonna get me a cow. As soon as I get a little more ahead, I'm gonna hire me some help and start on a house."

"Sounds like you're here to stay."

"I got to be," Rosebay said. "This land's all I own."

"It is not fitting for a woman to be alone," Rowell said. He thumped the handle of his knife on the table and stared fixedly at Rosebay.

"I wouldn't *be* alone if it warn't for what a man got me into," Rosebay shot back at him. "I'll take my chances."

Tim studied her other customers. To a man, they looked to him as if they would offer heart and hand in about two seconds if Rosebay Basham wanted to get married again. But Rosebay had a right to be cautious after the experience she had had.

"You stick to your guns," he said to her, half-joking and half-solemn. "Romance isn't what it's cracked up to be, and marriage is a sight too permanent."

She just looked at him sideways. "You been married?"

"I've been almost married," he said brusquely. "I got lucky."

"Oh."

"I was young and stupid," Tim muttered, feeling that he had been rude. "Don't pay me any mind."

Rosebay looked at Tim Holt with sympathy. She thought she detected the tone of a man who had been jilted. She couldn't figure why a woman wouldn't want to marry him. He was handsome and possessed an intentness behind his easygoing ways that seemed to leave a trail of sparks. The faint half smile on his face and the light in his blue eyes seemed to have a glow all their own. *Don't you go looking at him that way*, she told herself firmly. *He as good as said he wasn't interested.*

*   *   *

Rosebay's good cooking, however, brought Tim back with a regularity that generally not even love can manage. She quickly counted Tim and Peter among her regulars, with Hugo Ware and Wally Newsome. After dinner there would be what Rosebay liked best—a storytelling.

She would tell her own tales, gleaned from her grandmother, and then Hugo would look off into the distance beyond the campfire and talk about Normans and Saxons, Roundheads and Royalists, and battles lost and won until even cowboys like Wally Newsome got interested.

When Hugo got tired of talking, he would get out his pad and pencil and take notes as Tim Holt talked about Oregon and how his grandparents had gone there in a wagon train and built up a ranch out in the wilderness. Tim would describe life in Virginia City, Nevada, where a network of tunnels for the silver mines existed beneath the city and all the Cornish miners would leave bits of pasty from their lunch pails for the Tommyknockers, the little goblins who lived in the rock.

There was something about Tim's Nevada stories that Rosebay thought was incomplete, some subject that he skirted around. *That woman who left him,* she decided, but something more, too—something having to do with the darkness of the mines. He didn't like the dark, he'd said once, didn't like to be closed in. Tim was a tantalizing mystery.

If Tim was oblivious to Rosebay's speculations about him, Rowell was not. And because Rowell wanted her and had seen the way she was starting to look at Tim, he gave a great deal of thought to eliminating Tim Holt and also turning a profit at the same time. Rowell no longer wanted the town lot that he believed Tim had done him out of—bootlegging was a solitary business and had to be hidden in the woods—but it galled him that Tim was in possession of the lot, was building a new wood-frame office on it, and was setting himself up as a power in the town. And Rowell knew someone who might be willing to assist with Tim Holt's demise.

Since the government had been obliging enough to make whiskey illegal, thus ensuring a steady demand for it, Rowell had sold the whole of his first run through the back doors of Guthrie's saloons. Those who could afford it bought "prescription" whiskey at the drugstore. Everyone else went to the saloon and asked for a glass of "tonic" and got a dose of white lightning in a teacup. This system worked very well except when interrupted by periodic raids by Hodge Landrum's deputies. Landrum's efforts were in earnest but seldom amounted to much because most of the saloons had silent partners among the upright citizenry of Guthrie. The Yellow Rose, for instance, received timely communiqués from the mayor's office, prompting the barkeeper to hustle the whiskey jugs off the premises.

Dormer, a silent partner of the Yellow Rose, was less than amused to find the grimy specter of Rowell Basham in his office just before the day's end.

"What are you doing here?" Dormer demanded. "I told you to do your business with Mulligan at the Rose."

Rowell pulled up a straight chair, turned it backward, and sat down on it. "I been reading what Holt's been writing. He's been real uncomplimentary to you, Mayor." His teeth gleamed in a grin, feral and unappealing. "Thought I might help you out some."

"What are you proposing?" Dormer asked suspiciously. Men like Rowell Basham didn't do favors for friendship's sake.

Rowell leaned forward, smelling of sweat and the sharp odor of whiskey mash. "I just thought you might like to be rid of him."

"I won't condone—well . . . murder," Dormer said nervously. The watery gleam in Rowell Basham's pale eyes made him uneasy.

" 'Thou shalt not kill,' saith the Lord," Rowell said.

"I go by the Lord's word, Mayor. But the unrighteous shall be driven out with fire. Cleansed in the flame."

Fire. . . . Dormer thought hard. It wasn't something he would have done on his own, but with Basham handing it to him on a plate, the temptation was too much.

"You're missing your chance, Mayor," Rowell asked. "Water mains ain't in yet."

"What do you want for it?" Dormer said.

Rowell slipped through the darkness with a can of kerosene in his hand and the mayor's thirty dollars in his pocket. Dormer was a weakling, afraid to dirty his hands or kill a man who needed killing but not willing to say no to it, either. Rowell put the kerosene down and looked at the framing of the partially built office rising above him. Dormer had made him promise nobody would get killed, but fire went where it wanted to and would cleanse what needed cleansing.

There was a light in the tent where the press still stood. Rowell left the kerosene can behind a stack of lumber and slipped into the shadows to wait for the light to go out.

Tim yawned and stretched and started to pull off his boots. "Ready for bed, kid?"

"In a minute," Peter answered. "I can't find the contractor's accounts. I was going over the bills with him this afternoon. I think I left them outside."

"Get them in the morning," Tim said sleepily.

"You can say that because you don't have to do them over if they get rained on." Peter took the lantern off its peg on the tent post. "I'll be back in a minute."

Rowell saw the lantern move inside the tent and tensed when whoever was carrying it came outside. The bright sphere of lantern light illuminated the ground, leaving the carrier's face in shadow as he scanned the lumber pile. Rowell pressed himself farther back into the darkness. The figure with the lantern, apparently not finding what he was looking for, climbed up on the nearly finished flooring of the first story. The sanded planks had been laid across the joists and nailed down, with an opening in one corner where the cellar stairs would go. The man with the lantern found what he was after by the stairwell—a sheaf of papers held down with a rock. As he bent to pick it up, the lantern swung, and Rowell felt its light brush across his face. He ducked, but the fellow with the lantern saw the movement.

The man held the lantern high. Rowell knew he was caught, but it wasn't by Holt, as he had thought. It was that lippy kid. Rowell jumped through the framing with one lunge and wrestled Peter to the ground.

Peter struggled frantically, trying to bite the hand that was over his mouth. The man's other hand was around his throat, cutting off his wind. Peter dropped the lantern as he began to black out. He never saw his attacker's face, only felt himself falling as he was pushed over the edge of the cellar stairwell. His head cracked against the hard earth beneath, and then everything above him rose up in a burst of flame.

At first Tim took the sounds of scuffling to be Peter flinging lumber around, looking for his precious accounts. Then through the tent wall he saw the flare of fire. He ducked under the tent flap and ran barefoot into the yard to see the framing of his new building blazing like a pyre.

"Peter!" Tim screamed frantically, but there was no answer. He sprinted for the burning structure. *"Peter!"*

The boards around the cellar hole were an inferno. If Peter was under there, Tim knew that he would never get out. Tim could hear shouting for the water wagon in the distance, but the wagon would never arrive in time.

He ran back to the tent, stripped the blankets from

the cots, and plunged them into the water barrel in the yard. It was nearly empty, but there was enough to soak the blankets through.

Neighbors were beginning to arrive with buckets, but Tim didn't really see them. He pushed his way blindly through the crowd.

"Holt, come back!" someone yelled.

"Peter's in there!" Tim kept running.

"You'll never get him out. You'll burn to death!"

Tim flung away the hands that grasped at his arms. At the side of the structure, opposite the cellar stairs, was the hole in the foundation where the coal chute would go. The flames were licking at the wood above that, too, but the foundation was cement. Tim flung himself on the ground and began to inch through it, coughing.

The cellar was pitch black and stifling and thick with steam as the men above him began to hurl water on the flooring joists. Tim's nightmare caught him by the hair. He was underground again . . . underground in the Ninevah Mine in a caved-in caldron of heat and darkness. . . . He was paralyzed by that memory and the fear that had ridden on his back since then, of being enclosed in the dark.

There was a cough in the blackness and then silence.

Panic drove Tim on. He fought his way through his own demons and the smoke-filled air. The flooring joists above him were beginning to smolder. After sliding through the opening, he stood, wrapping one of the wet blankets around him and holding the end of it to his mouth and nose.

"Peter!"

Again a faint cough, then a moan.

Tim stumbled toward the sound and saw a blaze of flame at the other end of the cellar as the flooring around the stairwell began to collapse. He fell over Peter, who had passed out trying to crawl away. Tim bent and, by the hellish light of the stairwell, wrapped him in the other blanket. He managed to get Peter over his shoulder and started back, lungs burning and eyes swimming with tears from the smoke.

The opening in the foundation was twenty feet away, endlessly far, with the flooring burning above it. One step . . . another. . . . Underground. . . . The ghosts of Hobbs, who had died in the Ninevah Mine's subterranean cavern, and Shore, who had gone mad there, howled around his head. Another step . . . another . . . ten feet to the opening. A piece of flooring fell through, searing his arm as it crashed down. He was terror stricken that Peter, limp on his shoulder, was dead. The rest of the flooring behind him roared down with a billow of burning air. He was keeping just ahead of the flames. The rest of the building was getting ready to go.

And then there were hands reaching through the hole. Tim pushed Peter toward them and watched the inert body dragged through. He swayed.

"Holt!"

Someone grabbed his arms and yanked, and Tim felt himself hauled upward into cold night air.

It was Sid Hallam from the livery stable. "You lie still. The kid's all right," he said when Tim had stopped coughing. "They got it near put out," he added. "Didn't spread none. But your building's a goner."

"What about . . . my press?" Tim asked, gasping.

"Me and a couple of the boys drug it out in the street," Sid said. "Along with anything else we could lay our hands on. The tent was starting to burn. It's gone, too."

Tim lay on his back and looked up at the blackened, jagged remnants of the framing. The tent was a sodden, smoldering remnant of canvas off to his right. But he could see Peter, sitting up and gulping water from a dipper. And the press, squat and solid and unharmed, in the middle of the street. Tim closed his eyes again. "S'all right," he said.

"I didn't see him," Peter grated for the fiftieth time, pacing in the newly bought tent while workmen cleared out the mess from the foundation of the ruined building. "I didn't *see* him!" It infuriated him. "I know who it was, though!"

"You don't," Tim said. "You just think you know who it was. Oh, hell, maybe I think so, too, but it won't stand up as evidence just because we don't like him and I had a fight with him. Even Hodge won't go after him on that, and he hates Basham's guts. I told you, it's the function of newspapers to stir things up, and sometimes you don't know who you might have stirred."

Over the next few weeks nothing else untoward happened. Tim and Peter continued to take their meals at Rosebay's. Rowell was a constant and menacing presence, but he didn't slip up in any way that would have provided them with proof, either. Rosebay, sympathetic to their tribulations, gave them both the biggest wedges of pie.

A motive for arson occurred to Peter as he watched a sullen Rowell look at Rosebay, who had clear yearning in her eyes for Tim. Peter was unwilling to approach the subject directly with Tim, who was touchy and unreliable on the subject of love. Instead, he fished a little.

"What do you think about Mrs. Basham?" he inquired casually one morning while they were making up the *Recorder*'s front page.

"Huh?" Tim, unaware of being the subject of romantic speculation, knocked a line of type straight with his mallet and looked up with a vague expression.

Peter decided that that "Huh?" had answered his question. "I heard Wally Newsome asked her to marry him," he said conversationally.

"The devil he did," Tim said. "He's old enough to be her dad."

"He's not the only one," Peter volunteered. "Sid Hallam at the livery stable asked her, too. But she wouldn't have either one of them."

Tim groaned. "Don't tell me *you're* in love with

her. Aunt Cindy would hang me out to dry. Everybody already thinks Sam was my fault."

Peter looked scornful. "I don't mean me. From what I hear, the betting's running on Hugo Ware. He's over there all the time."

Tim shook his head. "Hugo won't ask her. He'll take a wife who could fit into his upper-class ways." He thought for a minute. "He'd better not lead her on, though, or he'll have to answer to me."

Maybe he is interested, Peter thought. "You ought to take her to see *Romeo and Juliet,*" he suggested.

Tim shrugged. "Hugo's taking her."

Peter gave up.

The Savoy Shakespeare Company arrived on the noon train, and their actresses had been the talk of the town ever since.

"They ain't nice, and that's a fact," said Mrs. Bennett, who ran the milliner's shop on the *Recorder*'s other side. "Their skirts were at least four inches above the ankle."

"But you're going anyway, aren't you?" Tim said.

Mrs. Bennett chuckled. "Of course I am. And Juliet bought one of my hats," she boasted.

Most of Guthrie turned out for the performance in the town hall. Tim saw Rosebay slide into a seat, escorted by Hugo Ware. He blinked. Hugo had chosen to attire himself in full evening dress, cutaway coat and all. He carried a tall silk hat under one arm and outshone even Mayor Dormer. The mayor was an imposing figure, but his coat and trousers were of less excellent cut than Hugo's, and the mayor's physique did not lend itself to such dashing attire.

"His shirt goes pop when he breathes," Peter whispered to Tim, meaning the mayor. "Did you hear it?"

"Boiled shirts are difficult to control," Tim said solemnly, "when one is of a portly nature."

"Jiminy, look at Hugo, though. He ought to have a monocle in his eye."

"Monocles require concentration. Hugo's too lazy to make one stay in."

"What do you really think of Hugo?" Peter persisted.

"I think Landrum was right," Tim said. "I think Hugo's a layabout." He grinned. "I've got to admit I like him, though."

Rosebay turned in her seat and waved at them. Her silvery hair was pinned up under a plain straw hat that did nothing to dim the glow of her face, and she had on what Tim thought must be her one good dress, a brown-and-white check with the tiniest line of lace around the high collar. She looked excited, like a child at the circus.

"Hugo tried to buy her a dress for tonight, but she wouldn't let him," Peter informed Tim.

"Do you know *everything* that goes on?" Tim demanded.

"Well, I get around," Peter allowed.

Tim, who ate and breathed current events, eyed him respectfully.

"And Rosebay talks to me," Peter added.

Rosebay? Tim thought.

"Since she doesn't have to worry about my courting her and getting jealous."

Well, thank goodness for that. "You'd be a hell of a reporter," Tim said, disgruntled. "I don't know why you don't give it a try."

"I'm a businessman," Peter said, then added happily, "I bought ten shares in the trolley company today."

"They haven't even laid the track yet."

"Always get in on the ground floor."

Tim grinned as the houselights dimmed. "As long as you're going to be a tycoon, buy yourself some clothes the next time you get paid. Those duds Rob Martin lent you are starting to look like they belong in the ragbag. Or wear what you brought from home."

"Tycoons," Peter informed him, "don't wear knee pants."

"Hey, pipe down!" An irritable chorus behind them shushed any further discussion.

The snake charmers began their act in front of the red velvet curtain. They were not particularly good, and the snakes looked stuffed, but everyone admired the curtain. It was Mayor Dormer's pride and had arrived in the nick of time on the morning train, accompanied by a good deal of discussion over who had authorized such a frivolous expenditure of city funds, until the mayor had said, just shut up, he'd pay for it himself if nobody else had any civic pride. When the snake charmers had jammed their charges back into the baskets, the curtain swished grandly away to either side, revealing painted flats representative of a castle in Verona. The narrator, in silken doublet, crossed the stage, and the audience settled into its seats with an expectant sigh.

Juliet looked closer to forty than fourteen, and the flats had a tendency to wobble, especially during the balcony scene, when Juliet, standing atop a stepladder behind the painted balcony, lost her footing and grabbed frantically at the railing, sending a flowerpot down nearly atop her lover's head.

"Lady, by yonder blessed moon I swear that tips with silver all these fruit-tree tops—*Goddamn it, Sophie!*" Romeo intoned, dodging the pot.

"O! Swear not by the moon— You watch your mouth!" Juliet hissed. "The inconstant moon, that monthly changes in her circled orb, lest that thy love prove likewise variable."

"Throw another one at him!" someone shouted.

Hugo Ware and Tim Holt had the look of men enjoying themselves hugely, but Rosebay sat entranced, eyes wide at the fight scene.

Rosebay's hands flew to her mouth when, in the last act, Romeo swallowed the fatal potion.

"Don't drink that, you damn fool!" another voice shouted from the back of the house.

Romeo lifted his head, glared at the interruption, and fell dead, leaving Juliet to wring her hands above his body and fall upon her dagger. Romeo was observed to flinch before she landed on him.

The houselights came up. Tim and Peter pushed their way through the crowd, most of whom were still arguing over the ending, to Rosebay's and Hugo's side.

Rosebay looked at Hugo, tears streaming down her cheeks. "That was the most wonderful thing I ever did see," she whispered.

"It was certainly unique," Hugo murmured. But he had a light in his eyes that was due partly to the play and partly to Rosebay's reaction to it.

"I'm going backstage," Tim said. "Would you two like to come?"

"Could we?" Rosebay breathed.

"Certainly. Privilege of the press." They climbed up on the stage, and Rosebay ran her hand over the painted flats.

"A whole castle, just painted on."

"Trickery, illusion, and deceit." Hugo smiled. He took her hand. " 'O! She doth teach the torches to burn bright!' That's true enough. 'Beauty too rich for use, for earth too dear.' "

"Beauty is soaking its feet in epsom salts," Tim remarked as they stepped behind the flats into the makeshift dressing rooms. He wanted to squelch that line of talk. Rosebay might not know Shakespeare from honest sentiment.

Juliet, her feet in a pan of water, received them regally. Seen close, her costume was threadbare, and half its milk-glass pearls were missing. She waved them in with a weary, queenly air.

"A triumph, madam," Hugo said, his eyes dancing.

"At least they didn't throw anything," Romeo said morosely from behind a screen. His doublet dropped over the top of the screen, and he could be heard hopping on one foot, trying to get his hose off.

"Tim Holt, *Prairie Recorder*," Tim said. He got out his notebook. "You folks making a lengthy tour?"

"As long as the money comes in," Juliet said.

"You've got some new actors since I saw you in Virginia City."

"All the time," Romeo muttered from behind the screen.

"Pay no attention to my husband," Juliet said. "He finds it wearing managing a company in these uncertain times. So you saw us in Virginia City?"

"I did. Tell me, what is an actor's life like?" Tim poised his pencil above his notebook.

"Oh, a vagabond's life, Mr. Holt. The freedom of the road." Juliet patted her hair and laughed gaily, but the sound was hollow. "We are gypsies, Mr. Holt."

"I thought you were wonderful," Rosebay said. "I cried at the end."

"Did you?" Juliet looked at her with a slightly sad smile.

"It all seemed so real." Rosebay struggled to explain. "All the quarreling and misunderstandings, and everyone so prideful and stubborn, just like real folks. Like a song my granny used to sing, about a man stealing his wife away and her pa and her brothers comin' after him. I don't guess folks have changed much since history times."

"Hardly at all," Hugo murmured.

Tim felt irritable. "And who told you that?" he snapped, thinking of Isabella Ormond, who sure hadn't made much of a Juliet.

" 'Young Adam Cupid, he that shot so trim when King Cophetua loved the beggar-maid,' " Hugo said, his eyes on Rosebay.

"You are familiar with the Bard," Juliet said with another jagged smile. "It's dangerous to take him to heart."

"Oh, I'm no king," Hugo said with a shake of his head. "*Au contraire*, I fear. And my true love's made of sterner stuff."

"Will you just pipe down long enough for me to interview this lady?" Tim said blackly, and Hugo subsided.

Rosebay looked at them both apprehensively, trying to catch the currents that were drifting in the air. Hugo seemed still caught up in the play or just in the language of it, but he always had a ready tongue for fine talk—as insubstantial as the Romeo, who had disappeared into a round little man in a grimy smoking jacket. But Tim, like a horse with its ears back, seemed to be actively fighting against the notion that a man might love a woman enough to lie down and die for her.

Surely not him for me, Rosebay thought with a sigh. *I'm done with men. I said I was done with men, and I'm gonna make it stick, however I feel about him.*

She looked at Romeo again and saw that, without his page-boy wig, he was nearly bald. The magic of the play shattered around her, like shards of glass sliding down to the floor.

VII

New York, May to September 1889

Heavens, Claudia thought as she surveyed the gathering in Lucy Woods's apartment. The guests looked wholesome enough, but there was certainly an air of Bohemian gaiety to the evening with which Cathy's own circle could not hope to compete.

Three raffish-looking but impeccably dressed young men in evening clothes were leaning on the mantelpiece singing "If We're Weak Enough to Tarry" from *Iolanthe* with a girl in a purple gown with a neckline that was far too low. Two other young actresses were giggling beside a portly man with a diamond stickpin. A young couple had rolled back the rug from the center of the room, and the boy was teaching the girl a dance step. Cathy sat just watching, eyes alight, while Lucy Woods presided over it all in an absentminded fashion.

"Champagne, Mrs. Brentwood?" One of the raffish gentlemen who had been singing Gilbert and Sullivan duets bowed and offered her a glass. He wasn't quite drunk, Claudia decided, but the light in his eyes said he was well on the way to it.

"Thank you," Claudia said gravely.

"Miss Martin's your niece, isn't she?"

"She is." She gave him a look that implied that any liberties taken in that direction would not be well received.

The young actor threw up his hands, laughing. "Oh, she's beyond my touch, ma'am. I'm just the third man in the chorus. These are my only good dress clothes, too," he confided. "All paint and no substance, that's me. In any case, Lucy—Miss Woods—already warned us off."

Claudia raised an eyebrow. "Thoughtful of her." She took the champagne and went to sit by Lucy on the chaise longue.

"I hope you aren't too bored, Mrs. Brentwood," Lucy said. "I'm afraid we can all be rather juvenile."

"Not at all." Claudia gave Lucy a sidelong glance. "I'm not as stuffy as I look. And you strike me as levelheaded."

"Well, I'm older than most of them," Lucy said. "I've managed to get my feet on the ladder. Precariously at times, but a rung or two up. It's a rickety profession."

Claudia pointed unobtrusively at Cathy, who had joined the singers by the fireside. "It might be an excellent idea," she said quietly, "if my grandniece saw more of the, er, rickety nature of your calling. I'm not advocating any unsavory associations, mind you. Just a little eye-opening."

Lucy looked at her with interest. "A vaccination?" she murmured.

Claudia was brisk again. "I have nothing against your profession. Her mother does, however, and I promised her mother to abide by her wishes. Cathy is young and has led a sheltered life. I want her to see certain things before she puts herself in a position of having to confront them unexpectedly."

"I understand." What might have been a shadow of anger, or only resignation, brushed across Lucy's face. "As it happens, I may be able to give her quite a good example in the morning."

Cathy looked around the anteroom excitedly. Two other women were already there—a young actress she had met before at Lucy's and another she didn't recognize. Although they sat side by side, their rivalry for the same role put an invisible shield between them. Lucy took a seat, and Cathy sat beside Lucy. Beyond them, behind a cluttered desk and a telephone, a bored secretary in shirt-sleeves ignored them all. To his left, a closed mahogany-paneled door guarded the office of the famous Mr. Ardry.

"Just like Ardry to have us all here at the same time," one of the girls complained.

"He always likes to let you know there's competition," the other girl said.

"They all do it," Lucy said quietly. "Get used to it."

"With you here I probably haven't got a chance," the first girl said and sniffed. She looked suspiciously around Lucy at Cathy.

"This is my friend Cathy Martin," Lucy said. "She's visiting New York for a while. Cathy, you've already met Jill Cabell. And this is Violet Ewing."

"You're not up for the part?" Violet said. "Well, in that case, welcome to New York."

Cathy smiled politely. She guessed that they were both dressed in their best, but Violet's blue gabardine suit had been turned once—taken apart when the material had grown faded, then restitched with the inner side out. Her hair was badly crimped, too, plainly the result of her own efforts and not of the ministrations of a professional hairdresser. Jill looked a little better off than Violet, but there was a hole in the sole of her black kid boot. With her newfound familiarity with the theater world, Cathy decided that they were ingenues or second leads, trying out for a leading role at this audition call.

"Who's in there now?" Lucy asked them.

"I don't know her," Jill answered. "But she won't get it. She's the wrong type."

Cathy wasn't sure what the right type was. The play was called *The Door of Heaven*, and Lucy had said that the lead was a novice nun.

Mr. Ardry's door opened, and a young woman came out. She was slightly overweight, with dark hair and thick brows, but prettily dressed. She pressed the producer's hand. "Thank you, Mr. Ardry. I just know I'd be right for it."

He held her hand and smiled. "That was a lovely performance, dear. We'll call you if there's anything." He was a sleek, dark man, short, with slicked-back hair and an appreciative eye that rested on the girl's figure just a moment too long. He gave a look of veiled interest at the other three actresses, then went back in his office. The dark-haired woman trotted out, with an anxious glance over her shoulder.

Jill gave a snort of apparent contempt, and Violet just looked grim.

"He's at it again," Jill muttered.

"Miss Woods," the secretary said.

Lucy stood up and went into the office.

"Do you think he'll try it with her?" Jill whispered to Violet.

"How do I know?" Violet snapped. "I have enough to worry about." She gritted her teeth. "I've *got* to get a job. I'm almost broke."

They heard a faint murmur of voices inside the office. And then Lucy's voice, pitched to carry, with the full weight of her theatrical training behind it.

"I shall never want any role that badly, Mr. Ardry!"

A cajoling murmur from Ardry, and then an angry one. The office door banged open, and Lucy emerged, head erect and her mouth set in a tight line.

She marched through the outer door. Cathy got up and hurried after her. The secretary said, "Miss Ewing, please," as the door closed behind them.

"Well," Lucy said when she and Cathy were standing on the pavement outside. "I trust that was educational." She adjusted her hat in the dusty glass of the window, above the elaborate gilt legend: Ardry Theatrical Productions.

"It sounded as if he . . . made advances," Cathy said.

"As a condition of employment." Lucy's nostrils flared, and she jabbed the hatpin through her black silk hat with a vicious twist. "He has a reputation for it." The anger faded, and disappointment took its place. "Oh, I did want the lead. It's a wonderful part." She turned from the window, chin up. "But I have *never* gotten a job that way, and I will not start now."

An empty cab came down the street, and Lucy raised her hand.

When they were inside, Cathy looked at her, indignant. "How dare he?"

"Because," Lucy said, "there is always someone who wants a part badly enough." She paused and gave Cathy a direct look. "Or is hungry enough."

Cathy thought about Violet Ewing's turned dress and desperate eyes and was silent.

Claudia had wasted no time in providing Cathy with an opposite object lesson to that offered by Lucy Woods the day before.

Awaiting Claudia, Cathy, and Eden in a private box of ornate gilt splendor at the Metropolitan Opera House was a party of Claudia's choosing: Mrs. Meigs, an old friend from years ago; her widowed brother-in-law Mr. Locke, who combined the ramrod carriage of an old soldier with the avuncular expression of a man with a lot of grandchildren; Mrs. McLeod, a younger acquaintance of Mrs. Meigs; and Mrs. McLeod's daughter, Cornelia, a wistful, dark beauty of Cathy's age.

Claudia felt satisfied with her efforts when Cornelia looked at Cathy shyly and smiled, and the two girls settled happily next to each other. Claudia had set up a household for her charges in a palatial suite at the Waldorf Hotel and installed a governess for Eden, a prim woman with a bun and an excellent command of French. But hotel company was not what she had in mind for either girl, and Claudia had lost no time in renewing old acquaintanceships and scouting *their* friends and relations for girls of Cathy's and Eden's age.

Claudia sank into her chair with a little sigh of contentment for all the pleasures New York had to offer. She was having the time of her life. And how pleasant, she thought, watching Eden sit smiling next to Mr. Locke, to be doing good thereby. All her qualms about the undertaking had faded.

Cathy knew what Claudia was up to, but she was having fun, and there was no reason not to enjoy herself in proper New York society so long as Claudia allowed her to go to the theater with Lucy, also.

She turned to Cornelia McLeod, ready to be friends. "I *love* New York," she whispered. "I'm nineteen. I'm done with school. How old are you?"

"I'm seventeen. I just came out. Usually we don't until we're eighteen, but Mama thought—"

"Mama thought you were much too pretty to stay in the schoolroom," Mrs. McLeod said indulgently, but Cornelia flinched.

The houselights dimmed, so Cathy kept any further questions for intermission. Gounod's *Faust* was being performed. The opera was a social occasion, and a great many people talked all the way through it, but Cathy, with Claudia at her elbow, knew better.

Mrs. McLeod and Mrs. Meigs, on the other hand, had no such compunctions. Cathy noted with some amusement that Mrs. Meigs's opera glasses were turned not on the stage but on the glittering company around them, and she and Mrs. McLeod kept up a running commentary on the dress, demeanor, and companions of everyone they could see.

"We were quite right to come," Mrs. McLeod announced. "There is Mrs. Astor."

At intermission everyone got up to exchange seats and gossip and make certain that they were seen with the right people. Claudia declined to move, and old Mr. Locke did likewise, announcing that anyone who considered him worth looking at could come to him. But Mrs. Meigs and Mrs. McLeod began a social round. Mrs. McLeod urged Cathy and Cornelia to accompany them.

Cornelia shrank back in her seat. "I'm tired, Mama. And these slippers pinch."

Mrs. McLeod smiled tightly and said, "Ah, the price of the social season. All the girls find it so exhausting. You rest, my love, and I'll make your excuses." She simpered at Claudia. "The young gentlemen always come to us, of course, but one must be polite to their mothers." She gave Cornelia a stern look as she left the box. "Don't talk too long to any one of them, dear. It doesn't give the right impression."

Cornelia had the look of a hunted rabbit as she watched her mother leave. Over half a dozen people popped in and out of their box until the lights dimmed again. Some were acquaintances of Mr. Locke's, but there was one pale young man with a faintly nervous expression who, Cathy noted, had come to see Cornelia and who had most certainly waited until Cornelia's mother left. He and Cornelia sat gazing at each other as if what they wanted to say could not be said in front of chaperons. They both started like burglars caught in the act when Mrs. McLeod returned, with a tanned, thirtyish gentleman in tow.

"Paul. How pleasant to see you." Mrs. McLeod gave the boy a frosty glare. "Allow me to present Paul Crawford to you, Your Grace. Paul, this is the duke of Manes." Mrs. McLeod exhibited the duke proudly.

"Good evening, Miss McLeod. You look very fetching tonight," the duke greeted Cornelia.

"Thank you," Cornelia murmured.

She didn't look overjoyed to see him, Cathy realized, and while the duke presented every appearance of a gentleman come courting, Cathy had the impression that he, too, wished himself elsewhere. She was acquiring somewhat of an education, as Claudia had intended, but what she was learning was different from Claudia's hope. Cathy felt that *both* the theater and society had good and bad aspects.

"Did you hear?" Jill Cabell asked Lucy. "Violet got the lead in *The Door of Heaven*."

Lucy and Cathy sat in the room that Jill shared with another girl, who was in the chorus of a long-running comedy. The room was crowded, with two beds bumping against a single sagging armchair. Coats and boots were strewn everywhere. Jill had made tea over a spirit lamp and now propped herself on the bed, her back against the wall, balancing the cup in her lap.

"I hadn't heard," Lucy said. "Poor girl."

"Do you think—?" Cathy, shocked, looked at Lucy. "I mean, did she—"

"I feel quite sure she did, dear," Lucy replied, stirring her tea. She was sitting next to Jill on the bed, feet straight in front of her, leaving the armchair for Cathy.

"She must have wanted it badly," Cathy whispered, stricken.

Lucy frowned and poked the spoon around in her tea. "I wanted it badly, too."

"At least you didn't *have* to have it," Jill said. "You can afford to be choosy now. You've got a rep."

Lucy raised her eyebrows. "You told Ardry to boil his head, too."

"How did you know?"

"Because Ardry would have given it to you if you had let him . . ."

Jill shrugged. "I had another offer I could take. Just a bit part, enough for rent money, but . . ." She shrugged again. "Maybe next time I won't be so lucky."

"You wouldn't!" Cathy said.

"How do I know what I'd do?" Jill, hearing footsteps coming up the steep stairs, got off the bed. "How do I know how badly I'm going to want it next time?" she muttered. "I'm not getting younger." She looked almost angry.

Cathy bit her lip. "I didn't mean to judge you."

"I know, dear. You're just green." The door opened, and Jill looked anxiously at the woman who came in.

She looked old, much older than Lucy, with tight russet curls around a face in which prettiness warred with the dark circles under her strained eyes and an erratic application of rouge on her cheeks and lips. She had a shopping bag over one arm and a shawl tied tightly around her shoulders. The shawl was grimy, but it had been expensive.

Jill took the shopping bag from the woman and peered intently at her face. "Oh, Claire!"

"Leave me alone, Jill." Claire lay down on the other bed with her back to them.

Lucy stood up, set her teacup on a small table, and motioned to Cathy. "We'd best be going. Mrs. Brentwood is expecting Cathy for dinner. Thank you for the tea."

Outside, Lucy paused. "Claire's addicted to laudanum," she said abruptly. "She isn't going to last much longer."

"Why doesn't she stop?"

Lucy laughed, a harsher sound than Cathy had heard from her before. "I don't think she cares. Claire's over thirty and stuck in the chorus. Her feet hurt—a dancer's always do—and she began to take it for that. Now I think it just dulls the pain of everything."

Cathy looked around at the dingy neighborhood. Three ragged children were playing with a ball in the middle of the street, dodging the milk wagons and drays that lumbered along it. Trash lay on the stoops of the peeling wooden buildings. A woman at a basement window screamed something at one of the children, and they turned and ran defiantly. If New York glittered on its outer surface, at its core lay defeat and misery.

"How can they live like this?" Cathy wondered.

"They have no choice," Lucy said, exasperated. "Haven't you ever seen poverty? Haven't you learned yet that poverty—and worse—are at the heart of an actor's life? You think you're going to live some stage romance—the leading lady is going to break her leg, and you, the understudy, will go on." Lucy flung her arms wide, theatrically. "Fame and acclaim, the instant star!"

Cathy hung her head, embarrassed. "I know I'm naive. I haven't had any chance to be anything else. But you did it," she said accusingly. "How did you do it?"

"I lived in a rattrap like this for three years," Lucy told her.

"But you aren't addicted to laudanum, and you're not dancing in the chorus, either."

Lucy sighed and relented. "I have more talent than Claire. I came from a better background. I knew I could fall back on my parents if I had to. And I was lucky. There are plenty of actresses with more talent than I who are living like Claire."

"I suppose it's harder for a woman," Cathy said.

"Much harder," Lucy agreed grimly. "Everything always is."

They began to walk toward the prosperous heart of the city. In the next block they hailed a trolley and settled into it, next to a woman with a chicken under one arm. Overhead, the elevated railway rattled and steamed, sending a shower of soot down upon them.

"May I go to the theater with you tonight?" Cathy asked her.

Lucy rolled her eyes heavenward. "After what you've seen, haven't you learned a thing?"

"I've learned a lot. And if I still want to be an actress, that ought to prove I'm serious."

"It ought to prove you aren't right in the head." Lucy sighed. "But maybe that's a prerequisite. *I* can't tell you not to do it. *I* wouldn't do anything else."

"Then I can come with you tonight?"

"No. I have an engagement tonight."

Cathy brightened at the hint of romance. "Someone special?" she ventured, smiling.

"No," Lucy said abruptly. "Just another man who likes a pretty actress on his arm and doesn't care to bring her home to his mother." Her lip twisted for an instant. "Another thought for you to ponder while you're socializing with your aunt's friends."

Cathy spent a week's visit with Cornelia at Zanzibar, the McLeods' Newport, Rhode Island, "cottage." The opulent palaces of the rich along Newport's Gold Coast, euphemistically referred to as summer cottages in the sense that Marie Antoinette had once styled herself a milkmaid, were like nothing Cathy had ever seen before. She had to force herself not to goggle as the McLeod carriage swept through enormous ornamental gates and up the curving drive to Zanzibar's terraced steps. Inside were sixty rooms, a ballroom large enough to hold three hundred, a solarium, a billiard room, a dining room that might have been lifted intact from Versailles, and countless drawing and reception rooms. Outside were tennis courts, chestnut-shaded carriage drives, and a stable much larger and certainly more ornate than Cathy's parents' house. Cornelia's slender form seemed almost lost among the vastness of the rooms and the constant swarm of people, including the duke of Manes, who came and went.

Claudia had provided Cathy with a wardrobe suitable for this excursion, and after lunch at a seemingly mile-long mahogany table, the girls changed into tennis whites and went out, swinging their rackets under the warm June sun. Cornelia seemed happy to escape from the house, and the hunted look left her dark eyes as she and Cathy smacked the ball back and forth over the smooth grass court.

After two sets, Cornelia laid down her racket and motioned Cathy into the shade of the summerhouse. "I'm not allowed to play longer than that," she confided. "Mama is afraid I'll freckle."

Cathy nodded wisely. Cornelia had the palest of fair skin, almost white against her dark hair, and freckles were anathema. Even at home, Kale Martin had always provided her daughter with lotions and veils against the prairie sun.

A footman appeared as if by magic, with a tray of lemonade and crisp biscuits. Cornelia nibbled the edge of one and put it down. "I'm so glad you're here, Cathy. Sometimes I feel just like a tennis ball, between Mama and the duke."

"You don't like him?" Cathy asked. "He seems pleasant."

"Nooo!" Cornelia wailed, tears spilling suddenly into the biscuits. "Mama wants me to marry him and have a title."

Cathy had seen enough of Mrs. McLeod to have decided that if she wanted something, the woman was capable of making everyone's life unbearable until she got it. Cathy supposed that if one had as much money as the McLeods, then the only thing left to yearn for was something unavailable in America—a title. "But surely he wouldn't want to marry you if you didn't like him," she whispered. "And he's so much older than you."

"It doesn't matter," Cornelia said dully. "He hasn't enough money to keep up his estates. It's a—business arrangement. I'll have to live in England and never see Paul again. I wish I could die."

Cathy had learned that Cornelia and Paul Crawford had grown up together. Their fathers had had business dealings. But now the widowed Mrs. McLeod held the family's financial reins, and Paul hadn't enough money to tempt her from the shining prize of a duchess's coronet for her daughter.

"You mustn't give in," Cathy urged, her eyes flashing with outrage. "When you're of age you can marry whomever you please."

"Maybe," Cornelia said wistfully. "Maybe."

"There you are, my dears!" Mrs. McLeod sailed across the lawn toward them. "You naughty children, you must come in and rest so you'll be at your prettiest tonight. We're going to have such a houseful, it tires me just to think about it." She shook her head indulgently at them. "But a girl's first season is so important. A mother mustn't consider her *own* health. And the duke is coming! *So* gracious of him to accept our little invitation," she told Cathy.

"Mama, I don't feel well," Cornelia said. "I think I ought to rest tonight."

Mrs. McLeod's eyes flashed, but she clutched her hand to her chest and swayed. "Oh, the pain! My heart! You undutiful child, you shall put me in my grave!" She sank to the grass, eyelids fluttering.

"Mama!" Cornelia jumped up and ran to her, feeling in her mother's pocket for her vial of smelling salts. "Oh, Mama, I'll come if you want me to," she said, looking up at Cathy, misery and desperation in her eyes.

*   *   *

Eden, blossoming under Claudia's care, was living strictly in the moment, hopeful that she was going to be allowed to stay with her grandmother always.

As she, Claudia, and Cathy rode through Central Park, their horses clip-clopping sedately along a bridle path, Eden happily absorbed all her cousin's stories of her grown-up doings and offered ready sympathy for poor Cornelia McLeod.

"Doesn't she have a brother?" Eden asked. "Won't he help?"

Cathy's lips compressed. "I've never met Edward. But Cornelia says he spends all his time with some very fast friends and won't open his mouth for fear his mother will cut off his allowance."

"Sam would never let someone do anything like that to me, would he?" Eden said.

Claudia had had a telegram from Sam to say that he and Annie were finally coming home. They had extended their European honeymoon and had been gone nearly a year. Eden realized that although she loved Sam and had shared the kinship of coming second to Franz, she didn't know him very well.

"I'll tell you a secret," Cathy whispered, giving Claudia a glance of sly amusement as their guardian expertly reined her horse a little closer to theirs. "Aunt Claudia has a beau!"

"Catherine Martin!" Claudia glared at her, embarrassed.

"Mr. Locke sent her a dozen roses!" Cathy said. "*Red* ones!"

Eden put her hand to her lips, giggling.

Claudia snorted. "I'm glad I serve as a source of amusement." She gave Cathy a stern look that wasn't quite as annoyed as she tried to make it appear. "If a certain person would pay more attention to the very pleasant young men she's been meeting, she might get roses, too."

"You don't want to go home, do you, Sam?" Annie

brushed out her long, rose-gold hair in their palatial stateroom and gave her husband a troubled look. "How bad can it be?"

"My darling family, do you mean?" Sam slurred his words just a little. He never got falling-down drunk or surly, but ever since they had boarded the White Star liner *Adriatic* in Liverpool, Annie hadn't seen him stone sober. "I wasn't much thinking of them," Sam said moodily.

"Oh, Sam." Annie laid the brush down. "I've always believed in truth telling. Are you wishing you hadn't done it?"

"Done what?" He stared at her levelly.

Making me spit it out straight, she thought. "Married me," Annie said flatly.

Sam grinned. His moods had always been as changeable as a March wind. "Married into the lap of luxury. Champagne and diamond stickpins. Gold cigarette cases." His dark eyes rested on the froth of lace and sheer silk on Annie's Paris nightgown. "Prettiest woman on the ship, too," he said ruefully.

Annie smiled. She knew she was pretty and knew that Sam always wanted her; he was young and as hungry as a tomcat. Some days they didn't get out of bed until noon. She wanted to say, *Then why aren't you happy?* But she knew why: Sam hadn't anything to do. He had thought that never-ending leisure would suit him fine when they had married, but it didn't. He felt like someone's kept mistress, and he was losing his pride.

The situation had begun to bother him more since they had started for home. It had been easy, on the Continent, just to spend money and enjoy themselves. Soon they would be back in the States, and Annie would be seeing about business and meeting with lawyers. It would be more obvious then that the money was all hers. Her house in Virginia City had been put on the market, so they would have to settle somewhere new; but neither of them knew where or how to choose. And that decision would be Annie's, as well, or at least

require her approval. Although she knew exactly why
Sam wasn't happy, there wasn't anything she could do
about it.

She got up and held out her arms. "Then come to
bed. It'll be early when we dock."

Sam took her hands and ran his lips up the inside
of her wrists. "I thought I'd go out for a little while
first."

Annie pulled her hands away. "If you go out, you
won't be back till four in the morning." The *Adriatic*
was a floating city, with plenty of saloons and gaming
rooms and convivial female company, in whose presence Sam could strut and spend money—and pretend
he held his own purse strings.

Sam's hands crept back to encircle her waist. "Sure
I will." He kissed her collarbone and buried his face in
the fall of lace. "Wouldn't miss the last night on the
boat." He laughed. "I like the way it rocks the bed."

"If you wake me up at four, I'll rock the bed for
you," Annie threatened, but it was so hard to put her
foot down when she knew how he hated to feel that she
was in charge.

"Word of honor," Sam said, insinuating his hand
down the front of the nightgown. "Just a quick drink,
maybe a game of baccarat." The hand cupped her breast
and then withdrew. He grinned at her, charming and
devilish, the look that had gotten him into her bed in
the first place, back in Virginia City. "Only trouble is,
I'm out of money."

"For God's sake, Sam." Annie tried to keep her
voice even. "You've gone through a whole quarter's
income since we sailed?"

"A whole quarter of *my* income, anyway," Sam said.

Annie's eyes flashed. "Which is a sizable portion of
my income. I'm not stingy with you, Sam."

"Certainly not," he agreed. "Oh, forget it. I'll be
penniless and penitent until my next allotment."

"Well, where did it *go?*"

"I thought the whole point of my having it was that
I shouldn't have to explain where it went," Sam snapped.

"You do if you want more."

"All right, it went for baccarat. And I bought some presents with it."

"What did you buy, a racehorse? Anyway, presents for your family shouldn't come out of that. They're from both of us. Or won't they take them if they're associated with me?"

"We bought things together," Sam acknowledged stiffly. "But I wanted something for Gran and Eden that came only from me—since I'd prefer to deserve the credit I'll get for them."

Annie bit her lip. Presents wouldn't have taken it all up. Nor, she thought, had baccarat, although probably it had taken far too much. She doubted that Sam could tell her where the rest had gone. When Sam had money, he spent it until it was gone. Often he spent it on other people—he was generous—but he spent it.

She went and got her purse, knowing that she shouldn't but loathing the resentment in the air when she said no. She wrote out a check and handed it to him. "Here. The purser will cash this. I don't want to know what you do with it, but I won't give you any more till quarter day, Sam, I swear it."

Eden anxiously scanned the docks. "It's been so long since I've seen Sam and Annie. Do you think Sam will be different?"

Claudia wondered much the same thing as they waited on the pier for the monstrous white and gold White Star liner to dock. And possibly more to the point, would Annie be any different? Would the time on the Continent with Sam have toned down her clothes and smoothed the rough edges from her speech? Unfortunately, it wouldn't have made Annie any younger, Claudia thought. Then she agonized yet again, *Oh, Sam, why did you do it?*

They were coming down the gangplank, Annie in a gown that looked as if it had cost nearly as much as the ship, and an enormous hat. Sam, behind her, looked dark, dashing, and tanned. Eden wriggled her way through the crowd, flung herself at Sam, and bore them back triumphantly to Cathy and Claudia.

Other than to exchange pleasantries, there was little chance to talk on the drive back to the Waldorf, where Claudia, at Sam's request, had arranged for a suite next to her own. Cathy had never met Annie and had not seen Sam for years. This would give them a fine opportunity to spend time together.

During the few glimpses that Lydia had allowed her during the newlyweds' ill-fated visit in Independence, Eden had thought Annie was the prettiest woman she had ever seen. Now Annie, seeing the way the little girl's eyes had lit up at the sight of Sam, let her sit by him in the carriage, taking for herself a seat opposite them. That meant that Annie had to sit next to Claudia, who was looking formidable. Eden grinned at Annie in appreciation of this sacrifice.

By the time they settled down for dinner in Claudia's suite—her habit, as she disliked the atmosphere of the hotel dining room—constraint had been eased somewhat by Sam's hilarious descriptions of their adventures as tourists on the Continent. They had strayed as far as Greece and wandered in the ruins by moonlight. Cathy sighed over the romance of that, and Annie laughed and confided that the entire time they had been there, her wish had been for an American hotel with a proper bathtub.

"It was very hot and dusty, and try as I would to look at all the marble pillars and whatnots, I kept thinking it was just like Virginia City, when I had to scoop all the dead bugs out of the rain barrel just to get part of me clean. That was before Joe and I made our strike. I always swore that if I ever got rich, I wasn't ever going to live anywhere I couldn't take a bath when I wanted one."

"Annie collects plans for bathrooms the way other women collect drapery swatches," Sam said cheerfully. "I expect there'll be five or six of them when we build our house. In Rome she was considerably more taken with the ancient bathing arrangements than the modern ones."

"Do you have an idea where you mean to settle?" Claudia asked. The ordinary bride went home to her husband's hometown.

"We're . . . talking about it," Annie said.

"We may stay here awhile and do the town." Sam poured himself more wine. "There's plenty we haven't seen in New York yet."

Sam would have stayed talking—and drinking—long after dinner, but when Eden was sent to bed, Annie pleaded a tiredness that Claudia was not sure she was feeling, and they retired to their own rooms.

Claudia looked thoughtfully at the closing door. Sam and Annie had been married long enough for the honeymoon mood to have dissipated—but there had seemed to be something between them that was neither the uncertain sexual tension of the newly married nor the relaxed camaraderie of an established union. And Sam had had far too much to drink.

Annie had been very sweet to Eden. . . . Sam had always been Claudia's darling. . . . Annie wasn't boastful about her money, just frank. . . . Sam had seemed reckless, burning a little too brightly. . . . *Heaven help me*, Claudia thought. *I don't know which of them has made the mistake.*

Cathy came in from kissing Eden good night and flopped down in a chair, then kicked off her shoes.

"Don't drop down like a pheasant that's been shot out of the air," Claudia said automatically. "Well, what did you think?"

"I think she's common," Cathy answered. "But I like her."

"A little common blood never did a family any harm," Claudia said because she knew that much. "It gives it heart and backbone."

"Have you explained this to Cousin Lydia?" Cathy inquired, a gleam in her eye.

Claudia snorted. "Andy's father, *my* Sam," she observed, "was hardly an aristocrat. Except of the spirit.

He and Toby's father, Whip, were self-made men. They would have liked Annie just fine. It's a shame that success goes to some people's heads. Makes them high-falutin and inclined to pretend their grandfathers were dukes and earls."

"Do you mean Mrs. McLeod?" Cathy asked.

"I find her behavior appalling," Claudia admitted broodingly. "Unfortunately, Lydia's grandfather *was* a duke. On balance, I suppose I prefer Annie." She got up wearily. "I'm feeling my years, child. I'm going to bed."

"I got a good look at her hair," Cathy whispered, kissing her aunt's cheek. "It's *not* dyed."

"Be that as it may," Claudia said, "it's still too bright." But she didn't think Annie's hair had much to do with the problem.

The next day Sam sent his father and Lydia a telegram to announce his and Annie's arrival. Neither he nor Claudia was surprised when it went unacknowledged. Sam packed off a box to Independence anyway, containing presents: a gold-headed walking stick for his father and a black shawl accompanied by an enormous onyx mourning brooch for Lydia, with a note expressing his hope that the gift would suit her sentiments upon the occasion of his return.

"Sam, that is extremely naughty," Claudia said, looking over his shoulder as he packed the box. But she didn't order him to rewrite it. "And *my* present suits my sentiments exactly."

They had brought her a fan, acquired in Venice—just the thing for the opera.

"She practically lives there," Cathy teased.

"Gran has a suitor." Eden giggled. She had been given a music box.

"At my age, one only has acquaintances," Claudia said firmly. "Of either sex."

"Ha!" Sam said. He ruffled Eden's hair.

"How's your parrot, Eden?" Annie asked. "The one we brought you last year?"

The girl sighed. "Mama is allergic to birds. I had to give him away."

Sam looked indignant. "Well, we'll get you another one, now that you're with Gran."

"Not," Claudia said quickly, "while we're living at the Waldorf." She smiled lovingly at Sam. He was rebellious and undependable, but he had a kind heart. Claudia sighed a little. She had never known whether kindness was his true nature trying to be let out or only the surface gloss of his undeniable charm. She looked at Annie and was fairly certain she had caught her wondering the same thing.

It wasn't long before Sam discovered charm worked in New York. It worked on his grandmother's high-society friends, and his chameleon instinct soon taught him to work it on Cathy's acquaintances from the theater world. He was attracted to the beautiful Lucy Woods, but she was popularly regarded as an iron maiden, invulnerable to anything but her ambition. He met others, however, who were more susceptible to his overtures.

Sam was soon introduced to the low side of theater life—the dime museums where the down-and-out acts performed alongside the two-headed calves and bearded ladies, and the music halls where the only slightly more successful made their living. Annie had no interest in those, but he had no desire to tour them with her; alone, he could be what he chose to be, without his wife's presence as a reminder of what he really was.

And so he took to stealing away, "slipping his leash" as he put it to himself, prowling the music halls and the gambling rooms, sitting in the smoky darkness drinking beer, and watching the soubrettes in their spangled costumes and flesh-colored tights. He learned which girls he could buy a drink for and which ones were spoken for—he had had a knife pulled on him once for mistaking that. Sam had pulled a knife of his own and knocked his attacker's head against a table. The big-boned man slumped to the floor, unconscious.

The girl for whom he had tried to buy the drink proved grateful.

"Clyde's had that coming for a long time," she said. "You want to come backstage?"

Sam grinned at her, knowing that the other customers were eyeing him warily now. She smiled invitingly through a heavy layer of paint and face powder, and he followed her, wanting desperately to make love to someone who was the supplicant, not the boss.

He made love to her on a dingy sofa, drunkenly and with vindictive satisfaction.

When they had finished, the man he had knocked out was pounding on the door. Sam got up, not bothering to button his pants. He wrenched the door open, and Clyde came barreling through it with his knife, lunging at Sam.

Sam swerved and stuck a foot out, and the man went sprawling. Sam laughed, but suddenly Clyde was at his throat. The alcoholic cloud receded just enough for Sam to realize that his opponent wanted him dead. All the pent-up rage he had been harboring against Annie flowed into his fists and his own sharp blade. Snarling, he grabbed Clyde's knife hand and bent it backward until the wrist snapped. Clyde howled in pain as Sam threw him to the floor. Chest heaving, Sam bent down and picked up Clyde's knife, then stood with a knife in each hand.

The girl pulled a dirty kimono around her, then bent over the writhing man on the floor. "Get out!" she hissed, with stark terror in her eyes.

Her image, wavering through the bloodlust, became Annie's and prevented Sam from committing murder, from stabbing to the heart everything that howled around his head.

"You're crazy, mister—get out!"

VIII

Eulalia hovered anxiously beside Lee's chair. "How are you feeling, dear?"

"Relieved that I'm not Theodore Roosevelt," Lee replied mildly. He was perusing the *Washington Post* while sitting by a sunny window in Toby's rented house on Connecticut Avenue. He laid the paper down on the carriage rug spread across his knees. "What do you think, Toby?" he asked as his stepson came in. "Are they going to throw him out?"

"The man hasn't been born who could remove Roosevelt from anything he didn't want to leave," Toby said. "He's caused an unholy stink, though, I'll admit that."

The political patronage and spoils system, a time-honored institution in the country's civil service, had been receiving loud criticism since the spring, in the person of newly appointed Civil Service Commissioner Roosevelt. With the fiery eye of the reformer, Roosevelt had rooted out illegally hired employees in the Indianapolis Post Office—regrettably the hometown of President Benjamin Harrison, who was, also regrettably, a personal friend of the postmaster there.

Moving on to Milwaukee, Roosevelt had called for the removal of the Milwaukee postmaster himself, for falsifying examination results in order to hire his cronies. Testimony to that effect had come from a subordinate, one Paul Shidy, who, on his boss's orders, had done the actual falsifying. Not unexpectedly, the postmaster had fired Paul Shidy the minute Roosevelt left town. And Roosevelt's enemies had seized gleefully on the fact that Roosevelt had found "Shady Shidy" another job—practicing exactly the political patronage he had been decrying.

The postmaster general of the United States had not looked kindly on Roosevelt's meddling and had pointedly suggested that a resignation was Roosevelt's only possible recourse. Roosevelt had declined. Now there was a move afoot to encourage his departure by more forceful means.

"He's rocking the boat too much," Lee said. "Got too many people mad at him. I'll bet they toss him."

Toby chuckled. "You're on. You don't know him like I do. And he's got more support than you think."

Lee raised his eyebrows. "Going to rock the boat a little yourself?"

"I've made a speech in his support, if that's what you mean. I honestly don't see what else Theodore could have done. He promised to protect Shidy if he testified."

Lee nodded. "Tricky ground. Well, I'll await a further editorial, with you as the subject." He flicked a finger at the newspaper.

"No doubt," Toby said. "I'll put it in my scrapbook." He departed, whistling.

His mother shook her head. "Everyone in Portland's going to be furious at him." Portland politics, like politics everywhere, ran on the smoothly oiled wheels of patronage.

Lee chuckled. "He has a secret weapon, my dear. He doesn't *care* if he gets reelected. The Portland Democrats talked him into this, and they should have known better. Toby's no politician. He'll vote his conscience every time. May the Lord spare me to watch it; I haven't had so much fun in years."

Eulalia gave him a worried look. Lee hadn't been well in months. He tired easily, and he was thin—almost gaunt—with his eye sockets hollow, his cheekbones sharply carved, and his lips pale under his drooping mustache. The mustache was nearly white now.

"I had a letter from Janessa this morning. She wants you to see a Dr. Amos. She says he's an excellent physician, although she doesn't like him as much as a person."

"If Janessa doesn't like him, what makes you think I will?"

"You don't have to like him. Just see him. Please?"

"Hmmm."

"Anyway, I've made you an appointment."

Lee smiled at her. "Managing female." He listened to the sound of Sally's laughter as she raced through the house somewhere above them with Juanita's heavy footfalls in pursuit. "The children do me good."

Eulalia laid her head against his and kissed his thin brow. "Have I told you how glad I am that I married you?"

"Tell me again," Lee said.

"Holt, you're going to live to regret this." Noell Simpson, Oregon's congressman from Portland, leaned both hands, palms down, fingers splayed, on Toby Holt's desk in the Capitol Building.

"Simmer down, Simpson. You look as if you're getting ready to spring at me." Toby leaned back in his chair and crossed his hands across his dignified senatorial waistcoat. He'd been expecting this visit. "Sit down, will you?"

Still glowering, Simpson hooked a chair leg with his foot and pulled it forward to sit as close to Toby's desk as he could get. "I don't recall discussing the wholesale dismantling of political institutions when we talked about getting you elected," he growled.

"I don't believe we did," Toby conceded. "I do recall saying I'd vote my conscience and not your pocketbook, though. Have a cigar."

"I don't want a cigar! I want to know why you're supporting that maniac Roosevelt."

"That maniac's got the law on his side. A certain

percentage of civil service posts are supposed to be free of patronage. If I had my way, they'd all be free of it. Handing out jobs to crooks as a reward for dubious political loyalty is no way to run a country."

"Now look here—"

"Oh, come on, Simpson. One of those men Roosevelt booted in Indianapolis ran a gambling den."

"All right. Maybe a few rotten apples do get in. But you're treading on a lot of toes. For God's sake, you stood up on the Senate floor and said every senator had a duty to support reform in his own state. You've got a lot of people worried."

"Good. There's nothing like a little fear to bring out the latent honesty in a local politician."

"Damn it, Holt. Local politics got you elected. You have no business throwing your weight around."

"Listen to me," Toby said, serious now. He took off his glasses and leaned forward to look Simpson in the eyes. "I've gotten a few telegrams from home, so I know they're angry. But I repeat: I won't vote against my conscience."

"Nobody's asking you to vote for anything. Just to shut up. This isn't a matter of supporting a bill; it's a matter of supporting that damned wild-eyed cowboy. And it isn't any of the Senate's business."

"Tell that to the senators who're lobbying to get President Harrison to fire him."

Simpson groaned and ran his hand across his forehead. "I know you're friends with Roosevelt. I understand your little girls are playmates. But this is politics, and he's dangerous."

"Only to the status quo," Toby said mildly.

"He's a Republican, too," Simpson muttered.

"That's the least of your worries," Toby said, smiling. "You don't know him like I do."

"I heard you put in a word for me," Theodore Roosevelt said, shaking Toby's hand on the spacious grounds of the British Legation. A reception was in full swing, taking advantage of the last of the good fall weather. The trees were ablaze with orange and scarlet, and Roosevelt looked like a man on fire himself. He always did. He was young, restless, and ambitious, and he burned with inner energy.

"I put in my two cents' worth," Toby said. "For whatever a junior senator's two cents are worth."

Roosevelt snorted. "From you, quite a lot." They both knew, although Toby was disinclined to make much of it, that he was a junior senator in name only. His last assignment had been a stint as commissioner of the West, which was a fancy name for a troubleshooter with some clout behind him, and he was a famous man. The young Theodore Roosevelt admired him tremendously. That they belonged to opposing political parties troubled Roosevelt not at all. Roosevelt's enthusiasms crossed party lines at will—a fact now unhappily evident to his President and fellow Republican, Benjamin Harrison.

"Well, I want to thank you," Roosevelt said, bouncing a little on the balls of his feet; he was always slightly in motion. Grinning, he looked around. "I think nearly everyone in the city is here today. Amazing place."

They contemplated the gathering on the legation lawn, in the lee of its palatial headquarters. Admirals of the navy mingled with senators, congressmen and their wives, broad-beamed lobbyists, their British hosts, and a colorful array of foreign diplomats. The subdued formal attire of the servants of Her Majesty paled in comparison with a high-ranking Chinese official in full regalia and the ambassador from Japan in kimono and hakama, two ceremonial swords stuck through his sash. Three embassy children in garden-party clothes were regarding the Japanese gentleman with wide eyes and giggles.

"Bad-mannered little devils," Roosevelt muttered.

"I don't think he minds," Toby said. "Alexandra tells me that in his own country we are regarded as quite peculiar looking."

"Your wife is amazing." Roosevelt grinned. "She is commonly regarded to be your greatest asset."

Toby chuckled. "True." Alexandra had taken hold in Washington society with ease and charm. Her dinner invitations were coveted. She had unexpectedly struck up a friendship with the Japanese ambassador, and Toby, to his amusement, had found that exotic and taciturn gentleman reading Japanese poetry to her at a White House reception.

"My foreman at home married a Chinese girl," Toby murmured, watching Alexandra now strolling on the lawn with the ambassador.

"Although I gather that Japan and China really aren't very similar, Mai has influenced Alex. She's developed a passion for expensive Oriental porcelain."

"Horrors," Roosevelt murmured. He had money troubles of his own. Neither man had recovered from the disastrous blizzard that had wiped out their Dakota ranches, and Washington was expensive. "You ought to call the man out if he's introduced her to a hobby like that."

"She's reasonably restrained." Toby remembered an interesting piece of gossip and lowered his voice. "Speaking of calling people out, I heard that our senator from Louisiana did just that last spring. Nearly killed a man."

"I believe it," Roosevelt said, casting a glance at Senator Leclerc, who was standing with his wife under a blazing maple tree. "That's a fine old tradition in New Orleans, and Leclerc has the temper of a fiend. His wife spends most of her time patching up his quarrels. Have you met her?"

"I don't think so," Toby said. Mrs. Leclerc had her back to them—a slim, elegant figure in a russet silk gown the color of her hair. The thick locks were piled under a dashing hat of russet and rose.

"Oh, you ought to," Roosevelt said. "Amazingly beautiful woman. I'll introduce you, since you have a weakness for redheads." He smiled at Alexandra's auburn head nodding at some pleasantry of the ambassador's.

"I've found it's a dangerous taste," Toby joked, but

he smiled, too. He did have a weakness for redheads, always had. Tim's mother had had red hair, too.

Theodore and Toby strolled across the lawn toward the Leclercs, dodging a lobbyist for the railroad companies determined to have a word with Senator Holt on an impending bill. The man had an air of bonhomie and a diamond the size of Toby's thumbnail in his cravat.

"In my office," Toby said firmly. "If you must."

"Good afternoon, Senator Leclerc," Roosevelt said. "Mrs. Leclerc, allow me to present Senator Holt from Oregon."

Mrs. Leclerc turned with a graceful nod of her head, and whatever pleasantry Toby had been about to make died on his lips.

Martha Leclerc was beautiful all right. She had also been his lover, and almost his wife, nearly twenty years earlier. But as he looked at her, choking, the years compressed and dwindled, narrowed into a vanishing point that hung between them like an electric spark, potent and crackling. She had flaming hair untouched by gray even in what Toby knew must be her forties, and her emerald eyes were deeper and greener than any Louisiana bayou.

He tried to jolt his voice into some kind of speech but failed, while Martha stared at him with a flash of—what? love? pain?—in those dark green eyes. Then she moved smoothly, inclining her head, offering him a polite smile of recognition suitable for a passing acquaintance.

"How nice to see you again, Toby. You're looking very well."

He wondered if Leclerc had seen. He smiled mechanically. "You're looking elegant, as always. I had no idea you were in Washington." A moronic and obvious remark. Toby got a mental grip on himself and forced his rigid muscles to relax.

"Martha has just joined me," Leclerc said. His dark, saturnine face looked marginally suspicious.

Roosevelt's bluff, friendly countenance was interested, too.

Toby was still struggling to balance himself against a sudden attack of vertigo and to frame his next words carefully before he spoke them, in the fear that he might blurt out something dreadful. There was no denying he had loved Martha—unwillingly at first because Tim's mother, Clarissa, was still alive—but in a driven, desperate way. Even worse, Martha's father had been a shadowy lord of the New Orleans underworld, and Martha was his partner.

When Clarissa died, Toby had been seized with a form of madness and made plans to marry Martha. He rationalized that her father, old Domino, who had helped Toby out of a scrape or two, was an honorable man—as criminals went.

But she had jilted him. He had come to New Orleans to plan their wedding and found her engaged to the leader of a Memphis gang. She had given Toby to understand that living out the rest of her life on an Oregon horse ranch under the gelid, disapproving eyes of his mother and sister had not been appealing. What she was doing now married to Lucien Leclerc, he had no idea.

"My father would send his regards," Martha said, "but he died several years ago."

"I'm sorry to hear that," Toby said.

"I wasn't aware that you were acquainted," Leclerc said. He did not look pleased.

"Well, it was a very long time ago." Martha spoke easily, with a faint touch of the old imperiousness in her voice, and Leclerc subsided. "A great deal of water under the bridge since then," she added. "It has been charming seeing you again. Washington is a lovely city. Not like my New Orleans, of course. I take my walks in Georgetown, along the canal bank, because it reminds me of home—especially early in the morning, when the mist is on it." The emerald eyes rested on Toby's for a moment.

He muttered some inanity and moved away into the throng, taking Roosevelt with him, refusing to give her any indication, if she had been looking for one, that he, too, might walk along the canal in the morning.

"She's a corker, isn't she?" Roosevelt said pleasantly, but his eyes were beady. "I gather you had no idea she'd married Leclerc."

"I knew her years ago," Toby said. "The last I knew, she was marrying someone else."

Theodore chuckled. "Maybe Leclerc killed him in a duel."

"I hope not," Toby said piously. Out of Martha's vicinity, he attempted to regain control of himself. He slammed everything that he remembered about Martha—which was an unfortunate amount—into the back of his mind and tried to put a lid on it. He loved Alexandra, not with the madness that he had loved Martha, but with a solid, steady passion that he had never experienced with any other woman. After fifteen years of marriage, Alexandra knew him right down to the bottom of his soul. If he wasn't careful, she would see Martha lurking there. Alex knew that he had had a broken engagement before he began to court her, but the thought of digging it all up again made his flesh crawl.

Toby collected his wife, made suitable pleasantries to the Japanese ambassador, then went home sweating.

Why, he agonized, looking out his bedroom window down onto the moon-washed avenue as Alexandra slept, *do I feel so haunted by Martha?* He had believed that her memory was laid to rest years earlier. Was he falling into the same madness he had known before? He didn't think so. He had not felt love when he had seen her—only shock and a sense of time unreeling and twisting into some alternate dimension, like reading Poe late at night. Whatever he was feeling wasn't love anymore, but it was strong and unnerving. Toby didn't know how to kill it, but he knew he was going to have to.

He got into bed but couldn't sleep, so he finally got up again and dressed. He slipped out of the house and around to the stables, then saddled his horse. The horse, startled and sleepy, snorted at him as he led it to the empty street and mounted. Washington by moonlight was as otherworldly as he felt his own predicament to be. *I don't know what I'm doing,* he thought. If he couldn't manage his own life without his mistakes rising to haunt him, how could he serve as a senator and speak for a country?

He turned the horse's head toward Georgetown, knowing on some level where he was going, even if he wouldn't admit it to himself. Across the Rock Creek Bridge, he rode down to the towpath beside the canal and sat on a mooring block, waiting for dawn.

She appeared just a little after the first light. Toby saw her walking toward him out of the mist, the specter of his past indiscretions, and kicked himself for coming.

"My poor man," Martha sympathized. "Your coat is soaked. You look as if you've been here all night." Her English held the faintest echo of French.

"I have," Toby said. "The better part of it anyway. I couldn't sleep."

"Not over me, I hope."

"Not exactly over you," Toby said. "Over . . . uncertainty, I suppose. Something needs to be said between us, and I thought the sooner said, the better."

"You're married now, too, aren't you?"

"For quite some time."

"Are you happy?"

"Yes." He cocked his head at her. "Are you?" *And if you are, why did you ask me to come here?*

"Reasonably. Red died," she said bluntly, "in a perfectly stupid fight with one of my father's men. And then my father died. I hadn't the heart to go on with it all, I suppose. So I bought respectability with Lucien. His family didn't approve, but Lucien wanted a political career, and politics requires money. Lucien's family haven't had that kind of money since before the war."

"Old Creole family?"

"Very."

Toby chuckled in spite of himself, imagining Martha planted like an exotic viper in their staid French bosoms, spending her father's ill-gotten fortune on Lucien's campaigns. "Does he know about me?"

"Up to a point," Martha said. "Too many other people in New Orleans remember you, if he should begin asking questions, for me to lie. I told him just enough, I think, to keep him from pursuing it. Lucien has a very hot temper, and he's inclined to be jealous."

"Oh, very good," Toby said sarcastically. A mule clip-clopped by, towing a coal barge, with a barefoot boy astride its back. In the light of dawn, some of Toby's moonlit uncertainties were beginning to fade. "Why did you come?" he asked abruptly.

"Because I've never run from anything, except once, and I didn't want to do it again."

"And now? Have you settled it?"

"I had better have. I have a lot invested in Lucien." She smiled, just a quick flash of resigned amusement, and then she was walking away from him down the path, disappearing into the thinning mist.

Toby had no idea what, if anything, their rendezvous had resolved. He rode back slowly along Virginia Avenue, heading for the Capitol. He would have breakfast there, he thought. That seemed an easier plan to him now than having to offer an explanation for why he had arisen and gone out.

When he returned that evening, Alexandra seemed not to have noticed his early departure or was being tactful about it.

"Am I old, Alex?" he asked her after dinner, with Sally dozing in his lap, and Mike, grown almost unrecognizably tall, reading by the hearth.

Alexandra chuckled. "Did you think it wasn't going to happen to you?"

She bent over his chair and kissed the streak of gray in his fair hair, and her touch solidified the world around him to a reasonable and manageable form. Having some inkling of the uncertainties this shift in his life to a statesman had brought him, she had been understanding and patient.

Toby closed his eyes. *God bless Alex.* "It's the permanence of it, Alex. Anything I vote on here becomes law for the country and affects everyone forever. How do I know I'm right?"

"How does anyone? I know this: There's no one I would rather trust than you to make the fewest mistakes possible—and certainly to have your country's good at heart." Then she bustled away to find Juanita and put Sally in bed with the brisk air of someone having settled a dilemma.

In some ways, she had. Toby had long felt a respect for his wife's good sense. He had a wild impulse to tell her about Martha, too, but suppressed it. The solution, he decided, was simply not to see Martha at all.

Avoiding Martha Leclerc was not quite as easy as it sounded, but over the next months Toby managed to stay away from her at parties and to cease to jump internally when he heard her voice. Martha seemed to have laid her own ghosts to rest with that single meeting on the towpath and didn't approach him again.

The functions of government, ponderous at best, slowed to a near standstill at Christmas. Powerful men drove back-room bargains and gained pledges of support in quiet corners at the President's New Year's Day reception, over drinks in the bar of the Whitney Hotel, and even in the elaborate marble bathtubs in the basement of the Capitol.

There were nine of these tubs, installed by a youthful country in the exuberant desire to give its own halls of government a touch of Roman magnificence. Toby found them a fine place to sit and think, and he was not the only one. One previous congressman, bathing when his vote was needed, was said to have wrapped himself togalike in a blanket, gone to the floor and voted, and then returned to his tub.

One afternoon toward the end of February, when

legislative matters had picked up again, Toby sank into one of the monstrous marble basins and found himself joined a few minutes later in an adjacent tub by Congressman Henry Cabot Lodge of Massachusetts.

Lodge settled into the water and heaved the sigh of a man much tried. "Roosevelt's in trouble now," he remarked. "They put Shidy on the stand this afternoon, and the man made it obvious he has the morals of a weasel."

"Aw, hell," Toby said. They had both been following the Civil Service Commission hearings. These inquiries had been ordered largely as a result of daily editorials by Frank Hatton, who was editor of *The Washington Post*, a former postmaster general, and a staunch advocate of the spoils system. In addition to hammering at the beleaguered Roosevelt about the Shidy affair, Hatton had accused Roosevelt's fellow commissioner Charles Lyman of employing a relative who trafficked in stolen examination questions. After condemning the commission for its inefficiency, corruption, and abuse of the law, Hatton was appointed assistant to the prosecutor. Toby thought this was like asking a fox to cross-examine chickens about their loyalty to foxes.

"He got that idiot Shidy to say he'd falsify government records again if his boss told him to," Lodge said with disgust. "Theodore should have dropped him off a bridge."

"Theodore's problem is that he has more conscience than Shidy," Toby said. "When are they going to put Theodore on the stand?"

"Tomorrow. Blast him, I warned him to look out, but he wouldn't listen to me."

Lodge applied a soapy sponge to his chest while Toby sank back down in the water of his own tub and waited. He and Henry Cabot Lodge were both friends of Roosevelt's, and Toby wondered if Lodge wanted him to speak up again for Roosevelt in the Senate. Because Toby had already done so at every opportunity, he doubted that was the point of Lodge's being here.

Finally the water began to get cold. Toby was halfway out of the tub and into a towel when Lodge at last turned his hooded hazel eyes away from soaping his toes and raised them to Toby. Seeing the senator from Oregon covered by neither water nor clothes, Lodge blinked. "For the love of God, Holt, what have you done to yourself?"

Toby grinned as he toweled his back. "Evidence of a misspent life," he said, pulling on his shirt over the numerous knife and bullet scars that had so impressed Lodge.

"Hmmm. Not a man to back off from a fight, obviously. We need more like you, Holt."

Toby pulled up his drawers and stepped into a pair of striped trousers. "Who are you planning to fight?" he asked suspiciously. "I'm already on Theodore's side."

"Theodore's going to have to ride it out himself now. No, I have something else in mind. I'd like a good man in the Senate at my back."

Toby adjusted his suspenders and waited.

"My crusade will have the champions of the status quo in a rage again," Lodge cautioned, "but I'm about fed up, and I think you're the man to help push it through."

"Could we get to the point?" Toby asked. "I didn't think you'd come down here to watch me take a bath."

Lodge sighed. "Another cowboy. You're too much like Theodore. All right, here it is: I'm going to sponsor a federal elections bill that will enfranchise the Negro in the South. Or rather, keep the southern states from disenfranchising him."

Toby whistled. "Tricky ground."

"Damn it, man, we fought a war to free these people, and most of them are no better off than they were under slavery. To our shame, some of that is our fault—I mean the fault of the North. Reconstruction was badly handled and only made enemies. If Lincoln had lived, things might have been better, but we can't change that. We can only move forward. These people have been given freedom; they must be given a voice."

"You might start a little closer to home," Toby murmured. More than ten years before, the citizens of Washington had disenfranchised themselves by turning the district over to the federal government's jurisdiction rather than allowing the large Negro population to achieve a possible majority.

"I can't mend that," Lodge said. "But, by God, I can and will mend the other. Every state in the South has some law that prevents a man from registering to vote unless his ancestors were registered before 1861. It's a very neat evasion of the intent of the law, and it's going to stop."

"You'll never do it," Toby predicted. "There's too much opposition, and not just in the South."

"Maybe not this go-round," Lodge agreed. "But I'm going to start it rolling. The country's collective conscience generally needs several kicks to get it moving. I'm going to give it the first one. Would you back me in the Senate?"

Toby sighed. It was going to make the folks back home in Oregon, with its large Chinese population and its own ingrained racial prejudice, even unhappier with him than they were now. But Lodge was right, and Toby himself had said much the same thing. "Yes, I'll back you. You knew I would, you devious old bastard," he added in a mutter.

Lodge's hazel eyes flickered with amusement, and he picked up a long-handled bath brush and began to scrub his back. "It is occasionally inconvenient to be a man of honor—especially when people like me get wind of it."

"It's going to be extremely inconvenient," Toby said. "And if you back down on this and leave me hanging from a rope, I'm going to drown you in that damn tub."

"Have you lost your mind? I think you've lost your mind. I *know* you've lost your mind!" Noell Simpson paced about Toby's office like a white mouse in a cage, scrabbling to find some path of reason. Senator Holt was not being cooperative, and Simpson was shortly up for reelection. The Oregon electorate was going to blame *him* for Toby Holt. He was opening his mouth for another try, when they both heard a scuffling in the next office.

"Holt, you conniving Yankee blackguard!" The door slammed open, and Lucien Leclerc hurtled through it. He raised his fist at Toby.

Simpson retreated edgily while Leclerc stood breathing fire and quivering like an unstable boiler.

Toby stood and took his glasses off as a precaution. "How did you get in here?" he demanded. "Watson!"

Toby's hapless clerk peeked around the door. "I'm sorry, Senator. I tried to tell him you were busy—"

"Louisiana will not allow a mockery to be made of cherished institutions. Louisiana will not allow the uneducated caprices of the Negro race to overthrow everything that decent citizens have built. Louisiana—"

"Louisiana had better save it for the Senate floor," Toby cut in. "And if you're worried about uneducated caprices, you'd better go home and put some effort into educating them."

"Pah!" Leclerc snapped his fingers under Toby's nose. "Every effort has been made to care for these people—freed wholesale and then left to starve by your army—by the white citizens of Louisiana. What did the Union ever do for them except encourage them to get drunk and vote for the first carpetbagger to put a dollar and a shot of whiskey in their hands?"

"Yeah, you folks are kindness itself as long as the Negroes don't want something unreasonable, like the right to vote." Toby was beginning to lose his temper.

"You have no right to meddle in our affairs!" Leclerc shouted. "First you support that scoundrel Roosevelt—"

"That scoundrel just came out of the hearings as clean as a whistle," Toby said.

"He's no cleaner than you are!" Leclerc shrieked. "Like you, Roosevelt meddles in matters that don't concern him—"

"Now, hold on. That's Roosevelt's *job*."

"It is not yours!"

Leclerc was beginning to look entirely demented. Toby wondered queasily if there was more than politics behind Leclerc's hatred. "Get out," Toby said. He didn't want to find out the answer in front of Noell Simpson.

Toby came around the desk and took Leclerc by the shoulders. Leclerc writhed in his grasp but was outweighed by nearly thirty pounds, so Toby managed to shove him through the door. Leclerc swung at Toby, who stuck a foot between the other man's legs and dumped him on the floor of the outer office in a windmill of kicking feet and thrashing fists.

"I'll have your blood for this, Holt!"

"You must be drunk," Toby grunted. "Go sober up." He got hold of Leclerc by the collar and threw him bodily into the hall. A trio of Senate pages watched with admiration until Toby fixed them with a terrible glare. "Go take a message somewhere," he snapped, and they scattered. Before Leclerc could get up, Toby slammed his outer door and bolted it. If Leclerc wanted to stand in the hall hammering on the door, he was welcome to do so.

"I don't want to see anybody," Toby snarled at Watson. He went back into his inner office and slammed that door, too. He glowered at Simpson while he got his breath back.

"Well, you got anything else to say?"

Simpson looked shaken. "That man's a maniac."

"Sounds to me like everything he said was right up your alley," Toby snarled.

"It was," Simpson admitted. He put his hat on his head and pulled the shreds of his dignity around him. "But I'll be damned if I'll use that lunatic to make my point for me. His animosity seemed as personal as it is political. And you might have mentioned the cause of it when we proposed you for election, Holt. I don't like having that kind of thing held back."

"What kind of thing?" Toby shouted, his calm now completely flown.

"Your association with Leclerc's wife," Simpson

said. "I was going to get around to that. I don't want to sound prissy, but—"

"Well, you do! I don't have any association with her. How the hell did you find out about it anyway?"

"Some day you will learn that the Washington grapevine is mysterious and unstoppable. And right now, Holt, on the heels of Roosevelt's troubles and your support of him, you cannot afford any hint of similar illicit—"

Toby started to say something, but Simpson's phraseology struck him as being odd, as if they might not be talking about the same thing. "Illicit what?"

"Connections with illegal activity," Simpson answered. "The rumor's gotten around that Leclerc's wife comes from an extremely shady background."

Toby let out a careful breath. "I see."

"Well, what do you think has Leclerc in such a taking? Apparently you used to know the woman. He probably thinks you spilled the beans but doesn't want to accuse you of it and draw attention."

Toby passed his hand over his forehead, relief sweeping over him. "Well, I didn't spill the beans. I'd be more inclined to suspect one of Leclerc's servants or a home-state political rival. If Leclerc had any brains, he'd know that."

"Well, he hasn't got any brains," Simpson said. "I don't like having him on my side, but I sure wouldn't want him for an enemy. Those Creoles have tempers like gunpowder."

"I'll see if I can scotch the rumors," Toby said, wondering how.

"If you're going to keep stirring him up with this federal elections bill—which is the biggest damnfool thing you've done yet—you'd better try," Simpson said, taking his departure. "This could be serious."

"Not as serious as it could have been," Toby muttered when Simpson was out of earshot. Just how efficient *was* the Washington grapevine? he wondered uneasily. Would it get ahold of the rest of the story?

* * *

Toby arrived home intending to consult Lee Blake, who had a level head and a talent for taking the long view. He found the family gathered in the parlor.

"Daddy! Come and see!" Sally grabbed his hand and towed him into the center of the room.

An empty packing crate was propped against the back of the piano, and leaning against its front, obscured by his whooping relatives, was something in a monstrous gilt frame. The family crowd parted, chortling with glee, to reveal a portrait, on silk, of Alexandra. Or at least the head was Alexandra's. From the neck down a delicate figure in a kimono clasped tiny, lotuslike hands over a silk obi. The figure was somewhat shorter and far more flat chested than his wife. The effect was of someone having her photograph taken behind a costume board at a county fair.

"It's Mama's birthday present," Mike explained, "from the mikado." Ever since they had seen Gilbert and Sullivan's new musical farce, the family had taken to referring to Alexandra's Japanese admirer in that fashion.

"I love it," Alex said, wiping her eyes. "I'm going to hang it in the parlor, and if one of you so much as winks an eye when he comes calling, I'll thrash you. I think it was sweet of him." She looked at Toby's stunned expression and burst out laughing again. "He asked for my photograph last fall. I had no idea why. But he sent it to Japan and had this painted there. It just arrived, with the most charming note. Apparently he's been worried it was going to miss the date."

Oh, Lord. Toby groaned. *He* had missed the date, what with one thing and another. He coughed. "Er, I'm afraid your present from me hasn't arrived yet. Some delay with the store I ordered it from. . . ."

Alexandra shook her head. "You forgot, you devil. You work too hard. Don't worry about it. Just make certain that it's something particularly splendid."

"You always did see through me," Toby said ruefully. "Although I can't compete with this. I'd get you a kimono, but it would never make your bottom half look like that lady's."

"Hmmph," Alexandra said. "You never used to find anything wrong with my 'bottom half,' as you so indecently put it."

"Oh, I don't," Toby assured her. "It's just that it's not quite so, well, straight up and down."

"This is a highly unsuitable conversation," Eulalia declared, trying not to laugh. "Children, you come with me and see about changing for dinner. And, Lee, I want you to rest."

Alexandra flicked a glance at their departing backs, then looked at her husband. "If you want a match for this," she murmured, "you could always ask Mrs. Leclerc to have your portrait painted. You could be a snake on the bottom."

Toby sat down suddenly in a chair. So much for wondering about the grapevine. "I hadn't seen her in nearly two decades," he said desperately. "That's been over for years. It was over before I met you. I wouldn't look twice at her . . ." He felt that the more he protested, the more he sounded like a guilty husband with his pants in his hand.

Alex nodded consideringly. "Of course, dear. And I'm sure you will continue to keep that in mind."

"Alex—"

"I trust you implicitly, of course," she said, looking very much as if she didn't, quite. "But you aren't exactly a monk. And as far as I can tell, your track record before you met me was quite phenomenal. In fact, it's probably something of a miracle that you haven't strayed."

"I haven't wanted to, damn it," Toby said, stung.

Alexandra looked down at him, hands on her hips, not angry but with a certain steely glint in her green eyes. "I just wanted to let you know that I am not uninformed," she said carefully. "It is very important, however, that everyone else in this family remain uninformed. Or rather that there not be anything to be informed *about*. Your mother met her, as I understand it, back then, and I will not have her worried about our marriage just now while she is so worried about Lee."

"Lee?" Toby sat up. "Is he worse? She hasn't said anything."

"No, she hasn't." Alexandra looked at the door to make sure they were still alone. "In fact she won't talk about it at all—not even about what that doctor of Janessa's said, and that is unlike her. I think she's frightened, Toby. Don't you dare do anything to worry her right now."

Toby passed his hand across his eyes. No, he couldn't ask Lee's advice now. But Alex had probably given him the best advice anyone could, which was to lie low and behave himself. He tried to summon up the righteous indignation of an innocent entrapped, to which he by rights should be entitled, but it wouldn't come. He knew that he would be far more comfortable in his own conscience if he had not fleetingly contemplated *not* behaving himself.

He went out the next day and bought Alexandra an extremely expensive Chinese cloisonné bowl and a dozen roses. They were white, for contrition.

IX

"Mr. Holt, you can either play your kazoo and teach these galoots the two-step, or you can let me fit you for this suit," Mr. Lomax, the tailor, muttered with his mouth full of pins. "But I don't see rightly how you can do both." He pushed a pin home through the black broadcloth, and Tim yelped as it took in a piece of his backside as well. "Told you so."

Tim tried to stand still, but it was hard not to move his feet, especially since he constituted the orchestra for the endeavor. Across the room— Tim's bedroom on the second story of the now completed *Prairie Recorder* building—Peter Blake and Wally Newsome lurched through the steps again. Peter was wilting in ostentatious feminine fashion in Wally's arms. Peter's stepmother had sent him to dancing school, but he had never tried to be a girl before, and as he had put on enough weight over the past year to be a little bigger than Wally, he found it hard going.

"Quit trying to lead, will you?" Wally complained. "I've seen heifers that were lighter on their feet."

"Somebody has to lead," Peter said. The lesson was for Wally's benefit. Wally had never particularly cared whether he could dance or not, but now he was under the influence of love. It was a waltz and not a two-step he was attempting to learn, although one wouldn't know it.

Guthrie was celebrating its first anniversary. The town now boasted electric lights, waterworks, a trolley company, and industry ranging from a cotton gin, grist-mill, and brickyards to wholesale firms dealing in everything from flour and meat to harnesses and lighting fixtures.

The central business district basked in the glory of stone and brick edifices of the latest gothic style. Official establishment of Oklahoma as a territory—and Guthrie as its capital—was expected within the next month, and the community was planning a celebration designed to show those hicks down in Oklahoma City how a *real* city went about its business. A parade, speeches, a rodeo, and a pageant would be capped by a display of fireworks and a grand ball in the Guthrie Hotel.

Tim planned to mark the occasion with a shift of the *Prairie Recorder* from weekly to daily publication and with a new suit to mark his change in status. And with the rather dubious achievement of teaching Wally Newsome to dance, if possible.

"There, damn it." Mr. Lomax took the pins out of his mouth and folded up his cloth, leaving Tim in his long underwear.

"Well, what do you think?" Tim produced three hideous bars of "The Blue Danube" on his kazoo and quit when Peter and Wally ran into the wall. "Am I going to dazzle them, Lomax?"

"You will if I ain't got one leg shorter than the other, with your jigging around."

"I can always lean to one side," Tim offered cheerfully. "By nightfall they'll all be leaning anyway." Once Oklahoma was no longer part of Indian Territory, whiskey would be legal. "You think you ought to make me two pairs of pants?"

"I reckon," Lomax said. "That way you can wreck one at the celebration and still have a pair left over for your sis's wedding."

"You've got a point." Tim put the kazoo to his mouth again.

Lomax fled, complaining that the only thing he'd ever heard worse was a bagpipe.

"All right, let's try it again," Tim encouraged. "Try to forget you're dancing with Peter. Put your arm around his middle and get a good grip. Rosebay Basham's a little bitty thing. If you want to dazzle her, you've got to be masterful."

Tim didn't think Wally had much chance with Rosebay, though. When he and Peter went to her house for dinner, he looked around her kitchen, impressed all over again. There were plenty of places to get a decent meal in Guthrie now, and Tim and Peter had a real kitchen in their own apartment over the newspaper office, but Rosebay was still the best cook in the area. Her pantry was lined with gleaming glass jars of preserves and vegetables, and Tim knew there was a cellarful under the house, too. Most of her land was planted now, in corn and wheat and garden truck, and the house rose solid and homey beside the kitchen garden—two bedrooms, a parlor, pantry, kitchen, and dining room, with sanded, oiled floors and rag rugs. She was too far out of town for electric lights, but coal oil lamps flickered with a cozy glow on the reds and greens and yellows of the stockpiled pantry shelves. Tim knew for a fact that she had plowed most of the land herself, and she didn't look to him like a woman who was getting ready to leave it and go live in any lonesome cowboy's sod diggings. Not that she hadn't had more elegant offers than Wally's. As far as Tim could tell, almost every man who ate dinner at Rosebay's fell in love with her.

Although she was sweet to them all, Tim couldn't say she encouraged anybody. If Rosebay had a spare minute, she spent it in planting something, not in flirting with any suitors. She had a lilac bush by the back door and a climbing rose on the front porch, and her immaculately hoed and weeded garden was a splash of color, with marigolds growing between the rows, and a scarecrow lady in an old red dress and flapping apron strings to shoo the birds away.

Tim guessed that Rosebay, who for most of her life

had shared a four-room cabin with eight or ten other people, was building a little kingdom just for herself. The only fly in the ointment might be said to be Rowell Basham, who didn't appear to have built anything or improved a bit in the past year. He was still eating at Rosebay's—for free, Tim suspected.

Rowell clumped in halfway through dinner, sat down in his usual place, and spouted hellfire in all directions at every opportunity. He punctuated his words by thumping his fist on the table, making the plates jump, or jabbing his knife at the diners in turn.

"The vengeance of the Lord will curdle the rich man's food in his stomach!" Rowell threatened, spraying spittle from his mouth. "And the fiery pit will swallow up the fornicator." His eyes glittered venomously at the men at Rosebay's table. "And the whore with him. Ye shall be sick to your stomach of your sins."

"I'm about to be," Sid Hallam grumbled.

He was a foul blast of malevolence, Tim thought. If Rosebay's customers hadn't loved her so much, not even her cooking would have made them eat with Rowell.

After she had served the pie and Rowell had wolfed his down, he jammed his hat over his eyes. "I got the word of the Lord to preach," he said. "But I'll be back, woman. You get these men gone."

"He means he's got a whiskey customer waiting on him," Rosebay muttered.

"Anything that gets rid of him," Peter said.

Tim looked at Rosebay, whose face was taut with irritation, her lips compressed. "You ought to quit feeding him," he said for about the hundred and fortieth time.

"He's kin," Rosebay said wearily.

"Let us not discuss yon surly lout," Hugo Ware suggested. "What's the news from Washington, Holt? Have they thrown all the rascals out yet?"

As the son of a senator, Tim was considered to have a private pipeline to news from the capital, but in truth most of his information came by cable service or the Readyprint, in more timely fashion than his father's occasional letters.

"No more than we have," Tim said. "Rascals are hard to dislodge. Witness Mayor Dormer, who has a new pair of spats and a diamond stickpin to magnify his stature."

"Magnify Dormer any more, and he'll block the whole damn horizon," Peter muttered. "Do you know he was going to foreclose on old Mrs. Lindsey just because she got one month behind in her payments?" Peter's eyes flashed with indignation. "He lent the Lindseys seed money last season, and then the old man died, and his widow hasn't got but half the land planted. There's no way she can pay it off if he won't give her some leeway."

"Dormer *was* going to foreclose?" Tim asked. "Well, did he?"

Peter quickly turned his attention back to his pork chop. "No. She, er, came up with the money."

Tim chuckled. "If you don't quit saving widows and orphans, you're never going to be a tycoon, chum."

"That farm's a good investment," Peter protested.

"And you got a good heart," Rosebay approved. "Tim Holt, don't you tease him for having a good heart."

"Not I," Tim protested, laughing now. "The kid's made more money than I have. If Peter says it's a good investment, it is. I never saw anybody with such a Midas touch. He'll probably have old Mrs. Lindsey wearing silk dresses and snooting Dormer on the street in a year or two."

"Devoutly to be wished," Hugo said. "What about your father's bill?"

Tim shook his head. "It's really Congressman Lodge's bill. Dad doesn't think it has much chance, but he's going to sponsor it in the Senate. I think they're hoping to stir up enough enthusiasm now for the idea to get around the southern legislators on the next try. I didn't know you were so interested in American government, Hugo."

"I'm a student of all things," Hugo replied, "but a

master of none. Since I'm marooned here, I may as well be informed. I might even surprise you and take out citizenship papers."

"That *would* surprise me," Tim said, grinning. "You're too lazy."

"Well, I'm interested," Rosebay said. "If they can give the vote to Negroes, I don't see why they can't give it to women."

"It's not the same thing," Hugo said, startled. "They're talking about a fellow's race, which is an iffier question than you might think, or people wouldn't be so jumpy about it. Gender is definable. And if the men vote, the ladies don't need to."

Rosebay slammed a cup of coffee down in front of him so hard that the coffee spilled into the saucer. "Hugo Ware, are you telling me I'm too dumb to vote?"

"Never!" Hugo said hastily. "Forget I spoke."

"You ought to talk to my sister Janessa," Tim suggested. "She holds similar views. Quite forcefully."

"She's a doctor, right? Lord, I can't imagine that." Rosebay poured Tim's coffee. "Though come to think of it, all the healer folk I ever knew was women. What about it, Hugo? You think Tim's sister is too dumb, too—"

"I do not," Hugo said. "I am biting my tongue at this moment. And if *I* ever get to vote on it, I shall vote for *you* getting to vote. Pax?"

"What does that mean?" Rosebay demanded suspiciously.

"It's Latin for *peace*," Hugo said. "And an apology."

"Well, all right."

"Tell us a story," Hugo requested with the air of a man thankful to have escaped the cliff edge. He brought out his notebook.

"I don't know why you're so interested in my stories," Rosebay said. "You know so many better ones, about knights and King Arthur and all."

"Ah, but I don't know all your stories. Did you know some of them almost parallel stories I heard from my nurse? I'm thinking about writing a book about the development of English songs and folktales in America."

Rosebay looked as if she didn't know whether or not to believe him. Hugo wrote in his notebook all the time, but he never seemed to do anything with it.

"Come on, Rosebay, tell us a story," someone else encouraged.

"You boys sound like my little brothers," Rosebay said indulgently, and Wally Newsome groaned.

"That ain't how Wally's been hopin' you'd look on him," Jeb Morrison said, laughing. Jeb, a big bluff man with curly brown hair encircling a bald spot, owned the carriage works in Guthrie.

"Well, let me think," Rosebay said, ignoring Jeb while Wally glared at him.

She scooted her chair back and got her guitar from the parlor. It was her treasure, the only frivolous thing she had bought herself in her life. Rosebay strummed the guitar a little for effect. "Well, this is one of them stephusband tales."

"Stephusband?" Tim asked.

Rosebay gave him a little grin. "You know, the one that steps in when the real husband steps out. Well, one time there was this woman. Her man was a pretty sorry fellow, and she had a roving eye and not so much willpower. Anyway, one time her husband had to go to town, and no sooner had he left than a stephusband comes up to the door, and that woman let him in. They got to playing, and in a little while here comes a horse riding up the trace. The woman says, 'Lord have mercy, it's my husband!' And her lover says, 'Where'll I hide?' So she puts him in this big old blanket box full of quilts and slams the lid down good, just as the horse gets to the door. But it wasn't her husband at all. It were another stephusband, and he was younger and likelier looking than the first, so she let him in, too. And *they* went to playing, just leaving that other poor fellow in the chest."

Hugo, with a slightly startled look, was scribbling frantically in his notebook.

"Then there was a tapping at the window, and a face looked in. It's another man yet. Well, I guess she had all she could handle, so she tells him, 'Go away,' but he just stands on his ladder out there in the dark and says, 'Gimme a kiss, or I won't go.' So the second man, who was in bed with her, says, 'I'll fix him.' He gets out of bed and pulls up his shirttail and sticks his bare bottom out that window—it was dark and all. And the fellow on the ladder, he kisses it, and then he's mad as spit. So he goes off and builds him a fire, and he heats up a red-hot poker, and he comes back asking for one more kiss . . ."

Wally and Jeb chuckled in delight, but Peter Blake looked at Hugo with suddenly raised eyebrows. Hugo nodded and grinned back.

"So the second stephusband gets his backside burned and takes off yelling 'Fire!' The man closed in the blanket box starts hollering for someone to let him out, cause he's thinking the whole cabin's ablaze. The second man thinks he's hearing a ghost, so he lights out screaming, wearing nothing but his shirttail. The third man, he's dropped the poker and run off already. So then the woman she lets the first stephusband out of the chest, and they get to laughing, and then to playing, and I reckon they're at it yet." She played a few chords on the guitar, picking quickly, lickety-split like the stephusbands running. "So I reckon it all goes to show what a danger it all is—or that's what my granny used to say."

Wally and Jeb howled with laughter, and Hugo put his notebook away. "Do you know that story's in Chaucer?" he asked.

Rosebay shook her head. "I don't know any Chaucer. I heard it from my granny."

Tim wrestled with a vague memory of an English literature class, through which he had sat dreaming of internal-combustion engines. "The fourteenth-century fellow?"

"There isn't but one," Peter said scornfully. "What did you do in school anyway? Chaucer was the greatest

English poet before Shakespeare. Rosebay, do you know how old that story is?"

"Old, I reckon. But if this English poet wrote it, how'd my granny hear it?"

"She heard it from her granny," Hugo explained. "And she heard it from hers, a long way back. I wonder where Chaucer got it. Maybe he didn't write it at all. Maybe he heard it from his granny, too." He looked at Rosebay, fascinated. "You know what you are, Rosebay? You're a throwback. That's what isolation does. It preserves things. While the rest of your country's been galloping along into modern times, your people have been saving its history for it."

She snorted. "And you sound like one of them teachers used to come from Richmond and look down their nose at everybody."

"No offense intended," Hugo said gently.

"Well, none taken, I guess. But you make me feel like a bug pinned in a book." Rosebay stared wistfully into the fire. "I don't live there now anyway; that's all gone from me." She smiled, and the smile was a little wistful, too. "I planted me an apple orchard this week. Thirty trees, over to the west of the house."

"Orchards take a long time to bear fruit," Tim said.

Rosebay nodded. "It's my sign to myself," she responded quietly, "that I got to stay here."

"Of course you got to stay here," Wally said. "You got to dance with me at the celebration. I been learning!"

In May, an act of Congress officially established the Oklahoma Territory, and the new territorial capital set its celebration for the Fourth of July.

The citizens, swelled with civic pride, believed that heaven smiled on Guthrie. The day proved fair. A few scraps of cloud floated under a round, gold sun, which embued the well-watered streets, scrubbed sidewalks, and the brick and stone buildings of the business district with a beneficent glow.

The jubilation in the air was echoed by the red, white, and blue bunting that hung anywhere that it could be attached. Flags snapped in the breeze, and Mayor Dormer had ordered that an appropriately bedecked podium be built in the middle of Oklahoma Avenue, from which he could deliver his reflections upon the occasion to his constituents.

The citizenry was more interested in the rodeo to be held in the stockyards by the depot than in Mayor Dormer's thoughts, but since the rodeo didn't start for an hour, they gathered to listen to him anyway.

Tim was in attendance because as editor of the *Prairie Recorder* he had to be, but his heart was with the rodeo. He had his eye on the fifty-dollar prize offered in the bronc-riding contest. While Mayor Dormer droned on to a restless audience, Tim scribbled automatically in his notebook and watched his staff slink away one by one toward the stockyards. He had a new cylinder press and a staff of five now and felt himself a successful newspaperman at last; but today his only longing was to play hooky.

When Dormer finally wound down, Tim stuck his notebook in his jacket and sprinted for the stockyards, dodging through the holiday crowd to draw his first horse.

The rodeo crowd was prepared to enjoy itself. The Yellow Rose and the Jack of Diamonds saloons had set up beer gardens beyond the new bleachers, and the Temperance Union was having an equally good time picketing them, outraged by the new legality of whiskey. Other enterprising souls were peddling ices, lemonade, and slices of pie. The Singer Sewing Machine franchise's demonstration booth had drawn a crowd of farm wives more interested in keeping their children clothed than in watching their husbands get rolled in the dust by a steer. Beyond the Singer booth—and from Tim's vantage point drowned out by the Guthrie Marching Band playing "The Star-spangled Banner"—a fiery-eyed Rowell Basham stood waving his arms in a revival tent, threatening the gathering with eternal damnation. Tim wondered how much the legalization of whiskey was going to cut into Rowell's income.

"You're crazy, you know that," Peter said when Tim had drawn his number and was inspecting his horse, a big sorrel with an irregular splotch like white paint down its nose. "If that demented-looking animal stomps you into jelly, who's going to run the paper?"

"You are," Tim said cheerfully. Then, "Horrible notion. Are you trying to jinx me?"

"You only entered because Dormer put up the prize and you don't like him," Peter said astutely.

"It will give me great pleasure to accept his fifty dollars. Now quit worrying. The boys are all trained to get the paper out; they've got to do it anyway while we're at Janessa's wedding. I might add, however, that no horse has stomped me into jelly yet." Whistling, he sauntered off toward the mounting chute. He supposed that a big-time businessman didn't take a chance on getting flattened by a horse. But what fun was life if you couldn't take any chances?

Hugo Ware appeared with Rosebay, and they and Peter found seats in the bleachers beside Sid Hallam from the livery stable. Hugo had brought his sketch pad. Wally Newsome was the first contestant. Peter watched as Hugo penciled a quick impression of Wally flying into the air just before the bell rang.

Peter chuckled. "I want a picture of the boss when he falls off. I'm going to frame it and put it on the wall."

"What makes you think he's going to fall off?" Rosebay asked indignantly.

The sorrel was in the chute now, with Tim on its back and a chute man holding a restraining rope around its nose. Tim's friends watched as he jammed his hat down on his head and nodded at the man. The gate went up, and the sorrel flew out, twisting like a rawhide spring. Tim's hat went up in the air, but the editor of the *Prairie Recorder* stayed on, although with gritted teeth. When the hat came down, the horse landed on it with both front hooves and then kicked it across the paddock, possibly because it was unable to do the same to the rider.

Rosebay bit her fingernails until the bell rang and breathed a sigh of relief when Tim leaped off, rolled, and came up in one piece. The sorrel swerved and chased him through the fence.

"I don't think that hoss likes you, Holt," the chute man said, grinning, as Tim dived between the rails and the sorrel skidded to a stop, snorting malevolently.

"Makes us even." Tim checked himself for damage and limped to the sidelines to see who else made it into the next round. Jeb Morrison and three men he didn't know lasted until the bell. The chute man came up with a hat filled with numbers to draw again. Tim's crew—three typesetters, a pressman, and a printer's devil (Peter having been promoted to advertising manager) —climbed up on the fence rail to cheer the boss.

The next round was a veritable picnic—a pinto with one blue eye who looked dangerous but whose heart wasn't in it. Tim actually managed to dismount instead of jump when the bell rang, to the disgust of the crowd.

"Put him out to pasture!"

"Sell him to the riding school!"

"Let him die of old age!"

The other contestants were not so fortunate. No one was left for the finals but Tim and Jeb Morrison, and when Tim drew his horse for the showdown, he found that his luck had been fleeting: He had the sorrel again.

"Aw, ain't that a pity?" Morrison drawled. "You want to bow out now, before he eats you for lunch?"

"There's not supposed to be but one ride to a horse," Tim protested.

"We ran short," the chute man explained. "So we put the sorrel back in. Mayor's orders." The man shrugged. "It's his prize money."

Tim glared at Mayor Dormer, who was smiling blandly from the reviewing stand. Dormer had developed a pretty consistent dislike for the *Prairie Record-er*'s editor, especially since the mayor had begun campaigning for reelection. Dormer had probably seen to it that Tim drew the sorrel after watching the horse chase Tim through the fence.

The announcer, who sat next to the mayor, put a megaphone to his lips. "No bell for the last round. Prize goes to the man who stays on the longest."

Morrison was up first, but Tim gave most of his attention to the sorrel that was being dragged, thrashing and snorting, into the chute. The horse didn't seem to have lost any of its fight, and if Tim had learned something about the sorrel from his first ride, then presumably so had the horse about Tim.

Morrison lasted twenty seconds—a good ride by any standards. Tim eased himself into the sorrel's saddle, most of his attention devoted to thinking of something unpleasant to do to the mayor. The sorrel was out of the chute almost before the gate was open, and Tim quit thinking about Dormer and started thinking about not getting killed.

The sorrel leaped and twisted, apparently trying to turn around and bite him in midbuck. Tim attempted to count seconds as he rode, having no desire to stay on the horse any longer than it took to beat Jeb Morrison, but it wasn't easy. The sorrel convulsed under him, threw itself up on its hind legs, and nearly went over backward. Tim leaned forward frantically in the saddle, and then they were coming down again, still right side up but with a sickening lurch and a bone-jarring thud that made Tim nearly bite through his tongue. He thought he had been on for twenty seconds—he felt as if he had been on for a year—but he found he had no idea about how to get off, given the sorrel's apparent desire not just to throw him off but also to kill him.

He thought that the sorrel was even more frenzied this ride than the first, and that didn't seem right because the horse should have lost some of his stuffing just from the exercise. As they careened past the reviewing stand, Tim saw Dormer looking at him with a malevolent smile. And then Dormer looked at someone else and made a little gesture with his hand as if he were telling that someone to get lost. The sorrel slewed, and Tim saw Rowell Basham slinking away from the chute across the arena.

There was no time to think further, other than to put two and two together. Tim didn't know what Rowell had done to the sorrel, but he obviously had done something that had sent the horse into madness. The sorrel heaved and twisted in rage, and Tim knew that he couldn't stay on much longer—and that if he fell or jumped off, he'd be dead before anyone could get to him. Tim thought about shouting, "Get a rope on it!" but no one could hear him over the roar of the crowd. They all thought he was going for a time record and were cheering him on.

He felt himself slipping off the saddle and could see the sorrel's flashing, iron-shod hooves beneath him. Having no weapon against the horse but to ride it to a standstill, Tim knew he wasn't going to make it. He was good, but not that good. The sorrel had gone insane, probably from the pain of whatever Rowell had done to it. There were plenty of painful things to do that wouldn't leave a mark.

Tim searched frantically for something—anything —to do and saw the solid bulk of the reviewing stand ahead of him. Maybe he could slam the horse into it and knock the wind out of the animal. The only trouble was that he himself might break a leg in the process. He dug his spurs into the horse's flanks anyway and was gratified when it leaped forward in the general direction of the reviewing stand. Dormer looked unnerved, and Tim thought vindictively that if he could give the fat bastard a heart attack in the process, at least he himself could die happy.

The sorrel executed a series of stiff-legged jumps, spun counterclockwise like water going down a drain, and then, spurred on by Tim, rocketed toward the reviewing stand again. They were too close to pull up, even if Tim had intended to. Dormer and the other dignitaries fled down the steps as the sorrel crashed into the wooden posts at the base. As the posts buckled, Tim grabbed the railing and swung out of the saddle, pulling himself up over the tilting platform as the sorrel dropped, momentarily stunned. When the horse got up again and began kicking the rest of the platform apart, Tim slid down the steps with not much less speed than the mayor had exerted.

At the bottom, he found Dormer picking himself up out of the dirt. Tim made certain he fell on him and knocked him down again.

"Have you told Rosebay?" Peter asked. Cleaned up, they were standing on the town hall steps watching the fireworks blaze red, white, and blue across the sky above the park. The mayor's fifty-dollar prize made a very satisfactory weight in Tim's pocket, even with the mayor's curse attached.

"No," Tim said. "I can't prove it. And Rowell's not her fault."

"Dormer's planning to have you arrested," Peter said, "if he can just figure out what to charge you with."

"He'll be cooled down by the time we get back. Maybe," Tim said. They were leaving on the morning train to see Janessa married in Richmond, where Charley's family lived, since most of her own family were closer to Richmond than to Oregon. It was Tim's guess that Dormer wasn't going to like his Fourth of July editorial.

"Are you sure the boys can handle the paper?" Peter asked for the fiftieth time. "Maybe I ought to stay."

"Janessa and Aunt Cindy would have my hide if you weren't at the wedding. And, yes, the boys can handle it. They've got the cable, and the Readyprint to fill in with, and they ought to be able to write up anything that happens in Guthrie during the next five days, among them."

"They can't write at all, among them," Peter said.

"Well, your mom and dad want to see you, and I'm more frightened of Aunt Cindy than I am of Janessa, so you're going. We have to prove that I haven't led you into evil ways. Now go on in there and dance with the girls. And stay out of the punch because I'll bet it's spiked."

Tim watched Peter amble into the hall. Uncle Henry and Aunt Cindy were in for a shock, he thought. The kid had grown at least six inches. He really wasn't a kid anymore. Peter made a courtly bow to a farmer's daughter a year younger than he was and swept her into the whirling dancers. Tim grinned. Wally Newsome galumphed by with Rosebay, unhandy on his feet but game. Tim sighed as the ghost of Isabella Ormond whispered past him. He oughtn't to laugh at Wally. Unrequited love wasn't funny.

Hugo Ware bent over Rosebay's hand as Wally relinquished it. " 'Alas poor Romeo, he is already dead—run through the ear with a love song.' That's a very fetching dress you're wearing."

"I made it," Rosebay said. "And you're making fun of me because I wouldn't let you buy me one."

"Never," Hugo denied. "Will you dance with me?"

She held out her arms, and they circled among the waltzers.

"You look very solemn," Hugo observed.

"I'm minding my feet. I didn't have to bother with Wally—he's worse than I am. But you know what you're doing."

"God help me, I hope so," Hugo replied fervently. The music stopped, and then the band struck up a reel.

"Now I can dance this," Rosebay said.

"So can I, but I don't want to," Hugo told her. "Come and talk to me instead." She looked at him, slightly puzzled, as he led her into another room, empty save for ladies' wraps thrown over a settee and an infant sleeping in a rush basket. He took both her hands and looked down at her solemnly. "Rosebay, have you ever thought about getting married again?"

She chuckled. "Now don't tell me you're doing Wally's courting for him."

"Would you please forget about Wally?"

"Well, I thought—"

"My beautiful darling, I'm speaking in my own behalf."

Rosebay's eyes widened. "Hugo Ware, you're plain crazy."

"Well, you must know I've been in love with you for a year."

"But I thought you just wanted . . . well . . . you know what I thought."

Hugo looked embarrassed. "Maybe that was all I wanted, to start with. But I finally figured out that wasn't all I wanted. And what kind of blackguard do you take me for, anyway?"

Rosebay took a deep breath, trying to think what to say. His blue eyes, normally so indolent looking, were intent on hers. But he *was* indolent, and she didn't love him. And what would his daddy the baron say? And what if Tim Holt was planning to ask her; that thought crossed her mind, unbidden.

"Hugo," she said finally, "I just don't love you, although I admire you for a friend. And your family would die if you married me," she added to soften it. "We don't come from the same world, you and me."

"You've left your world, Rosebay, and so have I. Couldn't we make a new one here?"

"No," Rosebay said sadly. "Hugo, don't ask me again."

He stood back from her, accepting but not quite resigned. "I won't for a while. I can't promise forever."

As she watched him go back into the other room, she wrapped her arms about herself, feeling small and mean. *Oh, Lord, why can't I love him? Lord Jesus, let me quit loving the wrong man.*

"What were you doin' in here with him?"

She spun around and saw Rowell glaring at her, as venomous as an adder and maybe a little drunk.

"What do you mean spying on me?"

"He ain't your kind." Rowell advanced on her. "And a wanton woman's an abomination."

"You get away from me!"

"I reckon you better have me, Rosebay. A man

ought to take to him his brother's wife, like the Good Book says. You read the Good Book, Rosebay?"

"More'n you, I reckon. Preaching with a skinful of whiskey! Makin' whiskey!"

"Money taken from the heathen ain't no sin. Got to support the Lord's work. You better listen to the Lord, Rosebay." He grabbed at her, but she twisted away.

"Rowell Basham, you touch me, and I'll scream! I'll have every man in this hall in here on you!"

"Can't nobody fault a man of God for counselin' his sister," Rowell said. "Abjurin' her to give up harlotry."

He lunged at her, and she drew back her fist and smacked him on the nose as hard as she could. Then she ran out into the hall, careening through the shifting figures of the reel.

The Santa Fe express train steamed out at mid-morning, bearing Tim Holt and a penitent Peter Blake, who had ignored Tim's strictures concerning the punch and was suffering his first hangover.

"I'm going to die," he muttered, wincing as the train rattled into full speed and the brassy Oklahoma sun blazed in his eyes.

"No, you aren't," Tim said, laughing. "You're just going to wish you would. You're lucky you didn't get in a poker game," he added reminiscently.

"I couldn't have read the cards." Peter leaned his head back and closed his eyes.

"I know," Tim said. "That's how I got in the newspaper business, remember?"

"Man, it's a good thing the boss is headed for Virginia. After yesterday, the mayor's going to split a gut when he sees this." Joey Garmer, Tim's newly hired junior typesetter, stopped with a half-filled type stick in one hand to read aloud. "Listen to this editorial he's gone and left me:

"Guthrie, now proudly a territorial capital, may one day be a state capital, and it behooves us to consider how any government may best serve all its citizens.

"As the federal government has just, shamefully in our opinion, refused to serve any but its elite, its white citizens, as demonstrated in the recent failure of the Federal Elections Bill, so do we detect a similar trend in Guthrie. The Federal Elections Bill was proposed primarily because of the notorious tendency of local government toward corruption for its own ends. This editor fears that Guthrie is no exception. We have here in Guthrie a government of the elite, by the elite, and for the elite: a small private club composed of Mayor Abel Dormer and certain of his cronies, who are now asking the citizens of Guthrie to reelect them.

"Campaign oratory is traditionally based upon reform—a better shake for the common man, a promise to throw the rascals out and start clean. Alas, Mayor Dormer's platform appears to consist of the effort to throw the rascals *in*."

X

The new graduates of the University of Southern California's Medical College came spilling down the steps of the three-story building that housed the entire college, diplomas in hand and mortarboards flying high into the air. They shouted to one another with raucous glee, slapping backs and dancing undignified jigs down the sidewalk.

"We're *doctors!*" one of them shouted, skimming his cap across the lawn.

Janessa Holt and Eliza Thoms, the two women who had survived the three-year course, moved more sedately, hampered by corsets and petticoats, but they, too, looked bouncy. Janessa had a spring in her step, and Charley Lawrence caught her by the waist and whirled her around exultantly.

The dean and professors watched indulgently from the porch, knowing from their own experience that these fledgling doctors' enthusiasm would tone down somewhat by the time they actually saw their first patients on their own. At that point, they would be stricken with stark terror, but they would get over that, too.

Janessa spun around in Charley's arms, knowing that his high spirits were not only for his medical degree but also for the fact that now they could get married.

"Come on!" Steve Jurgen pulled at them. "You can canoodle with each other later. You'll miss the party!"

"I'm the hostess," Janessa said, laughing. "You can't start without me."

"Watch us!" Steve said as he raced down the walk.

"We'd better go," Charley said, "and try to restrain these lunatics some."

The party was a barbecue in the backyard of the boardinghouse where Janessa had lived for three years. That she had invited these once-hostile males, and that they were coming, was a mark of how much her status among them had changed over those years. Some of them might still have reservations about the fitness of women in general for medicine, but they had none about Janessa Holt. She had worked side by side with them in the dissection room, over a malodorous cadaver, and had neither been sick nor fainted. She had been among them during a scarlet fever epidemic in the city, during which medical students had been called in, to work far beyond their strength and training. And she had graduated second from the top in her class. Even Mr. Felts, now Dr. Felts, who had spat on her skirt the day she had arrived, had no disparaging remarks to make over her medical abilities. He only thought that Charley Lawrence was crazy to marry a woman who had so far removed herself from her normal sphere. Janessa Holt might be an excellent doctor, but she wouldn't make anyone a biddable wife.

Mrs. Burnside, Janessa's landlady, had decked the backyard with calico streamers attached to a sort of maypole shaped like two entwined snakes with wings at the top, the symbol of a physician. Under its fluttering ribbons, her cook, Clarice, turned a whole calf on a spit. A table was laden with fruits and salads, an ice-cold crock of lemonade, and a tin washtub full of ice and long-necked beer bottles. Along the back of the table was a placard penned by Charley, who was a fair hand as an artist, showing each of the graduates in their presumed future occupation: Felts, in spats and a pince-nez, as a fashionable practitioner; Carstairs, in a country practice, surrounded by his wife and at least a dozen children; Janessa and Charley and Steve Jurgen, staggering under the weight of enormous epaulettes, as commissioned officers in the Marine Health Service, to which they were all three to report in the fall. To Eliza Thoms, Charley had given a blackboard and a stack of textbooks and something of the same expression commonly worn by Dr. Dunbar, who had made the students' lives a terror for three years. Eliza was going to teach at the Women's Medical College of Pennsylvania.

"Going to infest the profession with yet more females, eh, Miss Thoms?" Felts said jovially, uncapping a beer.

Eliza declined even to answer him, but Mrs. Burnside said, "Quite right, too. At my age one doesn't wish to confess the indignities that have been visited upon one's body to a male whippersnapper. Not to mention that's an uncalled-for remark while you're drinking Miss Holt's beer."

"That's all right," Janessa said sweetly. "It's quite understandable that most men prefer beauty to brains in a woman."

"That's my point exactly," Felts said happily. "A woman's sphere—"

"Considering that most men can see better than they can think," Janessa concluded.

Mrs. Burnside chortled. "I'm going to miss you, dear. You have enlivened my household. Now you enjoy your party. I'm just going to see how Clarice is coming with that barbecue."

She bustled off, and the guests milled across the lawn, exchanging addresses and promises to write, while Janessa's fellow boarders offered her their congratulations and advice.

"Take care of yourself out among the microbes." Mr. Pepperdine, who was tall and bony, bent to pat her hand.

"Of course you won't practice for long." Mrs. Bellow, stout and corseted, gave her an arch smile and glanced coyly at Charley across the lawn. She was envisioning, Janessa assumed, a hasty retirement for maternal reasons, but it wasn't considered nice to say so. Unmarried women weren't supposed to have any notion how you got pregnant in the first place, whether they had been to medical school or not.

"Shouldn't practice at all," Mr. Anderson grumbled. "That's what I always say."

"So you do," Janessa murmured. Mr. Anderson might have forgiven them for lancing his boil, but she was certain that he had not forgotten.

"But I wish you good luck all the same," Mr. Anderson added "I'll just have a word with that young man of yours, too."

He went off, presumably to remind Charley who should wear the pants in the family, and Janessa shook her head.

"He won't change," Miss Gillette said, glaring at Mr. Anderson's back. She was a librarian with suffragist leanings. "But I do admire you so!" She gripped Janessa's hand intently. "You are an example to us all!"

"I didn't really set out to be an example," Janessa said. "Just a doctor."

Colonel Hapgood put a frail arm around her while leaning on his cane. "My dear, you will discover that we are all to some extent as others see us. If Miss Gillette finds you an example, then you are one."

After the boarders had moved toward the other guests, Janessa thought about the colonel's remark. She looked at the other boarders and the doctors milling around her. How many people was she, then, according to Colonel Hapgood's theory? The feminine example for Miss Gillette; the wife as well as medical partner for Charley; the threateningly wayward female for Mr. Anderson; the embodiment of change if not outright revolution for these men she had been to school with; and soon something else entirely for her patients—the physician in whose hands they would place their trust. It was all very unnerving, but thrilling at the same time. She had a sense of being multifaceted, as changeable as the light flashing from Charley's ring on her finger. It

felt powerful, to present to the world the self most
useful at the moment, and with confidence.

She saw the dean beckon to her from the corner of
the garden. He was dark and elegant in a top hat
against a bright bank of Mrs. Burnside's canna lilies.
Beside him was a young woman whom Janessa had not
seen before.

She walked over and presented herself dutifully.

"An excellent party," Dr. Francis said, "and very
kind of you. I hope you're prepared to throw them out
when Mrs. Burnside has had enough."

The party was admittedly getting lively. Steve
Jurgen, Felts, and Carstairs had linked arms and were
singing "Froggy Went A-Courting" loudly and off-key,
with Felts hiccuping in time to the chorus.

"I expect I can manage them, sir," Janessa said
gravely.

Dr. Francis smiled. "I'm sure you can at that. Dr.
Holt, I should like you to meet Miss Lancaster. She is
enrolling with us this fall."

Miss Lancaster bobbed her head nervously and
held out her hand.

"Welcome," Janessa said. She cocked an eye at Dr.
Francis. Women at the medical college were an experiment that he was determined to make work. Janessa
suspected that he wanted to show Miss Lancaster a
woman who had survived the experience.

Miss Lancaster eyed the cavorting men, who by
this time were doing an Irish jig to Steve Jurgen's
banjo. Mrs. Carstairs, with a baby on her hip, was
watching her husband indulgently, and Eliza Thoms
watched with the expression of a woman who had no
time for foolishness. Neither was really a part of the
celebration. Mrs. Carstairs didn't mind, she had her
own world of babies and housekeeping. But Eliza Thoms
was neither a cuddly wife with a baby in a blanket nor a
man in this male world. Eliza was scornful of men,
having been given excellent reasons. On the other hand,
Janessa, who had tended toward the same sentiments
herself, had discovered in the course of the last three

years that she did like men—or at any rate she liked as many men as she did women. She wasn't ever going to like Felts or Mr. Anderson, but then she didn't like Mrs. Bellow, either. But Colonel Hapgood and Mr. Pepperdine were dear friends, and so was Steve Jurgen.

She linked her arm through Miss Lancaster's. "Let me get you some lemonade." She drew her a little away from the dean.

"The first year, they put a severed arm in my cupboard," Janessa confided in a low voice. "They'll do it to you, too. But if you can get through the pranks and keep a sense of humor, they'll change. Or at least most of them will."

"I'm terrified," Miss Lancaster whispered. "If I didn't want to be a doctor so badly, I wouldn't do it. But I live here, and I can't afford to go away to a women's college. My father won't give me the money. He says if I can't stick it out here, I have no business being in the profession. He's hoping I won't, of course."

"Well, if you do stick it out, you'll have a head start in dealing with disapproval afterward." Janessa handed her a glass of lemonade. "Not to mention the satisfaction of proving your father wrong."

Miss Lancaster laughed suddenly. "You have no idea how much I want to do that."

"I was lucky there," Janessa confessed. "My father was all for it. *I* was the one who held me back. Don't let your own fears do it to you. But don't let it make you hate men, either." She waved a hand to take in her classmates. "We're all what we're brought up to be, and it requires some kind of shock to make a person change opinions he's always had." She grinned. "It helps to get high marks, too."

"My father says they'll hate me for that."

"Some will," Janessa confirmed. "But the others will open their eyes very wide and say, 'Well, I'll be damned!' Excuse me," she added ruefully. "One thing coeducation does do for you is to give you a most unladylike vocabulary."

"I have a feeling I might need one," Miss Lancaster murmured.

Janessa chuckled. "Helpful in times of stress. . . ."

Miss Lancaster appeared to have brightened, and Janessa took her back to the dean, feeling rather like a mother duck encouraging her duckling into the pond. It seemed that she *was* an example, and maybe it wasn't such a bad thing to be.

Charley came up to her and kissed her surreptitiously. Or at least he thought he was being surreptitious, but Steve Jurgen shook a finger at them in mock admonishment, and Dr. Dunbar came over and bent his famous scowl upon Janessa.

"Dr. Holt, I hope I have not wasted three years on your medical education to see you spend the next three years in the nursery!" he snapped. Dr. Dunbar had none of Mrs. Bellow's reticence.

Janessa fled, leaving Charley to discuss their sex life with Dr. Dunbar, if he cared to. At least Miss Lancaster hadn't heard that, she thought, stifling a giggle.

All the same, Dr. Dunbar's indignation had touched on a subject that Janessa hadn't been able to bring herself to discuss with Charley. It wasn't a question of female modesty, it was simply that she did not know her own mind.

When the party was over, Charley sent home, and Mr. Pepperdine had helped her to sweep the last carousing doctors out the garden gate, Janessa went to her room and sat thinking for a long time. She had lived in this room for three years, except for flying visits home to the Madrona, the Holt family ranch in Oregon. The small bedstead and battered student's desk, the bookshelf with her anatomy, obstetrics, and pharmaceutical texts, were as familiar to her as her childhood bedroom had been. When she left here, she would be on a train for Richmond with Charley. She had no qualms about her future with him, but she had doubts. . . .

Finally she got up and pulled a wrapper over her nightgown, then tiptoed down the stairs. Mrs. Burnside was in the parlor, as Janessa had expected she might be. The landlady liked a quiet hour or two at night when her boarders were in bed and out of her hair. Fifi, a monstrous Newfoundland dog approximately the size of a small pony, was asleep on Mrs. Burnside's feet.

Janessa bent down and scratched Fifi's ears. "Was it a poor baby, shut in the house all day?"

Fifi had a tendency to munch on the contents of unattended plates and had been banished from the party. Now she lolled her tongue out happily and drooled on Janessa's toes.

Mrs. Burnside smiled. "Well, child, are you packed?"

"I'm dithering," Janessa said.

"Over packing or marriage?" Mrs. Burnside inquired. She reached into a cupboard beside her chair and took out a sherry decanter. She poured a glass for Janessa. "Dutch courage."

"Not marriage exactly." Janessa sat on the floor beside Fifi, who went to sleep again with her head in Janessa's lap. "Dr. Dunbar thinks I'm going to chuck it all and have babies," Janessa muttered.

"Mmmm. Do you want babies?"

"Yes, I do. But I don't want to be like Mrs. Carstairs with one every year until I fall down dead. Which," Janessa predicted darkly, "she's going to do if she doesn't put some space between the babies. But I do want children."

"I take it you know how to put some space between them," Mrs. Burnside murmured.

"Oh, yes." Janessa pushed her front hair, elegantly curled for the party, away from her forehead and stared broodingly into the fire. "It doesn't always work, of course. And even most of my professors think a woman's bound straight for hell if she tries. Charley doesn't feel that way. Not that we've actually talked about it," she added, embarrassed. "It's just that I know Charley."

"I don't quite see your difficulty, then." Mrs. Burnside tilted her head at Janessa, interested and sympathetic but a trifle bewildered.

"It isn't *not* having them," Janessa blurted. "It's having them. And practicing medicine. I don't know if I can do both, if it's fair, if I'll be too divided in my mind. Am I going to raise depraved delinquents because I have a profession, too?"

"There are plenty of mothers who do," Mrs. Burnside remarked. "Work, I mean."

"Most of them have to, poor things. And I haven't noticed their children turning out awfully well. May I have some more sherry?"

Mrs. Burnside refilled Janessa's glass without comment, waiting for the young woman to wrestle her way through her problem.

"Has it ever occurred to you," Mrs. Burnside finally said, since Janessa seemed to be making no progress, "that those children don't turn out well because of other factors, like poverty and despair and lack of education? And that the ones who do turn out well have their mother's strength as an example to sustain them?"

"Well, my aunt Cindy's children seem to be all right. She runs an art gallery. But you don't have to run out at midnight to deliver a picture. You can pretty much work when you want to."

"What about your own mother?" Mrs. Burnside asked gently.

Janessa's Cherokee mother had been a nurse and a medicine woman. She had not been married to Toby Holt and had raised Janessa alone until she had died when Janessa was a young girl. Toby had not been aware that he had a daughter until then. Mrs. Burnside was acquainted with the story, but it wasn't one that was mentioned often.

"Well, I suppose I did turn out all right." Janessa looked up at Mrs. Burnside. "But I honestly don't think I would have if she hadn't taken me to live with Dad when she was dying. I was a very bitter child and far too self-contained. I didn't really like anyone but my mother until I found myself in a real family."

"Family matters," Mrs. Burnside said. "Maybe it's family that counts, and not what the mother does. You won't exactly be in your mother's shoes, you know. I am aware that prevailing medical wisdom holds that working mothers give birth to two-headed monsters, but I never thought that *you* held those views."

"I don't," Janessa confessed. "It's just that I never had to apply my half-baked theories to myself before."

"Well, you will have to apply them to your patients," Mrs. Burnside remarked, "so you might as well start with yourself."

"Oh, Lord!" Janessa burst out laughing. "I suppose you're right."

"Oh, I am," Mrs. Burnside said. "I'll give you my own half-baked theory if you want to hear it."

"Please."

"I don't think it's children at all; I think it's Charley. This is something you're going to have to talk to him about, and you're afraid of what he might answer."

"Afraid that Charley will say I must stop practicing when I have children? And that I'll let him convince me?"

"Or afraid that you'll fight over it. Take my advice and fight over it *before* you're married. It's so much more pleasant than fighting over it afterward. Before the wedding, everyone is on his best behavior."

Janessa shoved Fifi away and leaned her head against Mrs. Burnside's skirt. "I'm going to miss you, Mrs. B.," she said sleepily. "You don't know how much I'm going to miss you."

In the morning, Janessa was lying in wait for Charley when he came to help her finish her packing. "I want to talk to you," she said. "Come out to the garden." The house was full of boarders, and their hearing was uncannily acute when it came to somebody else's business.

Charley raised his eyebrows, but he let her lead him out into the dusty sun by the canna lilies. Janessa stared at him and took a deep breath.

"I know," Charley said genially. "You're going to confess that you aren't really Janessa Holt. You're an opium dealer's daughter from Canton. You feel I ought to know this ere we wed."

"Oh, stop it." Janessa relaxed a little. *"The Ladies' Home Journal,"* she informed him, mock prim, "says that there ought to be no secrets or unanswered questions between a betrothed couple." She turned serious. "I want to talk about children. I don't know quite what to do about having them."

"The Ladies' Home Journal doesn't say?" Charlie inquired. He slipped his arms around her. "If we weren't in the garden, I'd be delighted to demonstrate."

"You aren't going to demonstrate anything until after we're married." Janessa pushed him away. *"Will* you be serious?"

"I'm trying to be," Charley said, "but I don't know what's eating you."

"I don't know if I can have children and practice medicine at the same time," Janessa whispered. "We've never talked about it."

"Well, speaking personally, I feel capable of being a father and a doctor simultaneously," Charley said.

"That's all right for you. You're a man."

"Oh." A certain amount of comprehension appeared in his eyes, with a faint light of indignation behind it. "And are you under the impression that when we do have a child—we, not just you—I am going to beat my chest and hand out cigars to the boys and have nothing further to do with the kid?"

"My father did," Janessa said. "I don't mean with me—he couldn't help that—but with Tim and to some extent with Mike and Sally. He's a good man, but he pretty much left their mothers to raise them. Most men do."

"Most men don't marry their business partner," Charley said. "Now look here, stop thinking about everyone and start thinking about us. I won't be out fighting wars and blazing trails or any of the other stuff your father has done. I'm a much duller fellow. I'll be around as much as you will, and we can strike some kind of balance if we work at it. We may have to quit government service or at least epidemic fieldwork when children come along, but that means both of us, not just you. Now, am I getting through to you?"

"Do you mean that? Do you seriously mean that?"

Charley found a lawn chair and sat down in it, with Janessa on his lap. A curtain twitched at an upstairs window, and he waved at it cheerfully. "Might as well create a scandal and give them something to remember us by," he said. He blew a kiss at the window, and the curtain snapped shut abruptly. "Janessa, I am not marrying you so you can clean the house and change all the diapers and raise kids who hardly know me. I'm marrying you because I worship the ground you walk on and because I want to be married to another doctor who'll understand why I've been out all night and am in a foul mood because a patient died. When we have children, I intend to see as much of them as you do. I'll admit I feel fortunate not to have to give birth to them, but that's all the one-sidedness I intend for there to be to the arrangement." He kissed the top of her head. "Here, are you crying?"

"No," Janessa said firmly. She ran her hand across her eyes, giving lie to that statement.

"Good," Charley said. "And if you think I'm too dumb to change a diaper, I resent it."

"I don't think you're too dumb. It just never occurred to me that you'd want to."

"I'm a pioneer. Now quit snuffling on my shirt and finish packing your trunk."

Janessa sat up. "You can help. Since we're partners."

Charley looked interested. "I've always wanted to see what you wore under that beetle shell." He poked her corseted waist.

"All my undergarments are pristine and ladylike," Janessa assured him. "One never knows when one may be hit by a train."

Rattling eastward on the Southern Pacific, she did feel rather as if she had been bowled over by something. The depth of her feeling for Charley was nothing new, nor was his respect for her as a doctor. But his theories on child raising were certainly avant-garde. What other undiscovered notions might he have? And how startling might some of them prove to be over the course of a married life?

Janessa was still wondering, bemused, as Alexandra twitched her wedding veil into place and Toby paced restlessly in the hall outside the dressing room.

"Alexandra?"

"Yes, dear?" Alexandra fiddled with the crown of lilies that sat atop Janessa's brown hair.

"How well did you know Dad when you married him? I mean, did you know everything about him?"

Alexanda paused. A dramatist would have described it as a pregnant pause. "I thought I did," she said after a moment, "but things have a way of . . . turning up." She looked cheerful, but Janessa caught an edge in her voice.

What on earth? "Is it awful, things turning up?"

"It can be startling," Alexandra said. "If you're expecting a life of placid certainty, don't get married."

"No. That would be awfully boring. Charley startled me a little. It was something I was glad to know, but it made me realize I didn't know everything about him. He has some rather unconventional notions."

"What, for instance?" Alexandra deftly poked a hairpin into the lilies. "Free love? Anarchism?"

"Of course not. Nothing that bad." Although she knew people who would regard the arrangement he had proposed as bordering on both.

"Good." Alexandra chuckled. "Seeing that *you* have always been the soul of convention."

"Ha!" Janessa threw her head back and laughed.

Alexandra pushed her through the door. "Marriage is an adventure, dear."

In the vestibule, Toby was waiting for her, and Tim was waiting to escort Alexandra to her seat. The bridesmaid, who was Charley's sister Nan, Janessa's oldest friend, had Sally firmly in tow. Sally was going to be flower girl and feeling very important about it.

"Late as usual," Tim said. "Lord, you look good. You make me want to get married myself."

"Have you got anyone in mind?" Janessa inquired as he kissed her.

"Lovely woman," Tim said, grinning. "She's about your age, and you hardly notice the third foot when she's sitting down."

Janessa snorted with amusement as he winked and went to take Alexandra to her seat. All the same, Janessa thought that Tim was drifting, romantically speaking, staving off any possibility of a real entanglement with his jokes about three-footed spinsters. It was that wretched Ormond girl. Being jilted took a long time to get over, as Janessa had cause to know.

The organist in the church faded into the last chorus of a hymn. Nan kissed Janessa and beamed at her.

"I'm so glad he's marrying you," Nan said. "We'd just about given up on him." Nan was married and considered it her womanly duty to marry off everyone else, too. Nan was a dear—a completely conventional wife and as happy as a clam about it. So was her mother. Where on earth had they gotten Charley? Janessa wondered.

Toby took her arm as the organist switched to the wedding march. The undercurrents of this family gathering and its assorted couples swirled around her bewilderingly. Janessa smiled at Toby with love tinged with speculation. *And just what is it that you've "turned up," Father dear?* There wasn't any use in asking him. Whatever Charley turned up wouldn't be the same. Marriage was an adventure, but all the adventures were different.

The big doors swung open onto the vestibule, and Sally stepped down the aisle, vibrating with excitement. The flower basket swung precariously. As Sally passed the front pews, Alexandra put out a hand and steadied it. Nan followed behind her, and then Toby with Janessa on his arm.

The church was packed with family and friends from Richmond and Washington, but Janessa didn't focus on any of them, just on Charley's face as he stood waiting for her beside the minister.

The light in Charley's eyes blazed up like fire when he saw her, and Janessa knew with a quick joy that filled her heart that whatever the adventure was to be, she was stepping into it gladly and with certainty. His eccentric viewpoints were a large part of why she loved him, in the same way that their eccentric courtship had been. He was safe and familiar in his oddities, and their friendship would outweigh the surprises.

"Bless, O Lord, this ring, that he who gives it and she who wears it may abide in Thy peace and continue in Thy favor until their life's end. . . ."

Janessa, her hand in Charley's, blinked back tears as she felt him slip the ring onto her finger. She had known Charley for years, ever since her college days— next year she would be thirty—and they had always thought of each other as friends. It was Charley who had encouraged her to go to medical school, to stand up to the prejudices of being a woman, half-Indian, and, into the bargain, illegitimate. He hadn't cared about any of that. It was even Charley, years ago, who had held and comforted Janessa when Brice Amos had jilted her because Brice *had* cared about those things.

"With this ring I thee wed."

Charley had even attended the University of Southern California with her, when he could have gone to the University of Virginia here at home, because Southern California admitted women and he had known she wouldn't go alone. Charley had cured her of all her fears.

Her fingers tightened around his hand now, and she looked up at him, not listening to the minister at all, just watching Charley's face, so familiar and dear.

"Those whom God hath joined together let no man put asunder. For as much as Janessa and Charles have consented together in holy wedlock and have witnessed the same before God and this company . . ."

"You look almost indecently gloating," Charley whispered.

"Oh, I am," Janessa whispered back. "I am."

The minister stared them into silence, but he didn't have the heart to frown. He motioned to them, and they knelt while he said his final prayer. Then they rose, and Charley pushed the veil back from Janessa's face and kissed her.

The organist began the recessional, and Charley took Janessa's arm while his sister, Nan, looped the heavy satin train over Janessa's other hand. They set off down the aisle past a sea of beaming faces and through the church doors.

Outside, while the bells pealed joyously, Charley bundled Janessa into the waiting carriage, and the wedding guests flowed after them. Then he got in, closed the door, and knocked on the roof at the driver. He put his arms around Janessa, to the detriment of veil and flowers. "I've got you!" he said exuberantly.

"Oh, you have," she agreed, and neither of them bothered to look up until the carriage rolled to a stop outside his parents' house.

With a smile, Tim watched them go. They looked exultant, certain that they knew what they were doing.

I couldn't do better than Charley, he thought, *not if I'd picked Janessa's husband personally.* And unlike the last wedding Tim had attended, Sam's to Annie Malone, both families were present in force, delighted with the outcome.

A mood of general bonhomie and congratulations prevailed at the reception, held at the home of Charley's mother and stepfather, Mr. Vernon Hughes. Toby and Mr. Hughes, a northerner who had lived in Virginia long enough to see things from a Richmond point of view, were deep in a discussion of the Federal Elections Bill. Both men knew it was bound to be resurrected.

"It's inevitable," Mr. Hughes was saying. "Our task is to see that it is instituted gently."

Alexandra, Cindy Blake, and Charley's mother were helping Janessa to cut the cake and fussing over the bride as if she were only sixteen. Mike appointed himself assistant to the photographer. Sally, who had been the flower girl, was clearly dazzled by the wonderful clothes and the beautiful cake.

Peter was talking earnestly to his father and to Charley's brother-in-law, who owned a carriage works. Tim caught the words "Benz engine," and the brother-in-law, George Eames, nodded sagely.

We've added another family to the clan, Tim thought. The Lawrences, the Hughes, and *their* connections were part of the web now, too. Tim visualized the family as a kind of net spread over the country, reaching from Richmond to Portland, tied together by relationships of blood and marriage and encompassing the whole history of the country back to Alexandra's great-something-grandfather who had been the governor of Plymouth Colony in the 1600s. Plymouth pilgrims, South Carolina planters, Indians, frontiersmen, all linked together, sometimes by relationships so complicated they could only be worked out on paper.

"You look as if you're off in another world, Tim," Charley's sister, Nan Eames, said. She linked her arm through his. She had only just met him, but she had been Janessa's best friend at college and seemed to feel that that gave her the right to be sisterly. "I'll introduce you to a nice girl."

As dutiful brother of the bride, Tim laughed and went and danced with the nice girl, and several other nice girls. It was pleasant just to sink into family ritual, with that family web close around him—a welcome change from Guthrie, where most people's connections had been broken. Tim thought about Rosebay Basham and, in the warmth and security of his own family, began to understand why she put up with Rowell, her last link to home. Even though she didn't like him, she couldn't bring herself to cut him away. There seemed a natural urge in man to hold to kinship, for good or ill.

He tried his theory out on Peter on the train back to Guthrie, more for something to talk about than from any serious philosophical bent, and was surprised when Peter nodded thoughtfully.

"I think you're right." Peter mulled it over for a moment. "Rosebay's just a born family woman. Look at the way she treats all her customers, as if she were their mother—even the ones who're trying to marry her. I guess that's why Hugo Ware is so hot after her. His own folks threw him out."

"Hugo's not in any position to be serious. And he'd better not make Rosebay think he is."

"You're mighty worked up for somebody who's not in the courting stakes," Peter commented. "She's bound to get married again."

"Well, it isn't going to be to Hugo," Tim said. "He'll break her heart. I'm just looking after Rosebay."

Tim arose the first morning back in Guthrie, intending to set Hugo straight, forcibly if necessary, the first chance he got. But after his five-day absence, there was the paper to be dealt with first. By midmorning he was still in the composing room. He heard the door's bell jangle in the front office but didn't give it much thought.

Thus it was that Peter, going over accounts at the front, was the first person encountered by an irate Abel Dormer.

"Ha!" Dormer erupted, as if he had discovered Peter at some disreputable activity. Peter noted that the mayor had a horsewhip and a crumpled copy of the *Prairie Recorder* in his hands.

"Can I help you, Mayor?" Peter asked, wondering what he ought to do with him.

"Where's your boss?" Dormer demanded, prepared to explode.

"Right here, Mayor." Tim came through the composing-room door. "What can I do for you?"

"So you slunk back into town, Holt."

"I wouldn't call it slinking," Tim said mildly. "I came on the train. Simmer down, Mayor, or you'll be too worked up to foreclose on widows and orphans."

Dormer brandished his horsewhip and advanced on Tim. "You watch your tongue, Holt, or you'll get more than the thrashing I aim to give you. I know you're behind this boy's bailing out every deadbeat the bank tries to get its just debts from, and now you've gone too far!" He flung the paper, with its offending editorial, down on the floor and stepped on it dramatically.

Peter, insulted, opened his mouth to protest, but Tim shook his head at the boy. And he waved away the interested men crowding through the composing-room door.

"I might say a man who tried to get me killed in a rodeo had gone too far," Tim observed.

"All right, Holt, that's enough!" Dormer shouted.

Tim backed off a little from the whip, then dodged like a rabbit around Peter's desk. "It's kind of crowded in here, Mayor: I hope you don't mind thrashing me outside. Away from this new, expensive office furniture." He feinted toward Dormer, then back again, and dived out the front door before the mayor could catch him.

Dormer came after him with the whip raised. "You're an impertinent scoundrel, Holt, and I'm going to teach you a lesson!"

Tim grinned at him. A crowd was forming. Two little boys sailing boats in the horse trough abandoned them and bounced excitedly on the inner edge of the circle. The mayor, who outweighed Tim by at least sixty pounds, came at him, and Tim dodged and rolled as the whip snaked out.

"It won't do you any good to run away," Dormer said. "You're going to get what you have coming."

Tim dodged again, circling back toward the side-walk. The whip cracked unpleasantly near him. He knew that being struck with a horsewhip probably hurt like hell, but if he ran, he would never live it down. Anyway, he didn't have any intention of letting Dormer hit him with it more than once. His eyes measured the distance to the horse trough, and he made his plan.

The whip snapped, biting into his arm like a strip of fire and wrapping around his back. But Tim got a grip on it, wincing, before Dormer could yank it back. He gave it a good tug, and the mayor was carried toward him into a collision that knocked Tim down. He managed to lever himself onto all fours and let Dormer roll over him, carried by his own considerable momentum. Tim twisted under the mayor and added just enough lift to topple that gentleman into the horse trough.

There was an almighty splash like a geyser, and Dormer surfaced, spouting warm green water, as the toy boats sailed over the lip of the trough on his wake.

Tim, hands on his knees, bent over, panting. Before Dormer could manage to get up, Tim found the horsewhip and tossed it to him. "Come back any time, Your Honor. We're always glad to know our editorials get some notice."

"Abel Dormer wants me to arrest you for tossing him in a horse trough."

Tim put down the catalog from the Mergenthaler Linotype Company and grinned at Hodge Landrum. "The horses been complaining?"

"He doesn't figure it accords with his dignity. Can't you be back in town more than twenty-four hours, damn it, without causing some kind of ruckus?"

"Dormer came in here with a horsewhip!" Peter protested.

"That's a time-honored method of dealing with uppity editors," Tim said. "Been done to better men than me."

"Well, I think you ought to press charges against *him*," Peter grumbled.

Landrum looked as if he didn't even want to contemplate that, and Tim took pity on him. "I think we can call it even." He chuckled. "My circulation's up twenty-five percent. You can tell old Dormer I said thank you." Half the town owed Dormer money. Half the town was also afraid of him, and Tim had given them considerable vicarious satisfaction.

"I'm trying to run a quiet, law-abiding town here," Landrum said. "And frankly, neither one of you is helping any. I came over here to ask you to lay off Dormer. You're making him look like a fool, and it's making the town look like a wild-west show."

Tim shook his head. "It's the function of a newspaper to rile up the scoundrels, not to be an out-and-out booster sheet. Landrum, I know you and the rest of the marshals have invested money in this town, and Lord knows I don't begrudge you a retirement fund. But you'd do better to pay more attention to what the citizens need than to the mayor's public image. Abel Dormer isn't synonymous with the well-being of Guthrie, and you know it."

Landrum looked uncomfortable.

"Unless you owe him money? . . ." Tim suggested.

"Nothing I can't pay off!" Landrum said angrily. "And I don't like your insinuation."

"I wasn't implying you're not honest, Hodge," Tim said quickly. "I know you are. But I think you're thick-headed, too. You've got worse things to worry about than a feud between Abel Dormer and me. If you want to do something for Guthrie, get rid of Rowell Basham—he's a disgrace, threatening to expose the sinners for the good of their souls unless they repent. Repentance generally means a good chunk of money in the collection plate. It's extortion!"

Landrum's eyes blazed. "I know what he's up to! I'd run him out of town on a rail if I could get away with it. But most folks figure a preacher can't do any wrong. Anyway, don't you lecture me about Rowell Basham! You're still having dinner at his sister-in-law's!"

"Rowell's a thorn in Rosebay's side, too," Tim said.

"I got no sympathy for either of them. They're

vermin, and if I ever get the chance to run Basham out of town, she goes with him."

Tim put down the catalog. "Hodge, when it comes to Rosebay Basham, you're all wrong."

"Like hell I am. That woman's too good-looking not to be trouble. She's already had two men killed over her. She ought to be married."

"Just because she's good-looking?" Tim asked.

"She's got half the men in town running after her. Why hasn't she married one of them? You tell me that."

"Maybe she doesn't want to get married," Tim said.

"That's what I mean," Landrum retorted. "What kind of respectable woman doesn't want to get married? Rowell Basham is uncivilized trash, and the woman is as bad, running around loose. You stay away from her, Holt. If she was a good woman, she wouldn't be carrying on with that damned remittance man." Landrum pointed a finger at Tim. "I don't like him, either."

Tim sighed. "You're the most unreasonable man I ever met, considering that I think you're a good lawman. There's more to the law and more to being an upright citizen than fitting people into little boxes with a shoehorn and making them stay there."

Landrum looked aggravated. "I'm talking about keeping order. You can't have law without order. There's times I feel like I'm standing in a high wind, trying to hold it all down."

Tim started to laugh. "You'd better brace yourself. I think the wind's picking up. You can enforce the law, but you can't live people's lives for them."

"Just see your wind doesn't blow the mayor into any more horse troughs."

Tim sighed. "Tell Mayor Dormer my arm hurts like hell. Maybe that'll cheer him up some."

"Reckon it will." Landrum stalked to the door. "I think you're a threat to order yourself."

"That's what we're here for," Tim called after him.

"Well, you'd better stay solvent," Peter warned

Tim as the door banged closed. "I can guarantee you aren't going to get a loan from the Bank of Guthrie."

Tim picked up his catalog again. He read about new equipment the way a farmer read seed catalogs. "How about the Bank of Blake? I tell you, Peter, this Mergenthaler's Linotype is going to revolutionize the newspaper business."

"You're still paying for the new press," Peter muttered.

Tim ignored that. "Just think, a whole line of type cast in one chunk. And when you're through with it, you just melt it down and start over. No more hand spiking, no more funny spelling when the font runs short—"

"No," Peter said.

"Aw, come on, you have a bank account that would put a nabob to shame. Now an investment in the newspaper—"

"This newspaper can't afford a linotype," Peter said. "As your financial adviser, I advise you that the new press is all you can afford for a while. I'm not going to lend you *my* money to go in hock with."

"Just what I need, a sixteen-year-old financial adviser," Tim grumbled. "And what, pray tell, are you going to *do* with all this money you're sitting on?"

"I don't know yet," Peter replied. "But I'm not lending it to you. One of these days I'm going to see something I'll want to put money into. And when I do, I'm going to have the money. Think of me as saving you from yourself."

"Oh, thank you, thank you." Tim grinned. He hadn't suspected he would have much luck, but it had seemed worth a shot. He got up and put his hat on. "I'll leave you to count your bags of gold."

"Where are you going?"

"To have my talk with Hugo Ware."

Tim found Hugo playing poker in the Jack of Diamonds and joined the game. What he had to say required some working up to. When the game was over,

Hugo and Tim lingered at the table, playing blackjack. The Englishman didn't have to be anywhere in particular in the morning and was feeling talkative.

While they finished the bottle Tim had bought, Hugo described the scene in the street after Tim had gone back in his office. "After the mayor hauled himself out of the horse trough, Sid Hallam told Dormer he'd pay double interest on his bank loan for three months if the mayor would try to horsewhip you again. And little old Mrs. Lindsey—the one young Peter bailed out of Dormer's clutches—had her hands clasped to her breast like somebody in church and a light in her eyes as if she had just seen the angel with the fiery sword driving forth the sinner." Hugo spread out his cards. "Can you beat twenty?"

Tim shook his head and tossed Hugo the cards. "You'd make a good reporter. You've got a way with words and a good eye."

"Are you offering me a job?"

"I would if you could bestir yourself enough to go to work," Tim said. "It might keep you out of trouble."

"What kind of trouble?"

Tim looked him in the eyes. "The kind you're going to be in if I hear you've done Rosebay Basham wrong. She's starting to get talked about."

Hugo blinked. "Are you asking me my intentions?"

"No. You're not in any position to have intentions. Just a warning: If you get that woman's hopes up and then leave her flat, I'll push your teeth in."

Hugo gathered up the cards and dealt them carefully. "It may surprise you to know that my intentions are entirely honorable. I asked Rosebay to marry me."

"The sun's fried your brains. What about your family? Damn it, Hugo, I'm going to punch you."

"She turned me down," Hugo said, "so you needn't punch me. And I don't care what my family thinks. What kind of bastard do you take me for?"

"I don't," Tim said, placating him. "You just took me by surprise. I won't have her talked about." Landrum was right about one thing, Tim reflected. Rosebay *was* too beautiful not to make trouble—but that wasn't her fault. "You just watch it, that's all," he muttered.

Hugo studied Tim thoughtfully, dealt himself another card, hit twenty-two, and flipped his two-bit stake in Tim's direction. Hugo began to wonder if Rosebay had turned him down because she was in love with someone else and if that someone else might be Tim Holt.

Hugo didn't say anything; he did not want to put that notion in Tim's head. He would just bide his time and ask her again. Against all odds and against all reason, Hugo was more serious about Rosebay than he had ever been about anything in his life. Maybe she was the *first* thing he had ever been serious about.

Rosebay woke up before dawn to milk her cow and mix biscuit dough for her breakfast customers.

She was just coming out of the little barn, which the cow shared with the horse and the plow mule, when a shadow fell across the pool of lantern light. She set the pail down with a plop and took a step back as Rowell's hand shot out and clutched her arm.

"Let me go!"

"I come to tell you something." Rowell breathed a cloud of whiskey in her face.

"Say it at breakfast. I got biscuits to make."

His eyes held a dangerous glitter as he yanked her to him. The milk pail was knocked over. The warm, frothy milk sank into the dirt and straw.

"Now look what you done!"

"You just shut your mouth." Rowell pulled her against him and bent her arm behind her back. "You're gonna marry me. The Lord tells me I need me a helpmate and a good house to live in. You got more here than what a single woman's entitled to."

He's off his head, she thought. She tried to think what to say as she stared at his face, the lank black hair hanging over pale, wild eyes. "You look like you been up all night. You get some sleep," she said, trying to stall him, waiting to feel his fingers loosen their grip on her arm. "I told you, I won't marry nobody."

The fingers tightened. "That's right," Rowell hissed. "You won't marry nobody if you don't marry me. I'll fix you so you *can't!*" He let go of her suddenly and flung her away, and she staggered back against the cow's stall. "I'll fix you good, Rosebay. So you better do what the Lord wants you to do."

Then he was gone.

He didn't come again, not for meals or even to speak to her, and Rosebay, used to keeping her own counsel and fighting her own battles, didn't tell anyone, even though she was frightened to death of him. Each day that Rowell didn't appear, she hoped that maybe he'd only been drunk, not crazy, and had forgotten all about it.

Then he did come again, and again, and again, waylaying her outside the barn in the dark of the early morning. Each time he voiced the same threat and wore the same vicious look in his eyes. She began to be afraid to go milking and started to carry a rifle with her. But he never did anything to warrant her shooting him. He just continued to threaten what he would do.

I can't take this no more, Rosebay thought, but she didn't know what to do. She couldn't ask Hugo to protect her and be beholden to him and then not marry him. Nor could she tell Tim Holt and make him feel responsible for her when she knew he didn't love her.

Finally, late in September, she stood in her kitchen listening to the cow bellowing to be milked for nearly two hours before she could get up the nerve to go out there with the bucket. When she had finished with the milking, she knew she had to do something. She put on her bonnet and hitched the horse to the wagon. Marshal Landrum hated her; she knew that. But she paid her taxes to pay his salary. Protecting citizens was his job.

Landrum shrugged his shoulders. "If he hasn't actually done you any harm, Mrs. Basham, I don't see how I can help you." He thought she had a nerve, but he didn't say so. He was trying to be businesslike and not pay any attention to that too-beautiful face, the cloud of pale hair, and the wide blue eyes. Not such innocent eyes, in Hodge Landrum's opinion.

"If he does me any harm, I'll be past helping, Marshal."

"I don't interfere in domestic disputes," Landrum said. "That's the province of a woman's husband."

"It ain't a domestic dispute! He ain't my husband!"

"Well then, maybe you ought to marry him," Landrum said. "I'll be frank with you, Mrs. Basham. You already caused the death of two men, and I've got no time for you."

Rosebay's face tightened as if she were trying not to cry, but her eyes filled with tears anyway. Landrum felt a faint flicker of unease, a suspicion that he might not be doing the right thing, but he squelched it. He turned his back on her and picked up some papers off his desk.

XI

Cathy Martin sat twisting the folds of her skirt. She couldn't stop herself. Beyond the closed doors of the theater manager's office, her fate was being decided.

Lucy had the lead in a new play, *Margaret Courtney,* and in it was a small part for which Lucy had persuaded the producer, the redoubtable Mr. Harry Lavering, to allow Cathy to audition. Now he was in his office talking to the author-director, Joseph Covey, and to Lucy, who, as the lead, was allowed to contribute her ideas about final casting of the minor roles. What was taking them so long?

Cathy stood and held up to herself a brocade and velvet gown that the wardrobe mistress had chosen for Lucy. Cathy pictured herself in it—or one like it—standing behind the footlights, brilliant and tragic and beautiful, captivating the audience.

The dressing-room door opened, and Lucy slipped through. Cathy put the dress down anxiously. "Did I get it? Did they like me?"

"Oh, dear." Lucy sat down and patted the settee beside her for Cathy to sit, too. Cathy's face fell. "My dear, I'm afraid you didn't."

Depressed, Cathy picked up the dress again and slowly hung it on the back of the door. Lucy reached out and pulled her back to the settee. "Now see here. You'll make yourself sick if you let this upset you."

Cathy burst into tears. "I wanted it so badly. I thought they liked me."

185

"I remember when I lost the first part I auditioned for," Lucy said gently. "I thought I was going to die. But it's a good lesson to get over with early. If you can't abide rejection, don't try to be in this business. It's no place for anyone who hasn't got the hide of a rhinoceros."

"This is an awful business." Cathy sniffed dolefully.

"Well, now, I told you it was," Lucy said, but she put an arm around Cathy.

After a few minutes of weeping, Cathy pulled a handkerchief out of her sleeve and wiped her eyes and nose. She looked broodingly at the floor. "I don't know what I did wrong. How can I do any better next time if I don't know what I did wrong?"

"That's more like it." Lucy gave Cathy a brisk pat on her back, then moved away. "To be truthful, I don't know if you'll do better next time or even if you'll get the part if you do. There are a lot of out-of-work actors. But I can tell you what you did wrong."

"What?"

"Well," Lucy said, "how did you feel during the audition?"

"Frightened," Cathy admitted.

"No doubt. Did you feel like yourself?"

Cathy looked puzzled. "Yes . . ."

Lucy smiled. "There's your problem. You were the very respectable Cathy Martin, reading tragedy out of a book. You weren't poor Lena Sholes, who had just had a child by another woman's husband. As an actress you have to *become* the character, right down to the heart, to make her real. You have to let go."

"Let go of what?" Cathy asked her, still baffled.

"Of yourself. And the audience. If the situation isn't real to you, it isn't going to be real to them. I'll let you watch rehearsals. Study the girl who did get the part. It will be painful but educational."

A week later Cathy was in Newport, sitting with Cornelia McLeod in a wooden swing in Zanzibar's garden. They pushed themselves back and forth over the fading grass with their toes, saying nothing. At last

Cathy sat up a little, looking with concern at Cornelia's pallid face and woebegone expression. Cornelia always seemed a little weighed down—who wouldn't be with Mrs. McLeod for a mother?—but today she seemed literally lifeless. "Is something wrong?" Cathy asked.

"Paul's gone out of the country," Cornelia answered. "I don't think he's coming back."

"Not coming back!"

"When I called on his mother before we left town yesterday, she said he might be gone a year or two. . . I hadn't had a letter from him, you see, and he always writes because Mama doesn't let me see him very often. I thought Mama might have stopped the letters, so I . . ." Cornelia buried her face in her hands. "Paul's mother didn't even want to see me. She said not to expect to hear from Paul again, that it was just a boy-and-girl romance, and . . . and those things fade away!"

"They don't!" Cathy said indignantly. "I've seen you and Paul together. I never saw two people so much in love."

"You don't know what it's like to be beaten down for years," Cornelia said fretfully. "Not to have any hope."

Maybe I don't, Cathy thought. *I don't seem to know anything about anything.*

"The duke's coming tomorrow night," Cornelia continued, "for Mama's ball."

"Cornelia, don't you dare marry that man."

"What difference would it make?" Cornelia asked dully. "Everybody wants me to. Even Edward's rung in on Mama's side and given me a lecture about it. I don't have anyone to help me."

"You have me," Cathy protested.

"You told Mama you have to go back to town tomorrow."

Cathy sighed. She just hadn't wanted to waste her time at a ball when she could be at the theater, wrestling with whatever it was that Lucy was trying to teach her. Now she felt meanspirited in the face of Cornelia's misery. "Oh, I expect they can do without me," she said lightly. "I'll stay if you'd like me to. I didn't bring a ball gown, though, and I can't get into yours."

"Oh, Cathy, please stay! Mama can send someone into town for you and take your aunt a note."

"Of course I'll stay," Cathy said. "And you brace up and don't give that duke the time of day."

"I don't know if I'm strong enough for that."

"I'm stubborn enough for two," Cathy said with more conviction than she felt. "You can borrow some."

The ballroom at Zanzibar was decked with hothouse ferns and roses. The smell of the roses was overpoweringly sweet and cloying in the crowded ballroom because all the windows were firmly latched. It was late in the season for Newport—Mrs. McLeod would close the cottage down for the winter after the ball and considered the night air to be full of diseases.

Cathy fanned herself, stuck as close to Cornelia as she could, and wished she hadn't stayed. She danced with a succession of men, including the duke of Manes himself, who moved stiffly, said a number of proper and unmemorable things, and seemed to Cathy as lifeless as a mannequin. His eyes were shuttered and almost vacant, as if he were getting something unpleasant over with.

At the end of their dance, Mrs. McLeod sailed over and detached him from Cathy with brisk condescension for Miss Martin and a fawning possessiveness for His Grace. *You can have him,* Cathy thought.

No one else seemed to find fault with the duke; indeed, they were congratulatory toward Mrs. McLeod, who wore a pleased, secretive little smile. There was no sign of Cornelia's brother. Cathy had yet to meet Edward but felt from what Cornelia had told her that she could well do without that pleasure.

"Are you all right?" Cathy whispered to Cornelia as they touched up their hair in the ladies' withdrawing room before dinner. Cornelia looked almost waiflike in her elaborate pink silk gown and choker of pearls, as if everything she wore were too big for her.

"It doesn't matter," Cornelia said. "What did I have to hold out for, besides Paul? I suppose I'll get used to it."

"Don't do it!" Cathy hissed, but she didn't think Cornelia had even heard her. As they left the room, Mrs. McLeod was waiting. She took Cornelia by the arm and propelled her toward the duke, her dinner partner. The light from the crystal chandelier gave a milky glitter to the pearl choker. It looked to Cathy, who felt suddenly sick, very much like a jeweled dog collar.

She decided to leave in the morning as soon as she was decently able. For Cornelia's sake Cathy would visit the McLeods again, but right now she didn't feel she could stand the sight of that opulent, bejeweled palace a moment longer.

"Money does fearful things to people," she announced to Claudia and Eden during lunch in their Waldorf suite. "I would sooner starve than be like Mrs. McLeod."

Claudia snorted. "Money does nothing of the sort. Mrs. McLeod would behave in the same way if she were a fishmonger's wife. Money merely gives her more scope." She cocked an eye at Cathy. "If you don't wish to benefit from your family's money, I could take rooms for us near the railway station."

"Oh, that wasn't what I meant. But if Cornelia didn't have money, then the duke wouldn't want her."

"If Cornelia didn't have money, her mother would be trying to marry her to someone who did, possibly someone less palatable than the duke. Cornelia's misfortune is not her money but her mother."

"Annie has a lot of money," Eden said reflectively. "Do you think that's why Sam married her?"

"Annie made her own decision," Claudia informed her, "which makes it an entirely different matter. Eat your fish, Eden."

Two weeks after New Year's Day, Annie Brentwood

decided she had better steel herself and talk to Sam's grandmother. The trouble between Sam and her was getting to be obvious, and the elderly Mrs. Brentwood was no fool. But Annie hesitated as she raised her knuckles to tap on the door. Mrs. Brentwood had certainly been nice enough, but Annie had no idea how the woman felt about her, and there was no denying she could be formidable.

Annie knocked and peeked around the door of Claudia's sitting room as the elderly woman called for her to come in. "Mrs. Brentwood? Have you got a minute for me?"

"Of course, dear. Do sit down."

"Thank you, Mrs. Brentwood." Annie sat and tried to figure out what to say next.

"Tell me, dear," Claudia said, "do you think it might be easier to call me something besides Mrs. Brentwood, after all this time?"

"What?" Annie asked. She wasn't going to presume and put her foot in it.

"Well, Sam calls me Gran, but you might not care for that. Why not just Claudia? Mrs. Brentwood makes me feel that I ought to call *you* Mrs. Brentwood, too, and then we would sound silly."

Annie laughed. "All right."

"Well, that's settled. Now, supposing you tell me what is troubling you?"

"You're pretty sure something is," Annie murmured.

"Let's say I have sensed a certain friction," Claudia said carefully. "If I had to hazard a guess, I'd say that money was part of it."

Annie spread her hands out unhappily. "It's not that I don't *want* to trust Sam, it's just that he's . . ."

"Unreliable. I'm his grandmother. I've known him far longer than you have." Her eyes misted. "He is my heart's darling. He always has been. But he has never learned to rein himself in. He's impatient and reckless and . . . oh, a lot of other things that make us both love him, I expect." She gave Annie a shrewd look. "I hope you tied up your money before you married him?"

Annie nodded. "I couldn't see my way clear without that. Sam knew I was going to. He said himself I probably should."

"It's beginning to chafe at his pride, isn't it?"

"It's getting worse since we came back," Annie said. "I've spent a lot of time catching up, writing to my lawyers and so forth. Sam's at loose ends." She looked at her hands in her lap. "It gives him a roving eye, too."

Claudia sighed. "You don't have to mince words with me."

Annie, still talking to her hands, twisted the gold band and the fat diamond on her ring finger. "I knew he would. I figured I could stand his stepping out on me some. But I care more than I thought I would."

"Tell me," Claudia said after a moment's thought, "do you love Sam?"

Annie looked her in the eye. "I didn't think I did this much, or I wouldn't have married him. I loved how he knew about all the things I didn't. I was born with nothing and never got through but fourth grade. And I loved the way he could make me laugh. I never could abide a solemn man. I was lonesome, and he was good company, and, well . . ."

"And extremely attractive," Claudia said. "In that devilish way that is such a snare to women." She smiled at Annie. "You're very pretty yourself."

Annie nodded knowingly. "He didn't marry me just for my money. *My* pride wouldn't have stood that." She smiled reminiscently. In bed there had never been any problem, but since coming to New York, it seemed that bed was the only place they did get along. And recently even that . . .

"I don't know how I feel about Sam now," Annie said. "Or how he . . ." Her voice trailed away. "I give Sam a liberal allowance. But it makes him feel like I'm his mother. Or so he says." Annie's mouth twisted.

"Well, dear, you *are* eleven years older than he," Claudia pointed out. "I know how irritating it is to have everyone keeping track of that, but I am not referring to appearances. You have had eleven years to gain the maturity that Sam lacks. And you probably had more levelheadedness to start with. I don't know what to tell you, except don't give in about the money. And if I were you, I would get Sam out of New York."

"Easier said than done," Annie said. "He likes New York. Well, I do, too. It's the life I've always wanted."

"It's bad for him," Claudia said.

"Maybe I'm bad for him." Annie stood. "Maybe he's bad for me, too." She thanked Claudia, feeling guilty that all she had accomplished was to make the old lady unhappy. Claudia had had no magic answers, just advised what Annie knew already: that she couldn't back down about the money.

"Where the devil is she?" Lucy Woods, hands on her hips, toe tapping the stage-front boards, glared over the Lyceum Theater's footlights at Joseph Covey. "I won't have this, Joe. I can't rehearse like this."

The houselights were up, too, and Cathy, in the front row, could see Joe conferring with Harry Lavering, the producer.

"I can't play a scene to the air," Lucy yelled over the empty orchestra pit.

Cathy could hear voices backstage calling "Mary Ellen!" but no Mary Ellen appeared. Cathy sank a little lower in her seat, ducking as tempers flared above her in a nearly visible arc.

"I know it's crucial," Joe shouted back. "I don't know where the hell she is!"

Lucy paced in a sulfurous cloud, and a stagehand quailed and got out of her way.

"Work with the understudy," Joe shouted at Lucy. He bellowed into the rustling darkness beyond the flats. "Annabelle! Get out here!"

A stagehand leaned around a door at the rear of the set. "Annabelle's gone to Macy's."

"Macy's!" Joe threw his hands in the air. "I'm not paying her to buy her Easter bonnet on my time!"

The stagehand retreated cautiously so that only his head showed. "You sent her to Macy's. You hated the ribbon on Miss Woods's hat in the first act and wanted another color."

Joe dropped back in his seat, his hands clutching his hair. "Oh, for Christ's *sake!*"

Lucy spun around in midpace and pointed a finger at him. "Don't you swear in my presence, Joe Covey!"

"Don't you get highfalutin with me!" Joe yelled. "You swear like a drunken sailor!"

Harry Lavering heaved himself out of his seat and got between them. "What is this, nursery school?" He pointed a finger at Cathy. "You. Get up there and read Maria."

Oh, no. Cathy started to say thank you, no, but they all looked so furious, she didn't dare. She edged out into the aisle and up the steps, and a stagehand came hustling in to give her a script.

"Just read it," Lucy said. Her voice sounded brittle, and her eyes shot sparks at Joe Covey.

Cathy stood on the spot on the floor at which Lucy pointed, and fixed her eyes on the script. " 'You,' " she read in a faltering voice. " 'You. How dare you come here?' "

"This woman's husband ruined your *sister*, for God's sake!" Joe yelled at her. "Put some *feeling* in it!"

Cathy's eyes flashed, and she began to share the general desire to kill somebody. Maybe it was that, or maybe it was only the charged atmosphere, but suddenly she was boiling mad, and wonder of wonders, she wasn't Cathy Martin anymore. She wasn't even playing to Lucy, but to the part of Margaret Courtney. She threw back her head and let Margaret have it.

" 'She is dead! Dead, do you understand? You who have never lost anything, who have always had everything? I wish to God she might have taken us both with her!' "

They played the scene to the end. Margaret fell sobbing at her feet.

Cathy jerked back to reality, and a small spatter of

applause came over the footlights. Joe and Harry were looking at her speculatively.

Lucy got up off the floor. "Thank you," she said brusquely, and went back to studying the blocking of the scene. She stopped and looked at Joe. "I'll need to do it again with Mary Ellen, but I think we have it."

Cathy slipped off the stage, excited and shaken, still feeling the character rattling around inside her somewhere. As she passed Joe and Harry, she heard the producer murmur, "What do you think?"

"I think she needs work," Joe said. He stood up. "Lucy, block the scene with me one more time, so we'll have it ready for Mary Ellen. . . ."

Cathy's face fell. They had forgotten about her already. She started for the front-office door. Aunt Claudia would have been expecting her half an hour ago.

"Hey! Hold on."

She turned back to find Harry Lavering giving her a conspiratorial grin. "I don't know what came over you since you auditioned, but you keep it up."

Cathy's face relaxed into an answering grin. "Thank you!" She ran away from him up the aisle, with a little wave of her hand. "I'm late," she called. "Thank you!"

She nearly danced down the street and, when she had hailed a cab, sank back against the cushions in a cloud of excitement. She had done what Lucy had said, slipped out of her own skin and into someone else's. It had been magical and strange. *I'm going to be an actress*.

She paid the cab driver and floated up the stairs at the Waldorf, trying to figure out, now that she had had a taste of it, how to get herself back up on the stage—any stage.

Margaret Courtney opened four days later, and cast, backers, friends, and relatives celebrated with an after-hours party at Delmonico's while they waited twitchily for the first reviews, in the early morning editions that came out shortly after midnight.

The restaurant was jam-packed, and the company was inclined to be giddy. Harry Lavering was trying to look unconcerned, even though he stood to lose a great deal of money. Joe Covey was in a corner diagraming a set change he wanted by tomorrow night, and a chastened Mary Ellen held his notebook for him as a sort of penance. All appeared to be forgiven between Lucy and Mary Ellen.

Cathy looked around her and shivered with excitement. This was her first opening-night party. Claudia, who found the theater crowd noisier than she cared for, had gone instead to the opera with Howard Locke, leaving Cathy to Sam and Annie's chaperonage. Sam had melted happily into the boisterous crowd, while Annie seemed content to sit at the table with Cathy, Lucy, and Harry.

"They liked it at intermission," Harry said for the fortieth time. "I was in front, and it was a good house."

"Winter will have hated it," Lucy said moodily. "He hates anything modern. He won't have liked the unhappy ending."

"I saw him," Harry said. "He looked pleased." Winter was the *Tribune*'s critic. "That's because he'd just thought up a nasty turn of phrase," Roderick Fitzhugh, who played Philip Courtney, said over Harry's shoulder.

"Here they are!" A murmur ran through the restaurant, and everyone crowded around the table to get a glimpse of the newspapers brought to Harry by a callboy he had sent to wait for them.

"Oh, Lord," Lucy said. "I told you!"

Cathy peered over her shoulder.

> A three-act dialogue called *Margaret Courtney* was obtruded upon the public notice yesterday evening at the Lyceum Theater, where it bored a small audience during several wasted . . .

"Forget Winter," Harry said. "Look at the *Times!*"

> Last night in the Lyceum Theater was produced one of the most radical and mesmerizing

plays from a native author-director ever performed in America. In *Margaret Courtney*, Mr. Joseph Covey gave to Miss Lucy Woods a role at last worthy of the talents of this multifaceted ornament to our New York stage.

"What did I tell you?" Harry demanded, pounding Lucy and Joe on the back, one with each hand. "Winter hasn't liked anything since *East Lynne*. People only read him to be sure to see the plays he's panned."

Everyone surged around them, passing the newspapers from hand to hand. One of Delmonico's waiters cracked the cork on a jeroboam of champagne and set it on the table.

"To *Margaret Courtney!*"

"To Miss Lucy Woods, our 'multifaceted ornament'!"

"To Joe!"

"To success, and bad cess to old Winter!"

Relieved, Lucy laughed, letting them toast her. She got up, kissed Cathy, and whispered in her ear, "I'm going home, dear, to sleep. I feel as if I've been dug up. You'll be all right here with Sam and Annie, won't you?"

"Of course." Eyes shining, Cathy hugged her. "Congratulations!"

Lucy slipped away, and someone put a glass of champagne in Cathy's hand. She sipped it, silently blessing Sam and Annie. Through the crowd she caught a glimpse of Sam, plucking a glass of champagne off a tray for the young actress who had played Lena. Lena still had on her stage makeup, and she looked up at Sam's dark, handsome face through fluttering lashes. Lena's roommate was with them—she had a part in the chorus at Weber and Fields—and she was admiring Sam, too. As Cathy edged her way toward them, the door opened again, and a crowd of young men came in—the kind of stage-door Johnnies that Cathy had seen before. They liked to go to theater parties and squire the actresses and chorus girls around. The girls always went along because the men showed them a good time and were generous with their presents. Lucy knew several girls who lived off the presents between jobs.

Cathy stumbled a little as one of them bumped into her, and he steadied her with a careless hand, then made an apologetic bow. "A thousand pardons," he said extravagantly and doffed his top hat. He had a round, not unhandsome face and tousled brown hair. His ears stuck out a little too much.

Cathy laughed. "It's quite all right. It's dreadfully crowded in here."

"Isn't it, though. Are you in Miss Woods's play?"

"No, not in this one," Cathy said, fudging just a little.

"Here, let me get you some champagne." His brown eyes took in her excited, friendly face. "I'll bet you're in some show, though, aren't you?" he asked admiringly. "You're too pretty to waste." He gave her a glass of champagne. "My name's Eddie Gamble." He looked at her hopefully.

He thinks I'm a chorus girl, she thought, and found herself disinclined to correct him. "I'm Catherine Salton," she said, picking her stepmother's maiden name at random and fluttering her lashes the way she had seen the girl do at Sam.

"Well, I'm pleased to meet you. *Real* pleased."

He moved a little closer in a kind of friendly way, and Cathy realized that he was looking at her bosom. Somehow that seemed funny. Maybe three glasses of champagne had made her feel naughty.

"I'm pleased to meetcha, too, Mr. Gamble," she said, trying out a faint New York accent. This was fun.

"Mr. Brentwood, you're just such a *card*!" The Weber and Fields chorus girl giggled and poked a finger at Sam's shirtfront. She squealed as he caught her finger and kissed the tip of it. The champagne in her other hand sloshed. "Now you look out!"

*   *   *

He'd better *look out,* Annie thought. She turned her back on Sam so she wouldn't be tempted to go over there and box his ears in front of so many people. This was too much, she thought, but it was too early to try and haul Sam away without making a scene. She'd do that later, he could bet his boots, when he had sobered up. She hadn't thought he'd flirt with his girlfriends right in front of her, as if he was *trying* to rile her. Maybe he was. And if he was, he had succeeded.

"Well, actually I'm between shows just now," Cathy confessed to Eddie Gamble while he poured her some more champagne. "Oooh, thank you. I just lost a job to another girl, so here I am, gadding about instead of getting my beauty sleep." She pouted with just the right mock seriousness.

His eyes admired her frankly. "I bet the director's wife was jealous."

Cathy laughed—a laugh quite unlike her own, a shade too loud. "Now I'm not a bit like that." She knew that everything about her said that she was.

Eddie was standing closer, the admiring eyes complacent. "Say, Miss Salton, can you sing?"

"Well, sure," Cathy said.

He grinned. "I might be able to help you out. I know the fellow who runs the Elysian. He's always looking for pretty talent."

Cathy looked blank.

"A music hall."

"Oh, of course." She knew the names of some of the bigger music halls, but she had never heard of the Elysian.

"I bet he could use a pretty soubrette with a class act." He was standing quite close to her now.

Cathy took a gulp of her champagne. It was hard to tell how much she'd had because Eddie kept refilling her glass. A music hall. . . . Aunt Claudia would never let her. But the thought of being up on any kind of stage beckoned through the bubbly glow of the champagne. Cathy Martin couldn't do it, but Catherine Salton could. It would be good experience, she thought, and it wouldn't do any harm.

"I could introduce you," Eddie suggested.

Miss Salton lifted her glass. "Okey-doke."

XII

Cathy tiptoed out the door of Claudia's suite and into the Waldorf's plush corridors. Everyone was still asleep except Eden, who was reviewing the high points of the French Revolution with her governess. Cathy inspected herself for a final time in the hall mirror and decided that she looked all right. She wore a dress of gray gabardine and had added a spray of pink cloth flowers, soiled and a little shabby, that she had unearthed from the bottom of a drawer, for the right air of jaunty poverty. Miss Catherine Salton, would-be soubrette, was on her way to an audition.

"Ground floor, please," she told the elevator boy. She had given Eddie Gamble an elusive giggle when he had asked for her address and arranged to meet him at the Elysian's manager's office on West Thirty-fourth Street near Sixth Avenue.

It won't do to arrive in a cab, she thought, and hopped on a trolley, feeling very much a New Yorker. Her enthusiasm waned, however, after she had walked the last few blocks to the Elysian. The theater looked dreary, with scraps of paper and trash blowing along the sidewalk. A sign below the marquee invited customers to hear the celebrated "female baritone" Mirella May and her all-girl orchestra.

Inside, a boy in a filthy apron was cleaning the tables with a greasy rag that left them smeared. Onstage, the name cards from the night before were still up. The last act had been trained dogs. *It doesn't matter where you start as long as you start,* Cathy told herself firmly.

"I'm looking for the manager," she told the boy.

"Mr. Swanson." The boy jerked a thumb at a door behind the tables to the left, and Cathy went through it and picked her way down a dim corridor with a threadbare carpet until she came to a door marked Management.

Eddie Gamble was already there, with his feet on the desk, drinking beer from a long-necked bottle. Mr. Swanson, behind the desk, was in his forties, with slicked-down black hair and garters on his sleeves. He was chewing on a cigar, which had gone out but still smelled foul. Neither of them stood up when she came in.

"This is Miss Salton," Eddie said.

"Sing something," Swanson grunted.

Here? Cathy had expected the stage, at least, maybe with a pianist to accompany her. She coughed and wished Mr. Swanson would open a window and preferably throw the cigar outside.

He relit it instead. "I ain't got all day."

"Oh. Sure." She coughed again, then sang "Carry Me Back to Old Virginny," which had been highly praised at the Cumberland Hill Academy's senior talent show.

Swanson grunted again and spoke to Eddie, not to her. "Her voice is all right, but she's got to have some material."

"They want something with some pep to it," Eddie told her.

"Maybe with a comic turn." Swanson winked. "A little sexy."

Cathy thought. "How about 'None Can Love Like an Irishman'?"

"Sing it."

She struck a coy pose and tried to forget the cigar.

"The turban'd Turk, who scorns the world,
May strut about with his whiskers curled,
Keep a hundred wives under lock and key,
For nobody else but himself to see;
Yet long may he pray with his Alcoran
Before he can love like an Irishman."

Swanson nodded, and for some reason he seemed relieved. "All right. Work up a couple more like that, and I'll give you a try. Since you're Eddie's pal." He winked at Eddie. "Fifteen dollars a week. Start Friday. Bring some sheet music for the orchestra in case there's something they don't know. You got a costume?"

Cathy looked at Eddie and bubbled happily inside. "The dress I wore last night?"

"Take up the hem about eighteen inches," Eddie advised. "Swanny's crowd likes a little leg."

"Oh. Sure." *Above my knees?*

"Now get out of here," Swanson said. "I got work to do." He pointed the cigar at Eddie. "You come back later. I'm counting on you."

"Never fear," Eddie said. "Never fear." He rose and gave Cathy his arm to escort her out.

She fairly skipped down the dingy hall to the front of the house. What did it matter if she had to hike her skirt above her knees? She was going to be onstage! Adah Menken had worn less than that in *Mazeppa* and been a smash.

"I'll take you home," Eddie offered. "We'll look at that dress."

If she let him take her home, Cathy knew that her aunt would find out. "Oh, I'm just exhausted," she pleaded coyly. "I've been up all night rehearsing. I have to have my beauty sleep now to do you credit on Friday." Cathy edged between the tables toward the door.

"Tell me where you live. I'll pop around and see you when you've rested."

"My landlady doesn't like gentleman callers." Cathy looked at her watch. "Jiminy, it's late! I got to run!" She dodged toward the door.

"Where can I find you?" Eddie called, exasperated.

"Right here on Friday!" Cathy laughed gaily and scooted out the door. She certainly had Eddie fooled.

Friday evening she informed the family as nonchalantly as she could manage that she was meeting Lucy at the Lyceum Theater. She would take a cab, and Lucy would send her home in one, so they needn't worry about her. Somewhat to her surprise, no one made any objection. Cathy didn't think that her aunt had really been paying attention—and certainly Sam and Annie hadn't. They just glared at each other throughout dinner, and Eden looked frightened by the tension.

As soon as dinner was over, Cathy decided to go while the going was good. She put on her wrap and picked up her bag with her sewing kit concealed inside it. She had a packet of pins, which, attached to the tapes she had already sewn inside her dress, would raise the hem the requisite distance above the floor. She had bought a pair of black net tights as well as black plumes for her hair.

Annie absently called good-bye to Cathy. She had been waiting for two days for a chance to let Sam have it, and Sam, well aware of her mood, had been conspicuously absent from the hotel, pursuing his own concerns and returning only when he was sure Annie was asleep. It was Claudia who had bidden him come to dinner tonight. Claudia was the only one he wouldn't cross.

When Cathy had gone, Claudia rose from the table and took Eden off with her to put the girl's hair in curlpapers. Tomorrow was her fourteenth birthday, and Claudia had arranged a lavish party. It was Claudia's wish that whatever Sam and Annie had to settle might be settled before the festivities, so as not to cast a pall on Eden's pleasure.

As the door closed behind them, Sam got up, too.

"I want to talk to you," Annie said.

"Going to call me on the carpet?" Sam grinned at her with sarcasm. He was furious that there was no escape from the confrontation. "Mother dear?" he added.

"I'm not your mother!" Annie shot back. "Even though you've been acting as if you're five."

"Been keeping tabs?" Sam looked rebellious. "Have you hired a Pinkerton man?"

"The only thing I need a detective for is to find your conscience. Do you think I didn't see you acting like a tomcat right under my nose? I was just plain mortified."

"And I'm not, I suppose? Coming to you hat in hand every time I want a nickel to spend?" Sam made an obsequious begging gesture.

"You get an allowance—a fat one. And I don't ask how you spend it."

"Shall I confirm your worst suspicions? I spend it on opium. Whiskey and sin. Harlots. I go out and prowl the Bowery every night. I'm sinking in iniquity."

"Oh, stop it," Annie said. "You bought my Christmas present with it. I know what that necklace must have cost. But why do you have to act like this?"

"Maybe because I'm choking to death on your damned diamond-studded leash," Sam snapped.

"Well, you didn't mind the diamonds when you married me," Annie retorted. "And you knew I was going to keep control of my own money. Don't be childish." She looked at his restive, angry face. "Aw, Sam, you know you aren't reliable. I'd be crazy to give you a free rein. You've never managed a business."

"Maybe I could learn," Sam grated. "You ever think of that?"

"Yeah, I've thought of it, and it gives me nightmares. You'd drain off my capital into every get-rich-quick scheme that came down the pike. Before we even left Virginia City you were after me to put money in that gold mine, and I *knew* it was salted."

"I knew it, too," he said, irritated. "But I could have sold it for a lot more than they were asking to somebody who didn't."

"Then you're just flat dishonest." Annie put her napkin down and looked at him over the table, trying to see some steadiness in him but not finding any. "And they'd have outsmarted you," she said gently. "I knew those boys from way back."

"Yeah, you always know it all. Maybe sometimes I just want to talk to someone who doesn't know so much."

Annie raised her eyebrows. "Like that little tart at the party?"

"She isn't a tart," Sam said defensively. "She's in the Weber and Fields show."

"And as pure as the driven snow," Annie said acidly. " 'Oh, Mr. Brentwood, you're just such a *card*!' "

"She doesn't mean anything to me, Annie." He came back over to the table, put his hands on her shoulders, and ran his fingers cajolingly along the back of her neck.

"I didn't expect you'd be faithful to me," Annie said stiffly, "but I didn't expect you to humiliate me."

"Now, Annie." He trailed his hands around to the front of her neck and over one breast under the tight silk bodice. He didn't have to feign his desire.

Annie pushed his hand away. "Stop it. You won't get around me like that. You haven't been home in two nights."

"Maybe I was afraid to." He tried to put his hand back.

Annie slapped at it and twisted her chair away. "You aren't coming into my bed out of someone else's. You stay home and sober a couple of nights, and we'll talk about it."

Sam backed off, his eyes blazing, his mood turning defiant again. "The hell with you." He turned on his heel and stalked into the parlor.

"Where are you going?" Annie was behind him in the doorway.

Sam snatched his hat off the coatrack by the front door. "Out!"

The Elysian's customers crowding through the front doors were noisy and seemed half-drunk already—even the women. And the alley by the stage door was very dark. Cathy made her way into the murky light of the backstage passageway, grateful to be inside.

Eddie Gamble was waiting for her by a dressing-room door. He preceded her into the room without ceremony.

"You're late," he said. "And I told you to take that dress up."

She looked at him with surprise. "It won't take me a minute." There was something funny about Eddie, less friendly and more demanding. She couldn't take her skirts up with him standing there, so she handed him the sheet music. "Please give this to the orchestra for me."

Eddie's hand rested on her wrist, caressing it. "You're on in fifteen minutes. They always put new acts on early." He smiled. "We'll have plenty of time to celebrate afterward."

"Oh, I'll have to go right home."

Eddie bent closer to her. "You aren't going to run out on me again tonight," he said distinctly. "Girls who get jobs are supposed to be grateful for them."

Cathy stared at him. The smile had grown wolflike and hungry.

"This job cost me a bundle," Eddie said. "So I'm expecting a whole lot of gratitude."

"Cost you—?" She felt frozen with Eddie bending over her.

"You dimwit, you don't think Swanny does anything out of the kindness of his heart, do you? He owes McCauley's gang money, and he's in too deep to pay it. I told him I'd square it for him if he'd give you a spot."

The realization that she had made a mistake hit her like a punch in the stomach. Cathy looked around the dingy room, but there was no way out past Eddie. "Well, just tell him I don't want the job," she said, panic-stricken.

Eddie laughed. "You tell him. If I don't pay off McCauley for him, Swanny's as good as dead. You've got the job. I'll pay up, then you can pay up." He loomed over her, and his hand slid up her arm. "Now get that skirt hiked up."

Cathy pushed at him. "All right, all right. Just go away."

"We'll settle accounts after your act," Eddie said.

She felt his hand caress her buttocks. "I guess I can wait that long."

When the door closed behind him, she looked frantically for a lock, but there wasn't one. Mechanically, she began pulling up the tapes inside her skirt and pinning them. She put on the black net tights and slipped her shoes back on. She looked into the cracked mirror and pinned the sad, silly black plumes into her hair. Her hands were shaking. There was no way out now except onto the stage. Somehow she would have to get away from Eddie after the performance. She didn't know how. Mr. Swanson wasn't going to help her; that was obvious.

Cathy looked at the closed door, scared to death of Eddie. If she wouldn't tell him where she lived—and she couldn't—he would take her someplace else. *Oh, why did I do it?*

The door opened without a knock, and Swanson glared around it at her. "Get out there. You're on next." He inspected her. "That goddam dress is still too long."

"I can't—it won't—"

"Move!" Swanson took one arm and pulled her out the door. Eddie was standing there, having given the sheet music to the orchestra. He grabbed her other arm, and together the two men hauled her down the passageway, past other dressing rooms filled with performers in various stages of undress; a contortionist in a spangled top and flesh-colored tights, just coming off, and a fat comedian in baggy pants sitting dejectedly on a pile of name cards. A canvas drop thumped down beside them, and Swanson pushed Cathy out onto the stage in front of it. The orchestra was playing the first bars of "None Can Love Like an Irishman."

"Ladies and gentlemen, for your particular enjoyment, Miss Catherine Salton, the New York Nightingale!"

The curtain rose. The air in the music hall was dim and smoky. The audience, a sea of pale faces in the gloom, drank beer at smeared tables and waited to be entertained. The orchestra leader looked at her, impatient. She nodded at him, her teeth chattering.

" 'The turban'd Turk, who scorns the world—' " She sang mechanically, knowing her voice was flat.

The audience began to shift in their seats.

" 'The gay monsieur—' " She lost the beat, struggled frantically to catch it, and stumbled over the next line. She looked into the wings and saw Eddie and a grim-faced Swanson watching her. Terrified, she looked out into the audience again. As if to set the cap on her horror, she saw that Mr. Smates, the corset seller from the train, was at a front table. She lost the beat again, and the audience began to boo.

Cathy tried to go on singing, but the words wouldn't come. She couldn't remember the next verse. Mr. Smates was pounding with his beer bottle on the table in an erratic rhythm, but half of the audience was standing up, shouting at her.

" 'Ask any . . . any girl you happen to meet—' " A piece of a half-eaten sausage bun smacked against the front of her dress, and a beer bottle landed at her feet.

She put her hands to her face and fled, sobbing, stumbling past the canvas drop. One of the tapes in her hem came loose so that it straggled about her ankles, nearly tripping her. Behind her she could hear the audience roaring and more bottles clattering onto the stage. The orchestra wound up the song with a crescendo.

Swanson was livid, shouting orders. "Get the curtain down! Get Mirella out there!"

The curtain hurtled down, then another canvas drop unfurled behind it, and Mirella May ran out in red spangles and white tights, shedding her kimono as she went. In the orchestra pit, the all-girl orchestra was taking its place in a flurry of sheet music, while the regular orchestra beat a retreat.

"Ladies and gentlemen, the management wishes to apologize— Ladies and gentlemen, the miraculous Miss Mirella May!" The curtain came up again.

"Damn you!" Swanson grabbed Cathy by the arm and yanked her into the wings, his fist raised. The orchestra had started up, but the audience was still booing. "I'm gonna bust your lying face open!"

She tried to tell him that it was the fact that Eddie was waiting backstage for her that had terrified her into paralysis, but she knew Swanson wouldn't care.

"Get her out of here, Swanny," the stage manager hissed.

Swanson started to drag her down the passageway when Eddie Gamble grabbed her other arm and pushed Swanson away. "Oh, no, you don't. I paid up, Swanny. You let her alone."

Cathy cringed between the two of them, knowing that Eddie was no rescuer. His next words confirmed it. "It's a shame you were such a flop, kid, but you're still a hit in my book. And you don't have to sing to pay what you owe *me*."

"Let me go!" She gathered her courage to struggle furiously, but Eddie just laughed. He held her by both forearms. "I'll let you go in a while. When we're square." He turned her around and shoved her down the hallway toward the door. The other performers gave her blank stares, unwilling to interfere. He dragged her out the door, and she saw with horror that he had a cab waiting.

She began to fight him again, and Eddie gave her a backhanded slap across the face that sent her reeling. As he jerked the cab door open, the driver looked in the other direction.

"My name's not really Salton," she wailed. "You don't understand!"

"I don't care what your name is. If you're on the lam, that's not my problem. Get in!"

She clung to the side of the cab, and Eddie's grip loosened just for an instant as the sound of running feet came pounding down the alley. Cathy jerked her head around, afraid that it was Swanson or some friend of Eddie's.

With incredulous disbelief, she saw that it was Sam. The chorus girl he had been with at Lucy's party was running after him, stumbling in her high-heeled boots.

Sam pulled Eddie off Cathy and swung an expert

punch at his jaw. Cathy leaned against the cab as someone else came huffing up behind them. It was Mr. Smates, red in the face and breathing beer.

"Which one of 'em you want me to hit, girlie?" he asked her.

Eddie and Sam were rolling in the trash of the alley, swinging at each other in fury. Cathy watched, her hands to her mouth, not answering Smates.

"That one," the chorus girl said, pointing at Eddie. "Hit him."

Mr. Smates pulled a full beer bottle from his pocket and picked his way across the alley.

"We were out front," the girl said to Cathy. "You got rocks in your head coming here, you know that? And with a guy like Eddie."

"I didn't know," Cathy whispered.

The girl shook her head. "Jeez, you're green."

Sam rolled away from Eddie and stumbled to his feet. As Eddie got up, too, Sam sent a hard right to his jaw. Eddie staggered backward, and Mr. Smates hit him with the beer bottle. Eddie dropped with a thud.

"Who the hell are you?" Sam demanded.

"Name of Smates. Just happened to be in town. Li'l lady's a friend of mine." He studied Sam. "And who might you be?"

"I'm her cousin," Sam snapped. He stalked over to the cab and looked up at the driver. "You get paid to abduct women often?"

"I get paid to drive," the man said. "I don't stick my fool nose in where it ain't wanted."

"Well, now you can drive," Sam said. He marched around the cab to Cathy. "Get in."

"You wanna go with him, girlie?" Smates inquired. "I'll hit him, too, if you want me to."

"No," Cathy managed to say. "It's all right. Thank you, Mr. Smates."

"This ain't a nice place," Smates confided. "I told you you should have let me show you around." Wreathed in a cloud of beer, he looked at her earnestly.

"Thank you, Mr. Smates. I believe we can manage," Sam said icily. He pushed Cathy into the cab and got in, too. "The Waldorf," he told the driver.

"What about me?" the girl demanded as Sam slammed the vehicle's door shut.

"Oh, Lord, I forgot about you." Sam opened the door again and pulled her in. "Twenty-ninth Street," he yelled to the driver.

"I've never been to the Waldorf." The girl sounded wistful.

"Well, you aren't going tonight, Sukie," Sam said.

Sam leaned back in the seat and ran a hand through his hair. He had lost his hat, and his dark hair hung limply in his filthy face. His shirtfront was torn to ribbons, and his knuckles were bleeding.

"All right, you putty head," he said to Cathy when he had gotten his breath back. "What the hell were you doing in that dump?"

"I wanted to sing," Cathy said, sniffling. "And don't you swear at me, Sam Brentwood."

"You could have been raped," Sam said grimly.

Cathy gasped. That wasn't a word she had ever heard spoken aloud.

"All right, he could have taken liberties with your person," Sam said sarcastically. "After what you've been up to, I didn't bother to mince words."

"What *I've* been up to?" she said indignantly, with a look at Sukie. "You're calling *me* on the carpet?"

"I wasn't going to be raped," Sam said, chuckling.

"You're horrible!"

"You're lucky I was there."

"Oh? Well, I'll be sure to tell that to Annie!"

"What are you going to tell your folks?" Sukie asked, interested. "You're aunt's going to just plain die."

"You stay out of this," Sam and Cathy said together.

The cab rolled to a stop outside the house on Twenty-ninth Street where Sukie had a room, and Sam deposited her on the sidewalk with a minimum of ceremony. "It's not your fault, kid," he muttered, "but I don't think I'll be coming around again."

"Naw," Sukie said sadly. "I guess not. Well, it's been fun."

"Look, do you think you could keep quiet about this?" Sam pressed some rolled bills into her hand.

"Sure," Sukie said. "I don't talk." She put the money in her dress.

"Buy yourself a present," Sam said. "Consider it from me." He looked up at the driver. "The Waldorf. And see if you can keep quiet, too."

When the cab deposited them at the hotel, Sam added another bribe as an aid to the driver's silence and handed Cathy down. She quailed a little at the brightly lit street. She had torn the rest of the tapes loose from her dress so that the hem reached her shoes, but she knew how she and Sam looked.

Sam pulled her into the shadows and repinned her hair as well as he could. On their way into the lobby, he threw the plumes into a potted tree with a gesture of disgust.

"All right, walk fast and keep your mouth shut." He guided her rapidly toward the elevators. The elevator boy goggled at them. Sam slipped him a bill, too. "Sixth floor, and the young lady is not feeling well, so please don't stop for anyone else."

As they got out, Sam took Cathy by the arm. "You're going to have to confess, so you might as well do it right off."

"What about you?" Cathy demanded.

"Grateful, aren't you?" Sam snarled.

"I like Annie," Cathy replied. "I think you treat her terribly."

"Oh, you do? Well, *I* think I should have left you in the alley. I bet dear old Mr. Smates would have brought you home. Where did you meet *him?*"

"I met him on the train. It's none of your business."

Sam pushed open Claudia's door, and they confronted a stunned tableau of Claudia, Annie, and Howard Locke.

"She was singing at a dump on West Thirty-fourth Street," Sam announced. "They threw sausages at her."

"*Oh!* Oh, I wish you *had* just left me there, and gone home with that—that *girl* from Weber and Fields!" Cathy screamed at him. She burst into tears and ran from the room. They heard her bedroom door slam.

Before anyone could say anything else, Annie snatched up a vase from Claudia's sideboard and hurled it at Sam. He ducked wildly, and it smashed into the door behind him in shards of china and sodden flowers. Annie picked up her skirts and ran through the mess, tears streaming down her face, too. Her flying feet echoed down the hall, and another door slammed.

Howard Locke took up his hat. "My dear," he said to Claudia, "I would stay and help clean up, but I expect you would rather do without me just now." He bent gallantly over her hand.

"Thank you," she said faintly. "I— It has been a most enjoyable evening. I do hope you will call again."

There was a twinkle in Mr. Locke's eyes. "Gracious lady, again and again, if you will let me. When one is my age, one has seen far too much of the world to worry about trifles." He departed with a tip of his hat.

"*That* is a gentleman," Claudia announced to Sam. She pinned him to the door with her eyes as if he had been a butterfly in a box. "I'm furious with you. I gather by your appearance that you got Cathy out of a scrape, but you've entirely negated your good deed with your boorish behavior. You are *not* a gentleman, and I am ashamed of you!"

"Gran—"

His grandmother's eyes bored right through him. "Don't talk to me. I'm too angry with you. When a man marries, he makes certain vows, and it is despicable not to keep them. To say nothing of throwing it in your wife's face."

"I didn't throw it," Sam protested. "That little devil in there did."

"I'll deal with her," Claudia said grimly. "My advice to you is to make your peace with your wife—if she will let you in. If she won't, you may sleep in the hall."

She pointed at the door and stood there until he went through it.

Claudia could still hear Cathy sobbing hysterically behind her closed door.

Now or in the morning? Claudia wondered. *Now,* she decided. In the morning they would be in a flurry with Eden's party. It was a mercy, she thought as she passed Eden's silent room, that the child slept so well. At least Claudia hoped she did.

She tapped on Cathy's door, and when Cathy sniffled "Go away," Claudia went in anyway.

"You'll make yourself sick," Claudia observed, sitting on the bed. Cathy was stretched full-length on top of the coverlet, her face in a pillow.

"It doesn't matter," Cathy moaned. "Oh, I wish I were dead."

"That would hardly solve your problems," Claudia said emphatically. "Then you would have to explain it all to Saint Peter instead of to me."

Cathy burrowed her face deeper into the pillow. "I only wanted to sing," she said through its enveloping billows of down. "I wanted to be on a real stage."

Claudia sighed. "The fact that you were unwilling to tell Lucy or me about your plans should have been enough to tell you they weren't proper."

Cathy rolled over and looked at Claudia miserably. Her face was red and splotchy and slick with tears. The green taffeta dress was a shambles, with a big greasy stain on the front. "I didn't know people could be so horrid. They threw things at me. And Eddie said . . ." She choked on tears of shame. "That girl who was with Sam said I should have known better, too. She knew, but I didn't."

"You've led a very sheltered life, dear. You've been protected from places like that. And from people like this Eddie, I expect, whoever he is. Suppose you tell me the whole story from the beginning."

"Do I have to?"

"You do." Claudia folded her arms and waited.

Once Cathy got started, the words flowed quickly.

Indignation took over, and she poured out not only her foolishness but also her affront at Eddie's deception, and Mr. Swanson's, and at Sam's having been there to rescue her not as a gallant knight in white but with a chorus girl on his arm.

"You weren't very gracious to him, were you?"

Cathy sniffled. "Should I have been?"

"Since he got you out of rather a bad spot, yes, I think you should."

"He was awful. Oh, everything was awful. The whole world is awful! Nothing is nice, the way it's supposed to be."

Claudia raised her eyebrows. "And how is it supposed to be?"

"Not like this!" Cathy wailed. "Look at Cornelia and her mother. She's going to *marry* that man. They've just beaten her down, and she won't stand up for herself! And Eddie, telling me all those lies and acting as if I were—"

"What you pretended to be," Claudia cut in grimly.

"Well, he shouldn't have taken advantage of it! Like that horrible Mr. Ardry and Violet Ewing. Even the family—Sam and Annie's fighting, and Sam's behaving like that. They're married! They're supposed to be *happy!*" Cathy began sobbing again, and the sobs abated into hiccups of grief and outrage.

Claudia produced a handkerchief from her sleeve and mopped Cathy's face. "This is life, child. You can't write a happy ending into the third act and make everyone see the light, any more than you can give people a conscience or a sense of responsibility. They have to develop that on their own. Dreadful things happen. Dreadful people exist. And sometimes things happen that aren't anyone's fault—or are everyone's fault. We must muddle along and do the best we can. But don't ever expect life to be lovely and equitable just because it ought to be."

Cathy wiped her eyes. "I suppose I *am* very naive."

"Not so naive now as you were this morning, I imagine," Claudia said gently. "I came in here to give you a number-nine scolding, but I'm beginning to think it would be superfluous."

Cathy's eyes welled with tears, silently now. "I'm sorry."

Claudia nodded. "All right, then. Now sit up and let me help you out of that dress, and we'll see what can be done about cleaning it." Her mouth twitched just a little. "Sausages, I believe Sam said. They're very greasy, aren't they?"

Cathy emitted a weak chuckle. "That was just at first. It was beer bottles afterward." She sat and turned around so that Claudia could unhook the back and unlace her corset. "Aunt Claudia, I do love you. And I am sorry. I don't suppose . . . that is, I expect you feel you have to tell my parents?"

"No, I believe I'll keep tonight's transgressions to myself," Claudia told her. "As a surety for your future good behavior," she added.

Cathy turned around and flung her arms around her aunt. "Oh, thank you! It would make Mother so unhappy. And you needn't worry about me, truly you needn't. I promise I've learned my lesson."

The next day was Eden's fourteenth birthday party, an elaborate gala at the Waldorf. The guests were eight young ladies in proper party dresses, and their attendant mamas or governesses. After the luncheon and a performance by a clown-magician, there was a final surprise, arranged with the assistance of Lucy Woods. The girls were beckoned into a side parlor, where the heavy curtains had been drawn and then overhung with lengths of black cloth. Three rows of gilt chairs had been set out in front of a square of framed white canvas on a stand. Behind the chairs was a mysterious box similar to a camera, but it shot a beam of light onto the canvas screen, making a bright two-foot square in its center. Tinkering with the apparatus was a man with a handlebar mustache, and a pair of pliers stuck in his back pocket.

The girls sat down, mystified. Claudia presented

Mr. William Kennedy Laurie Dickson, who, she told them, was going to present the very first *moving* picture ever to be shown, entitled *Fred Ott's Sneeze*. The guests stared expectantly at the screen, on which nothing was as yet visible.

I hope this works as well as he claims, Claudia thought. Dickson was an acquaintance of Lucy Woods's, who, Claudia had to admit, knew the strangest people. He worked in the laboratory of that ingenious eccentric Thomas Edison and was, so Lucy said, on the outs with his boss over the moving picture project.

Motion pictures had been discussed in theory since Eastman's perfection of celluloid roll film, and Dickson had now actually produced one in the Edison laboratory. The disagreement, as Lucy had explained it, stemmed from the fact that Edison, for reasons both artistic and financial, had decided not to exhibit the film on a screen for large audiences but through his peephole viewer, called a Kinetoscope. The clarity of reproduction in the little peephole machine was much better; and Edison, whose heart was really in his phonograph, not in pictures, thought that he would make more money showing the film to one person at a time, rather than to large audiences who would surely tire quickly of such a silly novelty. Dickson was violently opposed, and it was in the hope of demonstrating his invention's large-scale possibilities that he had agreed to condescend to demonstrating it for a children's birthday party.

At a signal from Dickson, Annie turned off the electric lights and slipped into a seat while Dickson turned the projection machine's crank and ran the film through it. It wasn't very long, and the image on the screen was grainy, but it moved. Fred Ott, in shirtsleeves and vest, looked at the camera, twitched his mustache, wiggled his nose with a look of comical surprise, put his hands to his face, and sneezed mightily. Then Dickson reversed the direction of the film, and Ott did it backward.

Eden clapped her hands and laughed with the rest of the girls and pleaded that he do it again. The fact that the sneeze was silent somehow made it funnier. Even the mothers and the governesses loved it.

Dickson was preparing to crank the film through for a fourth time when a crack of light split the darkness and a Waldorf bellboy slipped in.

"Mrs. Brentwood?"

Claudia frowned at him and then froze with a lurch in her heart when she saw the telegraph message in his hand.

"Which Mrs. Brentwood?" Annie asked quietly as Claudia joined her.

"Mrs. Samuel Brentwood," the boy said, which wasn't any help, since Claudia's husband had been Sam, too. "It's from Washington," he added.

"I don't know anyone in Washington," Annie whispered.

Claudia opened it slowly, in the light from the half-open door. People were beginning to turn to watch her. She read it and closed her eyes for a moment. Then she mustered a smile for Mr. Dickson and the party guests. "Thank you, Mr. Dickson. It has been a splendid show."

"What is it, Aunt Claudia?" Cathy asked.

"Your grandfather Lee is dying," she answered.

XIII

"My dear, you are not to grieve." Lee brought his hand out from under the blanket and took Eulalia's.

She sat silently holding it, cupped between both of hers as if she could somehow keep him from slipping away.

"You'll find everything you need in the desk in the sitting room," Lee said carefully. "My will. Insurance papers. A letter for Henry."

"I know," Eulalia said. How like Lee to have organized his affairs for everyone else's comfort. The only thing he couldn't prearrange for her was the regaining of his strength and health, and that was what she wanted. Henry, Cindy, Alexandra, and all the children were in the next room. She should let them come in again, but she couldn't bear to give him up. She knew she was being selfish, but she couldn't help it. Her first husband had gone so suddenly, taken from her by an avalanche; she hadn't even had time to say good-bye. Her impulse was to hold Lee to her, alone, as long as she could. The doctors had said he had only days left, if that.

Toby had had to go to the Senate, but he had been in that morning to tell her quietly that he had sent for Janessa and Tim and had telegraphed the Martins and the Brentwoods. They would all come to see Lee one last time.

Lee looked at her pale, set face, still beautiful under the wrinkles.

219

"You hold on," he said. "You're tough."

"Oh, yes," Eulalia said sadly. "I'm tough." She put her head down on his hand. He was so thin. He seemed to have faded from her already.

"There's something else. I want to ask you. . . ."

She had to lift her head, to hear him.

"Since I'll have the . . . good fortune"—he managed the ghost of a grin—"to die in Washington, I would like to be buried at Arlington."

Eulalia's eyes widened, but he didn't notice.

"I've earned a place there, I think. So many good men I knew . . . are there already. So many companions . . ."

His voice faded again, and Eulalia blinked back tears. "Of course, my dear." To be buried in Washington? Not at home in Portland, where she could visit with him, sit by his grave, and tell him the small news of her day, keep some kind of contact? To be like Whip, gone from her entirely? *Oh, no!* "I promise, dear."

The marriage of Senator Lucien Leclerc was a partnership, based upon mutual advantage to him and Martha; but a wrench in the works was the fact that the senator was, in his way, in love with his wife. The fact that he had not been her first husband gnawed at Leclerc's pride, and the appearance of an old and handsome acquaintance in the form of Toby Holt, whom he detested anyway, gnawed still further. Knowing that he should leave well enough alone, Leclerc had nevertheless perversely set out to learn exactly what Toby Holt had been to Martha, and she to him.

It was far easier even than Leclerc had thought. An interested crony from New Orleans reported that it was just as the senator had feared: Mrs. Leclerc, before her first marriage, had had a lover—perhaps more than one, but this one was known—and his name was Toby Holt. Leclerc paid the informant, now almost wishing that he hadn't asked.

He was waiting for Martha when she came home,

with her maid behind her laden with packages, and the flame in his eyes sent the maid scurrying upstairs.

"So Toby Holt was a business acquaintance of your father's?" Leclerc snarled before Martha had even taken off her hat.

Martha tensed, but she kept her face to the mirror as she lifted the hat off her hair and set it on a table. "Yes, of course he was. I've told you that."

"But you knew him, too!"

"I've also told you that."

"Knew him in what appears to have been a biblical sense!" Leclerc snapped.

Martha raised her eyebrows. "Any acquaintance I had with Toby Holt was before my first marriage, Lucien, and certainly well before my marriage to you. You knew you weren't getting a virgin bride."

"I expected a respectable bride, not some—some slattern! Admit it! Admit you were in Holt's bed!"

Martha's lips compressed. "Very well, I admit it. I've been faithful to you since we were married, Lucien. You aren't entitled to anything more."

Leclerc lunged at her, swinging his fists. She raised her hands against him, but he sent her reeling. She fell in the ashes of the hearth and rose with a poker in her hand.

"Hit me one more time, and you won't ever do it again."

Senator Leclerc stared, furious and wild-eyed, at his wife and then stumbled from the room, his hands to his face. As he crossed the threshold he looked up toward the landing, where Martha's maid, kneeling, watched through the banisters.

It didn't take long for word to spread. Forty-eight hours was considered the normal time for the Washington grapevine to disseminate information, but this news ran through it in twenty-four.

The Leclercs' cook did her marketing where all the other Capitol Hill cooks shopped, and the maid from Cabot Lodge's house had a brother who ran an elevator in the Capitol Building.

Toby heard it from his red-eared clerk, Watson, who "thought the senator had better know." An encounter on the stairs with a white-faced Leclerc convinced Toby of the truth of it, as did the number of people who suddenly appeared to hustle them off in opposite directions. To cap it off, Noell Simpson paid him a visit to inquire piously if Toby thought he could "keep it in his pants" for a while because Leclerc's support was needed for a piece of upcoming legislation to which Oregon lumbering interests would be particularly sensitive. Toby had all he could do to refrain from throwing Simpson down the stairs. After that, Watson told everyone that Senator Holt was indisposed.

When Toby got back to Connecticut Avenue, Alexandra was waiting for him at the door, a petite and bad-tempered avenging angel. Toby could almost hear a hiss of steam.

"Toby, how could you do this to me at a time like this?" she demanded before he had hung up his hat.

Except for Alexandra's simmering presence, the house was very still, shrouded in a layer of grief and apprehension over Lee. The uneasy silence grated on Toby's taut nerves. "I didn't do it 'at a time like this'! I did it nearly twenty years ago!"

"And the fact that you did is now known to every Tom, Dick, and Harry in Washington," Alexandra informed him.

Toby gave her a hunted look and tried to think of something to say, but nothing came. As they glared at each other, he heard a door open at the back of the house, where Lee's first-floor bedroom was. Eulalia came slowly down the hall, walking very carefully, as if she might crumble.

She looked at them through wet eyes. "Lee's gone," she said piteously.

Alexandra ran to her, and Toby closed his eyes and leaned his forehead against the cold plaster of the wall.

Toby stumbled up the steps to the Senate chamber

in a daze, feeling brittle and on edge with mourning. He had spent most of the night with his mother, letting her cry against his chest—and mourning Lee himself— once Cindy and Henry had come and gone home again and Alexandra had put Mike and Sally to bed.

The children were unhappy and frightened; they had seen death before, when Stalking Horse, the aged foreman of Toby's ranch had died, but that had not been as traumatic as losing their beloved Grandpa Lee. Because Toby had done it himself as a child, he knew that now they were tallying the ages of the rest of their family, afraid of whom else they might lose, and that their world seemed to them dangerously unstable just now. Sally had asked her father, clinging to his hand, how old he was himself. Toby had reassured her that he was only fifty, practically a spring chicken, but he didn't think she had been comforted. To Sally, that was a very great age, too.

Now, he felt a great deal older than fifty as his path crossed with that of the senator from Louisiana. The sight of Lucien Leclerc's pale face and hate-filled eyes roused in him an emotion that was half anger and half pity. Leclerc looked even worse then he himself did, Toby thought. He shrugged and turned away from the man. He didn't have the time, inclination, or energy for a personal confrontation; his was a house of mourning, and he wanted nothing more than to return to his family and grieve with them.

He would not even have come to the Senate that morning if a debate had not been scheduled on the possible revival of the Federal Elections Bill. That was too important to let go by, even if Toby did not harbor much hope for such a quick turnaround of opinion. He walked grimly to his seat, receiving murmured offers of sympathy from his fellow senators.

Leclerc's interest in the bill was now intensified by a raging hatred for one of its champions. The debate began along gentlemanly lines, but a nasty undercurrent caused some senators to shift uneasily in their seats.

Their heads jerked around abruptly toward the sound of a fist being slammed down upon a desk and the crash of an overturned chair. Leclerc stalked across the chamber toward Toby, eyes blazing, as Toby tried to ignore him and continue his speech.

"The senator from Oregon is very quick to tell the South how it should manage its affairs!" Leclerc seethed.

"Sit down," Toby said. "You'll have your chance."

"Mr. Leclerc!"

"Gentlemen, please—"

Leclerc looked wildly around the chamber. "Mr. Holt insults me personally!" he shouted.

"By suggesting that you're keeping half your population suppressed?" Toby inquired, goaded.

"By innuendo and false dealing! By interference in state affairs!"

"Now, Leclerc . . ." someone said.

"And by personal insult!" Leclerc drew his gloves from his pocket. "I demand satisfaction for it!" He made a gesture as if to slap Toby with the gloves, and everyone froze.

"Oh, stow the theatrics," Toby growled.

There was a soft intake of breath from the assemblage. The senators looked at each other, hopeful that someone would escort Leclerc out of the chamber.

Hurt pride and jealousy boiled over in a shrieking tirade. "I will have satisfaction, even from a slinking thief!"

Toby stiffened, but he got a grip on his own temper. "Nobody calls me that," he informed Leclerc. "Now, I understand you're wrought up, but I've done you no personal injury. And what's past is past."

" 'No personal injury!' There is none so personal as the sullying of a man's name and the sanctity of his family!"

Toby rolled his eyes at this high-flown declaration and mustered a final ounce of patience. "From what I hear, you sullied your own name by making a spectacle for your servants out of what ought to have been dealt with in private. When you hang out dirty linen, Leclerc, people are going to gawk at it." He was aware that that wasn't quite as patient sounding as he had intended, but he was sick to death of the man, and just plain sick at heart over the rest of it. "I haven't got time for you, Leclerc. My family is in mourning."

"I have no pity for your family, Holt!" Leclerc spat. "No pity for the just deserts of flagrant immorality." His face was sweating, and his eyes glittered brighter still. Leaning toward Toby venomously, he seized on a new insult. "No pity for a clan degraded at its very heart! For a woman who debauches herself with a heathen while her husband degrades honest men's wives!"

"Just what do you mean?" Toby asked quietly, but the menace in his voice stilled all sound in the chamber.

"Your wife, sir." Leclerc gave him a vile grin. "*Your* wife, who is known to be debasing herself with a man of color!"

"Now see here, Leclerc—"

There was a shocked ripple of protest from the senators. "Here, man, you're going too far!" said one. Mrs. Holt was known to be a friend of the ambassador from Japan, but nobody had even suggested— The senators looked appalled.

Toby could feel his anger boiling up out of control. He stood stock-still. Then with a lunge, he snatched Leclerc's gloves from his hand and flung them on the ground. "Name your friends," he said between his teeth. "Name your friends, or I'll take you apart right here."

"You aren't really going to fight a duel?" Watson stared at his boss in amazement and gave a little shiver of excitement. "Maybe chivalry isn't dead."

Toby didn't feel chivalrous. He felt trapped, hung up with a rope out of his own past. But there were some things a man couldn't let go by. He passed a hand over his forehead.

"He's right in here," Watson said to a man at the door.

Toby looked up to see Jules Amberand, one of Leclerc's aides. Leclerc was prompt, Toby thought sourly.

"Well! This is awkward!" Amberand said heartily.

"*Awkward* is not the word I would have picked," Toby informed him. "Your boss made a spectacle of both of us and insulted my wife—and his own wife, for that matter. If he wants to apologize, however, and withdraw his challenge, I'll be delighted to oblige him. We should both be too old and civilized for this idiocy."

Amberand coughed. "I didn't mean the challenge itself is awkward, exactly. I meant . . . er, how shall I put it? The information I want to convey. This doesn't come from Senator Leclerc's lips, you understand, but I can say that this—engagement between you and Senator Leclerc is only a formality."

"A formality with pistols," Toby said. "And you can go back and tell your boss I am a very good shot."

"That is it precisely. Senator Leclerc wishes to preserve his honor. He has no intention of actually trying to kill you."

Oh, very good. So I'm to make a public display of myself to salvage his stupid Creole pride. "In that case, I'd suggest he just call it off," Toby said. "I don't particularly want to kill him, either."

"Oh, that can't be done," Amberand assured him. "It's a matter of honor."

Toby glared at him. "All right. I want this taken care of by tomorrow morning. My stepfather's funeral is the day after tomorrow, and my entire family will be here by tomorrow night. I have no intention of involving them in this or further distressing my mother or my wife."

"Of course, of course," Amberand agreed. "I would suggest Bladensburg. Just over the district line, and quite traditional, I understand. There is an excellent inn there," he added hopefully.

"I'm not planning to stay for breakfast," Toby growled.

As he rode home, Toby fought off the temptation to shoot Leclerc anyway, out of sheer malice. But the man wasn't worth getting arrested for murder over, which would happen if one of them killed the other.

Dueling was completely illegal. They would be lucky to get away with a reprimand as it was. On the other hand, Toby couldn't back down if Leclerc didn't. The best he could hope for was to keep it quiet.

That proved to be a lost cause. The news reached home a full hour ahead of him. As Toby strode around the side of the house from the stable, his cook and his gardener, interrupted in a back-porch discussion of it all, stared at him goggle-eyed. And Alexandra was waiting again, her face white with fury.

"If you fight this man, I'll never forgive you," she said flatly. Her hands were balled into fists. "If you couldn't think of me, how could you do this to your mother?"

"I trust you aren't going to tell her," Toby said.

"I don't have to. She isn't deaf and blind."

Toby sighed. He drew Alexandra into his study and shut the door. "Alex, he has me in a box. I can't get out of it. But nobody is going to get hurt. He just wants to save his pride."

"Men." Alexandra gave him the look of loathing she might accord to something turned up under a stone.

"I told you, he isn't going to shoot me. And I'm not going to shoot him."

"Oh, no," Alexandra said vengefully. "You'll just give everyone a little more to talk about, about you and that woman."

They glared at each other, nerves rubbed raw by the multiple stresses of the past days.

"It's not entirely to do with Martha and me," Toby said. "Leclerc made some insinuations about you that I'm not about to let go by."

"Indeed?"

"He implied that you were carrying on an affair with the ambassador," Toby snapped.

"That is perfectly ridiculous. You won't distract me with that."

Toby himself didn't believe a word of the rumor about the ambassador, but he was in no mood to say so.

"All the same, I would prefer you didn't see him anymore, since it's causing talk."

Alexandra flung her head back, chin jutting out. "And *I* would prefer that you didn't fight this duel." She stalked out with an angry whisk of taffeta skirts and slammed the door.

Toby sat down at his desk, took a couple of deep breaths, and set about calming himself. It wouldn't serve any purpose to fight with Alex now. She would see reason when she had thought about it. He emerged an hour later, having squelched his temper to the point that he thought he could be civil to family and servants.

The house was subdued and empty. His mother would be in her room, and he could hear the children in the backyard. Juanita was trotting nervously back and forth with one of Alexandra's dresses, newly dyed black, as if she didn't know where to put it.

"Where's Miss Alex?" Toby demanded.

"She went out," Juanita said. "The ambassador asked her to tea. He sent a card this morning. A very quiet tea," she added hastily, seeing the blaze of pure fury in her employer's eyes. "All right for a lady in mourning."

Toby picked up a china card tray from the hall table and smashed it on the floor.

"An oasis of peace!" Alexandra settled herself on a cushion on the floor of the teahouse. The ambassador had personally supervised its construction in the embassy garden as a refuge from the pressures of diplomatic life. It was a warm day, with a springlike breeze to ruffle the maple trees outside the door. Alexandra arranged her black skirts to cover her stockinged feet and smiled at Mr. Nakamura. She knew that Toby would be boiling, but just now she didn't particularly care. "It was kind of you to ask me."

Mr. Nakamura smiled. "Genuine grief is very tiring. You loved your father-in-law." It wasn't a question. He could see it in her face.

"Yes, very much." Alexandra sighed. "I think we all feel a little lost."

Mr. Nakamura nodded. He poured hot water into the teapot and stirred it with a bamboo whisk. When the tea was ready, they sipped it in silence. Then Mr. Nakamura said, "Mrs. Holt, I fear that small-minded people have made a difficulty for you."

Alexandra marveled once again at the Washington grapevine. "You're very up-to-date."

He chuckled. "I am a diplomat. I am paid to be up-to-date. If our friendship troubles you, you must break it off."

"It doesn't trouble me," Alexandra said. She loved Toby and was loyal to him, but she would do as she saw fit.

Mr. Nakamura smiled. "Then we will finish our tea, and you will return to your duties perhaps a little rested by the serenity of my garden."

Alexandra returned rested, if not serene, and prepared to make amends with Toby. She would explain, with impeccable logic, that the invitation to tea had already been accepted when he had asked her to suspend her friendship with the ambassador.

But Toby wasn't home when she got there. He didn't even return for dinner. Nor did he return until after she had gone to bed, fuming all over again. Of all the stiff-necked, pig-headed . . .

When Toby climbed into bed, she had her face to the wall, and she kept it there.

Toby believed that Alexandra was asleep, and he was relieved. He was too angry with Leclerc, and the world in general—and so, he thought, was she—to risk another quarrel now. All the same, he didn't sleep much.

He got up again at four to ride to Bladensburg. With luck, he would be back home before anyone took much notice. He slipped down the darkened stairs and out the kitchen door. His nerves were on edge, as anyone's might be who was going to let someone fire a pistol at him, however wide the shot might go.

When a shrouded figure slipped out of the shrubbery and waylaid him, he jumped nearly a foot. It was a young black woman, in a dark cloak and hood, her face nearly indistinguishable in the predawn.

"What do you want?" Toby demanded. "What are you doing here?"

"You Senator Holt?"

"I am. Who sent you?" As his eyes adjusted to the darkness, he could see a starched gingham dress and an apron under the cloak. She looked like someone's maid.

"Mrs. Leclerc send me to give you this." She handed Toby a square white envelope. "She say to tell you it's for true, and you read it right away." She edged away from him. "I got to go. Lord help me if he find out I been here."

Toby went into the stable and lit a lantern. He sat down on a hay bale to read the missive.

> My dear Toby,
> Whatever Jules Amberand has told you of Lucien's intentions, believe this instead: Lucien means to kill you and take his chances with the police.
>
> M.

The Washington Inn in Bladensburg exuded the seedy grandeur of a hostelry whose glory days had passed it by. Built in 1732, it had been renamed in later years for the first president, who had once spent a night there—as he appeared to have done, Toby thought wryly, in nearly every other structure in this part of the country. The inn's fame hadn't come from Washington's slumbers, however, but from the hundreds of duels fought with sword and pistol in the tree-shrouded ravine that lay just off the main road to Baltimore. Far from being embarrassed by this, Bladensburg had done everything but advertise its amenities on poster boards. Dueling brought guests to the inn—both participants and spectators—and kept the local livery stables and undertakers occupied.

As dueling went out of fashion, the inn had declined. Perhaps that accounted for the fact that the current proprietor, standing on the long porch and wiping his hands on his apron, looked so delighted.

Six men, talking under the shade of the inn's ancient sycamore trees, turned to greet Toby as he dismounted. Jules Amberand was with Leclerc, as well as another man whom Toby didn't recognize and who carried a flat wooden box under his arm. Watson and Amberand had arranged for the pistols. A fourth man, looking disgruntled and scornful, set a black satchel at his feet, introduced himself as Dr. Bellow, then announced that he hadn't time for this damnfool practice, and if anyone got killed he was calling for the police. Watson cheerfully assured the doctor that the duel was a formality, and his presence was required only in the event of an accident.

Toby blinked with surprise when he saw that the sixth man was Theodore Roosevelt.

"Theodore, what the devil are you doing here?"

"Came to talk you out of it," Roosevelt said.

"Well, you can't. Talk Leclerc out of it."

"I tried. The man's as unstable as a volcano."

"Let's get on with this," the doctor said, scowling. "I have a clinic full of patients to see."

Toby couldn't blame him. Like the rest of them, Dr. Bellow knew the morning's events to be a charade—a sop to two men's honor and an outdated code. Except for Bellow, they laughed and chatted as they strolled across the road and down the slope to the ravine. Martha's warning hammered at the back of Toby's mind.

On the flat grass at the bottom of the ravine, Watson and Amberand, as seconds, made the requisite but futile last offer of calling off the duel by apology, should either side wish to do so.

The man with the boxed pistols, who proved to be a gunsmith named Hilbert, opened the case for Toby's and Leclerc's inspection. It held old-fashioned single-shot pistols with elaborate silver-mounted grips, practically antiques but in excellent condition—a product of the days when dueling pistols were a part of every gentleman's accoutrements. Under any other circumstances, Toby would have taken a connoisseur's interest in them. Now he gave them the most thorough going-over they had probably ever had. Then he and Leclerc took a pistol each and stood back to back. Toby could feel the brutal energy of the man pulsating behind him. He knew Leclerc's reputation as an excellent marksman. Toby wasn't afraid to die, but this seemed such a stupid way to do it—and too soon, with only half his life used up.

"When the handkerchief falls, march ten paces as I count them, turn, and fire," Watson instructed.

Amberand held the handkerchief, hesitated, and let it flutter to the ground.

"One . . . two . . . three . . ."

On the other hand, Toby realized, he didn't want to kill Leclerc, either. In the course of an adventurous life, he had killed enough men, but never in cold blood. A duel with Leclerc wasn't worth dying for, and killing Leclerc wasn't worth getting tried for murder, either.

"Seven . . . eight . . . nine . . ."

How did I get into this?

"Ten!"

Toby spun, aimed as carefully as he could, and fired, trying to twist out of the way of Leclerc's shot as he did. There was a double crack of gunfire, and something slammed into his shoulder, knocking him backward. As he fell, he saw, with a kind of frozen-motion clarity, Leclerc's pistol spin from his hand and arc upward against the bright sun. It fell then, turning end over end, while Toby watched it, hypnotized, as little sparks of light began to dance in front of his eyes.

"Hold still, damn it. You're bleeding like a pig!"

He found himself on the ground, the smell of wet grass all around him, and saw through the bright haze that Theodore was kneeling beside him, pressing a wadded handkerchief to his shoulder while Dr. Bellow came sprinting with his bag in hand. Toby's shirtfront was scarlet with blood. Gritting his teeth as the first numbness began to wear off, he closed his eyes. The pinpoints of light still danced behind his lids.

"That son of a bitch was trying to kill you!" Theodore said, outraged.

"He will have if we don't get the bullet out and stop the bleeding," the doctor grunted.

"What about . . . him?" Toby managed to ask as the doctor held chloroform-soaked cotton under his nose.

"The bullet took him in the hand," Theodore said. "I doubt he'll ever fire a pistol again."

I am a better shot, Toby thought as he slipped into unconsciousness. *I hit what I was aiming for.*

Toby woke up in Theodore's carriage. "Where's my horse?" he demanded.

Theodore chuckled and turned in the seat to inspect him. "You're either very rational or delirious from fever," he remarked, "depending on how strongly you feel about your horse. Watson has him. He went on ahead to tell Alexandra to get a bed ready."

Toby groaned.

"And to reassure her that I'm not bringing home your corpse. Small thanks to Leclerc," he grumbled. "I can't believe the man would actually try to kill you."

"Isn't that supposed to be the object of a duel?" Toby muttered. His head felt light from the chloroform, and his whole chest hurt.

"In 1891 there aren't supposed to be duels among civilized men," Roosevelt said. "No one present this morning thought there was going to be any bloodshed. You and Leclerc are both far too good shots to hit someone by mistake."

"Leclerc's done it before," Toby said through gritted teeth. "And not by mistake." The world seemed to have become real and solid again.

"That wasn't how these proceedings were billed,"

Roosevelt said. "Not by Amberand anyway. And I'll swear he wasn't lying. He looked flat stunned." Theodore narrowed his eyes at Toby. "You didn't hit Leclerc in the hand by accident, either, did you? How did you know he was lying?"

"I didn't like his looks," Toby said. As an explanation, that held water like a colander and he knew it, but he wasn't about to admit that Martha had warned him.

Theodore snorted, but he didn't ask again for further explanations. It was obvious that the truth had already occurred to him.

The gates stood open at Toby's house, and the stableman came running to take the reins. The front door flew wide, and Alexandra ran down the steps, with the children behind her and Eulalia and Juanita following them.

Alexandra peered into the carriage, her eyes searching Toby's face. When she saw that he was pale but not dead, her green eyes flew to Roosevelt's.

"I'm grateful to you, Theodore," Alexandra said quietly.

"Be grateful to whoever warned him about Leclerc," Roosevelt said just as softly.

Her eyes flared. "I'm trying to."

There wasn't much you could hide from Alex, Toby thought, almost unbearably thankful to see her again and to feel her cool, soft hands on his arms as she and Theodore helped him from the carriage.

"Can you walk?" Theodore asked. "It would probably hurt more to carry you."

Between them, they got him up the stairs, while a white-faced Eulalia held the children back, pulling them to her with quiet, comforting words.

When they had gotten him undressed and into bed, Roosevelt picked up his hat and tipped it to Alexandra. "I'll pop in tomorrow. I'm going to go see what dire threats and cajolery I can offer the *Post* to exercise restraint over this."

"Thank you," Alexandra said.

Roosevelt grinned. "Well, they don't like me much. But deals can be done."

"He'll probably manage it, too," Toby said when Theodore had gone. "More than I deserve." He looked up at her wearily. "You're more than I deserve. Alex, I'm sorry for this."

"I am, too. And I'm sorry about yesterday." She sat gently on the edge of the bed. "I've never been so terrified in my life. When Watson rode up with your horse, I thought I had lost you." She shuddered, and her hands jerked in her lap in remembered fear. "Toby, I won't visit with Mr. Nakamura anymore if it truly bothers you."

Toby grinned weakly. "You go on and be friends with him." He held out his hand. "Now are you going to kiss me, or are you just waiting until I'm well so *you* can shoot me?"

She kissed him carefully. After a long while she said, "Can I send in the children? They both need to know you're all right. And so does your mother."

Toby nodded contritely. He felt desperately sorry for his mother, with worry over him to add to the loss of Lee. Sorry for all of them, in fact, except for himself. He figured he had had it coming. Stupidity had a way of catching up with people. "Send them all in," he whispered, suddenly wanting nothing more than to have his family around him, warm and comforting and infinitely more valuable than pride.

XIV

Toby never found out what "deal" it was that Theodore had made for his benefit, but Theodore Roosevelt was a rising star in Washington these days, and even though Frank Hatton of the *Post* didn't like him, there were excellent reasons to oblige a man who was becoming a valuable news source. The *Post* confined itself to a small paragraph at the bottom of page eight.

Janessa and Charley arrived on the evening train to be greeted with the news that the staid and respectable head of the family had been in a pistol duel and was now lying in his bed upstairs, greatly embarrassed by it all. The newlyweds ran up the stairs, and Janessa ordered her father so authoritatively to strip off his nightshirt that Toby didn't argue.

Janessa and Charley peered at him professionally. The shoulder was healing nicely with no sign of infection, but a bullet wound, she informed her father briskly, was nothing to fool around with.

Then Janessa shook her head. "Honestly, Dad, at your age!"

Toby narrowed his eyes at her. "I begin to think that there may be something in the notion that women should not be educated," he informed her.

"Hmmph!" Janessa said. "Now you watch what you eat while that's healing. No rich food."

Charley winked at her. "Oh, absolutely," he said solemnly. "Thin gruel, I should think."

Toby chuckled. "At your peril." He held out his

hands to them. "I'm glad you're here. A sad reason for a visit, but you look fat and sassy. Marriage agrees with you."

Janessa smiled. "It does."

The door bumped open, and Tim stood on the threshold. When he had been hugged by his sister and had shaken hands with his father and Charley, he said, "There are about eighty people downstairs. Aunt Claudia's arrived with Eden and Cathy. Rob and Kale are here. Andrew and Lydia and Sam and Annie are all staring at each other like gorgons. I hope some of them are sleeping at Henry and Aunt Cindy's house."

"I think Andy's taking Lydia to a hotel," Toby said.

"Dad, I want to talk to you about Lydia," Janessa said.

Toby groaned. "I suppose she's wearing a long black veil, and it all reminds her of the lamented Franz."

"No, Dad, listen," Janessa said. "I think there's something really wrong with Lydia."

Tim snorted. "I could have told you that."

Janessa gave him a squelching look, but he didn't appear to be squelched. "I mean more than just histrionics. She's as thin as a rail and looks ready to dissolve. If Andy doesn't do something, I don't know what's going to happen to her."

Toby looked at her, serious now. "Do you think she's really physically ill?"

Janessa glanced at Charley. "I think—we both do—that it's mental in origin. We know so little about diseases of the mind, but a mental illness can very definitely have a physical effect."

"Have you told Andy about this?"

Janessa bit her lip. "Do you think I ought to? You can tell he's worried to death just by looking at him, but he's been living with her for so long, he may not see it clearly. And I don't know how he'd accept it."

"Unburden yourself to Aunt Claudia," Tim suggested. "If ever there was a stout soul in a crisis, she's the one."

"I think Tim's right," Toby said.

Janessa looked relieved. "Oh, what a good idea." She bent and kissed her father. "You rest now. That horde of people can wait to see you until tomorrow."

"We'll have your gruel sent up," Charley said.

Lee Blake's funeral was postponed for two days to allow Toby's shoulder a chance to heal. Alexandra and Eulalia knew that he would attend, no matter what condition he was in.

To Claudia, the family gathering had a sad echo of that Easter visit nearly two years before at the Martins'. Lee's absence was a tangible hole in the fabric of the family. In some ways he almost seemed still to be here, in memory and in conversation. "Do you remember—?" the talk often began. Claudia worried that it might make Eulalia sadder, but instead she appeared to draw strength from it and from their shared love of Lee.

There were undercurrents, of course. Everyone was very interested in Annie, whom most of them had never met but of whom they had all heard a great deal. In spite of the continuing tension with Sam, Andy, and Lydia, Claudia thought that Annie was holding up remarkably well.

"Andrew won't see it, of course," Claudia said to Alexandra as they wrestled with the mountains of food sent from the kitchens of nearly everyone in Washington. "But to my mind, Annie is the best thing that could have happened to Sam. I only hope she doesn't get fed up enough with him to leave him before he realizes that."

"You mean divorce him?" Alexandra looked shocked. "Nobody in our family has ever gotten a divorce!" They all counted themselves as kin by right of their tangled connections by marriage.

Claudia opened the tin pie-safe looking for someplace to put an apple tart. Alexandra's cook was on the back porch plucking a chicken, and they kept their voices low. "Annie will do what she has to do. I just hope it doesn't come to that." Claudia shook her head sadly. "She's a breath of fresh air. Almost a gale-force wind, in fact."

"She hasn't said two words to me," Alexandra observed.

"She's waiting to be snubbed," Claudia said. "Once bitten, twice shy, I fear."

"Oh, poor thing." Alexandra was instantly sympathetic. "I'm going to get to know her." She inspected a covered dish. "Edith Roosevelt has sent a rhubarb pie. Oh, dear, no one will eat it. Everyone hates rhubarb."

"Serve it after the funeral," Claudia advised. "There will be more people here then; someone's bound to favor it."

"What a blessing you are," Alexandra murmured. "I'm so used to conferring with Eulalia about these practical matters."

"Well, bless you, too," Claudia responded warmly. "I only wish I could deal with Andy as easily as I can dispense with the rhubarb pie."

"Andy?"

"Janessa thinks that Lydia is seriously ill in her mind. Quite frankly, she has only confirmed what I've been wondering myself."

"Have you talked to Andy about it?"

"Only peripherally. This isn't the best time. But it has convinced me of one thing: I must keep Eden with me. Lydia hasn't even argued about that, which further confirms my fears, I'm afraid."

"Have you said anything to Eden?"

"Only that she is to stay with me awhile yet."

Eden's eyes gleamed ecstatically. "I'm going to stay with Gran," she whispered to Mike. "From now on, I think, though no one will say so."

"Don't try to make them say so," Mike advised, "or they may balk."

Eden nodded. After a few minutes' initial shyness, they had gravitated toward each other and were sitting in the little summerhouse at the end of the garden, soaking up the first spring sun. Mike was nearly fifteen now, even taller and leggier than he had been, and possessed of an urgent desire for his first pair of long pants, still more than a year away. Even so, Eden thought he looked very grown-up and was glad for the new longer skirts to her frocks.

Mike held out his palm shyly. Gold gleamed there. "I still have your locket," he said.

He leaned forward, and she leaned forward, too, and with an elaborate pretense at accident, his lips brushed hers.

Eden smiled when they sat back. "I have something else to tell you about." She had been saving it up, like a present. "I saw a moving picture!"

"Where? When? What was it like?" Mike stuffed the locket back in his pocket. "Tell me everything about it!"

Although Eden's reunion with her troubled parents had been brief and almost perfunctory, Cathy Martin and Peter Blake were unabashedly delighted at seeing their own parents and were recounting their adventures with such happiness that neither the Martins nor the Blakes could bring themselves to try to draw their offspring home again.

Cathy had edited her own tale somewhat, leaving out Eddie Gamble, but a new adulthood and solidity shone in her face.

"I think our bird has flown, dear," Rob said good-naturedly to Kale. If Cathy's passion for the theater had been going to wear off, as they had hoped, it would have by now. "And when may we expect to see you in a starring role?" he inquired, making himself sound cheerful about it. He might as well.

"Not for a long time, probably," Cathy said, realistic now. "But you will."

"You're nearly eighteen now, Peter," Henry Blake told his son. "When you're twenty-one you are going to have to go to Germany and discuss the future with your mother's trustees."

"When I'm twenty-one, I'll be ready to," Peter said, grinning. "And they had better look out."

Henry thought that they had indeed. He still felt a little at sea with Peter, but his son appeared self-assured, at ease with the dictates of his own nature, and exceedingly grown-up in a dark broadcloth suit, which he had purchased himself.

"Are you sure that this newspaper is where you want to stay?" Henry asked.

"Oh, not permanently," Peter said. "But it's good business experience. The trustees won't be able to say I haven't had business experience when I tackle them."

"I could still get you a commission in the army," he ventured hesitantly.

Peter shook his head. "I know how you feel, Dad, but no. I'd join in a minute if we were at war. But as a career, I can't see it. Maybe my mother's blood is too strong in me."

"Maybe." Henry smiled, remembering his first wife, for whom the term "iron-willed" might have been coined. "If that's it, maybe we won't try to fight it."

With the funeral postponed, the household was restless, alternating between tears that would seize them without warning and the fidgets of enforced confinement. Being stuck in any house for any period of time tended to make Tim pace. When the next morning's *Post* announced the exhibit of a German Benz carriage with an internal-combustion engine at the Smithsonian Institution, he found it a welcome outlet. He sought out Peter to go with him and discovered him in the garden with his parents.

"I don't think Grandpa Lee would have minded, sir," Tim said.

"No," Henry agreed, suffering another sharp stab of grief, thinking of his father. "In fact, I wish you would take the children with you. It might do them good."

"It would do *you* good," Peter said. "Come with us."

Henry hesitated, but Cindy put her arm through his and gave him a little push. "Let's," she urged. "Please? I feel so dreary. And you can't expect Tim and Peter to watch children. They'll get to looking at the engine and forget they've got the children with them."

Eden and Mike, who were reading Rudyard Kipling aloud to each other in the summerhouse, declined the invitation, which prompted Tim to raise an eyebrow, but the rest piled into Toby's town carriage. It was a tight squeeze, with Sally Holt and Midge Blake each positioned on an adult's lap, and Midge's brother Frank complained of having his sister's elbow in his ear. At the last minute, Cathy Martin joined them, too, climbing up on the driver's seat beside Tim. She had put on a black dress gown—all the closer relations were in mourning—but Tim decided that she looked surprisingly attractive in it . . . now that her parents had apparently decided to let her pursue a career in New York and not marry her off to him.

With that pitfall averted, he felt free to give compliments. "You look very elegant," he observed. "New York suits you."

"You haven't seen me in years," Cathy said. "I *hope* I've improved."

"Last time you had braids, and mud on your nose," Tim remarked. "Eden's growing up, too."

"She has an acute case of puppy love over your brother Mike," Cathy said.

"Horrors, they're precocious." Tim said, shuddering. "When I was Mike's age, all I wanted to do was study mechanics—the noisier and smellier the better. I had no time for girls."

Cathy gave him a bland look. "It doesn't look to me like you've changed much."

"I know more," Tim said darkly.

"Are you going to stay in Oklahoma? My mother says your newspaper is very successful."

"I'm going to stay until it's extremely successful," Tim said. "Then I'm going to buy a paper somewhere on the West Coast, settle in, and make it the biggest thing anybody ever saw."

"You know where you're going, don't you?" Cathy remarked. "I do, too—at least I hope so. Aren't you ever afraid you won't succeed?"

"All the time," Tim confessed. "If I don't, though, I'll die with my boots on."

Cathy laughed. "If you could bottle that attitude, you could get rich selling it."

Tim laughed, too. She was really very pretty, and there was more to her than he had thought.

Compared to the gleaming black Benz carriage parked in front of the Smithsonian Institution's red gothic spires, however, his momentary interest in this collateral cousin faded. The Benz was built very much like an ordinary phaeton except that it was so obviously designed to move without a horse. The engine, in fact, when cranked over, emitted a cloud of smoke and a rattle and clatter that would have sent any horse into hysterics and had much the same effect on Toby's team.

"I told you," Cindy murmured as Henry grabbed for the reins. "Tim and Peter have abandoned both horses and a carriageful of relatives to make a beeline for that monster."

The Benz carriage had been imported from Germany for the exhibit and was accompanied by a German engineer and his assistants, knowledgeable-looking men with linen dusters over their coats. Peter, who spoke fluent German, edged his way through the crowd and struck up a conversation with the engineer while Tim peered into the machine's inner workings, crawled under its carriage, and shouted occasional questions at Peter, who served as interpreter.

Tim's interest was mostly theoretical, stemming from his love of all things mechanical, particularly things that moved. He began to toy with the notion of trying to put one together himself. But Peter had a different gleam in his eye. Peter was talking cost and fuel consumption and patent rights with the chief engineer.

Cindy and Cathy each took a small girl by the hand

and stood at a respectful distance from the chugging and the smoke. Frank Blake wanted to know if anyone was allowed to ride in it. When told no, he looked downcast. Cindy, however, had no intention of allowing any child of hers to be involved with what she regarded as a very dangerous invention. Henry had his hands full keeping Toby's horses from kicking their own carriage to pieces in their desire to bolt.

"All right, folks, clear the way, and we'll give you a demonstration." An official of the Smithsonian waved a hand to move the crowd, most of whom stepped back with alacrity. One stout woman, who assured everyone that the carriage could travel of its own will in any direction, went up the institution steps, thus indicating that she considered the contraption capable of pursuing her even there.

The chief engineer climbed into the driver's seat and moved the steering levers. Slowly, the carriage began to lurch forward, belching smoke. It rolled down the Mall, with the assistant mechanics running before it to clear the way.

Peter watched it intently. "That is the future of transportation," he announced to his father. "In twenty years, every household in the country will own one."

At the far end of the Mall, a policeman's horse was trying to flee at the sight of the machine.

"Certainly," Henry said with asperity. "It will have frightened all the horses to death." He still kept a firm grip on Toby's team, calmer now as the Benz carriage retreated.

It turned and began to come back, then stopped with a sputter and a grinding of gears. The mechanics ran up to it.

"And killed half its owners," Henry added as a mechanic tried to crank the engine over and was sent sprawling in the dirt. The engine caught, and the mechanic rolled out of the way in the nick of time. Three small boys ran behind the carriage, cheering.

"It's going to revolutionize warfare," Peter predicted, looking for bait to hook his father.

"It will if you can arrange to equip the enemy with it," Henry said as the carriage chuffed and snorted its way back down the Mall. "That way we'll see them coming. I'll keep my faith in the cavalry and the railroad."

Now I know what I'm going to do with my money, Peter thought.

"If that thing is the future of the world, I don't want to be here for it," Cindy declared as they climbed into the carriages for the long, sad drive to Arlington the next morning.

"Too late," Toby said. He grinned at her, seizing the excuse to lighten the moment a little. "It's here. One of you is going to have to back down."

"Never," Cindy said. Then she sighed. "I feel ancient, Toby. I sound like old Mrs. Burkett, who's afraid the telephone is going to electrocute her."

"We're all getting on," Toby said, shifting uncomfortably against the cushion that Alexandra had propped behind him. "Some of us more than others," he added ruefully.

Henry and Cindy and their children had spent the night in town, so as to join the funeral cortege at Toby's house with the rest. The line of black carriages rolled down Connecticut Avenue toward the river and Arlington, behind the hearse with its flag-draped coffin. Lee Blake had been accorded full military honors, befitting a man who had served his country long and well. Born in 1804, he had been eight years old when America fought the War of 1812 and had joined the army at the earliest possible moment thereafter. He had fought with Andrew Jackson, escorted the first wagon train across the Rockies to Oregon, and commanded Fort Vancouver there. He had served the Union with distinction in the Civil War—a conflict whose wounds were only now beginning to heal. But Lee Blake had been such a man that there was no other man of honor, even on the losing side, who had truly wished him ill.

When he was laid to rest in Arlington Cemetery the president of the United States was among his mourners. Theodore Roosevelt was there, too, out of respect for the old man's reputation as much as his friendship with Toby. There were many others—senators, congressmen, and judges, officials and foreign ambassadors. Mr. Nakamura, in a snow-white kimono and hakama, made a startling contrast to the black-garbed Americans. White was the color of mourning in Japan, Alexandra told Eulalia, touched by the ambassador's show of formal respect.

And the army was there. Hundreds of soldiers in their dress uniforms—old men who had served with Lee in their youth, middle-aged men who had fought under his command, and young men who knew him only by reputation.

Oh, my dear, Eulalia thought. *So many people to say good-bye to you, but that doesn't make it easier.* Lee had lived so long. She knew he had been very tired, and it was time he rested. He had seen a greater sweep of history and change in the world than probably any man before him—the wars that had rocked a new country, the advent of the railroad and the telegraph, the first use of electricity, the centennial of the United States. A long, full life. Eulalia wiped her eyes. *But that doesn't make it easier.*

Claudia was at her elbow, and the two women mourned together. *We are almost the last,* Eulalia thought. Except for Rob Martin's parents in Portland, no one was left of that historic first wagon train. Claudia's sister, Cathy, and Whip Holt had been gone many years, as had Eulalia's brother, Claiborne, and his wife, who had farmed a land grant next to the Madrona Ranch that Eulalia had begun with Whip.

"So many gone," Eulalia said softly to Claudia. "So many gone."

Claudia put an arm around Eulalia's thin waist and the yards of black widow's veiling fluttering in the March wind. "We've made history," Claudia said stoutly, fighting back tears. She managed a crooked smile. "I intend to be reincarnated in the twentieth century and see what they have done with it." She nodded at the children, at Sally and Midge and Frank, and at Mike and Eden side by side. Eden solemnly comforted Mike. They were bereft now, but they were resilient, and they came from strong stock, people who had weathered the worst and made something enduring of it. *Maybe*, Claudia thought, watching Sam with Annie at his side, *I'll live long enough to see that come out in Sam. It must be in him somewhere.*

As the carriages began to roll out of Arlington again, it seemed to Alexandra that the echo of the last salute, fired by the army guard of honor, still reverberated in her ears, as solemn as a drumroll.

"I'm exhausted," she said to Cindy, sitting with Henry, opposite her, Toby, and Eulalia, in the first carriage. "This has been a sad and dreadful week. I don't know what other awful thing could possibly befall us, but I feel as nervous as if it were lurking on the top of the carriage."

Eulalia was lost in her own thoughts, but Cindy looked at Alexandra with worry. "That doesn't sound like you. I'm afraid I have let too much of the burden fall on you."

Alexandra tried to smile. "I expect I'm only tired."

"Grief is exhausting. You need to rest. We all do." Cindy reached across the carriage and took Alexandra's hand.

The steady motion of the carriage faltered, and they looked out, trying to see what was wrong. The procession was making its way through thin traffic that nevertheless came to a halt amid a jumble of carriages. Someone was screaming loudly, maniacally—it was impossible to tell if it was a man or a woman. Then, over the swelling of confused voices in the street, the screaming coalesced into a single word: *"Holt!"*

Toby struggled to get the carriage door open with his good arm, then climbed down and looked around him.

"Oh, my God."

The others pinpointed the man at the same time

Toby did. Leaning precariously from the rooftop arches of the Bureau of Engraving and Printing, a disheveled figure shook a bandaged fist at the street and clung with his other hand to a struggling woman. He jerked her closer to the roof's edge and wrapped his arm around her throat. They saw the flash of sunlight on a knife.

"It's Leclerc," Henry Blake said.

"I've been waiting for you, Holt!" Leclerc screamed. "I wanted you to watch!"

Below him windows were beginning to open and heads to lean out, craning upward.

"Watch what?" Toby shouted. "Come down from there, you fool!"

"You're responsible for this!" Leclerc tightened his grip on Martha. His voice rose and fell, shrieking and moaning. "My honor . . . lost, lost. You thought I didn't know . . . my wife sending secret messages to my enemies? You didn't think I loved her, did you?" The voice rose in an anguished howl, and he leaned forward again while Martha scrabbled frantically against the stone arch, trying to hold them both back. "I can die with honor, Holt! I can do that!"

"My God, he's going to jump!" People in the street began to scream, and someone was shouting for the police.

"He isn't going to wait until the police get here," Toby said. "We've got to get him down from there."

Henry Blake nodded and stripped off his coat. Toby did likewise, although gingerly, and found Tim blocking his way.

"You can't go up there in your condition, Dad," Tim said.

Toby glared at him, momentarily diverted from Leclerc. It was like scowling at himself—a younger self, admittedly. "He'll listen to me," Toby said, wriggling out of the rest of his coat.

"More likely he'll try to throw you off, too," Tim said. "I'll get him."

"I'll come with you," Peter volunteered.

"You stay put," Henry said to Peter.

Toby, accepting that the situation was partly his responsibility, and Henry, who was only forty-one, were not going to have their noses rubbed in middle age by their offspring. But whoever went up there was going to be in danger. Alexandra and Cindy stood by dubiously, knowing better than to interfere. Alexandra took Cindy's hand and clenched it.

"I'm not too old to whip *you*," Toby said to Tim. "Go find your sister and Charley and a medical kit for me."

"Set foot on that roof, and you go back to military school," Henry informed Peter.

They set off across the street at a run. Tim looked at Peter.

"If too many people go up there, I think Leclerc will jump," Tim murmured.

"Are we just going to stand here?" Peter demanded.

"Not exactly." Tim saw Janessa and Charley pushing their way through the crowd. "All right, they're found," he muttered grimly. "Let's go."

Toby and Henry strode through the halls of the Bureau of Engraving and Printing with a flutter of clerks at their heels.

"Where are the stairs to the roof?"

Someone pointed.

"How the devil did he get up there?"

"Tours," a clerk replied. "We give tours."

"To a man waving a knife?"

"There were a lot of people," the clerk protested. "I didn't see any knife."

Toby emitted an aggravated growl. Henry was halfway up the stairs, and Toby sprinted after him.

The stairs came out on the rooftop in the shadow of the bureau's tall, square tower. Leclerc had vanished. A whimpering cry from the tower sent them racing up those stairs, too. The tower, an architectural obelisk, had open, glassless arched apertures at its summit.

"Stay away!" Leclerc shrieked as he heard their

footsteps. He was crouched under the pointed roof of the tower, his arm still around Martha's throat.

"Toby, go away!" she yelled as he and Henry rounded the last curve. Leclerc dragged her closer to an open arch.

"Let her go," Toby said as calmly as he could manage.

"My honor. My wife," Leclerc grated, his eyes glittering madly. "You stole them both, Holt. But I can take them back!" He made a desperate gesture at Toby with his bandaged hand. "The doctors say I'll not fire a pistol with this hand again."

Toby thought Leclerc probably knew that that had been his intention. In the distance, he heard the clanging bell of a police wagon; they weren't going to be in time.

Henry heard it, too, and began to edge around the inner circumference of the tower while Leclerc's eyes were on Toby. Worse than not being in time to help, the bell was likely to provoke Leclerc into jumping. It was plain that he intended to take Martha with him.

"Let go of Martha," Toby said. "It's me you want."

"Go away," Martha said faintly.

Her green eyes were wide with fear and despair, Toby thought. Whatever the outcome, there was nothing left of her life with Lucien Leclerc to salvage. However, her own life could be saved.

"I never meant you harm," Toby said. "Let the past die, man, can't you?"

Leclerc's head swiveled, and Henry froze. "Stay away." His eyes turned back to Toby. "You are mistaken," he said thickly. "I don't want you. I want Martha."

"Not that way!" Toby screamed as Leclerc pulled her with him into a tiny balcony that projected from the tower arch.

Toby and Henry jumped Leclerc at the same time, flinging themselves across the remaining distance and wrestling frantically in the open archway. Forty feet below them, the flat rooftop spun dizzily as they hung halfway through the tower arch and over the low balcony wall.

Toby got his hands on Leclerc's knife hand and held on, setting all his weight against gravity and momentum as Leclerc tried to drag Toby through the opening with him and Martha. Henry smacked the back of his hand against Leclerc's bandaged one, distracting him just enough to haul Martha away and send her slamming against the opposite wall.

Leclerc wrenched his other hand free, and the knife sliced past Toby's face. As Leclerc overbalanced and slid through the arch, Toby felt himself losing his balance, too. The roof, far below, seemed to rise up to meet him as he scrabbled for some purchase on the balcony floor with the thin, slick soles of his dress shoes.

Henry flung himself at them again and grabbed Toby around the waist, momentarily stabilizing the combatants. Toby flailed with his fist and caught Leclerc in the jaw. The jolt knocked the knife from Leclerc's hand and sent it spinning down into the air. Toby, knowing that in another second he and Leclerc would go with it, felt Henry pulling at them both.

But Leclerc, intent on killing himself, kicked out, and his foot caught Henry in the chest, knocking him backward. Henry pulled himself up and watched in impotent horror as Toby and Leclerc teetered on the edge of the archway.

Footsteps pounded up the stairs, and Tim and Peter hurled themselves at Toby as Leclerc began to fall backward through the arch, with Toby holding onto him. For a moment the men seemed suspended between the sky and the slates of the roof below. Then Tim and Peter hauled the combatants onto the balcony floor. Tim grasped Leclerc by his flailing wrists, and Peter dragged Toby into the safety of the tower.

Leclerc toppled inward on top of Tim, writhing furiously. Tim, breathing hard, punched him in the jaw, rolled him over, and sat on him. Leclerc bucked and twisted under him until Peter sat on him, too, and then the man lapsed, glassy eyed, into a stream of incoherent French. Spittle ran from the corners of his mouth. Martha came forward and knelt by his side.

Toby found himself sitting with his back against the tower wall while Henry stood bent, his hands on his knees, drawing ragged breaths past the bruises in his chest caused by Leclerc's kick.

"I told you to stay down there," Toby said to Tim. "Who do you think you are, the cavalry?"

"That's us," Tim said, getting his own breath back. "To the rescue."

Toby looked down and saw that the bullet wound in his shoulder had opened up again and his shirt was thick with blood. "Well, I'm damn glad to see you," he muttered.

More footsteps came up the tower stairs, and Janessa and Charley appeared with a gaggle of clerks behind them. Janessa looked at Leclerc's glazed eyes and twitching body and took a small, dark vial out of her handbag. She bent over the man.

"What is in that?" Martha dragged herself from the floor and stared at Janessa.

"Laudanum," Janessa said, tipping the contents into his mouth. "I'm going to knock him out." She gave Martha a sympathetic look. "I've sent for an ambulance, which will take him home. But I wouldn't advise being alone with him when he comes around." He was unresisting now. Then she turned to look at Toby. "You're bleeding. You need that seen to."

Toby pulled a handkerchief from his pocket and pushed it under his shirt, wincing. "In a minute." He looked at Henry and Tim implacably. "Get him out of here."

Janessa looked ready to protest, but Charley took her by the arm.

"Come on." Charley's adamant glance took in Peter as well.

Janessa nodded. The men picked up Leclerc and carried him down the stairs, leaving Toby alone with Martha Leclerc.

Toby and Martha sat on the floor of the tower, facing each other. Martha's silk gown was ruined. Her hair hung in her eyes, and Toby noticed, for the first time, fine threads of silver along the temples and the hairline. That silver struck him as being unutterably sad. He couldn't imagine Martha with gray hair. He looked at the floor and saw spatters of his own blood on the ocher tiles.

"What will you do now?" he asked her finally.

"Go home with him, of course," Martha answered.

"Go home with a man who tried to murder you? Why did you come here with him?"

"I had no choice. If I had resisted, he would have killed me at home and then shot himself. I thought that if I stalled for time, he would change his mind before he actually killed me. When I saw that he wouldn't, it was too late. He found out I had warned you. Odd, isn't it? I never thought Lucien loved me, but it seems he does."

"Do you want that kind of love?" Toby asked.

Martha didn't answer.

"It's a high price for a social position, isn't it?" Toby asked grimly. There wouldn't be much left of that position now, even if Leclerc did recover his wits.

"I believe in abiding by my decisions—even if they may be mistakes." Martha's eyes, miserable and defiant, caught his just for a moment, and Toby knew that one of those mistakes had been in not marrying him when she could have. From Martha's point of view, at least. He realized, sadly, that he was appallingly grateful that she hadn't.

He stood up. "Come on," he said quietly. "I'll take you down."

"I think if you could possibly manage it, sir, you ought to stay off rooftops until this heals," Charley said, retaping the bandage on Toby's shoulder while Janessa collected the old bandages in a basin.

"I'll work on that," Toby said. "It's not a habit of mine."

"I don't think you've done yourself any permanent damage," Charley continued, "but—"

"If you say 'at my age,' " Toby warned, "I'll get out of bed and strangle you."

Eulalia peeked into the room. "Your clerk is here to see you, dear."

Toby beckoned, and Eulalia ushered Watson in, preceded by a gigantic basket of hothouse flowers.

"Glad to see you looking chipper," Watson said. "Everyone's talking about it. The betting's running two to one that Leclerc's never going to be right in the head again. His wife's taking him home to New Orleans tonight."

Toby thought about Leclerc, who would now spend his days watched and guarded by his family, a prisoner of the demons in his own mind . . . and of Martha going home with him to "abide by her decision." He stared at the flowers. "Get those out of here," he ordered. "Send them to Leclerc."

Claudia pressed Janessa's hand as they boarded the New York train at the Baltimore & Ohio station on New Jersey Avenue below the Capitol. Janessa and Charley, who were between assignments for the Marine Hospital Service, were traveling back to New York, to the headquarters hospital on Staten Island, with Claudia, Sam and Annie, Cathy, and Eden.

"I spoke to Andrew," Claudia told Janessa. "After seeing that poor madman yesterday, I felt I must. Andrew didn't take it very well, but I think he'll try to get Lydia to some sort of doctor who understands these maladies. I wanted to tell you before we settled in." She glanced apprehensively down the aisle at Eden. "I don't want Eden to know."

Eden was hanging out the window, waving at Mike, who stood on the platform. Janessa nodded. "I think that's best for now."

As the train pulled out, another slipped by them headed in the opposite direction, and Tim and Peter leaned out their own window to wave. Eulalia, Alexandra, Cindy, and the smaller children waved back.

"How's Uncle Toby?" Peter asked as their train sped out of the station.

"Crotchety." Tim laughed.

"It doesn't seem right," Peter said doubtfully. "All this happening in the middle of Grandpa's funeral. It's as if, well, he didn't matter."

"Life goes on," Tim said. "In a weird way, I think the crisis with Leclerc helped to cushion the shock."

"I wish that Grandpa could have seen that motorcar," Peter said suddenly. "Dad thinks it's a flash in the pan, but Grandpa would have loved it. He just missed it." He was silent for a moment. "Do you think Grandpa still knows everything that's going on?"

"I'm sure of it," Tim answered. He wasn't sure of it; how on earth could anyone know anything when all the important things seemed to boil down to a matter of faith? But Peter looked comforted by Tim's certainty. So he didn't retract it.

XV

Guthrie, Oklahoma, March 1891

Rowell Basham looked through the lighted window of Rosebay's house at his sister-in-law. She was taking a bath. The shade wasn't quite pulled, and he could see her standing over the washtub by the kitchen stove, sponging the soapy water down her legs. The firelight flickered on her wet skin. He couldn't see all of her—just her legs—unless she bent down. He crouched for a better angle.

She ought to marry him. Then he could look at her whenever he wanted to. And he'd have a house and some land, too. Since the selling of whiskey had been made legal, the price of bootleg liquor had dropped, and the price of free-lance preaching wasn't up any, either, what with a new church being built every day.

I ought to have this house, Rowell thought. Rosebay bent down again, the yellow light rippling along her arms and swaying breasts. *And I ought to have her*. She was saving it for Tim Holt, he thought venomously. But Holt was out of town. Rowell felt let loose by that, freed of the nagging fear that Holt might be a better man. *That prideful woman needs a lesson*, he thought, watching Rosebay step away from the washtub and the white folds of a nightgown drop down around her bare feet.

There wasn't any use knocking; she wouldn't let him in—not at this hour, not when she was all alone—since he'd taken to scaring her in the barn in the mornings when he thought she needed it. Rowell took off his battered slouch hat, put it over his hand, and punched out the window glass.

Rosebay spun around at the sound, but he was through the window before she could run. He grabbed her, trying to rip the nightgown loose from her neck. Her skin was still damp from the bath, and she felt cool to his touch, hair showering a mist of water into his face as she struggled with him.

She screamed once and then fought him silently, saving her breath to lend her strength. This far out of town there was no one to hear her.

"Rowell, no! Please!" The nightgown ripped down the front, and he pushed her down on the floor, feeling under the cloth.

Rosebay writhed beneath him, terrified.

"Gonna teach you who you belong to," Rowell grunted.

"No!" His touch sent her into a thrashing frenzy. They rolled on the floor, into the searing heat of the potbellied stove and the open hearth beside it, knocking over a broom and shovel. Rowell dragged her backward and pinned her to the floor, his hand pressed to her throat.

Rowell fumbled with the buttons of his trousers and released Rosebay for a moment. She leaned her head forward and sank her teeth into his shoulder. He howled and lashed out at her, and as he moved off her just a little she got one knee up and jabbed it into his groin, but not hard enough to disable him. The pain only made him rock backward. But as he raised his arm to hit her, she twisted from under him, scrambled to her feet, and made a frantic grab for the shovel.

When he came after her again, Rosebay swung the shovel in terror and desperation. The flat of the blade caught him on the side of the head, and he dropped. She raised it to hit him again, but he began to crawl away. She ran for the parlor door, snatched up the rifle from the wall, and pointed it at him, shaking.

"Get out, Rowell. Don't come back. Not ever. I'll kill you next time, I swear."

Rowell pulled himself up by the kitchen doorjamb. Blood was running down his temple. "You're gonna burn in hell, Rosebay," he threatened.

In the morning, with her skin still crawling because Rowell had touched her, she swallowed her pride and told Hugo and Wally what had happened. It was almost more than she could bear.

"I don't want you to tell anyone else," she whispered. "Folks always think the woman started it. Marshal Landrum would. But I'm too scared to stay alone out here anymore. I thought there might be someone I could hire."

"Hire, hell," Wally protested. "We'll fix that bastard. I'll fix Landrum, too, if I have to. This has gone too far."

Hugo got up grimly. "I want you to stay in town today," he told Rosebay.

"But I got to cook!"

"Not today, you don't. I'm going to take you to Sid Hallam's, and you sit there until we find Rowell and I come to get you."

Something in Hugo's face looked different to her—a decisiveness she hadn't seen in it before. But she didn't know what he thought he could do. "I'm not going to tell Sid," she said, quailing because Sid's livery was next door to Tim's newspaper. At least Tim wasn't in town.

"All right, I understand," Hugo said gently. "But you're misjudging Sid."

"I ain't misjudging people," Rosebay said. "Rowell's a preacher. If it gets out, he'll act pious and blacken me."

"We'll just say somebody, not Rowell, tried to break in," Hugo suggested. "And when we find Rowell, if Landrum doesn't act, I'll drag Rowell to the governor if I have to. Why the devil didn't you tell me what he was doing?" Hugo looked hurt and bewildered. "This has been going on for six months!"

Rosebay looked at her feet. "It didn't seem right to get you into it," she whispered.

"You thought I might want to collect on the favor? Well, I'm no Rowell Basham!" Hugo snapped. "Now let's go. I'm taking you to Sid's for the day."

It was nearly nine o'clock when Rowell stopped outside Rosebay's house in the shadow of the porch. No lights showed inside. The broken window had a piece of board nailed up over it. There was no way to tell if she was inside.

Her dinner customers would have come and gone. Rowell had known better than to get near while they were around. He had been hiding in the woods by his still all day, just waiting.

Rowell gripped the can of kerosene tightly. This time it would do its job: burn her in the flame for going against him, when she should have come to him after Wedge died. She had no business going to some other man—no business living here alone, either. Rowell poured the kerosene around the porch. He went to the back door and soaked that, too, and all the window ledges. If she was inside, she'd burn in the flames of hell. Rowell lit a match. He wasn't doing this to her. She had done it to herself.

He watched the flames blaze up like a bonfire, then, satisfied, went to crouch in a ditch by the road and watch the fire. He drew out his thin silver knife in case Rosebay did manage to escape.

Hugo, bone tired and frustrated, headed back toward Sid Hallam's after a day of looking for Rowell Basham. He reined his horse tightly when the fire engines rumbled out of their shed and turned in his direction.

"It's Mrs. Basham's house!" someone shouted in the gathering crowd.

"Rosebay!" Hugo wrenched open the door to Hallam's office, where he had deposited her that morning. She wasn't inside. Sid came in on Hugo's heels, carrying a basket.

Hugo turned on him. "Where is she? What do you mean leaving her alone?"

"I just went out to get us some supper," Sid said. "She was here when I left. Jesus! That's not—?"

"Oh, God, *Rosebay!*" Hugo ran outside, flung himself on his horse, and yanked the animal's head around toward the distant flames.

When the night train from St. Louis steamed into the Guthrie depot, the first fire engine was racing past, bells clanging, the firemen clinging to its sides. Tim, with a newsman's affinity for disaster, sniffed the air and looked south where an orange glow spread across the prairie sky.

"Fire," Peter said. "A big one."

Tim shoved his carpetbag at Peter. "Find our trunks. I'm going to see what's happening."

Tim grabbed on to a fire engine as it went by, so the men had to pull him up. "Are you crazy?" a fireman asked. "Oh, it's you, Mr. Holt. Well, what the hell do you think you're doing? You trying to get killed?"

"Got to get there," Tim panted. "Don't happen to have a horse." By now he guessed whose house it was, and fear for Rosebay clawed at him.

Rosebay ran frantically through the darkness that lay beyond the streetlights. Her breath was coming in gasps, and her ribs ached. She hadn't stopped to saddle her horse, which was loose in Sid's corral; panicked, she just started running. She knew exactly where the house she had labored so long to build stood on the prairie skyline. Panic drove her on until she could almost feel the searing flames devouring everything she owned. She knew who had set the fire, too, and a vengeful fury nearly as hot as the flames went through her. *I should have shot him where he stood and taken my chances with the marshal.*

Another fire engine went past at a headlong gallop. "Stop!" she screamed. "Oh, please stop! That's my house!"

But the engine company didn't even hear her against the rumbling of the wheels and the clanging of the bell. They hurtled on, leaving her in darkness. She gathered up her skirts and ran after the engine. Her mule and cow were in the barn . . . her guitar that she had scrimped so long for . . . her garden and the put-up vegetables in the cellar . . .

The house was still a quarter mile away. She heard another drumming of hoofbeats behind her, but she didn't bother to look back.

When the engine Tim was riding pulled up outside the flaming building, the first crew had already run its hoses to the creek. The house was engulfed in a sheet of fire.

"Where's Rosebay?" Tim yelled. "Anybody seen Rosebay?"

Wally Newsome emerged from the smoke, as black as a miner and coughing. "She's in town. Been in town all day. But her stock's in the barn."

"Come on!" Tying a handkerchief around his mouth and nose, Tim headed for the barn with Wally. The fire that had claimed his half-built office two years earlier crackled in his mind's eye. He had gone into that one for Peter, and some men might say a cow and a mule weren't worth it, but he could hear their terrified screams. He couldn't leave them to burn.

Between them, Tim and Wally got the barn door open. Thick smoke billowed out. Tim scooped water from the trough outside with his hat and poured it over his head. Choking, he pushed his way inside and began to wrestle with the bars on the cow's stall. She lowed in panic, her eyes bright with the orange glow of the flames.

"Come on, Bossy." Tim choked. Flames were licking at the door frame, and the animal wouldn't budge. Tim found a milk bucket and clanged it against her rump, and she lurched through, galloping into the chaos outside. Tim followed her and took deep breaths of cold air. It was laden with ash, and he choked again. From inside the barn, he could hear the mule's braying and the thud and clatter of kicking hooves. After taking another breath, Tim plunged back inside.

Wally was hanging from the mule's halter as the plunging animal reared and twisted. A section of the roof above them dropped a flaming beam across the mule's back, and Wally fell under the thrashing hooves. Tim pulled the handkerchief from his mouth and got it around the mule's eyes, trying to shield Wally with his body from the iron-shod hooves. He could feel cinders in his hair and smell singed flesh. The mule quieted as the flames disappeared from its view. Tim kept a hand on the mule's halter and pulled Wally to his feet. Wally fell again to lie limply against the side of the stall.

"Damn it, don't die on me now!" Tim dragged Wally to him, got one arm under the man's shoulder, and hauled him and the mule both toward the door. Once out of the stall, he set the mule's nose to the doorway and hit him with the milk pail, too. The mule shot out of the barn in a shower of sparks. Tim picked up Wally and ran as the barn roof crashed down behind them.

When Rosebay stumbled into the yard, the barn was a pile of blackened cinders, and the engine company was pouring water on the flames that had spread to the grass around it. The house was a pyre, and ash rained down around her. In the glow she could see flames licking along the edge of her garden, lighting her apple trees until their flowers looked like blossoming fire. Anguished, Rosebay searched for something to wet them down with and found a milk pail on the scorched ground. She snatched it up, filled it at the trough, and ran for the trees.

Hugo slid from his horse. His eyes searched through the hellish light, where shadows leaped and fell with the flames. He saw Tim Holt, fanning his hat over Wally Newsome, who lay choking and gagging.

"Have you seen Rosebay?"

"No! I thought she was in town!"

Hugo ran on. Beyond the light of the burning house and the muddle of firemen and hose, he thought he saw a flicker of white among the little apple trees. He started to shout, but then he saw a dark shadow that slid from the woods at the edge of the orchard, coming between them, stalking Rosebay.

It was Rowell. Firelight ran like blood along the knife in his upraised hand. He had his back to Hugo and was no more than five feet from Rosebay. Hugo pulled his pistol from his pocket and fired a single shot. Rowell pitched forward.

No one had heard; the shouting firemen and the cracking of burning timber were too loud. Rosebay moved away unknowing, to pour the last desperate ounces of water on her trees, while Hugo, white-faced, turned and slipped into the line of men who were trying, with buckets and shovels, to halt the advancing fire line.

The house and barn were gone. Hugo, with Tim, Wally, and Peter Blake—who had saddled his horse and ridden after them—battled the fire in the grass and the dry leaves of the woods until it, too, was dead. Rosebay fought it with them. Everything she owned was gone, but she was grimly determined that the fire shouldn't spread to anybody else's land. When it was out, they stood in the harsh moonlight, leaning on shovels or against the fire engines. The engines were still now, their hoses coiling uselessly into the creek. The mule and cow were God knew where. Rosebay looked at the blackened faces around her. Everyone's eyes were streaming. Tim had a red weal across his forehead, and his traveling clothes were in shreds. Hugo's chest was blistered raw, and she could tell his hands were burned too, by the way he held them.

"I want to thank you," she said. "All of you." She looked at the grimy firemen. They were volunteers. Nobody paid them for this.

"How did this start?" Hodge Landrum demanded.

His face was blackened too, and he looked at her accusingly.

"I wasn't here," Rosebay said wearily.

"Rowell Basham set it, that's how it started," Hugo said.

"You got proof?" the marshal demanded.

Tim looked at Hugo. "What the devil happened? I just got in."

Hugo shook his head. "You'll have to ask Rosebay."

"You might as well tell him," Rosebay said dully.

As Hugo gave Tim and the marshal a terse account of the day, a shout sounded from one of the firemen standing amid the apple trees.

"Marshal!"

They followed Landrum as he strode through the ashes and knelt over Rowell Basham's body.

"There's justice," someone said. "You reckon the fire got him, Marshal?"

"I reckon it didn't," Landrum answered in a low voice. The moon was bright enough to see the hole in Rowell's back. "You take the law into your own hands, Mrs. Basham?" Landrum asked evenly, but his face was hard.

"No!" Rosebay put her hands to her mouth.

"You own a gun, Mrs. Basham?"

"I didn't shoot him, Marshal."

Landrum stood up, looming over her. "You want to tell me who had better reason? He was shot in the back." Landrum spat. "That's a woman's way with a gun. That's the way they do it back in your mountains, too, isn't it?"

"Now just a minute, Hodge," Tim said.

"You butt out. I'm talking to Mrs. Basham."

Rosebay began to tremble.

"I did see her out by these trees," one of the firemen said slowly.

"I was putting water on them!" Rosebay cried.

"I kind of thought I saw a *man* with a gun, back earlier," another offered dubiously.

"You 'kind of thought'?" Landrum's voice held elaborate sarcasm.

"I didn't look close. We were fighting a fire, Marshal."

"Well, *I* kind of think that isn't evidence. Mrs. Basham, I want you to come along with me."

Tim stepped between Landrum and Rosebay. "You haven't got any evidence, either. How the hell do you know what went on in the middle of that fire?"

"I know a man got shot," Landrum said. "And I know who's going to stand trial for it."

"I didn't!" Rosebay cried. She looked at Landrum with terror-stricken eyes.

"There *was* a man with a gun," Hugo Ware said quietly. His expression impassive, he stepped forward. He didn't look at anyone but Hodge Landrum. "You let her go. I shot him."

Landrum and everyone else stared at him.

"Basham had a knife," Hugo continued calmly. "He was right behind Rosebay with it. He was crazy."

Rosebay moaned and staggered slightly. Tim caught and held her around her waist.

"Where's the gun?" Landrum demanded.

"I threw it in the fire," Hugo said. "I thought maybe I could get away with it. It never occurred to me you'd be fool enough to suspect Rosebay."

"Here's the knife, though." A fireman straightened up from beside Rowell's body. "Looks like that was true."

"Or he drew it to defend himself," Landrum said. "Only I reckon he didn't get much chance." He looked at Hugo with disgust. "Was he already running when you shot him in the back? Or did you just sneak up on him?"

"I already told you," Hugo said. He held out his hands for Landrum's handcuffs, with no motion to defend himself.

"Hodge, you might at least listen to him," Tim protested, furious. "Basham set this fire. Would you put it past him to try to kill her when he found out the fire hadn't done it?"

"She's alive, isn't she?" Landrum retorted. "And he's dead." He pointed at Rowell.

"Hugo!" Rosebay cried as Landrum marched him away.

Hugo's shoulders flinched, but he didn't look back. The others looked after him, stunned. The last embers of the fire settled with a sound like a sigh in the cold night wind. Whatever Rowell Basham had been or had done was negated now by the fact that he was dead, that someone had committed murder. There wasn't any other word for it.

"What will they do to him?" Rosebay sat huddled in a blanket on Tim's bed in the apartment above the newspaper office. Tim had moved his things in with Peter's, but he was afraid to leave her alone.

"They'll try him, honey," Tim said. "We'll get him a good lawyer."

"Can the lawyer prove he didn't shoot Rowell?" Rosebay whispered.

"Not if he stands by his confession," Tim said reluctantly. "And I don't think he's going to take it back. I don't think he can if he wants to." Landrum wasn't going to turn Hugo loose even if he recanted. And Hugo wouldn't recant because the only other suspect was Rosebay. "At least Hugo knows he really did it." Tim took her hand. *He must really love you,* he thought. "If Hugo hadn't come forward, it would be you in that jail."

Rosebay's hands flew to her face. "Maybe it ought to be. It was my fault!"

"No, it wasn't," Tim said. "Don't torment yourself with that. We're going to do everything we can."

He made her lie down. He had given her one of his nightshirts to wear, and she looked tiny and child-like in it. He pulled the blankets up around her, then left. But that night he didn't sleep much, and he was certain that she didn't, either.

*   *   *

In the morning Tim put the *Prairie Recorder's* voice to work, as loudly as he could, listing Rowell Basham's sins. Then he took Ben Abbott, reputed to be the best lawyer in town, to see Hugo.

Hugo was in a cell at the back of the jail. His face looked blank, as if he had shuttered himself against the world. His fair skin was still blistered from the fire, but Tim saw with relief that Landrum had sent for a doctor to bandage his hands and chest. Hugo was wearing clean clothes. Landrum was a stiff-necked moron, but at least he wasn't sadistic.

"How is Rosebay?" Hugo asked.

"Pretty upset," Tim said.

"You try to distract her, will you?" Hugo requested. "And if they hang me, I want you to get her out of town before it happens."

"It's not going to come to that."

"Damn it, Holt, pay attention! And don't you bring her here to see me."

"You know she won't stay away," Tim said. "There's more to Rosebay than that." *And a lot more to you than most people thought*, he decided, looking at Hugo's determined face.

"It's too soon to be talking about a hanging," Abbott said with professional cheerfulness. "Holt's filled me in on last night, but I want to go over it carefully with you. Since you admit you shot Basham, it's not a jury we've got to sway here; it's the judge. Now you say that Basham pulled a knife on the woman?"

"I say it." Hugo leaned back on the cot in his cell and stared at the wall. "But she can't. Rosebay never saw it."

Abbott wasn't ready to talk about a hanging yet, but everyone else in town was. Landrum looked up from his desk as Tim passed by him, having left Abbott with Hugo.

"I told you to stay away from that woman," he observed. "She's vermin, and she attracts vermin."

Tim spun around, his hands clenching into fists in spite of himself. "Rosebay told me that she asked you to keep Rowell Basham off her back months ago, and you wouldn't do it. Now whose fault does that make this?"

"The fault of the man with the gun. Don't you push me, Holt. Guthrie's a territorial capital, not some loose-living frontier town. People who can't uphold the law don't belong here."

"And what would the law do if Hugo Ware hadn't shot Rowell Basham and Basham had killed his sister-in-law?" Tim leaned over Landrum's desk, wanting to punch him.

"Then I'd hang Rowell Basham, with pleasure. But he didn't. He got a bullet in his back because someone else went outside the law, and now I'm going to hang the other party."

"And if the law had done its job six months ago instead of mouthing a lot of sanctimonious platitudes," Tim snarled, "it wouldn't have come to this. I hope you can sleep at night, Landrum!"

Landrum's mouth snapped closed, and he stared at Tim icily until Tim stalked out.

On the sidewalk, Mrs. Bennett from the milliner's shop rushed past, intent on the latest news.

"Have you heard?" Her eyes were round and shocked. "They're saying at the post office he shot him down in cold blood. Jealousy, I expect." She nodded briskly. "That's what everyone's saying, how they both wanted to marry her. And that poor dead man a preacher, too!" She hurried on.

Tim stared after her, defeated. Rowell Basham had been about as saintly as Beelzebub, but that wasn't going to count now. He began to pace down the street, trying to think of something that would help Hugo.

Wally Newsome and Sid Hallam and the others who knew Rowell were more sympathetic, but their opinion wasn't going to count for much, either. Nobody's was except Hodge Landrum's and the judge's.

The judge was a crony of Abel Dormer's, and as such he wasn't going to have anything to say to Tim Holt.

While Tim was snarling over that, Dormer himself sauntered by, fat and pleased with himself, as if a good splashy murder case with a hanging to end it proved that Guthrie was an up-and-coming town where justice was sure and the righteous could safely settle.

Dormer had the noon edition of the *Recorder* under his arm, and he smirked at Tim. "This won't get you anywhere, Holt." He passed on through the doors of the Yellow Rose, where he could be heard informing the clientele that it was just as he had always maintained: The *Recorder* was soft on criminals, preferring instead to harass innocent and upstanding citizens.

"Got your mind made up already, Mayor?" Tim heard the bartender ask.

"Justice will be done," Dormer replied with satisfaction.

When at length Tim came back to the jail, heavy with hopelessness and fury, he met Abbott coming out. Out of the prisoner's sight, Abbott had abandoned his optimism. "I'll do my best, but they're going to hang him."

XVI

New York City, March 1891

On her return to New York, Cathy Martin received an invitation to visit from Cornelia McLeod. The missive was so incoherent and tearstained as to be almost illegible.

"It looks as if that harpy has done it," Claudia said, reading over Cathy's shoulder.

"May I call on her?"

"Most certainly," Claudia responded. "In fact, I'll go with you."

But when the two of them arrived at Mrs. McLeod's imposing city residence on Madison Avenue, they were informed by the butler that Miss McLeod was "not at home" to visitors. Madam would receive them in the drawing room, however.

Since there was no way out of that, they spent the requisite fifteen minutes allotted to a formal call drinking tea with Mrs. McLeod and making noises of forced politeness when she informed them that dear Cornelia had not been well—so much excitement and too many late nights. But she would be herself again soon, and Mrs. McLeod confidently expected a wonderful announcement to be made shortly.

Cathy and Claudia fled in disgust. At the Waldorf, Claudia didn't even bother taking off her hat before she telephoned Howard Locke, who always knew everything.

The gentleman said he was charmed at an excuse to see Claudia, escorted her and Cathy to the park, and explained what had been the talk of New York society for the past four days.

"She has that child under lock and key, doesn't she?" Claudia asked.

Locke nodded. "She does. Of course nobody wants to admit knowing about it; it would make it very awkward to go to the wedding."

"She's not going to marry that man?" Cathy wailed.

"I'm afraid she is," Locke answered. "Cornelia hasn't the strength of the ladies of your family. And certainly her mother hasn't the character." He made a gallant bow to Claudia. "You see, young Paul Crawford was sent away by his family—everyone knows that now."

"Cornelia thought he didn't care for her anymore," Cathy told him. "You mean her mother arranged that?"

"She did indeed. She has business dealings with the Crawfords, in which she has the upper hand. It wouldn't have been difficult—just a genteel combination of threats and bribery. When Cornelia found out, she had a terrible row with her mother in public and hasn't been seen since. I imagine that you'll receive a wedding invitation before long."

Two days later Cathy received an invitation to be a bridesmaid. Mrs. McLeod had won and launched Cornelia and Robert, the duke of Manes, into an endless round of teas and luncheon parties. Cornelia walked through them as if she were a mannequin.

Weeks later, at the rehearsal dinner, the best man stood up to toast "a lifetime of happiness," and the bridal couple looked at him with eyes that might have been carved out of wood. When he had finished, the duke took a photograph from his pocket, tore it into a myriad tiny pieces under the table, and left them scattered on the floor.

"It was a picture of a young woman," Cornelia said desolately to Cathy a few minutes later as the wedding party began to move into the ballroom. "I saw it."

"You mean he's lost someone, too?"

"I think so. My God, what's going to become of us?" Cornelia looked at her bridegroom with sadness.

"You can still refuse to go through with it," Cathy hissed.

Cornelia shook her head. "It's too late. For both of us." She glanced at the doorway, and her eyes flashed. "Well! It's about time. It's my brother, Edward. I thought he wasn't even going to bother to come!"

Cathy looked up and recoiled in sheer horror. "Brother Edward" was Eddie Gamble.

Cathy managed to survive the introduction without fainting or otherwise disgracing herself. Eddie looked at her, startled, then slyly and secretively.

"Actually, he's my half brother," Cornelia said. "Mother has been widowed twice."

"Come and dance with me, Miss . . . Martin," Eddie invited.

She could not gracefully refuse. They circled the ballroom while Eddie grinned at her viciously. "I've been wanting to meet you again."

"I should think you'd be ashamed to!" Cathy hissed at him.

"Me, ashamed? That's rich. Fancy finding little Miss Salton the chorus girl in my sister's wedding party."

"I told you my name wasn't Salton! You wouldn't listen."

"Easy is as easy does." Eddie licked his lips. "You still owe me, too. Double now, I'd say." His arm tightened around her waist. "Why don't we just slip out of here? If you make it up to me nicely, maybe I won't tell on you."

The music ended, and Cathy detached herself from him with as much speed as she could. "Stay away from me!"

Eddie grinned.

Someone else asked her to dance, and she found herself in the duke of Manes's stately and protective arm. *Well, thank goodness,* she thought. Eddie wouldn't annoy the duke, because that would annoy Eddie's mother, who held the purse strings.

"You appear to be preoccupied, Miss Martin," the duke murmured. "Or is it only loathing for my person?"

Cathy's eyes flew up to his and saw a kind of weary humor in them. "Not at all, Your Grace," she said. "I'm only minding my steps." Eddie leered at her over the duke's shoulder. She had to fend him off only until after tomorrow's wedding, she thought. With Cornelia in England, Cathy didn't care if she ever saw the McLeods again.

In the morning while Sam and Annie were dressing for the wedding, Cathy managed to catch her aunt alone and announce her discovery about Eddie Gamble.

Claudia sniffed. "You did just as you ought," she approved. "You'll continue to ignore him, and with any luck that will make him feel very small indeed."

"Sam didn't see him last night," Cathy said. "But he's bound to today."

"You may leave Sam to me."

"Aunt Claudia . . ." Cathy twisted her new white elbow-length gloves between her fingers. "Is everything I ever do going to come back to haunt me like this?"

Claudia's imperious expression faded, and she laughed. "Probably!" she said at last.

Cornelia McLeod became the duchess of Manes in St. Thomas's Episcopal Church on Fifth Avenue. A thirty-piece orchestra drowned out the bride's sobs as she went up the aisle.

Cornelia, nearly as white as her gown and thin to the point of emaciation, murmured her responses in a barely audible whisper. The duke held up somewhat better. He, at least, had been coerced only by circumstances and had had fifteen years more of life to learn how to bear his burdens.

The reception was held in the ballroom of Mrs. McLeod's Madison Avenue mansion, where the mother of the bride complacently accepted congratulations upon having captured a title for her daughter. By nearly anyone's definition she had scored a victory, regardless of the tactics she had used.

Claudia Brentwood did not congratulate her; nor did she let her friend Mrs. Meigs do so, either. "Why didn't she simply have him stuffed and put in the hall?" Claudia asked icily. "It would have served the same purpose."

The cake was cut, the ritual wedding waltz was danced, and Cornelia retired to change into her going-away costume. Cathy had very little opportunity to speak to her, with Mrs. McLeod's hovering about them. The girl looked utterly terrified. In a moment she would be alone in a carriage with her husband, a stranger.

I'll bet her mother hasn't even told her anything, thought Cathy, who had grown up on a farm and knew something more about the relations between the sexes, in theory at least, than city girls.

Cornelia descended the stairs, threw her bouquet with an aimlessness that landed it at her mother's feet instead of among the bridesmaids, and embraced Cathy with a shuddering hug. "Write to me, *please!*"

"Of course I will." At length Cornelia had to let her go and allow her husband to lead her down the steps in a shower of rice. An enormous crowd of gawk-ers stood on the sidewalk, pressed against the iron railings in front of the house, with three city policemen trying to keep them back. Cathy turned away from the door. She didn't want to see Cornelia drive away.

A hand caught her arm. "I don't know that I want you writing to my sister," Eddie Gamble said, pulling her back toward the ballroom. "Maybe I ought to tell my mother what you're really like."

Furious, Cathy tried to jerk her hand away, but Eddie tightened his grip. She looked around for help, but everyone else was watching the newlyweds depart in their carriage.

"I don't care what you tell your mother!" Cathy retorted.

"You'll care," Eddie threatened, pulling her closer. "Because if you don't take care of me, I'll tell everyone about how I found you singing in a cheap music hall and how you slept with both me and the manager to get the job. Then just see how many society parties you get invited to." He leaned his face toward hers, ugly and threatening.

Cathy stamped down hard on his instep with her high-heeled shoe, and Eddie yelped. He jerked her arm roughly, and Cathy drew back her other fist and hit him as hard as she could.

"Why, you little bitch!"

Their scuffle began to attract notice. The carriage had gone, and the wedding guests were diverted by the sight of one of the bridesmaids and the bride's brother wrestling in the ballroom doorway.

Cathy saw Sam hand his top hat to Annie and stalk toward them. She knew that until now he had been restrained from mayhem by Claudia, but by his expression, it was clear that the time for restraint had passed.

Sam collared Eddie by the back of his tailcoat and spun him around, leaving Cathy to stagger away, rubbing her bruised arm. Eddie swung at him as the wedding guests scattered with shrieks of consternation. Sam ducked and tried to get a grip on Eddie again. He was a little startled to find the elderly Howard Locke at his side, brisk and competent.

The wedding guests scattered again—only far enough to be out of harm's way—as the combatants tumbled into the ballroom. Mrs. McLeod was clutching her chest and screaming incoherently, while the guests were enjoying the novel entertainment.

When Eddie tried to punch him again, Sam managed to grab one flailing arm and twist it. Howard Locke caught Eddie's other arm and bent that, too.

"We're going outside," Sam grated, panting, "and then I'm going to beat you to a pulp."

"You'll be sorry," Eddie warned. "When I tell—"

"You'd better not open your mouth!" Sam twisted his arm harder. Eddie yelped in pain. "Let's get him out of here," Sam grunted to Locke.

"On the contrary," Locke said. He was panting,

too, but his grip on Eddie was solid. "There's a big enough crowd outside to fill a circus tent. The New York papers would like nothing better than to hear about this. Let's keep this situation inside."

He swung his fist hard into Eddie's chin, and before a startled Sam could argue further, Locke shoved Eddie hard. It might have been sheer evil chance that Eddie landed in the remains of the wedding cake. On the other hand, Howard Locke was a tough old fellow, and his aim was good. Eddie fell with a splat, and the table buckled in a river of champagne and frosting. When Eddie didn't move, Locke dusted his hands and motioned for a pair of footmen to remove both Eddie and the table.

Sam was a rumpled mess, but Howard Locke had somehow remained his usual urbane self. He was even preening a little under Claudia's admiring eye.

"Everyone will know," Cathy moaned later, in their suite in the Waldorf. "I won't be able to go anywhere."

Mr. Locke patted her hand in an avuncular fashion. "Of course you will. After being made to look ridiculous by an eighty-year-old geezer, everything Eddie says will sound like sheer spite—especially when the geezer has an impeccable reputation and Eddie's is somewhat sullied. No one is going to believe a word he says."

"Geezer, indeed," Claudia said. "Howard, you amaze me."

"It's all in the approach," Howard replied, taking up his hat and edging toward the door. "Sam did all the work. I just provided the coup de grace."

Cathy sat looking at the closed door after Howard's departure. "Aunt Claudia, are you going to marry him?"

"At my age?" Claudia murmured. "And what about Eden?"

"I like him," Eden said. "I think Sam likes him, too."

"Children," Claudia said in a stern voice, "should be seen and not heard. You may be sure I will inform you if I contemplate any such step." She turned with relief when there was a knock at the door.

Lucy Woods came in, flinging a Chinese shawl onto the settee and casting her eyes around the drawing room. "And where are the heroes of the hour? I suppose you know that the story of Eddie and the cake has already entered into legend?"

Cathy groaned again.

"Mr. Locke has likely gone to take a bow before the gentlemen of his club," Claudia said. "And Sam is letting Annie put a steak on his eye. He's going to have a shiner."

"Badge of honor," Lucy said. She looked at Cathy's miserable face. "Buck up. Eddie Gamble may have to leave the country and change his name. No one can talk about him without laughing. Anyway, forget him. I have good news for you."

"News?"

"Joe Covey has recommended you to Madame Anna Glispenskaya."

"She's an acting coach, isn't she?" Claudia inquired.

"*The* acting coach," Cathy breathed.

"Madame only takes pupils with great promise, and they have to come with a high-placed recommendation." Lucy smiled.

Cathy's eyes glowed.

"You'll need great dedication," Lucy said solemnly. "I warn you, Madame would make Napoleon look relaxed. You'll have to buckle down."

"Oh, I will." Cathy hugged herself, delirious with pleasure. "Oh, I just can't wait!"

Lucy chuckled. "You haven't met Madame."

In the morning, with her lunch in a string bag and a new notebook in which to write down Madame's words of wisdom, Cathy ascended the steps of the brownstone house that contained Madame Glispenskaya's apartments. Madame had been born in Russia and achieved stardom in St. Petersburg. When she married an American naval officer, she had given up her career for him. Now widowed, she reverted to her maiden name and made her living instructing the New York theater's young actors and actresses. Some successful students, grateful for her training, still invited her to their openings and sent her lavish gifts at Christmas.

Cathy rang the bell and found herself looking down at a stoutly corseted figure nearly six inches shorter than she was. Madame wore a black dress with a frill of antique lace and a pince-nez on her nose. She inspected Cathy from head to toe and snorted.

"So you want to be an actress." There was a faint note of derision in her voice. "And what makes you think that you are tough enough? Well?" She thumped an ebony walking stick on the floor when Cathy failed to answer.

"Be-because I want it so much," Cathy stammered.

"Hmm!" Madame backed up a little and let her in. The apartment was dim, full of overstuffed furniture. Over the mantel was a portrait of a delicate young woman with a fairylike face. Cathy realized with a start that it was Madame.

"Joseph Covey tells me that you are scatterbrained," Madame announced.

Cathy jerked her attention away from the portrait and back to the five-foot tyrant before her.

"And possibly unreliable."

"Oh, no, Madame!"

"I will expect you here three days a week. You will practice five hours a day on other days, Sundays included."

Cathy gulped. "Yes, Madame."

"Take off your shoes. First you must learn to walk not so very much like a duck."

Cathy unlaced her boots with shaking fingers.

"Tell me," Madame Glispenskaya said, "do I frighten you?"

"Yes," Cathy confessed.

"Good." Madame Glispenskaya nodded. "We shall get along excellently."

*   *   *

"And where is our young ingenue?" Howard Locke inquired of Claudia. It was a warm evening, and they were riding at a sedate pace in Locke's phaeton through the moonlit grounds of Central Park.

"She has gone to bed with an ice bag on her head," Claudia answered.

"Ah. Life can be very tumultuous for the young."

"Life can be reasonably tumultuous for the elderly," Claudia murmured.

"Dear lady, am I to interpret that as encouragement?"

Claudia sighed. "I'm old, Howard."

"And set in your ways?"

"I truly don't know. I've been widowed for twenty years."

"And yet you have rearranged your life to take the incorrigible Miss Martin under your wing. And your granddaughter."

An owl swooped by them, hunting something, and the horse tossed its head. "Howard, if you are proposing marriage, you must realize that I would still have them—or at least Eden. I truly don't know what will become of her mother."

"One does not get to be our age without encumbrances, either," Howard said. "I like young Eden."

"She has recommended you to me," Claudia confided.

"A perspicacious child."

"There's Sam, too," Claudia said, trying to be sure she listed all her burdens.

Howard chuckled. "Sam and I have thrown a fellow into a cake together. I consider that a bond."

Somewhere in the bushes a whippoorwill sounded its triple note. They listened to it in silence for a few minutes as the horse clip-clopped through the park. At length, Howard drew the horse to a halt and wrapped the reins around the whip socket. He fished in his coat and pulled out a little velvet box of the kind instantly recognizable to ladies of any age.

"I'm not going to put it on," he said, quietly handing it to her. "That's your decision." He shook out the reins with a cluck to the horse, and they rode on while Claudia sat balancing the box in the palm of her hand. "I have a strong dislike of being told that I am too old to do things," was all he said.

After a moment, Claudia opened the box and took out a sapphire encircled with diamonds. "Oh, my dear," she said gently, slipping the ring onto her finger, "that is the last thing I would ever tell you."

XVII

Guthrie, April 1891

At very much the same time that Claudia and her Mr. Locke were riding through Central Park, Tim was driving Rosebay Basham into Guthrie to see Hugo. It had been nearly a month since the fire, and Rosebay's house was rebuilt largely with the labor of sympathetic friends and lumber paid for by Peter Blake. It was a loan, Peter had sworn when she protested, but Tim knew that it wasn't a transaction that Peter carried on his books.

Hugo Ware was to stand trial for murder in two days. Ben Abbott, the lawyer, had postponed it as long as he could while he searched for some witness who might have seen Rowell Basham stalking Rosebay with his knife, but all he had found was the lone fireman who had thought he had seen Hugo with a gun—not that he could swear it had been Hugo; but Hugo had done that.

Tim didn't hold much hope, and he was bitterly aware that while his ceaseless campaign in the columns of the *Recorder* had done a lot to influence public opinion, it had only made Hodge Landrum more recalcitrant.

Rosebay sat huddled on the wagon seat with a basket of fried chicken and pie on her lap, while Tim drove her mismatched team—the mule and the piebald horse he had saved from the fire. He could see that it was all she could do not to start crying. She had put on her best dress for Hugo and tried to look as if there were still some hope.

"Are you all right?" Tim asked quietly.

Rosebay wiped the back of her hand across her eyes. "I wanted Rowell dead," she whispered. "I prayed for it. Now he *is* dead, and it was my wishing that brought it about."

"Rosebay, no!"

"My granny always said never to wish for a death. 'A death will bring a death. God hears prayers, but the devil hears you wish for a death,' she always said. Rowell was the devil's, and now the devil has him, but he's going to take Hugo, too, for payment."

Hugo was waiting for them, playing solitaire in his cell while one of Hodge Landrum's deputies kept watch in the front office, feet on the marshal's desk, reading a dime novel. He poked around Rosebay's pie for hidden weapons, then ordered Tim to relinquish his pistol and holster.

Hugo put the cards away and stood up smiling, ushering them to seats on the cot with the same gentle gallantry he might have used to welcome them to his father's manor.

"The accommodations aren't good," he said gravely, "but the company is excellent. Do I smell chicken?"

"I brung—brought a pie, too," Rosebay told him. "It's peach."

Hugo's burns had nearly healed, and his face had returned to its normal hue, its pallor accentuated by having been indoors for almost a month. There were dark circles under his eyes, too, and the gold signet ring he always wore looked loose on his hand. But his pale hair was neatly brushed, and his shirt and trousers were spotless. Tim had no idea how Hugo could contrive to look like that after a month in jail but decided it was one of the ways in which Hugo's upbringing crept to the surface.

Tim wondered if Hugo had written to his father, but he wasn't going to ask. If Hugo hadn't, Tim would see to it that the old man knew. Coming from the Holt family, Tim had no capacity to understand Hugo Ware's father; he could think of no action he could perpetrate that would cause his father, Toby, to forsake him.

The marshal's unbending rules allowed them to stay only ten minutes. Hugo patted Rosebay's hand and kissed the top of her head, then sent her out with Tim, who marveled at the Englishman's calm resignation.

After they had left, Hugo picked up the cards and let them trickle to the floor in a flutter of red and black and stiff, painted faces.

In weary bitterness, he lay down across the cot. It had been a long time since he had cared for anything; in fact, he had been startled when he realized how much he cared for Rosebay. But now he felt such a longing to see England again, just once more, that it nearly overwhelmed him. His brother had considered him to be the family's black sheep for so long, he had come to accept Gerald's assessment. But now, in the gathering shadow of a noose, he knew that he had lied to himself even in that, goaded by his own rebelliousness and his loathing for Gerald. He *did* have substance. He *did* feel devotion to the ideals, standards, and principles the family held right and proper. His present behavior was certainly proof.

He would see Rosebay safely into Tim Holt's care. How could any man not love Rosebay? Tim would wake up eventually. But England . . . Gerald would have that and value it not from love but only from propriety.

Hugo closed his eyes and wished desperately for some drug that would make him sleep and not dream.

"You look done in," Tim said as he pulled the team up in Rosebay's yard. His own horse whickered at them from the barn. "Go on in and go to bed. I'll unhitch them."

"Thank you." She slid wearily down. "Come in, though, when you're done, and I'll give you a drink. I don't think I could sleep yet."

Feeling a black depression settle around him, Tim led the team into the rebuilt barn. He knew that Rosebay and Hugo's friends were enveloped in it, too.

When he had rubbed the team down, he found her in the parlor getting out a glass and the whiskey bottle she kept for company.

"You have one, too," he said brusquely. "It might help."

"I don't drink liquor."

"Tonight you are. Call it medicinal." He got out another glass from the set that Wally Newsome had given her, to help refurnish the house. Peter had replaced the parlor sofa and rug, and Sid Hallam had given her an old brass bed. Tim had bought her lamps and a big oak table, but now he thought he should have given her a guitar. The house was eerily quiet.

He poured a healthy shot of whiskey into both glasses and pushed one into her hands. She turned it around and around, looking at it.

"You all have been such good friends," she whispered. "Better than I deserve."

"I don't want to hear any talk about not being deserving. You don't value yourself enough, Rosebay."

She took a swallow of the whiskey and then another, grimacing, but she kept drinking. "Maybe I got good reason. How can I value myself when I couldn't even love poor Hugo?"

"That's not your fault. You never did Hugo harm."

"Oh, didn't I?" Rosebay's eyes were filled with misery. "He's gonna die for me, isn't he? I could have loved him. He could at least have had that."

Her glass was empty, and Tim poured more whiskey in it and in his. "You can't make yourself love someone," he said. "Or make someone love you," he added somberly.

Rosebay choked on tears. "But I could have pretended. Why couldn't I just have pretended?"

"Oh, honey." Tim felt her sadness nearly swallow him up. He put his hand on her shoulder.

"It wouldn't have been hard," Rosebay said, sobbing. "I've been so lonely."

Tim put his glass down, empty again now, and put

his arms around her. "Here now, don't cry like that. You've got friends. You've got me. I'll see you through."

Rosebay laid her head on his chest, put her arms around his waist, and cried. "Just hold on to me. I need someone to hold on to me." Her own empty glass dropped from her fingers and rolled on the rug, and she wept against him.

Tim pressed his lips to her forehead, trying to comfort her, and she raised a tear-streaked face to his. His mouth came down on hers, and the whiskey in his blood blurred the edges of good sense. The next thing he knew, they were in Rosebay's bedroom, standing by the foot of the brass bed, and he was undoing the buttons that ran down the back of her calico dress. Underneath was just a thin cotton shimmy. He unhooked her petticoat and, when she turned to face him, pulled the shimmy down over her breasts. She was so God Almighty beautiful. . . .

Rosebay never said a word. She reached out pale bare arms for him when he had stripped his trousers off. As he pressed her to the bed with all the urgency of a man who had been trying to pretend to himself that he was immune to women and the drives of his own body, the thought crossed his mind that Isabella Ormond would never have let him undress her, even if he had married her. And then he forgot about Isabella, forgot about everything but a shared hunger and the beautiful sylphlike body in his arms.

Whatever had driven them together lasted the night, and he went to sleep with his hand tangled in her corn-silk hair and his head on her breast.

In the morning it all came back to him with a rush, like something he thought he had dreamed but then woke to find waiting like a monster by the bed. He sat up and looked with horror at Rosebay asleep beside him, wrapped only in the blankets.

Awww . . . Tim buried his head in his hands, calling himself all the evil names he could think of. He had taken advantage of her unhappiness. And Hugo!

He called himself Hugo's friend! The whiskey didn't excuse it. Nothing would excuse it.

Rosebay opened her eyes, and Tim sat up, with the sheet around him, feeling on the floor for his drawers. "Oh, God, Rosebay, I'm sorry," he said abjectly.

"Don't be," she whispered. "It wasn't your fault."

"It was my fault," Tim said grimly. "Don't blame yourself." He found his drawers and pulled them on, then reached for his shirt. "I never should have given you that whiskey. I knew you weren't used to it. We were just feeling so sad, we took comfort where we could. I used you to keep the demons off. I ought to be horsewhipped."

"To keep the demons off." Rosebay looked at him sadly. "Yeah, I reckon you did." She bit her lip. Then she lifted her chin. "Maybe I needed to keep 'em off, too."

"Maybe you did," he said gently. "But that doesn't excuse me. I just hope you won't hate me for it."

"I couldn't do that," she said dully as he raced out the door.

No, she couldn't, he thought savagely as he saddled his horse. She was too nice a person. And he was a son of a bitch. He spurred his horse out of the yard, trying to get back to town before her customers showed up for breakfast or met him on the road.

He got home just as Peter was going out to breakfast. They bumped into each other in the hall.

"You've been up all night," Peter observed.

"How the hell do you know?"

"That's what you were wearing last night."

"Oh. I couldn't sleep. I kept wanting to break into Hodge Landrum's house and beat his brains in. If Landrum had done his job in the first place, this would never have happened. Then Rowell could have gone on and gotten shot by whoever else was bound to do it eventually. Someone would have done it, that's for sure."

"You could probably have gotten people to stand in line for the privilege," Peter said. "Are you coming to breakfast?"

"No."

Peter went out, and Tim stomped up the stairs. On the third step he halted, with Peter's penultimate remark reverberating inside his head like a gong. It was the truth: Hugo Ware had just had the misfortune to be in the right spot at the wrong time and to have enough conscience to confess afterward. Tim shot down the stairs at a dead run.

Tim caught Sid Hallam as he was getting on his horse and dragged him into the livery-stable office. When he was through with Sid, he headed for Jeb Morrison's carriage works and waited amid the sawdust and turpentine scent of the finishing shed for Jeb to get back from breakfast. Naturally everybody he wanted was eating as Rosebay's, but Tim didn't think he had the guts to show his face back there yet. Eventually Jeb, well fed, rode in, and Tim grabbed his arm and spoke to him, then headed for Wally Newsome's spread.

Wally was branding calves in a cloud of dust and singed hair. He listened with interest to what Tim had to say, and then he grinned while the tied calf, abandoned for the moment, rolled on the ground and bawled for its mother.

"I'll do it," Wally agreed. "But I've got to do these calves first."

Tim departed, satisfied, and headed for the marshal's office before Peter found out what he was up to. Given the fact that it might backfire, he didn't want Peter involved.

About lunchtime, Marshal Hodge Landrum was in his office having a friendly chat with Mayor Abel Dormer.

"Once you convict this Englishman," the mayor said, "Holt isn't going to have any reputation left in Guthrie. Folks will see how he's been trying to run honest officials out of office."

"I'm not going to convict Ware," Landrum said. "That's the judge's business."

"Well, you made the arrest," Dormer pointed out. "I always said you were a sound man."

"I do my duty," Landrum said uncomfortably, not liking the implication that he had done his duty to suit the mayor—particularly since, as Tim Holt had once suggested, he owed the mayor money. "I wouldn't have arrested him if I hadn't thought he was guilty, damn it. He confessed!"

"Of course he did," Dormer said soothingly. "You're a good man, Hodge."

The bell on the office door jangled. "I act on my convictions," Landrum insisted to the mayor, and looked up to see who else was coming to annoy him. He wanted to eat his lunch.

"I wouldn't count my convictions before they're hatched." Tim Holt stood looking down at the pair of them. "I've got to talk to you, Landrum." He flicked a glance at Abel Dormer to indicate that he could do without Dormer's presence.

Dormer harrumphed, and Landrum said, "You got anything to say, you can say it in front of the mayor." Landrum thought that Holt looked embarrassed.

"I can't square it with my conscience any longer, to let you try Hugo Ware for murder. I shot Rowell Basham."

"You didn't!" Landrum said, but the mayor put a hand on the marshal's arm.

"Now, Hodge, let's hear the man out."

Tim took a deep breath, a man steeling himself for confession. "Basham had it in for me ever since we had a fight over a claim the first day in Guthrie. He's the son of a bitch who set fire to my newspaper office. When he set Rosebay's house on fire, I knew I had to do something."

"You never told *me* he set the fire at your office," Landrum complained.

"I couldn't prove it. And knowing your upright character as I do, Marshal, I didn't bother to try."

"Horse shit," Landrum said. "I don't know what you're up to, Holt, but I don't believe a word of this."

"Let's not be so hasty." Dormer looked positively jubilant.

"You might as well believe it," Tim said, "because I'm going to stick to it. Hugo was just trying to shield Rosebay when he confessed. He didn't know it was really me. I thought you'd have sense enough to know he was lying and let him go. But since you haven't, I can't let you hang him for a crime I committed."

"You telling me you want me to hang you?" Landrum demanded.

"Not particularly," Tim said. He looked depressed. "But better me than him, I guess. Now get him out of that cell and put me in it."

"I'll put you in a cell," Landrum said. "With great pleasure. You're a headache, Holt, that's what you are. But I ain't letting Ware go. The judge can sort it out."

"Makes it kind of complicated," Tim suggested.

"I don't give a damn!" Landrum got up and snatched the gun and holster that Tim meekly held out to him. He took Tim by the arm, propelled him down the hall to a cell adjacent to Hugo's, and locked him in. "I hope you won't regret this, Holt."

"Yeah, me, too," Tim murmured.

Hugo was leaning on the bars, his face grim. "Have you lost your mind?"

"Not yet," Tim said. "Ask me in a couple of hours."

"You can't confess!" Hugo hissed. "You *know* I shot him!"

"Nope," Tim said. "*I* did. Now for God's sake, just shut up. Dormer's out there, too."

The news traveled fast, possibly given wings by Abel Dormer, and to Tim's dismay, Peter showed up before anyone else did.

"Get out of here," Tim told him. "And whatever you do, don't tell Rosebay."

"Did you really shoot him?" Peter asked seriously.

Tim looked him in the eyes. "Just go home."

Something in Tim's expression made Peter obey, but he didn't go home; he paced in agitation in front of the marshal's office, which served to draw attention to the situation. By the time Wally Newsome showed up, a crowd was gathered. Landrum shut the door in their faces.

"And what the hell do you want, Newsome?"

Wally scuffed his feet on the floor. "I came to tell you I shot Rowell Basham," he said quietly.

Landrum exploded. "Are you trying to make a mockery of the law?"

"No, sir," Wally said earnestly. "I shot him. Well, you know I wanted to marry Rosebay—Miz Basham— and that Rowell was after her all the time, trying to make her marry him. And, well—well, his brother killed my buddy Yates. He was a good boy, old Yates, when he wasn't drunk, and it seemed to me like they was two of a kind. So when I got the chance, I shot him," he added ingenuously.

Landrum riveted him with a piercing look but said nothing.

"Everyone was right busy with the fire and all," Wally babbled. "I didn't think anyone would see me. But I never thought you'd latch onto someone else instead. Or that my buddy Tim would step in and take the blame." Wally squared his shoulders. "My conscience just couldn't take it no more."

"Are you under the impression that you're going to keep me from hanging him?"

"Well, hell, I don't know which of them you're aiming to hang," Wally admitted. "But I did it."

Landrum pushed Wally into a third cell, across from the other two. As he banged the door shut he turned and shouted, "I'll get to the bottom of this!"

"Enter the third murderer," Tim said when Landrum had vanished down the hall in a sulfurous cloud of irritation.

Hugo got off his cot and looked at Wally uneasily. "Just what are you two up to? You're taking a hell of a chance."

"Just hold on," Tim murmured. He grinned at Wally. "Glad to see you, chum."

"I said I'd come," Wally replied, grinning back. "I think Landrum's about to bust a gut."

Tim had to admit to a certain feeling of relief. With three of them in there, the possibility of a backfire, with a hanging noose attendant upon it, seemed more remote. He settled back on his cot and waited. In a few minutes Tim was gratified to hear shouting from the front office.

Sid Hallam stood truculently in front of the marshal's desk, his muscular blacksmith's forearms crossed on his chest. "I ain't goin' away," he announced. "I come to confess, and I'm going to confess. I don't care how many dang fools you got in there claiming to have done it."

"Just suppose you tell me why *you* did it," Landrum said from between clenched teeth.

"Well, I done it for poor little Rosebay, of course," Sid answered. "Fat lot of help she got from you. I been sweet on her, you know that. Somebody had to get that bastard away from her. And it's a sin and a shame the law in this town can't be counted on to help a woman in distress."

Before Landrum could answer, the bell jangled again, and Jeb Morrison came in.

"What do *you* want?" Landrum screamed.

"I came to tell you I shot Rowell Basham," Jeb said. "My conscience wouldn't—"

"Your conscience wouldn't stand it," Landrum said sarcastically. "If you boys think you're being funny, you'll find out different. But just for the record, suppose you tell me why *you* shot him. You never picked up a gun in your life, Jeb Morrison, and don't think I don't know it."

Jeb blinked. "That's right. I'm a churchgoing man, as you know, Marshal. I was brought up in the Friends' Meeting, though I have to say I've slipped a little. But that Rowell Basham was giving religion a bad name, calling himself a preacher and the law standing by. Well, I was brought up to disrespect civil authority when it goes against the Lord's word, and when the law won't even protect a poor widow, a man has to take a stand. God will chastise me, but thee ought to be ashamed, Hodge Landrum," he added, lapsing into the dialect of his youth.

Landrum glared around him and found a lone deputy goggling at them all from the other side of the office.

"You go get me our witness. That fireman—what's his name? Williams?—who saw Ware with the gun."

"He didn't say it was Ware," the deputy corrected. "He just said it was someone."

"Well, I'm going to give him some some*ones* to look at," Landrum retorted. "I'm going to get to the bottom of this! And bring me a sandwich. I haven't even had lunch."

"Yes, sir, Marshal." The deputy scooted out the door.

Fuming with disgust, Landrum herded the two of them down the hall. "Jeb Morrison, *you* ought to be ashamed of yourself."

"I am," Jeb said piously. "But thee knows I'm not a fighting man. I had to gather my courage."

"You give me any more of that Quaker talk, and I'll give you something to worry about," Landrum screamed. "Get in there!" He held open the door of Wally Newsome's cell and shoved Hallam and Morrison both into it.

The only other available cell was occupied by a drunk who had slept through the proceedings so far. Now he opened one eye and looked around him. "Mighty crowded," he mumbled, and went back to sleep.

Williams the fireman arrived with Mayor Abel Dormer on his heels, a presence that did nothing to please the marshal.

"All right, get in there and look at them," Landrum told Williams. "I want to know which one of those lying bastards you saw the night of the fire."

Williams studied the three cells full of men. "Could

you maybe line them up, Marshal?" he asked finally.
"And it ought to be darker. He was kind of a silhouette.
It would help if there was a fire," he added.

Landrum ordered the five out at gunpoint into the
front office, where he closed all the windows and produced a pair of kerosene lanterns. He looked as if he
could cheerfully set a fire and let them all go up in it.

"Could you turn kind of sideways?" Williams
requested.

They obeyed while Landrum stood fuming and
Mayor Dormer looked hopefully at Tim's profile.

Finally Williams threw up his hands. "I don't know,
Marshal. They're all about the same height."

"They aren't the same build!" Landrum erupted.
"And what about their clothes? What was he wearing?"

"It was dark," Williams said plaintively.

"You said it was Ware!"

"I just said it could have been him," Williams
reminded the marshal. "But I ain't going to say it wasn't
one of them, either." He looked stubborn. "Not over a
hanging matter."

"Your witness appears to have gone down the drain,"
Tim remarked.

"You keep quiet!" Dormer said. "You're charged
with murder."

Landrum ignored him. He stared at the five of
them in the glow of the lanterns.

"It was Holt," Dormer said. "He's the one with the
biggest grudge."

"Mayor, will you just butt out," Landrum said.
"You can't prove that."

"He confessed!"

"So did the rest of them."

"Marshal, if you don't do your duty, I'll do it
myself." Dormer pointed a finger at Tim. "Holt, you're
under arrest for the murder of Rowell Basham." He
looked at the deputy. "Lock him up, boy."

Landrum finally snapped. He turned on the mayor
with fire in his eyes. "You don't have one ounce of
authority in my office, Dormer. You couldn't arrest a

hop toad without my permission. I'm here to uphold the law, not fight your private grudges for you, and I'm getting just as sick of you as I am of them. Now shut up."

"I'll have your badge for this!"

"You try me any further," Landrum shouted, "and I'll arrest *you* for tampering with the law. You have three seconds to get out of my office! One . . . two . . ."

The mayor looked as if he might argue, but then he stalked out the door and lurked instead on the sidewalk, trying to hear what was going on.

The fireman looked after him apprehensively. "Can I go too, Marshal?"

"Yeah, git." Landrum opened the shutters and blew out the lanterns while he got his temper back and did some hard thinking. Asking the judge to settle guilt between Hugo Ware and Tim Holt would have been one thing. Presenting him with five confessed murderers would just make the marshal a laughingstock and annoy the judge something fierce. Despite the mayor's loathing, Tim Holt was an influential man. And Jeb Morrison was a churchgoing pillar of Guthrie. The judge would let them all go, probably with a public dressing-down for Landrum for allowing matters to get to this point.

In the back of his mind, Landrum knew that he should have listened to Rosebay Basham, whether he liked her or not. He'd known it since Rowell Basham got shot. If he pushed this case any harder, everyone else would know it, too, and there still wouldn't be a conviction.

Landrum gritted his teeth and scowled at the five confessed murderers. "Get out of my sight. All of you. And if you know what's good for you, you won't cross my path again this side of doomsday."

XVIII

"In a cavern, in a canyon,
Excavating for a mine,
Dwelt a miner, forty-niner,
And his daughter Clementine— "

The murderers were celebrating in the Yellow Rose Saloon, standing at the bar, their arms linked across each other's shoulders.

"Why didn't you *tell* me?" Peter demanded, outraged. "I would have been in on it!"

"Because Aunt Cindy would skin me alive," Tim said, extricating himself to pour another drink from the bottle on the bar.

"Well, it's not fair."

"I take that kindly," Hugo said. "Have a drink, Peter."

"One," Tim said.

"Thou are lost and gone forever,
Dreadful sorry, Clementine!"

"Has anyone told Rosebay?" Peter asked.

"You do it," Tim said. He pushed Peter toward the door. He was still afraid to get anywhere near Rosebay. He threw his arm around Jeb Morrison's shoulder, and they began singing again.

"Light she was and like a fairy,
And her shoes were number nine,
Herring boxes without topses,
Sandals were for Clementine."

"You boys want to tone it down a little?" the bartender said. He was as burly as a moose and doubled as the saloon's bouncer. "You'll have the marshal in here, and I reckon you've seen enough of him."

"Let 'em sing!" someone shouted.

"Give 'em a drink on me!" someone else yelled. "And none of that bootleg hooch!"

"We don't buy bootleg," the bartender said, affronted. "Well, not since whiskey got made legal."

"You mean not since Rowell Basham got shot," the other man hooted. "Old Abel's going to have to find another source, or he won't be able to cheat his customers."

"Now you cut that out," the bartender warned. "The mayor's business investments ain't your business."

Tim took another swallow of his drink and gave the bartender a sodden grin—he was acting a lot more inebriated than he really was. "Hell, what's a little bootleg between friends? The way I figure it, whiskey's whiskey."

"Damned government wants a piece of everything," the bartender grumbled, nodding. "They'll put a tax on breathing next."

"That's right." Tim smiled at him drunkenly. "An' everybody does it. Bought a little myself from time to time. Not from the dear departed, of course. Here, buy yourself a drink."

"Thank you." The bartender poured himself a shot and raised the glass. "To poor ol' Rowell." He chuckled. "Dangerous son of a bitch, but he made good whiskey."

"I'll bet," Tim murmured.

When the bartender peered at him suspiciously, Tim slumped against the bar and allowed the whiskey to slosh out of his glass and onto his hand.

Sid Hallam slapped Hugo across the back. "Hey! Let's have another song. Sing us 'Loch Lomond.' I like a good love song."

"That's a damn dirge," Hugo protested. "It's about

some poor Scot who's gotten killed a million miles from home and his ghost is going back to the highlands."

"Sing it anyway."

"No." Hugo shuddered. "That's a little too close to the bone." He stood back from the bar a little. "I haven't thanked you all properly because I couldn't think of the words to say it with. I still can't. I owe you my life, and I found that it means a lot more to me than I thought it did. All I can say is, I don't think a man ever had such true friends."

"Whoever shot Rowell Basham," Sid said quietly, careful not to be too explicit in the bartender's hearing, "did what any of us would have done."

"That's right," Jeb agreed. "The love of a good woman ought to be a bond between men, not a black jealousy. It wasn't fair to let you take the blame."

"True comrades all." Hugo smiled wistfully, and they sang "Barbara Allen" instead, in a mood of mixed brotherhood and unrequited love, until Peter came back. They saw that he had brought Rosebay with him.

"Oh, my friends," she said softly, when they had fallen silent. And then she ran across the saloon floor and threw her arms around all of them, one after another.

Tim flinched, but she didn't look at him funny or even seem to be mad. He let out a sigh of relief at her happily shining eyes. Whatever he had done last night, he had redeemed himself this afternoon.

"You oughtn't to be in a saloon, honey," Wally said when she had kissed and hugged him.

Rosebay looked at them all lovingly. "Any place you boys are is good enough for me."

"Hugo?"

"Yes?" He turned to Rosebay at the first sound of her voice, his eyebrows raised at the hesitancy in it. He had stayed to help her wash the dishes after breakfast as he often did, and he had soapsuds to his elbows.

She studied his face. He was almost his usual urbane self again, although he was thin, and there were fine lines around his eyes that hadn't been there before.

"Hugo, you ain't—you haven't asked me to marry you again."

"No," he said quietly.

She knew he wouldn't; she was beholden to him. He had nearly died for her. Hugo wasn't a man to take advantage of that.

"I was brought up to think it wasn't fitting to ask a man yourself," Rosebay said quietly. "But I'm going to. If you still want me."

"*Want* you?"

"And if you think your family won't flat disown you."

"They already have. Are you sure it isn't because you feel obligated?"

Obligated? I owe you my life, and I'm going to pay for it the only way I know.

"I don't want a beholden wife," Hugo continued, searching Rosebay's face when she didn't respond.

"No," Rosebay said. "No, I love you." And if she did right by him, he wouldn't ever find out that was a lie. She had done a night's hard thinking about that. "I love you, Hugo. It just took me awhile to figure that out." And knowing for sure that Tim Holt wasn't ever going to love her had helped a lot.

"Oh, my darling." Hugo pulled her into his arms, with almost a sob, holding her close. A flurry of soap bubbles drifted around them. "I love you more than I've ever loved anything or anyone." He held her tighter, bent his head, and kissed her.

Rosebay lifted her face to his and felt his strong hands on her back. After a moment they began to move urgently over her body. By the time he lifted her in his arms, his eyes shining with delight, she could let Tim Holt slip from her mind—at least for now . . . at least while Hugo made love to her. And if there was a baby, she wouldn't ever know it wasn't his. . . .

"Well, congratulations." Tim blinked with surprise and then genuine delight as he took in Hugo's beaming countenance. They had come hand in hand to the

Recorder office to give him the news. Tim knew that he would never think of Hugo Ware as a lightweight again, and if Rosebay had seen that, too, he was happy for them both. He was also relieved that his own ill-timed antics hadn't spoiled her chances for happiness with Hugo.

"Wally Newsome's going to be mighty cast down." Tim chuckled.

Hugo grinned. "Probably try to put me back in jail."

"No," Tim said, "I think those boys all knew you had the inside track. There won't be any hard feelings."

"There will be if Rosebay goes out of the restaurant business," Peter said. "Oh, that's a horrible thought. Rosebay, we're all going to starve!"

"No, you won't," Rosebay said. "I like cooking. Nobody ever paid me for doing it at home."

"Rosebay's a worker," Hugo said. "I think if you told her she had to sit idle, she'd go mad." He sighed elaborately. "I expect I'll have to get a job, too. I wouldn't feel right with such a hardworking wife." He smiled down at Rosebay. "And I'd rather have a job than plow that field. I draw the line at that—we'll pay someone to plow."

Rosebay nodded. "Get us a hired hand. It would be a help."

Tim laughed. "Well, if you want to get out of plowing that badly, I'll give you a job. I always said you'd make a good reporter, and I need someone else on the staff who can write without having to chew up two pencils for every line and then have me fix his spelling. We might even run some of your sketches. I've got the equipment to print them now."

"All right," Hugo agreed, grasping Tim's hand to seal the agreement. "You've got a deal. Lord knows what else I'd be any good at."

Rosebay smiled at him proudly. "You'll do just fine. You don't value yourself like you should, Hugo."

"Maybe I do now," Hugo said, "since you do." He kissed the top of her head.

"Good," Tim said. "That'll give you the courage to learn to use this thing." He pointed at the new type-writing machine on his desk. It was squat and efficient looking, with rows of black keys springing up like mush-rooms across its front.

"Qwertyuiop," Hugo said, reading the top row. "What the hell does that mean?"

"Lord knows," Tim said. "I can't figure anything on it."

Hugo sat down at the machine, intrigued. He picked out "i came, i saw, i conquered," with one finger.

"Here, this gets you capitals." Tim punched the shift key.

"Aha."

"There's a booklet on the finger positions. You're supposed to memorize them so you don't have to look at the keys."

"I suppose this is a condition of employment?"

"It is. Your handwriting's even worse than mine."

Hugo looked thoughtful. "All right. I'll bet you: Dinner and champagne, and not at Rosebay's, for the first one who can type an error-free page without looking."

"All right, you're on. You're doomed, Hugo."

"Probably. You'll have more chance to practice. But think how good it will be for you. What a sterling example you will set." He stood. "And now I am going to take my intended wife and go have a short chat with a preacher. We are going to have a large and splashy wedding. Rosebay didn't have much of one the first go-round."

"I don't want to put on the dog," Rosebay said uncomfortably.

"Well, I do. I don't know much about planning these things, but we shall take the preacher's advice."

Tim smiled. He knew Hugo would pick a church that Rosebay felt comfortable in—Hugo was probably Church of England himself, which was so high a church as to be next door to Rome—but he was right about opting for the big wedding. It would get Rosebay off on the right foot and squelch any gossip. People who went to your wedding were honor bound to wish you well.

"I wish I could lend you my grandmother," Tim said. "She's an old hand at weddings. But you'll do fine. Who's going to give the bride away?"

Rosebay looked at her feet. "I was wondering if you would," she murmured. "It doesn't seem right to ask Wally or Jeb or Sid. I mean, they asked me to marry them themselves."

Tim gulped. "Of course." It was plain she hadn't told Hugo what had happened, and thank goodness for that. That would be no way to start a marriage. "I'll be glad to. I'm tickled you finally made up your mind. It took you long enough," he added teasingly.

Rosebay smiled at him calmly. "It just took me awhile to figure things out." She gave Hugo her arm. "Let's go see the preacher."

Tim stood in the office doorway and watched them walk arm in arm down the sidewalk. She looked awfully calm for a woman who was about to get married, he thought. Nothing like Janessa had looked, or even Annie. Rosebay's cornflower eyes had seemed, well, determined rather than elated. Tim shrugged and quit trying to figure it out. Rosebay had been through a lot; maybe this *was* a calm time in her life.

"Well," Tim said cheerily to Peter, "we have a wedding present to buy. What do you think about silver candlesticks and a new guitar? I want to give her something expensive and something frivolous. That kid hasn't had near enough foolishness in her life."

"She's had you, you moron," Peter muttered under his breath. Aloud he said, "Yeah, I think those would be fine."

"Good. And we've got type to set." Tim raised his voice a little. "If the boys in the back room will quit sighing over romance and shake a leg."

There was a flurry of activity from the composing room.

Tim began to whistle. "Guthrie won't want to miss the story of the five murderers." He sat down at the new typewriter, his mind already on other matters. "Do you think it would annoy the mayor," he inquired over his shoulder, "if we insinuate that *he* might have done it? I found out the old reprobate was buying Basham's whiskey."

"I expect it would raise his blood pressure some," Peter said. "If that's your goal."

"Oh, it is. A story always ought to have pepper." Tim began to poke at the typewriter. Maybe Dormer would try to horsewhip him again. That would be fun.

Shearer, the old pressman, watched the boss whistling at his work and consulted his conscience. Everything had turned out fine. It ought to be okay to sweep a few odds and ends under the rug. Shearer shuffled his feet, stared at the toes of his boots, then stared at the big new press. It was the best press he'd ever worked on; a man ought to be proud to be associated with it. It seemed to look back at him reproachfully. *Oh, hell,* he thought, *I been a newspaperman too long.* He threw down the oily rag with which he had been cleaning the cylinder and cleared his throat. "Uh, boss?"

"Yeah, Shearer?" Tim looked over his shoulder.

"Uh, I was in the Yellow Rose this morning—"

"In the *morning*?" Tim gave him an awful glare.

Shearer looked at his shoes again, trying to repent. "I saw the mayor. That's why I'm telling you."

"Drowning his sorrows," Peter suggested to Tim. "It must have been a real disappointment to him not to be able to hang you."

"No, he was talking to the bartender," Shearer said. "The big night man, the bouncer. They were in the office, but the door was open, and the mayor was chewing him out something fierce. So I snuck around behind the door where I could hear 'em."

"Attaboy," Tim commended. "You're forgiven for drinking in the morning. This time."

"They were talking about you," Shearer continued. "The bartender seemed to think he'd let something slip to you last night when you was in there, and he must have decided he'd better warn old Dormer."

"Ha!" Tim said jubilantly. "That proves it. He told me Dormer was buying bootleg from Rowell Basham, the thieving hypocrite."

"No wonder," Shearer said. "Dormer was in an awful snit about Basham's still and was going out to bust it up. You reckon he was dumb enough to let Rowell keep account books out there?"

"Dormer's dumb enough for anything," Tim said. "I wonder why he didn't bust it up sooner." He thought for a moment. "I bet there was a batch of mash in it he was trying to salvage." Tim abandoned the typewriter and stood up, a study in frustrated energy. "Tarnation, I wish I knew where that still was. Landrum's been looking for it for over a year. It'd be better than a birthday present to give him Dormer and the still together." He scowled at the thought of this incriminating scene slipping through his fingers.

Shearer sighed. "That's why I told you, boss. I know where it is."

"It better be there," Hodge Landrum informed Tim for the fifth time as they picked their way in Shearer's wake through the trees along the riverbank. Past the trees they could hear the burble and rush of the Cimarron River.

"Shearer's got a nose for liquor like I never saw," Tim said. He shook his head. "Blasted old rummy. I can't fire him now, though."

"It better be there," Hodge said again.

Tim knew that finding Basham's still had been an obsession with the marshal, but Landrum would have been a lot happier if anyone besides Tim Holt were delivering it to him.

Tim slipped through the newly greening woods and cast an outdoorsman's eye at the dense shrubbery. An undergrowth of briars and vines and odd bits of river debris caught at their ankles. It looked to Tim as if something else had come along this way before them—

something about the size of an elephant. Tim felt wickedly hopeful. He hadn't mentioned the mayor to Landrum. Surprises were always nice.

Tim stopped at Shearer's side. The pressman pointed, and Tim and the marshal followed the line of his finger. The still was there, but they never would have found it without Shearer. Even with the woods still nearly winter bare, the tangle of shrubbery and driftwood flung up by the river hid the equipment until they were on top of it.

It didn't hide Mayor Abel Dormer, however. Coat off and sleeves rolled up, the mayor was swinging an ax at a four-hundred-gallon copper pot that rested on a ring of stones above a blackened fire pit.

Landrum stared, outraged. "Dormer, I'm going to nail your hide to the courthouse wall!" he bellowed.

Tim caught a flicker of pure panic in Dormer's eyes and wondered if he had erred in not telling Hodge his suspicions. Tim had always thought of the mayor as malevolent but physically ineffectual. Now, as the mayor's eyes bit into him, Tim realized that any cornered animal was dangerous.

"Get down!" Tim shouted at Shearer as Dormer drew his arm back and hurled the ax. He gave Shearer a shove into the trees, and they both hit the ground as the ax landed where they had stood. Tim saw Dormer pull a small pearl-handled pistol from his pocket.

"Don't do it, Dormer, you damn fool!" Landrum shouted.

Tim pushed Shearer to safety behind a fallen log, then he drew his Colt and zigzagged forward toward Dormer. A bullet whistled past Tim's head, and he dodged behind a tree. Out of the corner of his eye he saw Landrum, also behind a tree, checking his pistol.

The mayor was crouched behind the still pot. Tim began to edge around to the other side, leaving Landrum to keep Dormer pinned down. Dormer fired at Landrum, emptying his gun in a blind panic, and Tim, counting the shots, crept forward. Behind him, he could hear Shearer, lying low behind his log, assuring the Lord in a quivering voice that he would swear off whiskey forever if the Lord would just kindly get him out of this in one piece.

Tim chuckled. *I've almost got you,* he thought, eyeing the flapping tails of the mayor's coat, just visible behind the huge copper pot. And then he heard an explosion of sound and a howl from Landrum. Tim swung around to see the big-boned bartender from the Yellow Rose standing above the marshal with a stout length of tree branch in his hand. The man had sneaked up behind Landrum from what Tim could now see was a supply shed. As Landrum tried to writhe out of the way, the club came down again hard across Landrum's hand, then his head. The marshal collapsed. The jolt knocked the gun from his fingers, but as the bartender reached for it, Landrum, in a last effort, snatched it and flung it into the underbrush before he passed out. Tim, with a furious howl and a blazing gun, rushed at the man. The bartender dived for cover in the trees. Tim's last shot was lost into the woods.

Dormer rushed out from behind the pot and snatched up the ax. Tim cursed himself for having been cocky enough to have come out with only a gun in his pocket and no gun belt. He prayed that Shearer wouldn't do anything stupid. The old drunk was no match for the bartender and a madman with an ax.

Tim stumbled, his heels catching in the thickets and the tangles of driftwood. If Shearer survived, he thought, scrambling backward and frantically trying to lay his hand on something to fight with, at least he could testify to Dormer's guilt—small comfort that would be to himself and Hodge Landrum, who would both be dead.

Tim's hand closed around a rock, a good sharp one. He heaved it at the bartender, and it took him in the chest. The man doubled over but didn't drop his club. The mayor was nearly on Tim now, smiling victoriously, the ax raised. Tim knew that Dormer would split him in half, then use it on Landrum. Abel Dormer had either lost everything, or he had lost nothing—there would be no middle ground, and it all depended on whether or not he could kill Tim.

Tim hurled another rock, then fled, circling around, trying to get the still pot between himself and Dormer. The briars caught at his boots and wrapped themselves around his ankles. Tim felt cold, and when he thought he saw Rowell Basham's eyes glitter at him from the mayor's face, he blinked hard to clear his head.

"Let it go, Dormer!" Tim shouted. "It isn't worth it!"

Dormer just grunted and came after him, heaving himself through the woods. The sun slid along the ax blade. Tim worked his way toward the pot and the shed, moving backward, never taking his eyes from the ax.

At the shed's doorway, he glanced inside for a weapon. He saw a two-by-four inside on the ground, quickly grabbed it up, and ran back out before they could corner him in there. He swung the board around his head. It was longer than the ax, and he caught Dormer in the arm with it, but before Tim could grab for the weapon, the bartender rushed him. They grappled, stumbling down the bank from the still, falling, rolling in the vines of the river's edge.

The bartender outweighed him, but Tim was more wiry and agile. He wriggled in the man's grasp, swung a good left to his jaw, and then felt around desperately for a rock. His hand closed around a flat, current-washed stone. Tim cocked his elbow and hit the bartender with all his strength. The man sagged limply, and Tim rolled out from under him, gasping for breath.

Tim slumped, his face nearly in the water. It was the reflection of the ax blade that he saw first. He staggered up on the muddy bank as the ax went past his ear, cutting the air with a shriek that was part the passage of the blade and part Abel Dormer's whistling breath. Tim grabbed a stone and threw it, and as Dormer dodged, Tim butted his head into the mayor's stomach before Dormer could swing again.

Dormer grunted and slipped on the slimy mud of

the riverbank. He didn't let go of the ax, though, until a barrage of rocks hurtled down on them. Tim ducked, hands over his head, then realized that he wasn't in the direct path of the rocks. A big rock thudded into Dormer's back, knocking the mayor to his hands and knees. Tim kicked at the mayor's chin, then brought his boot down hard on Dormer's hand. When the ax slid from the man's fingers, Tim pushed him onto his back and sat on him.

It was only when he had gotten his breath back and punched Dormer one more time to make sure he didn't get up—and for good measure—that he saw Hodge Landrum beside him, a bloody lump the size of an egg on his head, flexing his lacerated fingers to pick up the ax. Shearer, a rock in each hand, slithered down the bank to join them.

"I thought you was a goner," Shearer said.

Tim groaned and climbed off Dormer. "I thought I was, too."

He stood over Dormer, hefting the ax, while Landrum put the handcuffs on the mayor and dragged the bartender by the scruff of the neck up the bank. Then, after using the mayor's suspenders to secure the bartender's wrists behind his back, the marshal propped them both against a tree.

"Well, Dormer," Landrum said, gingerly feeling his head, "as far as I'm concerned, you're as guilty as hell."

"I've been framed." The glittering light in his eyes had died, and he had only the look of a frightened man trying to defend himself. "I don't know what this criminal has told you"—he nodded at Tim—"but he's been running this still with the Basham woman, Marshal. I was going to bring you the evidence."

Landrum didn't bother to answer him.

"Basham's account books?" Tim suggested. "For instance?" He went to the shed and returned with a fly-specked notebook, which he waved at Dormer. The mayor blanched.

Shearer sidled up to them. "I, er, I reckon my name's in there, too." He shuffled his feet hopefully.

Landrum sighed and looked at Tim. "Oh, all right, blast it. I owe you one."

"He can shy a rock with the best of them, too," Tim said, grinning.

Landrum pointed a finger at the old pressman. "Shearer, you're a federal witness. If you testify, I won't charge you."

Shearer heaved a sigh of relief.

Tim jerked a thumb at the still. From a gash midway up its side, the copper pot was leaking a dark brown viscous fluid that smelled of fermented corn. "What about that?"

Landrum hefted the ax.

Shearer and Tim watched the ax blade bite into the pot and the mash flow out into a pool around their feet. Shearer sighed at all that whiskey flowing away, but as Tim watched it he was reminded of water washing something clean. The last of Rowell Basham, flowing out into the leaves. The air was thick with the smell of it, but the wind was already blowing even the scent away.

When Landrum was through destroying the pot, he wrenched the coil out of it and chopped that into handspan-size pieces, too. Then he started on the doubling keg and the cooling box.

"Want some help?" Tim asked.

Landrum shook his head, and Tim realized what was going on. As a method of working out bad temper and a worse conscience, there was nothing like chopping something into smithereens. Tim could almost feel the breeze blowing away the bad blood between himself and the marshal, too. Landrum was pigheaded, but he was a good man, and he'd be a better lawman now that he'd learned he wasn't infallible.

When Landrum was through, he wiped his face with the back of his arm and dropped the ax into the wreckage. He prodded Dormer and the now conscious bartender to their feet, and went away without looking back at it.

The return of Mayor Dormer in handcuffs—and smelling strongly of corn mash—was witnessed only by those lucky few citizens who happened to be on the street at the time. But a full account was provided in the next day's *Prairie Recorder,* and it was read with avid interest, particularly by the mayor's debtors. It was a lively piece of copy, full of action and daring feats of strength. One might almost have thought that the publisher, who had written it himself, had been present, but all the credit had been given to Hodge Landrum.

When the marshal read it, he frowned in puzzlement, reread it, threw up his hands, and went out to buy Rosebay Basham and Hugo Ware a wedding present. It was all he could think of to do.

The bestselling saga of the intrepid Holt family
continues with

THE HOLTS:
AN AMERICAN DYNASTY
Volume Three
CAROLINA COURAGE

by Dana Fuller Ross
author of the 25 million copy
WAGONS WEST Series

Turn the page for an exciting preview of
CAROLINA COURAGE . . .

*Due to Lydia's debilitating obsession with her infant
son's death, Andrew's life has become impossible. After
Lydia's suicide attempt he is desperate, and on the advice
of Dr. Janessa Holt Lawrence he arranges for his wife
to see a specialist.*

"Never!" Lydia Brentwood's round blue eyes stared accusingly at her husband from her retreat in a wing chair in the parlor. She had her gloves and hat on, but she wasn't moving. She flattened herself against the chair. "You want to take me to this doctor so he can put me away in some asylum and you'll be rid of me!"

"I don't want to be rid of you," Andy muttered. "I want our life to have some kind of sanity to it."

"Then you do think I'm insane." Lydia fluttered thin fingers at him pushing away his unspoken accusation. "You all do. Your mother does, and that daughter of Toby Holt's. They don't understand. I'm not strong. They've never had as much grief to bear as I have, Andrew."

"They've had plenty of grief to bear," Andy said, trying to keep his voice level. "No one gets through life unscathed, especially my mother, who's lost two husbands, and Janessa Lawrence, who lost her own mother under the most tragic circumstances."

"Janessa's mother was an Indian," Lydia retorted. "They are not a delicate race. They don't feel things as I do."

Andy's eyes flared. He took her by the wrist and pulled her out of the chair. "You are coming. I've let this situation go on far too long, and it was probably my fault from the start. I was young and foolish, and I've paid for it all my life. You aren't strong enough to cope with things, and I should have realized that before. It's the only hope we have."

Lydia looked up at him, blue eyes welling over. "You hurt my wrist," she whispered.

Andy let her go. "Lydia, you drank a whole bottle of laudanum and nearly died. What do you expect me to do? Just go on with my life, wondering if you're going to do it again?"

Lydia walked to the window and stared out it. It was

raining, and the gray light outside made her seem even slimmer and more delicate, frail enough to wash away in the rain. "I don't know," she said. "I thought if I could see Franz, I could tell him why I left him."

"Lydia, for God's sake—" But he thought she was really trying to give him an honest answer. He also thought that before she had tried to kill herself, she had pictured him weeping over her lifeless form, guilty forever. But since there seemed little point in saying that, he took her, gently this time, around the waist, and walked her to the waiting carriage.

New York

Sam Brentwood read the letter from his father: Andy was taking Lydia to Germany on the advice of a doctor who specialized in disorders of the mind, to visit Franz's grave. The doctor had said that Lydia was unable to put the past behind her and accept that Franz was dead. Sam tossed the letter in the wastebasket. He didn't know why his old man had bothered to tell him, since the only possible interest Sam could have in the venture was if his father took Lydia to Germany and left her there. A pity she hadn't drunk more laudanum, he thought vengefully.

He stood up and paced uncertainly about the suite of rooms, now littered with dirty clothes and a miscellany of empty bottles, playing cards, and overflowing ashtrays filled with cigarette stubs and half-smoked cigars. Dickie Merrill and a couple of other cronies had come by last night for a poker game. Sam had won enough from them to pay the hotel bill a while longer, and there were still plenty of things he could sell: a gold cigarette case, his signet ring, a set of diamond shirt studs. Annie had been generous with her presents.

Maybe he would go out again tonight, he thought. There was a new show at Weber and Fields that Dickie was hot to see. Dickie had telephoned earlier to sing its praises: "Best-looking chorus in town. Well-fed, long-stemmed beauties, and they're not above slipping out the stage door afterward for a drink, either."

Sam poked through the debris on the parlor table and found a stale biscuit in a dish. He bit into it moodily. *Fancy free, that's me*, he thought. *No more dog collar, and I still have money in my pockets.*

So why wasn't it more fun? And what was he going to do to kill the afternoon until he could go out and not have fun? He looked at the mantel clock, but it had stopped because no one had bothered to wind it. He opened his pocket watch, and Annie's face stared back at him from the miniature inside the lid: smiling, beautiful, and with a glint in her eyes like granite.

Sam sat down in a chair, still looking at the miniature. He hadn't heard from Annie in a week, not since she had left. The porters, for five dollars apiece, had told him that they had taken her things to the Fifth Avenue Hotel.

The telephone rang, and he got up and lifted the receiver, but it was only Dickie Merrill again.

"It's all set, old boy. Two of the little darlings are going to meet us afterward for dinner. Prettiest pair of the lot, too."

It didn't seem worth the trouble—too much trouble to bathe and dress. "Count me out tonight," Sam said. "Maybe next time."

"Are you all right?" Dickie's voice squeaked with surprise. "You don't sound well."

"Maybe I'm coming down with something," Sam muttered.

"Well, put a mustard plaster on it," Dickie said. "Or a little champagne inside it. That's the ticket."

"Yeah, I'll do that."

"Well, the girls'll be disappointed."

The girls would find another stage-door Johnny with no trouble, Sam thought. *Dime a dozen, that's me.* Annie would find someone, too, he supposed. The thought rolled over in his mind like a wave of nausea, and he flung his head back, startled by the intensity of his reaction. Oh God, Annie . . .

"I wasn't supposed to miss you!" he shouted at the empty room.

No one answered. A hotel maid, coming in to clean, took one look at his face and backed out again. With one arm Sam swept the debris of last night's game off the table, cards and ashes spilling to the floor. *Let her clean that up,* he thought savagely.

Annie . . . She wasn't coming back, or she would have come by now. And he wasn't fool enough to think that it wouldn't all start up again if she did. His father was taking Lydia to look at a grave, but there wasn't any cure for Sam and Annie.

He found a whiskey bottle that miraculously still had something in it and took a swallow out of the bottle. Nausea receded into a faint ache and then numbness. Sam went into the bedroom, taking the bottle with him, and rummaged through his jewelry case. There was a pawnshop on Thirty-fourth Street that would give him enough for his shirt studs to buy a lot of whiskey. He couldn't think of anything else he wanted, except Annie.

He looked up at the mirror over the dresser. There were dark circles under his eyes. He picked up his hat and set it at a jaunty angle, mocking the reflection. "Goodtime Sam," he told it. "Always a barrel of laughs."

From the porthole of Andrew Brentwood's stateroom, the North Atlantic Ocean looked greasy with white foam, rolling and swelling against the steel hull of the *Germania* with an unending motion that had reduced Lydia to a quivering misery and made Andy wish he had not eaten breakfast. He would not have chosen a November crossing, but it had taken a full two months before he could arrange his business affairs to a point at which he could be comfortable leaving them in the hands of his vice presidents for an extended period.

Lydia was as thin as a wraith, and her eyes shone with a feverish blue glow that unnerved him. He didn't think she had eaten a full meal since they had boarded the *Germania,* even though Andy had decided against the master's stateroom on one of his own company's sturdy cargo vessels in favor of the opulence and comfort of a Cunard liner.

He sat down on the bunk and took her hand. The cabin blazed with electric light, and a bowl of fresh hothouse roses sat on the table, but Lydia's face was shadowed with demons that even the light couldn't burn away.

"Would you like to go out on deck?" he asked her. "A breath of air always helps."

Lydia shook her head. "No. I must just endure it."

"In God's name, why? You will want a hair shirt next. Lydia, you must realize that what happened to Franz was . . . fate. They call it *karma* in the East. What will be. We did everything we could. Scarlet fever isn't confined to Germany." They had been through it all so many times before. He looked at her without much hope. When she didn't answer, he said, "Lydia, if I could turn time back and do it differently, I would."

"If I could turn time back, I would not have lived out my life in an uncultured country where everyone hates me!" Lydia snapped.

Andy sighed. "They don't hate you, but you haven't made it very easy to love you," he said bluntly.

"Even you don't love me, Andrew." Her voice was doleful and set his teeth on edge. "I did," Andy said. "I do," he amended. "And you haven't lived out your life. We have a lot of good years left. They could be happy years. Think of our daughter."

"Your mother has taken her away, just as the count stole our Franz to raise."

Andy sighed. "We didn't do very well by Eden. Mother was right."

Lydia sat up, pushing the lap robe away. "You never loved Franz! You had Sam, so you never cared that I had lost Franz!" Her voice was rising hysterically. "Well, see what Sam has become. And married to that *woman*! Bringing her to our house and flaunting her!"

Andy winced at the memory of what had probably been the most unpleasant Christmas of his life, when Sam had brought his bride home. Annie Malone, now Brentwood, was not the wife that even Andy, who was no snob, would have picked for his son: She was undeniably common, undeniably his senior by at least a decade, and had, since her first marriage and widowhood, "seen life" as the ladies' journals phrased it. She brought with her ten trunks of clothes that were still being talked about in conservative quarters of Independence, and unsuitable presents for Eden—notably a parrot, which had belonged to a miner and had been taught to screech "Fire in the hole!" at unnerving moments. Lydia had banished Eden to the nursery for fear of corruption and taken to her own bed with a sick headache in the most pointed manner possible. The newlyweds had not stayed long.

Andy ran his hands through his hair. "Annie has a good heart," he muttered. He had learned that much by now. "And Sam's our fault, too. He may be past redemption, and I blame myself for that. It was no way for him to grow up, shunted aside while we were trying to get Franz back from the count."

Lydia's eyes spilled over. "You didn't love him, did you? Because he was a child of my—my sin and degradation!" She balled herself into a huddle on the berth. "You never loved him, but I loved him. Why won't you let me go to my baby?"

"That's where I'm taking you," Andy said grimly, almost to himself; Lydia wasn't listening. "I wish to God I thought it would work."

He got up and put on his coat and hat. "I'm going out for air," he said as gently as he could. "I'll be back soon."

The night air was icy outside on the promenade deck. Wisps of cloud scudded before the wind, and the stars flung among them looked like the cold lights of houses seen from a distance. Andy leaned against the rail and pounded his fists on it. A few people passed by him— courting couples . . . an elderly gentleman in a caped greatcoat, puffing a cigar. On the deck below he could hear the notes of a concertina and the laughing voices of dancers warming themselves to its music.

What would happen when they actually got to Germany, he wondered, and unexpected tears, as cold and salty as the sea spray, ran down his face for Franz, whom he had loved. But it had been so long ago, and eventually their desperate quest to gain custody from the powerful count had obliterated all feelings but determination. What would Lydia do when actually faced with Franz's grave? Repeated visions crossed his mind: Lydia, shocked to sanity, gradually growing well again, welcoming their daughter home, allowing him to make his peace with Sam . . . Lydia, driven over the brink, mad and uncontrollable, being dragged back to Independence in a straightjacket. He looked up at the stars again as if their cold light might spell out some answer.

The salt spray lashed his face as the ship rolled. The wind was coming up, and the sea was rising. He turned to go in and saw a white figure slip like a shadow along the rail. At first, in his despondent mood, he almost thought it was a ghost—some past happiness fleeing from him. Then he lurched forward.

"Lydia!"

The figure turned toward him, gestured at him to stay away, and began to climb the rail, pale velvet skirts gleaming in the moonlight.

"Lydia, no!" Andy began to run. The ship rolled, pitching him from side to side. He stretched out his hands, stumbling, too far away. Someone at the other end of the deck was screaming.

She scaled the top of the rail, precariously balanced astride it, and unspeaking, turned to look at him. Then slowly she toppled over the side.

He reached her just in time to feel her velvet skirts brush against his hand. People were rushing to the railing, shouting questions and orders at one another.

"What is it?"

"She's gone overboard!"

"A woman's gone overboard!"

Andy snatched at a life preserver hung from the rail and flung it, its tether line uncoiling into the darkness. Lydia was floundering in the water, buoyed up for the moment by air trapped in her heavy skirts and petticoats—a tangle of clothing that would sink her as soon as they were soaked through. People were still shouting orders, and a ship's officer had appeared. The steady clatter of the engines slowed and stopped, and a siren was shrilling. The officer was ordering a boat lowered.

Andy knew it wouldn't be in time. Already Lydia was slipping away in the liner's wake into the icy darkness. Her white skirts floated like a ghost on the water. She made no move toward the life preserver and in that frigid water might not have been able to grasp it if she had wanted to.

Oh, God. Andy looked up for a moment at the night sky, some desperate, unspoken prayer on his lips. She had wanted death, and he knew how much easier his life would be if she found it. And who would blame him, in that raging North Atlantic Ocean, for leaving the rescue to the ship's crew who knew their business? If Lydia drowned it would be an unutterable relief to him. And because he knew that, he could not let her, could not face his God in some later year if he let her die.

With an agonized cry he tore off his coat and ran to the stern. Hands pulled at his arms.

"Get back, sir! You'll drown for sure."

The lifeboat was halfway down the side. Lydia was only a pale splotch, like a pool of moonlight on the water, the spreading skirts beginning to sink around her.

"Get back!" Someone tried to drag him from the rail. Andy lashed out at the unseen face, heaving himself over the side. With a moan, he pushed himself from the railing and plunged into the water.

The sea was frigid beyond bearing, and he surfaced nearly numb with shock. Desperately he began to swim toward that floating patch of white. The lifeboat was behind him. If its occupants were calling to him, their voices were drowned by the roar of the sea that buffeted him, slashing his face with icy salt water, forcing it down his throat. He choked and floundered, trying to make his limbs obey as his muscles cramped with the terrible cold. The swell of the liner's wake rolled him under and lifted him again, eyes blinded with salt. He tried to see Lydia but could see only the life preserver that someone had thrown to him. He put out a hand for it, but already the cramped muscles had gone numb and would not move. His hand brushed against something that felt like seaweed, and Andy clutched at it, his hand entwined with Lydia's hair. She lay facedown in the water, unmoving, a single pocket of air beneath her petticoats holding up the almost weightless body. Andy tried to lift her from the water as the lifeboat struggled toward them, but then the swells rolled him under again, turning him over and over in the endless, icy sea.

Sam let his grandmother Claudia Brentwood in. She had just received the news by transatlantic cable. In her state of grief for her son's death, it took her a few moments to see that the suite was a shambles and that Sam was drunk.

"Uh, Gran. I wasn't expecting company," he said defensively. "Sit down."

Claudia took a deep breath. It wasn't in her to scold him for being drunk. "Sam, your father is dead."

He stopped in the motion of sweeping newspapers off the settee. Slowly he straightened. "How?"

She told him as gently as she could manage and saw his mouth twist when she came to Lydia's part in it.

"He should have let that she-devil drown," he said viciously.

"Sam, don't. It won't do any good."

"Nor any harm." He seemed half shocked into sobriety. "How's Eden taking it?"

"Badly."

"Poor kid."

"I'm afraid she feels much as you do but has more conscience about it." She tried to gather her thoughts now that his attention was focused on her. "Sam, I've seen Andy's will. There's a trust for Eden, but everything else— the house and his share of the company— goes to you."

Sam closed his eyes.

Claudia looked at him doubtfully. "Where's Annie?"

"Uh, visiting friends. In Virginia City."

"You'll need her, Sam. She has a good business head. Your father always ran the shipping business. It has to be run, and I'm too old to do it. Andy didn't expect you to have to, yet, and he had hoped—"

"That I'd turn out better?" Sam suggested.

"Oh, don't, Sam. You know you've always been my darling, from the time you were a baby. You've taken the wrong road somewhere, but now you've got to turn back. The business has to be run, and you have to do it. I'll teach you as much as I can, but Annie will help if you'll let her. You're going to need her."

"Well, it's a risky proposition, Mr. Brentwood, and as I happened to be in New York"— Fingall, the eldest of the three Brentwood Shipping Company vice presidents quivered his white mustache at Sam with the resolute obduracy of a terrier— "I did feel the decision should be yours."

So it's my fault if the blasted deal lands us belly up, Sam thought, but he knew that his father would have made the decision. "What about insurance?" he asked Fingall.

"I'm afraid that no one wants to insure livestock of such prohibitive value and in that condition for a midwinter voyage."

The livestock in question were racehorses, three of them mares well into foal, being shipped to England by an owner who wanted the shipping company to bear the risk but was willing to pay an exorbitant shipping fee. If the transport was successful, the breeder promised a great deal of future business. And no, the owner wasn't willing to wait until spring . . . something to do with the regulations of the English stud registry and upcoming races.

"Oh, hell," Sam said, and ignored Fingall's raised eyebrows. He looked at his watch. He could call Gran and see what she thought, but he wasn't willing to do it under Fingall's beetle-browed gaze. And in any case, Gran was taking Eden shopping for what promised to be the family's grim Christmas. "All right, do it," he said abruptly.

"If you're certain," Fingall said.

"If you didn't want to ship the damned horses," Sam said, "you wouldn't have come here to ask me about it; you'd have turned him down. So do it."

When Fingall had departed, Sam looked miserably at the latest set of account books and tried to figure how bad it would be if the cursed nags damaged themselves midvoyage. It made his head ache like fire, and he thought wistfully that Annie would have nosed through those account books like a beagle and told him a figure—*and* what the figure meant—in two minutes.

Annie . . . When someone told him a joke, he thought of how Annie would have laughed. Shopping for Eden, he saw hats that would have suited Annie. He saw a dud of a play and thought of how Annie would have described it; he rode through the blaze of autumn leaves and knew how Annie would have loved it.

He hadn't had a drink in three weeks and he had plenty of money in his pockets, but he still missed Annie. Was there any way to tell her that it wasn't the money he cared about, it was *her*? And would she believe him if he did? It was not the kind of problem that Sam, in his wayward life, had ever wrestled with before, and he found that he needed a shot of whiskey for courage as he got out a pen and notepaper.

Her answer arrived on New Year's Day, all of one line long, and the paper spattered as if she had gouged it with the pen. She wanted nothing to do with him ever again. So much for auld lang syne, he thought bitterly, and crumpled the paper into the fire.

He was in a tricky mood when he got to his grandmother's house for New Year's dinner and took in her somber expression, framed by the black mourning dress and cap, without really seeing it. He poured himself a cup of eggnog and added a stiff dollop of whiskey.

"Sam, I must talk to you privately. Please don't drink that."

He put the cup down and stared at her. There was more agony in her eyes than the last time he had seen her. Grief should be fading, not growing stronger. Or was it the season? It had been a dismal Christmas.

"Come in here before Eden sees you."

He followed her into her sitting room and stood dutifully in front of the fire as she closed the door. She motioned him to sit, and he sat.

"Sam, is Annie coming home soon?"

"Yes, I think so." *No, she's never coming home, but how can I tell you that?*

"Thank goodness. I've got to lay another burden on you, and on Annie."

He looked closely at her and saw that her eyes were hollow and dark circled. She looked, for the first time he could remember, her true age. "Gran—"

"It's Eden," Claudia said. "I want you to take Eden to live with you. No, hear me out; if I don't keep talking, I'll break down. My husband has a degenerative heart condition. Howard has been complaining of shortness of breath, and today the doctor—a dear, good man to come out on a holiday—became convinced of it. I don't grasp all the medical details, but we don't know how long he has. Thank the Lord he isn't in any pain." Her voice wavered, and she put her hands to her face for a moment. Howard's sapphire ring quivered on her finger, the only item she wore that was not the dismal black of mourning. "I've been so happy with him."

"Does he know?" Sam whispered.

"Yes, but Eden doesn't yet. She loves him, Sam. I cannot bear to have her watch him die—not after losing her parents. And I'm nearly eighty-three. I want her guardians to be young, young enough to give her something to cling to."

"Gran, I'm not—"

"You are. I've watched you over these last six weeks."

"Six weeks?" Sam stared at her, shaken. "Six weeks against how many years? What makes you think I'll even stay sober?"

"You probably won't," Claudia said with a touch of her old spirit. "Not all the time. But I truly believe you've reached a turning point. Eden needs you, and maybe you need Eden. Responsibility seems to do you good. And she will have Annie, too."

Sam groaned. "Gran, I can't—"

"You can. I've thought it out. There's more, Sam: I am going to take Howard on an extended tour of Europe. We many not come back until—" Her voice broke. "He says

. . . he says he has no wish to spend the time that's left being pushed around in a bath chair. It's what he wants."

Sam stared at her, then stared past her into the fire, trapped.

Independence

"Miss Eden! Mr. Sam!" Hattie, the housekeeper, came down the steps as the carriage rolled up in front of the three-story frame house wrapped around with a two-sided veranda and set above a sloping green lawn. The lawn was mowed and the hedges trimmed, but the front of the house looked shuttered and dismal.

It wasn't much better inside. All the furniture was draped in dust sheets. "I'd of had these off," Hattie said, "but you didn't say if you'd be staying."

Sam sighed. The house held nothing but unpleasant memories for him, but he'd decided on the train that Eden had to have a solid footing somewhere.

"We're staying," he said, and saw Eden's stiff shoulders relax a little in relief. "And you can get that down, too," he said suddenly, pointing to the portrait of one-year-old Franz, which hung, wreathed in dusty crepe, above the parlor mantel.

"Yes, sir."

"And open those shutters. The place smells like a tomb."

"Mr. Sam, I got a home to go to. I couldn't be staying here all the time, not knowing if anyone was coming back to it."

"No, I know you couldn't. But for God's sake, let's let some life into the place."

"There'll be plenty of that," Hattie said. "When folks find out you're back."

"I didn't know I was so popular," Sam remarked. "I'd rather expected offers to ride me out of town on a rail."

"Your circumstances have changed some," Hattie said cryptically. "You'll see."

The next morning the vice presidents were lying in wait for Sam. They reminded him of octopi, encircling as he stepped through the office door, waving contracts and bills of lading, their round, bespectacled eyes peering at him solemnly through clouds of ink. He spent the morning at his father's desk, feeling unpleasantly small for his father's shoes. He made his escape at two and went home to find Eden sitting morosely in her mother's bedroom.

"You look awful," Sam said. "The first thing we have to do is get you out of those hideous black dresses."

"Sam, don't you know anything? I have to wear them for a year. Maybe I can wear white or lavender by the summer, but not before then."

"You're too young to look like an old crow. I hate mourning," Sam muttered. He twitched at the folds of crepe trim that added a further note of gloom to Eden's dress. "Are you sure?"

"I think so," Eden said doubtfully. "I wish Annie was here. I need some more stationery, too. There'll be more notes to answer, now that we're home."

"Your mother must have had something you can use."

"It has to have a black border," Eden explained.

"Oh, for—"

"And I have to have some new . . ." She looked embarrassed. "Well, chemises. I've outgrown all mine."

"Do they have to have a black border, too?" Sam demanded, exasperated.

"Of course not."

"Maybe Hattie can take you." Sam went to find Hattie and encountered her coming up the stairs to fetch him.

"I got this house to straighten out," Hattie said after hearing his request. "You want some ladies' help, you got plenty in the parlor."

"What do you mean?"

"Ladies come to call on you and Miss Eden," Hattie answered. "I told you so."

Sam and Eden descended the stairs to find the parlor inhabited by what appeared to Sam to be half the matrons in Independence, accompanied by their daughters. The mothers pressed his hand condolingly and called him "dear boy" while the daughters fluttered around Eden, sympathizing solemnly and casting bright-eyed glances over their shoulder at her half brother. All were older than Eden, girls in their first season or well beyond. There were several whom Sam distinctly remembered not being permitted to dance with his wicked self some years before.

He wondered briefly if his new status as owner of Brentwood Shipping cast an aura of respectability about him, and then realized that it was also the absence of his wife that had brought out not only the mamas but their hopeful daughters. The mothers sounded him out delicately.

"Mrs. Brentwood is not with you?" Mrs. Cleery tut-tutted and patted his hand. "Poor man, such a dreadful time for you. But we're all so glad to have you among us again. Do you plan to reside here? I was saying to my daughter Betty that we must do all we can to make you feel at home. And dear Eden, too, of course—Betty always thinks of her as a little sister."

They had all heard that the unsuitable Mrs. Brentwood had left him—that much was plain, and it wasn't any use in wondering how. The matrons would have a friend in New York or a cousin who had visited in Virginia City, and any news as interesting as marital difficulties would have traveled at top speed. Sam gathered that a divorce was considered imminent. Shocking, of course, but he was only a boy and wasn't to be held permanently to blame for youthful mistakes.

They stayed no more than the requisite fifteen minutes, but all departed with considerable groundwork having been laid. The restrictions on gentlemen during mourning were not so confining as those imposed upon women, and Sam found himself pressed with warm invitations to small teas, musicales, and sleighing expeditions that "would do Eden so much good."

Sam accepted the invitations because he hoped they would indeed help lift Eden's spirits. Unfortunately, his experience of fifteen-year-old girls had been confined to putting mice in their desks when he had been fifteen, too. He couldn't tell what his half sister wanted or should have and felt himself on swampy ground when it came to her wardrobe and her schooling, the necessity for piano and art lessons, and whether she should be allowed to put up her hair.

As the winter turned to spring, it was clear to him that Eden needed more than he could provide. She wasn't happy. She was thin, and her face was bereft and bewildered, despite the efforts of the older girls to make a pet of her and the introductions they offered to their own little sisters.